ABOUT THE AUTHOR

Nancy Carson lives in Staffordshire and is a keen student of local history. All her novels are based around real events, and focus on the lives of the people of the Black Country.

By the same author:

The Dressmaker's Daughter
The Factory Girl
Rags to Riches
A Family Affair
Daisy's Betrayal
The Lock-Keeper's Son

NANCY CARSON

Poppy's Dilemma

avon

AVON

A division of HarperCollins*Publishers*
1 London Bridge Street,
London SE1 9GF

www.harpercollins.co.uk

First published in Great Britain by
Hodder & Stoughton in 2003 as *Poppy Silk*
First published in Great Britain by HarperCollins*Publishers* 2015
This paperback edition 2016
Copyright © Nancy Carson 2016

2

Nancy Carson asserts the moral right to
be identified as the author of this work

A catalogue record for this book is
available from the British Library

ISBN-13: 978-0-00-814687-0

Typeset in Minion by Palimpsest Book Production Ltd,
Falkirk, Stirlingshire

Printed and bound in Great Britain by
Clays Ltd, St Ives plc

MIX
Paper from
responsible sources
FSC **FSC® C007454**
www.fsc.org

POPPY'S DILEMMA

Chapter 1

She did not really want to be there, but Poppy Silk loitered compliantly with her friend Minnie Catchpole outside the alehouse, which was called 'The Wheatsheaf', but somewhat appropriately known by some as the 'Grin and Bear It'. Poppy was wearing the only reasonable frock she possessed; second-hand and made of red flannel with buttons down the front. It was a size too big for her slender figure and had cost her mother a shilling. Her black worsted stockings and inelegant clogs were made more conspicuous by the frock's short skirt. Despite the frock, and despite her reluctance to be among her own kind, Poppy had seldom been short of admirers lately. She had the face of an angel, strikingly beautiful, manifesting all the innocence of the unenticed, and yet she was much too worldly to warrant a halo.

There was a stiff breeze, not uncommon for the middle of May, and the evening sky was shredded with sprinting clouds. The road, growing dustier and more uneven the longer the dry spell lasted, was strewn with old news-sheets that flapped like misshapen birds against the wind.

The Wheatsheaf stood alone, surrounded by wasteland on one side and the Old Buffery Iron Works on the other. Within spitting distance was a collection of wooden shanties that lined the Blowers Green section of the Oxford, Worcester and

Wolverhampton Railway, which was just another of the huge civil engineering enterprises under construction.

The event was payday and it only occurred monthly. A horde of railway navvies had assembled in blustery sunshine two hours earlier at The Wheatsheaf, Poppy's and Minnie's fathers among them. The tavern was where they reaped their monetary reward for four weeks' gruelling labour minus, of course, what they owed in truck to the contractor. Most were the worse for drink. Their pockets were bulging with money, which was begging to be spent on beer, whisky, or whatever other libation would intoxicate them into sublime oblivion and render painless their aching backs and limbs. Some had ventured further afield in their search for it, but were now returning, having boisterously worn out their welcome at other public houses and beer shops, and even wobble shops, which were illicit drinking houses.

Poppy and Minnie were not the only girls aware that it was payday and hoping to be treated at least to a drink; many neighbourhood girls had gathered, hoping some of the navvies' hard-earned money would trickle down to them. Minnie, the flightier and more buxom of the two, struck a pose calculated to attract the favourable eye of the young workmen who were there in abundance, and she was flattered when some young buck whistled his approval. Poppy, though, was not so sure about those others who sidled up and made bawdy suggestions, even though those suggestions elicited girlish giggles, or feigned indignation, depending on what was being suggested and by whom.

'I reckon our dads have forgot we,' Minnie commented.

'They forget everything once they've got the beer in 'em,' Poppy replied realistically. 'Shall we go inside and ask 'em for money so's we can buy our own?'

A particularly well-built navvy, who looked old enough to

be her father, suggested something spectacularly indecent to Minnie. She stared at the man in mock outrage for a moment or two, yet inwardly remained unruffled, before she turned round to reply to Poppy's question. 'I ain't going in there. We'd get mauled to death by this lot o' dirty buggers. I don't mind somebody young, but not that lot o' dirty old buggers.'

'Well, I ain't stoppin' here much longer,' Poppy said, glancing apprehensively at the same man. She turned to Minnie. 'They ain't doing to me what they done to that Peggy Tinsley the other week down by the Netherton turnpike. Seven of 'em, there was, she reckoned. They just left her there lying in the grass after. She couldn't walk properly for days. *And* her best bonnet blowed away in the wind.'

'Poor soul,' Minnie commented, but with little sympathy. 'Still, I'm glad it wasn't me. If they'd done to me what they done to her, and Dog Meat had found out, it would've spoiled me chances.'

'Why do they call that chap o' yours "Dog Meat"?' Poppy asked. 'Does he eat dogs or summat?'

'Course not. It's 'cause he used to sell meat for dogs to the swells afore he was a navvy. Any road, it's just a nickname. Everybody's got a nickname.'

'I ain't got a nickname, Minnie.'

'Nor me, but your dad has – "Lightning Jack".'

Poppy smiled and her blue eyes sparkled. 'So's yours – "Tipton Ted" . . . Come on, where shall we go? We ain't gunna get a drink here. And I want to be safe in me bed asleep come turning-out time when they're all drunk and a-fighting.'

'Let's have a walk up the town,' Minnie suggested with a gleam in her eye. 'Let's see what the swells am up to.'

As they were about to go, a packman carrying a case came up to them. He opened it up and displayed rows of necklaces, earrings, bangles and other trinkets.

'Buy a necklace, Miss?' he suggested to Poppy. He lifted one out and held it before her throat where it tantalisingly out-glittered the glass and paste example she was already wearing. 'It'd look a treat on you with your pretty face, wouldn't it?' He regarded Minnie beseechingly, in an attempt to elicit her support. 'Wouldn't she look a picture, eh, miss?'

'I got no money,' Poppy informed him.

'Got no money? Well, it's soon got, a pretty wench like thee.'

'It's me dad what's got the money,' Poppy replied, the innuendo lost on her. 'But he's making sure he spends it on himself.'

'What about you, my flower?' he said, addressing Minnie.

'I got no money neither.'

'The men got paid tonight, didn't they?' the packman queried, placing the necklace back in the case and closing it up again. 'I daresay I'll be able to prise a sovereign from somebody afore I'm done.'

Poppy and Minnie turned to go. They were content to leave behind the hawker and the local girls who were making up to the young navvies, content to leave behind the guffaws and the swearing, the shouts and the bawling, which were increasing in direct proportion to the amount of beer being drunk. A hundred ordinary workmen, each with a pocketful of money, in even a large public house, could wreak havoc. A hundred drunken navvies, with their own brand of disregard for order and serenity, could triple the chaos. Poppy and Minnie were well aware of it. They were all too aware that towns which were being linked to the railways did not altogether embrace the arrival of hundreds of burly, uncouth men, some with their so-called wives, however transient their stay. It was commonly believed that the shanties they erected alongside the railway workings were hardly fit for pigs, let

4

alone people. And heaven protect decent, God-fearing folk from the unspeakable goings-on inside. But how those men could shift earth!

The girls left the turnpike and walked steadily towards Dudley up a track known as Shaw Road that ran alongside the new cutting the men had been excavating. As they passed the gasworks, chattering amiably, Minnie imparted some very personal secrets about herself and her man Dog Meat.

Poppy giggled in disbelief. 'You don't do that, do yer?'

'Course we do. It's nice.'

They sauntered between the houses, factories, shops and alehouses of Vicar Street. The granite spire of the recently built St Thomas's church came into view, pointing the way to heaven as it gleamed ethereally, caught by the sun's dying orange glow. It was good to be away from the rabble and babble of the navvies. Here was the chance for Poppy to derive some notion of how civilised society functioned.

They reached the church, turned right and headed downhill towards the town hall and the market square. The market square occupied the area that split High Street into two carriageways before joining up again to form Castle Street. Poppy and Minnie nudged each other at the sight of bonneted women in fine dresses and handsome men in cylindrical top hats. A carriage passed them coming in the other direction, its wheels clattering over the uneven surface. Neither girl would have known whether it was a barouche or a phaeton, a landau or a clarence; the only horse-drawn vehicles they could recognise were the tip-trucks that conveyed spoil from the cuttings and the tunnel. Poppy marvelled at the pristine goods on display in shop windows. Soft feather mattresses adorned with clean white sheets and pillowcases lay on bedsteads fashioned from glistening brass. There was highly polished furniture you could almost see your face in. Shoe shops displayed modish boots, cuffed and lace-edged, with delicate heels. Poppy drooled over elegant white dresses – the height of fashion – and beautifully tailored coats, and bonnets bedecked with colourful ribbons and flowers. Oh, it was a fine town, this Dudley, both Poppy and Minnie agreed.

'If me father's got any money left after his randying I'd like to get me mother to come here and buy me a pair of them dainty boots,' Poppy said, knowing it to be a vain hope. 'I'd love a pair of new boots.'

They ambled on, past the old town hall and market. Things were subtly different in this part of the town. The street was busy with people. Even this early in the evening, several people were stumbling tipsily as they entered or left the profusion of noisy public houses. A few were sitting in sluggish stupors adorning alcoves, or lolling against convenient walls. Women and girls stood around, gossiping animatedly, cackling like hens in a farmyard. Some were overtly trying to tempt men with coquettish looks. Here and there a glimpse of some well-turned ankle promised heaven. Poppy and Minnie giggled at the sight and sound of an old man emptying his nose into the gutter with a voluble snort; that sort of action would hardly offend them, used as they were to witnessing far less refined behaviour. They chuckled even more at the pettiness of a woman walking behind them, who tutted self-righteously and muttered, 'How disgraceful!'

They walked past the frontages of some more tightly squeezed shops, inns and houses; a succession of stone and red-brick porticoes, forming an unbroken way on both sides of the wide Georgian street. It narrowed as they approached St Edmund's church, with its red-brick tower overshadowed by the cold grey stone of the old Norman castle on the high adjacent hill.

'Shall we turn back?' Poppy suggested. 'We don't want to

walk down the hill towards the station, there's no shops down there.'

'Only the new railway bridge.'

Poppy chuckled. 'Remember when the first one they built fell down? It's lucky we weren't under it.'

They turned around and retraced their steps. As they passed The Seven Stars opposite the town hall and the market place, four youths who were loitering around the doorway called after them. They made disparaging comments about the girls' clogs, and their unusually short skirts which revealed their shins.

'Show us your drawers!' one called, and laughed with satisfaction at his own bravado. Rumour was rife that some working girls were wearing the long johns of their menfolk.

'Show us your pego, then,' Minnie replied with equal bluster. 'If you've got e'er un worth showin'.'

With a cheeky grin, the lad put his hands to the fly buttons of his trousers and, fearing Minnie had failed to call his bluff, Poppy turned and walked on. Minnie, laughing, caught her up.

At the side of the road in front of the town hall a woman was arguing with a hawker about the price of a coal scuttle. A middle-aged man with sunken cheeks was sitting on a step, lecherously stroking the blooming cheeks of a full-bosomed woman sitting next to him. A couple of urchins in rags and tatters, who had been nowhere near a bar of soap in a fortnight, rolled over in the gutter and came to blows, one of them squawking with hurt pride.

After only a few minutes, Poppy and Minnie realised that the four youths were following them.

'Quick, let's hurry up,' Poppy urged.

'Let 'em come,' Minnie said, unabashed. 'Mine's a nice-looking lad.'

'Oh?' Poppy queried. 'What about Dog Meat?'

'Sod Dog Meat. You take your pick of the other three.'

'What if Dog Meat sees yer with one of 'em? What if he finds out?'

'He won't. He'll be fuddled out of his mind by now. Any road, I always deny everything.'

'Are yer gunna go with *him* then?' She tilted her head to indicate she meant one of the four lads following at no more than ten yards' distance now.

'If he asks me. If he buys me a drink. You want a drink, don't you, Poppy?'

'I'm parched.'

'Well, I'm parched an' all, and *we* ain't got no money to buy one. So let these.'

Minnie stopped and waited for the boys to catch them up. 'D'you want to buy us a drink?' she asked forwardly, catching the eye of the lad she fancied.

'Will you show us your drawers after?'

'Who says I've got any on?'

'Show us then . . .'

Minnie shrugged and cocked an eyebrow suggestively. 'That depends.'

'Depends on what?'

'On whether I like yer enough.'

'Then what?' the lad asked provocatively.

'Depends on whether I like yer enough.' Minnie tantalised him with an alluring look of devilment. 'Tek me and Poppy for a drink and then it'll be dark. Who knows what hidey-holes there am round here.'

'They'm navvies' wenches, Tom,' one of the lads murmured apprehensively to the one in charge of these delicate negotiations. 'From that new cutting down Blowers Green. Yo'll get yer yed bosted.'

'They'll have to catch me fust.' With a grin, Tom turned to Minnie again. 'Come on, then. We'll goo in The Three Crowns.'

It was of no consequence to Poppy and Minnie that The Three Crowns was scarcely more refined than The Wheatsheaf, with its sawdust floor and its spittoons not so strategically placed. Oil lamps hung from hooks screwed into the beams of the low ceiling. The lads barged a way through to the bar and the girls followed compliantly. Soon they were handed a tumbler of beer each, which they quaffed eagerly. They stayed for about an hour, laughing with the lads and their increasingly bawdy humour, until Poppy said it was time she went back to her mother and her brothers and sisters.

'Stop a bit longer, Poppy,' Minnie entreated.

Minnie had been getting on famously with Tom; she was obviously equal to his probing indelicacies, and their rapport showed immense mutual promise.

'No, Min, not with me father out on a randy,' Poppy insisted. 'I want to go to my mother.'

'Luke'll goo with yer,' Tom said, keen to part Minnie from her companion and so boost his chances further.

Luke was keen to oblige. He hadn't taken his eyes off Poppy's lovely face the whole time but, because of his complete lack of conversation, he had made no impression on her.

'I'll walk with yer, Poppy, if yer like,' he mumbled.

She gave her assent and he finished his beer. Outside, darkness had fallen.

'So what's it like, being a navvy?' Luke asked.

'How should I know? You should ask me dad. He's the navvy.'

'They say it's hard work.'

'The hardest job in the world, me dad says.'

'But they get paid plenty.'

'And spend plenty,' Poppy replied, and her contempt for the fact seeped through in her tone. 'All on beer. They got paid tonight and they was all drunk two hours later. None of 'em will be sober till it's all spent. About Wednesday at the latest, I reckon. Then they'll all have to live on truck till the next payday.'

'What's truck?'

'Vouchers,' Poppy explained. 'They can buy food, boots and clothes from the contractor's tommy shop with the vouchers, and then it gets docked off their next wages.'

'Sounds fair,' Luke commented.

'No, it ain't fair, Luke. Some of the contractors charge a pound for fifteen shillings' worth of goods. That ain't fair at all.'

Poppy spied a group of navvies walking towards her and Luke. Even in the darkness you could tell they were navvies by their distinctive mode of dress. They wore white felt hats with the brims turned up, bright neckerchiefs and waistcoats, moleskin jackets and trousers, and big boots. She hoped they wouldn't recognise her as they approached.

'You'd best leave me now,' Poppy suggested, fearing for Luke's safety.

'Not till we've gone past this lot.'

'No, they're navvies from the Blowers Green cutting. If they recognise me, they'll make trouble for you.' She looked around for some means of escape. 'Quick, let's hide in that alley, out of the way.'

She shoved him into it unceremoniously. There was a gate at the top and he took the initiative and opened it, leading her quickly through. He put his forefinger to her lips, gesturing her to remain silent, and pressed himself to her while they waited. The warmth of his body against her made her heart pound with a bewildering mixture of pleasure at his closeness, and fear at the sound of footsteps, scuffs and the navvies' muttering and swearing in the alley. But the men were too drunk to know what they were doing or who they had seen, and quickly lost interest in their search. Poppy and Luke lingered a minute longer, enraptured by this enforced intimacy, yet lacking the confidence or know-how to exploit it.

'You'd best go back,' Poppy said, when they were out in the street again. 'I'll be all right from here. I know the navvies. They won't hurt me, 'cause of me dad, but they'd kill you if they saw you with me.'

'Any chance o' seein' you again, Poppy?' Luke asked.

Poppy smiled appealingly and shrugged. 'You never know. If me and Minnie come up to the town again.' Luke seemed a decent lad; he'd shown her consideration and a heart-quickening, gentle intimacy she'd never experienced before. 'Thanks for walking me back.' She turned and gave him a wave as she hurried on down the road.

The hut Poppy shared with her family and eight other navvy lodgers was a ramshackle affair. It stood amongst a muddle of shacks huddled together in bewildering confusion, as if they had fallen randomly from the sky and been allowed to remain just where they had landed. Heaps of disused planks, discarded bottles and all manner of rubbish littered the place. The huts were owned by Treadwell's, the contractors, and had been dismantled and reconstructed several times in several parts of the country before their sojourn at Blowers Green in Dudley. Although built predominantly of wooden planking, they were a mix of other waste materials such as engineering bricks and refractories, stone, tile and tarpaulin. Over the door of the hut occupied by Poppy and her kin hung a piece of wood that bore the name 'Rose Cottage', nailed there by some joker who'd been blessed with the ability to read and write. At least one of the four panes of glass in each window had been broken; one was replaced with a wooden board, the other a square of cardboard. Rose Cottage had three rooms. One was the communal living room that served as kitchen, dining room, brewhouse and gambling saloon. There was the family's bedroom, and another separate bedroom for the lodgers, crammed with eight bunk beds and such other accoutrements as the navvies deemed necessary. The kitchen area was nothing more than the space at one end of the hut that had a fireplace. Also crowded in was a stone sink that emptied into the dirt outside, a copper for boiling vast amounts of water, a rickety table and a row of lockers that were the lodgers' personal tommy boxes. Every navvy provided his own food, which he called his 'tommy', and which he paid for in either cash or vouchers from the tommy shop. It often fell to Sheba, Poppy's mother, to cook it.

When Poppy returned to the hut, Sheba, a mere thirty-one years old, was sitting on a chair in the communal living room nursing her youngest child; her fifth that had survived. Another woman, a neighbour from a similar hut, was with her, smoking a clay pipe they called a 'gum-bucket'. While they gossiped, they shared a jug of beer tapped from the barrel that stood cradled in a stillage against one wall. Neither woman was drunk but the beer had loosened their tongues, and they were talking over each other in their eagerness to chatter. Poppy undressed herself in the adjacent family bedroom and put on her nightgown. She could hear the women's conversation clearly, but took little notice as she clambered over the rough, bare floorboards to the two dishevelled beds that were shoved together through lack of space. She slid into the one she shared with her two younger sisters and her younger brother Jenkin, better known as Little Lightning.

Poppy had consumed two half pints of beer and the effect

of the alcohol was making her drowsy. The drone of the women's voices became indistinct and in no time she was dreaming of Luke and his unexpected chivalry. She did not know how long she had been sleeping when she was awakened by the urgent shouts of agitated men and the sudden, alarmed crying of one of the children. Poppy raised her head off her pillow and tried to understand what was happening in the darkness. A lamp flared into life. Men were gathered in the open doorway, and her mother looked anxious as she stood at the bedroom door.

'What's the matter?' Poppy asked as she rubbed her eyes.

'They've got your father.'

'Who's got me father?'

'The night watch. He's in the lock-up in Dudley.'

'Why, what's he done?'

One of the navvies answered. 'Nothing, as far as we can tell. A packman come in the public house selling baubles. Your father asked to see one and the packman handed one to him. When he asked for it back, Lightning Jack said somebody else had took it to have a look. But he accused Lightning of pinching it.'

Poppy looked with bewilderment at her mother, then at the navvy. 'And had he pinched it?'

'Nay,' he answered. 'Oh, somebody did, but I don't reckon it was yer dad. He just passed it to somebody who asked to see it. Any road, the packman went out and the next thing we knowed, the police was there. The men am up in arms, and in the right mood. There's gunna be trouble aplenty.'

Poppy quickly got dressed. Already she could hear the shouts from an army of angry men outside. Because they were navvies, they were regarded by those who didn't know and understand their isolated way of life as the absolute dregs of society. Well, the navvies knew and understood their own

13

way of life well enough and they stood together nobly, especially when one of their number was locked up for supposedly committing some felony of which he was innocent. The news had quickly spread. Those navvies who lodged in houses close by had been knocked up from their beds. They answered the call as well and joined those from the encampment, grabbing whatever they could that would serve as a weapon. It was time to set the record straight.

Poppy ran outside. Every man from the encampment still capable of standing must have been there. The ringleader was a ganger she knew only as 'Billygoat Bob'. In the darkness, she could see that he was standing on a box as he incited the men with his ranting about injustice and bigotry. For the benefit of men who had been drinking elsewhere, he was explaining what had happened at The Wheatsheaf.

'Nobody thought anythin' on it, till the packman come back to the Grin and Bear It half an hour later with three bobbies. They came in like three devils, clouting everybody wi' their blasted copper-sticks. The damned packman pointed out Lightning Jack and Dover Joe, so they dragged 'em out and chucked 'em in the Black Maria. Afore we knew what had hit us, they was away.'

The men were sufficiently inebriated to accept with fiery enthusiasm his tirades on the police and on the packman, which fed their lust for revenge.

'If any one of you was in trouble, would ye not look to we, your own kind, to help yer in yer travail?' Billygoat yelled over the hubbub, and there was a thunderous response of accord. 'Well, Lightnin' Jack and Dover Joe am innocent, but they'm in that stinkin' gaol. It's up to we to fetch 'em out afore they come before the beak and get sentenced. If we fail, they'll end up doing penal servitude in Australia – that wilderness on the other side o' the world . . . And they've both got women and families . . . It could have been you dragged out of that public house, mates. It could have been any one of you . . .'

A raucous jeer rang ominously through the night and a forest of arms shot up, most wielding pickaxe handles, shovels or hedge-bills. Billygoat stepped off his wooden box and led the incensed army away from the compound and up the hill towards Dudley. One or two stumbled and fell in their drunkenness, but they got up or were helped to their feet by mates bent on avenging this savage oppression.

Poppy followed behind. She had a vested interest. The other women, however, keen to witness some action, were caught up in the fervour of the moment as they hurried to keep up with the men, forming a separate, more passive group. The ragtag army fell more or less into step as they slogged on. Poppy had no idea of the time, but the streets were deserted except for the horde. They strode through the sleeping town, led by Billygoat Bob and those who knew the way, having deliberately followed the Black Maria which carried their comrades to the lock-up.

The two-hundred-strong mob reached the police station in Priory Street, a castellated, red-brick building with a mock portcullis through which they teemed. Hearing the commotion, the two policemen that were on duty presented themselves at the door on the other side of the yard that had rapidly filled up with the ranting crowd. One of the constables asked what the trouble was.

'We want our two mates, Lightning Jack and Dover Joe,' Billygoat Bob replied, with all the aplomb of a victorious army general negotiating a surrender. 'They've been locked up for pinchin' trinkets, but they took nothing. They'm innocent.'

'Not according to what I've been told,' the policeman said defiantly.

'Then what you've bin told is a pack o' lies. Some of these men here was in that public house, and they'd swear on their lives that them two men you'm holding had sod-all to do with any theft. Have you found the evidence on 'em?'

'No, but they could've jettisoned that when they saw the arresting officers arrive.'

'No evidence, eh?' Billygoat called, loud enough for the throng to hear. 'No evidence!' He turned back to the policeman. 'It strikes me as you should let 'em go, if you got no evidence.'

'That ain't up to me,' the policeman said. 'There's nothing I can do. They'll appear afore the magistrate tomorrow and he'll decide what should happen to 'em. I'm just doing me duty.'

Billygoat turned to his men. 'You heard what the constable said,' he shouted. 'He's got no evidence, but there's nothing he can do about it. There's nothing he can do for us or our mates inside. He's just doing his duty. Well, men . . . we have a duty as well . . .'

A roar of assent went up and the men surged forward in a mass. The policemen, realising that it was impossible to stand in the way of the mob and live, stood aside while the navvies poured into the police station. Inside, huge muscle-bound men wrenched open doors, pulling some off hinges, until one group came across the cells. Another policeman was on duty there. One of the mob asked him to unlock the padlock and set the prisoners free or be killed. Bravely, he refused. Acknowledging his courage and application to duty, Billygoat gave the order to leave him be. They would wrench the cell door down with physical force.

It took no more than five minutes. The two prisoners were helped out, to broad grins and triumphal cheers.

*　　*　　*

As the triumphant navvies and their women lurched back to the encampment, they dispersed into smaller groups. Poppy had gone up to her father as soon as she could get close to him and asked him if he really was innocent of the accusations levelled against him.

'I'm innocent, my wench,' he answered, 'but I doubt the law will ever regard me as innocent. I had a necklace in me hand, I admit it – I was gunna buy it for you, my flower – but somebody snatched it from me and I don't know who . . . Where's your mother?'

'She stayed with the kids.'

'Good . . . I'm glad.'

'You look worried, Dad . . .'

'If I do, it's 'cause we ain't heard the last o' this.'

'What do you mean?'

'What I say. The line will be crawling wi' police tomorrer. They'll never be able to let us navvies get off scot-free. They'll never let us get away with this.'

They walked on together, silently considering the implications, and Poppy was touched that her father had been about to buy her a necklace. A few of the men were singing lewd songs as they trudged drunkenly homewards. Then, as the various clusters of navvies and women lumbered down Vicar Street towards Blowers Green, Poppy was aware of somebody else at her side and turned to see who it was.

'What's goin' on, Poppy?'

'Minnie! Where did you spring from?'

'From that alleyway.' She pointed over her shoulder. 'I was with that Tom. So what's up?'

Poppy told her, then asked what she was doing out so late.

'That Tom,' Minnie whispered behind her hand, rolling her eyes self-consciously. 'He's a bit of a buck. We was having it against the wall in that alley when we heard this commotion and saw all the navvies marching towards the town. I knew Dog Meat would be among 'em, so I thought it was a good time to leave Tom and get back in bed afore Dog Meat got back. Anyway, at that, Tom says, "Hey, I ain't finished yet," so we settled back to doin' it again. It took longer than I thought . . .' Minnie giggled unashamedly. 'So if Dog Meat ever asks, I was with you on the way up to the gaol, as well as on the way back. I've bin with you all night. All right?'

Poppy chuckled. 'You're a crafty one, Min, and no two ways. Are you seein' him again, this Tom?'

'Who knows? I might. He's worthy.'

Sheba, who had waited up anxiously for news of Lightning Jack, was overjoyed when he returned to Rose Cottage. She took his arm with concern and drew him to her proprietorially as he entered the hut.

'Are you hurt, Jack?' she asked, with sympathy in her eyes. 'Did the police hurt you?'

'I copped a clout across the shoulder, but I daresay it's only bruised. Nothing to fret about.'

'Oh, Jack, I was that worried. Thank God you'm all right.'

'Aye, I'm all right, my wench. But I'm famished. Get me summat t'ate.'

'There's some bread and cheese.'

'That'll do.'

Two loaves of bread stood on the table in the communal living room. Sheba cut a hunk off one and handed it to Lightning with an ample lump of cheese. She poured him a glass of beer from the barrel, and treated herself to a smaller one.

While her father ate his supper, Poppy returned to the bed she shared. As she slid between the sheets, her sisters and brother roused but did not wake. Before long, her father and mother came in, carrying an oil lamp. Lightning Jack had sobered up following his experience in the gaol and was conducting a whispered conversation with Sheba. Then he blew out the flame and clambered into the adjacent bed, followed by Sheba. Poppy heard their stifled grunts and the squeaks of the iron bedstead as they performed their inevitable horizontal exercise. In the adjoining dormitory, the navvies who lodged with them clumped about as they stumbled over each other and swore profusely before they settled down. Poppy pulled the pillow over her head to shut out the various violations of her peace and tried to drift off to sleep, to the accompaniment of her own imaginings. It had been an eventful night.

Chapter 2

Morning came. Sheba and Lightning were up and dressed by the time Poppy awoke. Lightning was tying his clothes up in a bundle and Sheba was regarding him fretfully.

'I'll be back as soon as it's safe,' Poppy heard him say.

Alarmed, she sat up in bed and called, 'Where you goin', Dad?'

'I'm goin' on tramp, my wench. The police'll be swarmin' round this place like flies round shit, afore you can catch your breath. If they find me they'll arrest me again. I'm gunna mek meself scarce. In the meantime, I'll find work on another railway. The bobbies won't know where I've gone and they won't send men everywhere just to look for me. I'll either send for yer all or, if the job's no good, I'll come back when the dust has settled.'

'Will Dover Joe go with you, Dad?'

'He'll leave here if he's got any sense, I reckon. But it'll be best if we don't go together.'

'Oh, Dad, I shall miss you,' Poppy declared with a flush of tenderness for this man, who protected her from the perils and coarseness of living among so many uncultured men. 'Come back as soon as you can.'

He smiled, but sadness showed in his eyes as he ruffled her wayward fair hair. 'I'll be back for you, my flower. I'll be back for you all. Have no doubt.'

'You'd best be back soon an' all, Jack,' Sheba said. 'Else we shall be turned out o' this shant as sure as night follows day. Don't forget as it's owned by the contractors. Don't forget we're only tenant landlords, and that if you ain't workin' for the contractor we've got no rights being here.'

'Ask Dandy Punch to cover for us,' Lightning said. 'He might ask a favour in return, but that's fair enough.' He arched an eyebrow, giving Sheba a knowing look.

Dandy Punch was the timekeeper. Poppy did not like Dandy Punch.

'Tell him I'll repay him handsomely as well for his trouble when I get back. Do whatever you think's necessary, Sheba.'

Lightning kissed each of his children, gave Poppy a squeeze and clung to Sheba for a few seconds in a parting embrace. Then Poppy watched him turn around and walk out of the hut. Outside, he fastened a length of rope to various points on his wheelbarrow, creating a harness by which he could carry the thing on his back. He picked up his shovel, his pickaxe and his long drills, and tied them together and carried them on his shoulder like a soldier would a rifle. He threw his bundle of clothes over his other shoulder; a stone jar full of beer hung from that. Sheba handed him his straw bag, called a pantry, which held food to sustain him for a day or two. Then, heavily laden, he walked away from them, kicking up the dust as he went.

Poppy imagined that he had not turned around to wave lest they should see tears in his eyes. More likely, he would have seen theirs and, seeing them, might have been tempted to stay. But he could not stay. To stay might mean transportation. Transportation meant she would never see him again.

Through a haze of tears, Poppy watched him go. Lightning was a big man, tall and muscular. He was thirty-six years old, or so he believed, but because arduous work had taken its toll he looked nearer fifty. As a child, he had been a farm labourer in Cheshire. He had started work on the railways as a nipper, as a fat-boy greasing axles. Then, at twelve years old, on the construction of the Bolton and Leigh Railway, he'd been promoted to tipper boy, working with a horse and tip-truck, tipping the spoil from cuttings into wagons to be used subsequently as infill on embankments. After that, he worked on the Liverpool and Manchester till its completion. Lightning went back to farm labouring, but it could never offer enough, either in monetary terms or in excitement. So, when he heard about the starting of the London and Birmingham Railway, he tramped to the capital and worked the whole length of that line, starting as a bucket-steerer, but ending up as an excavator. Poppy recalled him telling her once how, at a place called the Kilsby Tunnel, he had witnessed three men, the worse for drink, fall to their deaths down a shaft as they tried to jump across its mouth, playing a game of follow-my-leader. When the London and Birmingham was finished, Lightning eventually joined the construction of Brunel's Great Western Railway from London to Bristol with its controversial broad-gauge track.

Poppy turned to her mother, who was holding the youngest in her arms. 'I wonder just how long it'll be before we see him again.' She had heard so many tales of men jacking up and going on tramp, leaving wives and families behind, never to be heard of again.

'Within a month,' Sheba replied with confidence. 'Barring accidents. I know your father. He's a man of his word.'

'Tell me about how you came to be his woman, Mother.'

'I was fourteen,' Sheba said. 'Two years younger than you are now. My own father was working on the London and Birmingham, but he'd gone off on tramp and left us. Lightning asked my mother if he could take me off her hands. She said yes, and he gave her a guinea for her trouble. She was glad of it as well.' Sheba laughed as she recalled it. 'That day we jumped the broomstick and the shovel together – the nearest a navvy ever gets to being proper wed – and that night I slept in his bed.'

'But did you like him, Mother?'

'Oh, I liked him well enough. He was strong and handsome with his long curls and drooping moustaches, and yet kind and gentle – not like some of them rough buggers. I caught straight away with you, our Poppy, and I had you when I'd just turned fifteen.'

'I don't know if I want to be a navvy's woman, Mother,' Poppy said, almost apologetically. 'I reckon there's a better life to be had.'

Sheba laughed and sat down, unbuttoning her dress to feed the baby. 'Oh, there's a better life, I daresay, but I wouldn't know where to find it. This life is hard, though, tramping from one end of the country to the other, sleeping rough, just looking for work. I have to admit, no change could ever be a change for the worse. But getting away from it is another matter. Lord knows, everybody shies away from us as if we're lepers when they know we're navvies' women. And yet a good many are glad to become navvies' women – you only have to look how many wenches the single men pick up from the towns.'

'Last night, me and Min went up into Dudley town,' Poppy said. 'We looked in the shops. They was full of stuff – beautiful stuff – shoes, frocks, coats, furniture, pots and pans, lovely crockery. And you should have seen how some of the women was dressed . . . the men as well . . .'

'The shops in Dudley don't do truck, do they? With no money coming in now, how am we supposed to get food and clothing except by truck?'

'But that's what I mean, Mother. If we didn't have to rely on truck we could have what we wanted.'

'Then you'd best find a feller who don't drink every penny away in a couple of days, like your father does,' Sheba said. 'Somebody who won't expect you to live on truck for the rest of the time, like most of 'em do.'

'Yes, that's what I'm saying, Mother. I don't want to end up with a man that lives like that. So I don't want to end up with a navvy. I want a house of my own. I want to sit in front of me own fireplace with a good husband and me kids safe abed upstairs.'

'Dreams, our Poppy. And easier said than done. Any road, somebody's already asked if he can have you.'

'Who?' Poppy asked with alarm.

'Never mind. Your father wouldn't agree to it.'

The rest of the hut's occupants were stirring. Poppy heard the coughs and groans of men emerging from sleep with thick heads and wondered if it had been one of them that had asked for her. Through the thin partition she could hear the robust breaking of wind, followed by puerile laughter from those who thought it funny, and strings of abuse from those who considered the ensuing stink an intrusion. Somebody stepped outside and, through the small window, she glimpsed Tweedle Beak – so called because of his beaked nose – his back towards her, urinating into a patch of grass. Poppy was maybe the richer for having experienced this life, for nothing shocked her.

'Shall we have some breakfast?' she suggested. 'Then I'll scrub the floor.'

'There's plenty bread and cheese,' Sheba said. 'I'll get some eggs today and some bacon.'

'Did Father leave you any money then?'

'About ten shillings. But I'll have money from the beer we sell as well, and from the beds.'

Something else caught Poppy's eye through the window. Towards the turnpike road she saw about a dozen policemen assembled, standing alongside a Black Maria and four horses. One of the policemen was clearly giving instructions to the others. Another man in a tall hat, a gentleman by his bearing, accompanied them. Her father had been right.

'The police have come,' Poppy warned her mother.

'Let 'em come. They'll not find my Lightning Jack here. He left just in time.'

The navvies lodging in the same hut grew strangely quiet; the irreverence and laughter were suspended, pending the intrusion of the police, whom they had evidently also seen. One thing was certain, however: if any of them knew anything about the missing trinkets, they were not about to confess it.

Soon they heard a loud rap at the door and it flew rudely open. A policeman was standing there with a young official employed by Treadwell's, the contractors. Sheba withdrew the child from her breast and buttoned herself up, indignant at the interruption.

'Are "excuse me" two words you've never heard of?' she asked sarcastically. 'Is there something you want of me, since you feel entitled to barge into my house?'

'Good morning, ma'am,' the police officer said, failing to sound deferential. 'We are looking for two men who live in these barracks. They gave their names as Jack Silk, better known as "Lightning Jack", and Joseph Wright, who is also known as "Dover Joe". I suspect you know why we want them.'

'You can suspect all you like, but there's no Jack Silk here,' Sheba said coldly. 'Nor no Joseph Wright either. But if you want to check for yourselves, I won't be able to stop you.'

'I'm told Lightning Jack lives here.'

'He used to,' she responded defiantly. 'But, thanks to you

damned lot, he's jacked and left us. Lord knows when we shall see him again – if we ever will.'

'He should've thought of that afore he committed the crime,' the policeman said, and nodded to the contractor's man, who was young and handsome, and vaguely familiar to both Sheba and Poppy. Both men stepped inside the hut. The young man doffed his hat respectfully, but the policeman did not. Poppy appreciated this little demonstration of good manners from the young man and rewarded him with a brief smile, which he returned.

'They've committed no crime,' Sheba retorted. 'It's the pack-man's word against theirs, but it suits you better to believe the packman, eh? Nobody ever believes there's any good in a navvy.'

The policeman ignored her jibe, pulling sheets and blankets off the beds. He bent down to look under them.

'Who's in the next room?'

'Lodgers,' Sheba replied. 'The men you're looking for ain't there either.'

The policeman opened the door and was greeted by eight surly, unshaven men leaning against their disorderly bunks. A birdcage with a tweeting canary hung from one beam; pairs of boots tied together and bags of kit hung from others. The constable spoke to the men and got several grunts in response as they shifted in turn so that he could search through the bedding. A small dog yapped from under a blanket, indignant at being so rudely disturbed.

The policeman turned to the contractor's man. 'Mr Crawford, do you recognise any of these men as the prisoners who were sprung last night?'

Mr Crawford shook his head solemnly.

The policeman then addressed the men. 'Do any of you know where these two men, known to you as Lightning Jack and Dover Joe, might be hiding?'

All shook their heads and looked suitably solemn.

'Well, we shall find 'em. Be sure of it. And woe betide 'em when we do.'

This encroachment on the navvies' early morning routines as they prepared for work was not being well-received in other areas. Many had gathered together in the centre of the encampment and were muttering their dissatisfaction to each other. More joined them and the atmosphere thickened with a menacing air of belligerence. The policemen regrouped, truncheons drawn, the law firmly on their side, watching defiantly, until a lump of wood tossed from somewhere among the navvies hit one of them on the chest.

The older person, who was dressed in the top hat like a gentleman, moved to the front at once and shouted to make himself heard. He announced himself as a magistrate and told the men that unless they dispersed immediately and went about their business, the consequences for each of them would be serious. They must back off. Nothing was to be gained. The men the law was seeking had given them the slip. Why provoke more trouble?

So the navvies slowly dispersed. They took up their picks, their shovels and their barrows, and commenced work.

Only two days before his temporary incarceration at the Dudley lock-up, Lightning Jack had spoken to a navvy who had passed through the Blowers Green workings on tramp. The man had been looking for good, dry tunnelling work and had been disappointed to discover that the Dudley tunnel had already been completed. He'd told Lightning that he'd been working on the Oxford, Worcester and Wolverhampton at Mickleton, but had got into trouble with a card school to whom he owed some unpaid gambling debts, so he'd sloped off. Recalling what this man had told him, Lightning decided to head south and try his luck at Mickleton. That first Saturday, he walked about twenty miles and was refreshed and victualled at a public house in Ombersley, Worcestershire.

Afterwards, he found a suitable hedge under which to sleep, the weather being settled. Next morning, he awoke under a blue sky and took in a great gulp of the cool morning air, so fresh with the promise of summer, and free of the stench of coal gas that had normally greeted him at Blowers Green. The sight of the leaves stirring gently on the trees, and of the ordered pattern of fields that adorned the landscape, set his heart singing after the muck and filth of the Black Country. Maybe he should have gone on tramp before. He finished what food he had in his pantry, gathered his things together and set off again, intent on reaching Mickleton later that day. At Evesham, stopping for a gallon of ale at a beer shop, he met another navvy on tramp and they got talking. The stranger told Lightning that people knew him as 'Bilston Buttercup'.

'I've never seen anybody less like a buttercup in all me life,' Lightning said, genially, as they supped. 'Buttercups are pretty, dainty flowers. You'm as plain as a pikestaff and as ungainly as a three-legged donkey.'

The stranger laughed good-heartedly at Lightning's banter. 'That I am, and no doubt about it. Here . . . fill thy gum-bucket with a pinch or two o' this best baccy.'

'Ta . . .' Lightning helped himself to some of the tobacco the man was offering and filled his clay pipe. 'So you're a Bilston bloke, eh?'

'Bilston born and bred,' the plain man said, filling his own gum-bucket. 'Though I've been most places.'

'So where are you heading for now?' Lightning asked.

'The Oxford, Worcester and Wolverhampton. They say there's work on the Mickleton tunnel near Campden.'

'That's where I'm headed. We might as well tramp there together, if that's all right by you.'

'Let's have a drink or three together and celebrate the fact,' suggested Buttercup.

So Lightning Jack and Bilston Buttercup drank. They drank so much that they lost their resolve to reach Mickleton and, instead, discussed where they would doss down that night.

'Under the stars,' declared Lightning. 'There's nothing like it, and the weather's fair.'

'Then maybe we should find somewhere afore darkness falls. We can always find an inn afterwards for a nightcap.'

So they finished their drinks and set off in search of a place to sleep, into countryside that was wearing its vivid green May mantle. They pitched camp just outside a village called Wickhamford, alongside a stream that was invitingly clear. Buttercup contemplated building himself a sod hut, constructed by cutting turf from the ground and stacking it into walls, to be roofed with a tarpaulin.

'So where's your tarpaulin?' Lightning enquired.

'Oh, bugger!' Bilston Buttercup replied with a laugh of self-derision. 'I ain't got ne'er un, have I? Damn it, I'll sleep in the open . . . Like yo' say, Lightning, the weather's fair. Tell thee what – I'll go and catch us our dinner. Why doesn't thou gather some wood and kindle us a fire, eh?'

Lightning did what his new friend suggested. He collected some dry sticks of wood and had a respectable fire going in no time. He carried in his pantry a small round biscuit tin in which he kept his mashings, which was tea leaves mixed with sugar and wrapped in little parcels of paper screwed together at one end. From the stream, he filled this biscuit tin with fresh spring water and set it over the fire to boil. He stood up and stepped back to admire the fire. In an adjoining field he could hear the lowing of cows and knew at once where to get his milk. He took his metal tea bottle, rinsed it in the stream, and clambered through the hedge that surrounded the field. Startled rabbits bolted before him, but the cows regarded him with that indifferent curiosity of which only bovines are capable as he strutted towards them. Already he had picked his cow, its udders bulging.

'Here, come to daddy,' he said softly and stooped down alongside the compliant animal. As Lightning returned to the campfire with his bottle of fresh warm milk, he saw that Buttercup had arrived back also, and was feathering a chicken.

'Bugger's still nice and warm,' he said. 'Feel.' Lightning felt. 'There's another, yon, for thee.' Buttercup gestured his head towards the ground behind him. By the flickering light of the fire, Lightning could just make out another chicken lying forlornly dead, its neck broken.

'Feather it, and I'll draw the innards out for thee,' Buttercup offered.

'Where did you pinch these from?' Lightning asked, collecting the chicken from the ground.

'Some farm, yon. I picked up some eggs as well.'

'Let's hope no bugger heard you or saw you,' Lightning said, recalling his brief stay in Dudley gaol for allegedly stealing something of similar value.

When the men had finished plucking feathers, Buttercup drew the innards out of both chickens and washed the hollow carcasses in the stream. Lightning constructed a spit from wood, on which they could cook the two fowls over the fire. Meanwhile the water in the little tin was steaming promisingly. Lightning watched his companion's face by the light of the flickering fire as he rammed the chickens on the spit and began cooking them.

'What brings you on tramp?' Buttercup asked his companion.

Lightning Jack filled and lit his gum-bucket and told his

story. 'But it's hard to leave a woman and kids. It is for me, at any rate. Some buggers couldn't give a toss, but I think the world o' my Sheba. I shall send for her and my babbies just as soon as I got meself settled at Mickleton. What about you, Buttercup?'

'Me? I'm single, me.' Buttercup turned the chickens on the spit and the fire crackled as it was fuelled with a further sputtering of fat. 'I wouldn't be in thy shoes, tied to a woman's apron strings all thy natural. I've seen it all afore, watched men and women and seen how as they make each other as miserable as toads in a bag of flour. Look at another woman and just see how they moan. They swear as yo'm having it off. Dost ever look at other women, Jack?'

'That I do. Show me a bloke as don't and I'll show you an elephant that can purr like a kitten.'

'How old is your old woman, Jack?'

'Not so old. Thirty-one. And not bad looking, considering she's had seven. Two of 'em died, though, Buttercup.'

'Aye, well when she's forty-one her teeth'll very likely fall out and all her hair. Then you'll be gawping at even more women . . . younger women . . . and wondering why on earth thou ever messed with her in the fust place.'

'Well, she was a right pretty young thing when we jumped the broomstick,' Lightning said. 'Fourteen, she was, and pretty as a picture. I was about nineteen.'

'Aye,' replied Buttercup. 'But, by God, how quick they go to seed. The time will come when thou would'st rather kiss a scabby hoss.'

Lightning laughed. 'Who knows? Mebbe . . .' The water in the tin began bubbling. 'I'll drum up.' His pipe clenched between his teeth, he poured some of it into his metal bottle and followed it with his mashings.

'Just think,' Buttercup said. 'You and that Sheba o' thine

have got nothing to look forward to now but the workhouse or the grave.'

'That's it, cheer me up,' Lightning said. 'And what have you got to look forward to?'

'Whatever I set me mind on,' came the reply. 'And if I want e'er a woman, I'll have one, without it laying on me conscience.'

'Have you never loved a woman, Buttercup?'

'Oh, aye, to be sure. When I was younger and a lot safter than I bin now.'

'Have you ever thought what it'd be like to have a little house o' your own? To have the woman you love bring you your dinner on your own best bone china while you was warming your shins in front of a blazing fire?'

'Oh, aye,' Buttercup replied. 'I was close to it once. Sadie Visick was her name. Met her while I was working once diggin' up Wiltshire. Any road, I put Sadie in the family way . . .'

'Then what?' Lightning asked. 'What steps did you take?'

'Bloody big steps. I bloody well hopped it, sharp. I couldn't see meself tethered down by e'er a wench and a screaming brat. Any road, as a navvy, what chance hast thou got o' living a decent life? All around it's dirty and depraved. Filthy, unkempt men like me and thee, Lightning, wi' no money, one shirt to we name and a pair of boots what leak like a cellar in a flood. When was the last time you ever saw a priest?'

'You mean one o' the billycock gang?'

'Aye. Some churchman who'd have a good try at saving thy soul, putting thee on the straight and narrow?'

Lightning shrugged. 'Dunno if I want to see any o' them stuck-up bastards. Dunno if I believe in God, to tell you the truth, Buttercup. I'd rather there was no God. If He's keeping a tally on me and my misdeeds, I've got a fair bit of accounting to do come judgement day.'

'Aye, me an' all,' Buttercup confessed. 'Like I said, I never did right by Sadie Visick, though her was comely enough and pleasant with it. I wonder whether her had a little chap or a wench . . .'

'Does it matter after all them years?' Lightning commented. 'It's history now.'

Eventually, the chickens were cooked. The two navvies ate well and drank their hot tea, talking ceaselessly. So engrossed were they in their conversation that they stoked up the fire and their gum-buckets and talked into the night, never once thinking about beer. Tired, they eventually fell into a contented silence, firm friends, and slept soundly on the ground till daylight, awaking to air that was as full of the sounds of spring as it was of perfume. The ardent songs of nesting birds was as strange to both men's ears as the whisper of water from the stream as it lapped over the stones and gravel of its bed.

They rekindled the fire and Lightning fried the eggs Buttercup had stolen in a bit of fat left over from the chicken, using his shovel as a frying pan. While they ate, they consulted the dog-eared map that Buttercup pulled out of his pantry, and pored over it.

'Why . . . Mickleton's no distance, judgin' by this,' Buttercup said, looking up from the map. 'We'll be there by drumming up time. I just wish I could read the blasted thing.'

Chapter 3

According to the navvies' convention for nicknaming, anybody who was short and stocky was liable to be called 'Punch'. But, to differentiate between the several Punches inevitably working together on the same line, they had to be further identified by some other pertinent feature. Thus, Dandy Punch was so named because of his taste in colourful and fancy clothes, as well as for his stockiness. He was about forty years old as far as anyone was able to guess, but he might have been younger. He was employed by Treadwell's, the contractors, as a timekeeper, and one of his tasks on a Saturday was to collect rent from those workers who occupied the company's shanty huts as tenants. Lightning Jack had been gone a week when he called on Sheba.

Poppy answered his knock and stood barefoot at the door of the hut, her fair hair falling in unruly curls around her face. Her eyes were bright, but they held no regard for Dandy Punch.

'Rent day again,' he said, a forced smile pinned to his broad face. His eyes lingered for a second on the creamy skin of Poppy's slender neck as he tried to imagine the places covered by her clothing. 'Comes around too quick, eh? But never too quick to see you, my flower. Heard from your father?'

Poppy shook her head.

'Well, no news is good news. Is your mother here?'

Sheba had lingered behind the door, and thrust her head around it when she was summoned. 'You've come about the rent . . . As you know, Lightning Jack has made himself scarce. He asked me to say that if you could put the rent down as owing . . . he'd look after you when he got back.'

'When's he coming back?' Dandy Punch asked.

'I don't know.'

'You don't know, eh? Has he jacked off for good?' He arched his unpitying eyebrows and fumbled with the thick ledger he was carrying, which bore the records of what was owed.

'No, he's coming back. For certain. I just don't know when.'

Dandy opened his book, licked his forefinger and thumb and flipped through the handwritten pages unhurriedly. 'He already owes a fortnight's rent. Ain't you got no money to pay it?'

Sheba shook her head. 'He said you'd be able to cover it somehow, till he got back. As a favour.'

His eyes strayed beyond Sheba, into the hut, drawn by the sight of Poppy. She was pulling on a stocking as she sat on a chair in the shabby living room, and had pulled the hem of her skirt up above her knee. Dandy Punch tried to see up her skirt, but the dimness inside thwarted him.

'I owe Lightning Jack no favours,' he declared, irked. 'D'you think you'll be able to pay me next week?'

'I doubt it. With Lightning away, how shall I be able to? But he'll pay you when he gets back. He'll have found work. He'll have been earning.'

'I bet you charge these lodgers fourpence a night to sleep in a bunk,' he ventured.

'Or a penny to sleep on the floor.' Sheba was trying to hide her indignation. 'But that's got nothing to do with you. None of 'em have paid me yet for this week . . . or last.'

'Well, all I can do for now is enter in me book that you

owe me for this week as well. Let's hope Lightning's back next week so's he can settle up.'

'Let's hope so,' Sheba agreed.

Dandy Punch touched his hat, taking a last glance past Sheba at Poppy, who was pulling up the other stocking, unaware of his prying eyes.

Sheba shut the door and sat down. Her two younger daughters, Lottie and Rose, were outside playing among the construction materials stacked up in the cutting. The baby was propped up against a pillow on a bed. Poppy adjusted her garter and let the hem of her skirt fall as she stood up.

'I wish I knew what me father was doing,' she commented. 'If only he could write, he could send us a letter.'

'Even that wouldn't do us any good,' Sheba replied, 'since none of us can read.'

Poppy shrugged with despondency. 'I know.' She grabbed her bonnet and put it on. 'I'm going into Dudley again with Minnie Catchpole now I've finished me work. Can you spare me a shilling?'

'A shilling? Do you think I'm made of money? You just heard me tell that Dandy Punch as I'd got none.'

'Sixpence then.'

Sheba felt in the pocket of her pinafore. 'Here's threepence. Don't waste it.'

A Staffordshire bull terrier scampered through the dust of the camp in front of Poppy and Minnie as they walked along the Netherton footpath towards Dudley town in the afternoon sunshine. After a morning scrubbing the wooden floor and laundering the men's available rags, the prospect of seeing Luke once more was appealing.

'Why didn't you tell me you'd been seeing this Tom on the quiet?' Poppy asked, as they began the climb to Dudley.

''Cause I want to keep it a secret. Dog Meat would murder me. Don't breathe a word. Not to a soul.'

'As if I would.'

'And that Luke asked specially if I could bring you with me today. He took a real shine to you, you know, Poppy.'

Poppy smiled shyly. 'He seemed decent an' all. I liked him . . . But I couldn't do with him what you do with that Tom – or with Dog Meat.'

'Nobody's asking you to.'

'As long as he don't expect me to. I see and hear enough of it with me mother and father going at it nights. It always seems as if me mother don't like it, the way she moans. As if she's just putting up with it to save having a row with me father. As if it's her duty. It don't appeal to me at all.'

Minnie burst out laughing. 'Oh, you'll change your mind all right once you've got the taste for it,' she said. 'Everybody does. And I'm sure your mother likes it as much as anybody.'

'Maybe she does. Was Dog Meat the first lad you ever did it with, Minnie?'

Minnie laughed again. 'No. I did it first with Moonraker's son, Billy, when I was thirteen.'

'And did you like it?'

'Course I liked it. Else I wouldn't have done it again. You do ask some daft questions, Poppy.'

'But what about if you catch, Minnie? What about if you get with child?'

'There's ways to stop getting with child. It pays to know how if you'm going with chaps regular.'

It amazed Poppy how canny Minnie was for a girl of sixteen. She cheated on Dog Meat without a second's thought, and he had no idea just how she was carrying on with other men.

'Don't you ever feel guilty?' Poppy enquired. 'Going behind Dog Meat's back while he's at work?'

'Why should I? He'd do the same on me. He very likely does, if he gets the chance.'

Their conversation continued in the same vein until they reached The Three Crowns, where Minnie had arranged to meet Tom and Luke. The two lads were already waiting when the girls arrived. Poppy smiled bashfully at Luke and he smiled back, baring two front teeth that were black as coal.

'It's nice to see you again, Poppy,' he said. 'I didn't really expect to, after the other Friday.'

But her eyes were fixed on his gruesome black teeth and she could not avert them. Why hadn't she noticed those teeth before? He must not have smiled. He must have been too self-conscious of them and kept his mouth shut every time she looked his way. And besides, it had been dark when they walked down Vicar Street that night. Thank God she hadn't kissed him. The thought of kissing him with those tarred tombstones in his mouth was repulsive. So Poppy quickly lost interest in Luke.

'I fancy a walk round the town,' she said experimentally, trying to extricate herself from his company. 'I got threepence and it's burning a hole in me pocket.'

'I'll come with yer,' Luke said. 'Tom and Minnie won't mind being on their own together.'

She finished her drink, resigned to the idea that Luke was not going to be that easy to shake off. They walked around the town for a while until Poppy decided she really must go. Luke was uninteresting, he had little to say and, while she allowed him to walk with her as far as the gasworks, she pondered on the density of men in general and of this Luke in particular.

As Poppy walked down Shaw Road, she saw Dog Meat walking almost parallel with her below in the cutting, having just finished his shift. It was inevitable that they would meet before either reached their huts.

'Hello, Poppy.' He greeted her with a friendly grin that concealed his fancy for her.

'Hello, Dog Meat. How's the work going?' she asked, hoping to divert him from the inevitable question about Minnie's whereabouts.

'It's good,' he answered in his thick, gruff voice. 'I've bin labouring for the bricklayers . . . Hey, I thought you was going out with Minnie this afternoon.'

'I had to be back early,' Poppy lied. 'I just left her. She'll be back in a bit.'

The following Monday, a young navvy tramped into the encampment at Blowers Green looking for work. He was tall and lean and his broad shoulders gave no impression of the toil of carrying his wheelbarrow and tools over the miles. His very appearance was a monument to his strength and fitness. His eyes were a bluish grey with the glint of steel about them. He asked somebody to direct him to a foreman and found himself in an untidy office with Billygoat Bob, the ganger.

'So what's your name?'

'They call me Jericho.'

'Jericho what?'

Jericho shrugged. 'Just Jericho.'

Billygoat tried to read the young man's mind, thinking that he must be hiding his real identity for some reason, like so many of the navvies, but there was something about the lad that led him to believe he was not hiding anything. His hair was long, which meant he hadn't been in prison recently. The name Jericho must be the only one the lad knew, but such a thing was not entirely unusual for somebody who was navvy-born.

'I take it you've worked on the lines before?' Billygoat asked.

'Aye. I've been on the Leeds and Thirsk. But 'tis finished now. Afore that I worked on the Midland.'

'What work have you been doing, lad?'

'I done excavating, barrow-running, shaft-sinking . . .'

Billygoat eyed the younger man assessingly. 'I can find you work excavating, Jericho. Your pay will be fifteen shillings a week for shifting twenty cube yards a day. Anything more will get you a bonus. Can you manage that?'

Jericho smiled. 'I can manage twenty cube yards easy. I'll take the job. Do you know of a hut where I can get lodgings?'

'You'll get a lodge over at Ma Catchpole's.' Billygoat pointed to a shanty that he could see from his office, and Jericho leaned forward to get a glimpse of where he should be heading. 'They call it "Hawthorn Villa".' Billygoat smiled at the irony. 'Tell the old harridan I sent you.'

'Can you sub me a couple of bob till payday?' Jericho asked.

'I'll see as you get a sub – as soon as you've finished your first day's work.'

So Jericho collected his things from where he had dropped them outside and made his way over to the hut that Billygoat had pointed out. He knocked on the door and a pretty young girl with dark hair and brown eyes answered it. Her hands were wet from the work she was doing and she wiped them quickly on her apron as she smiled at him with approval.

'Yes, what do you want?' the girl asked, and self-consciously tucked a stray wisp of hair under her cap.

'Is this Hawthorn Villa?'

The girl nodded. 'That's what everybody calls it.'

'Good. I'm after a lodge. Billygoat told me that Ma Catchpole might have a spare bunk.'

'Ma Catchpole is me mother,' the girl replied. 'I'm Minnie. Am you new here?'

'I just got here.' He smiled and his magnetic steel-blue eyes transfixed Minnie.

'What's your name?'

'Folk call me Jericho.'

'Jericho, eh? Well come in, Jericho.' She stood back to allow him in and he towered above her. 'I bet you're thirsty after your walk. Fancy a glass of beer?'

'I could murder a glass of beer, Minnie.'

She went over to the barrel that was standing on a stillage beneath the only window on that side of the hut and took a pint tankard, which she filled. She handed it to Jericho with an appealing smile.

'How much do I owe you?'

'Nothing. You can have your first pint free.'

He quaffed it eagerly and wiped his lips with the back of his hand. 'Thanks. I don't get a sub till I've finished me first shift.'

'Then you'd better get a move on.'

Jericho emptied his tankard and handed it back to Minnie. 'Can you show me the bunk I'll be sleeping in?'

'Gladly.' She glided over the floor to the dormitory the lodgers occupied and opened the door, which creaked on its hinges. 'That one, I think,' she said, pointing. 'Fourpence a night. Have you got fourpence for your first night?'

He rummaged in his pocket and pulled out a few coppers. 'Just about.' He handed her fourpence. 'Where do you sleep, Minnie?'

She looked at him knowingly, then tilted her head towards the door. 'In that bedroom there . . . with me mother and father and the kids . . .'

During the afternoon on the same day, Poppy had to go to the tommy shop owned and operated by the contractor, to buy beef, bacon, tea, condensed milk and bread. Minnie had also gone to the shop and Poppy entered just as Minnie was being served.

41

'I'm glad I've seen you,' Poppy whispered. 'I wondered what had happened after Saturday. Did Dog Meat tell you I saw him after I left you and Tom? It was just as he was finishing his shift. Did he ask you where you'd been?'

Minnie grinned artfully. 'There was no harm done, Poppy. He didn't have any idea as I'd been with another chap. Even if he had, I would've denied it. He's easy to fool, that Dog Meat.' She collected her purchases and stuffed them into her basket. 'I'd better go. I've got a load of work to do yet. We got a new lodger in our hut. Calls himself Jericho. He's young and . . . well, Poppy . . . I come over all wet-legged when he's near me. I don't half fancy him.'

'That's a bit too close to home, don't you think, Min?'

'I only said I fancied him.'

Poppy chuckled. 'You're a right one, you are. Listen, will you be about tonight if I call for you? Or will you be with Dog Meat?'

'Call for me.' Minnie gave Poppy a wink and said she'd see her later.

Back outside, the blue sky had given way to dark clouds that threatened rain for the first time in ages. Poppy, carrying her loaded basket, stepped onto Shaw Road to return to the hut. Over to her right stood the head gear and the horse gins of several pits, the tall chimneys of ironworks volleying ever more coal-black smoke into a leaden sky that was already full of it. She was contemplating Minnie's voracious appetite for men when she heard the rattle of wheels trundling over the uneven surface. Poppy turned to look, expecting to see a carriage. Instead, she saw a man wearing a top hat and frock coat, astride what looked like a hobby horse. As he drew closer, she recognised him as Mr Crawford, the considerate young man from Treadwell's who had entered the hut with that arrogant policeman on the morning of her father's unscheduled departure. She watched him and, as he overtook her, she caught his eye and smiled, and he smiled in return. A few yards further on, he drew to a halt and turned around, still astride his two-wheeled machine, waiting for her to catch up.

'You're Lightning Jack's daughter, aren't you?' His voice was rich and his accent was definitely not working class. Yet he seemed pleasant and his smile was friendly.

'Yes,' she replied, a little surprised that he'd taken the trouble to stop and speak. 'I'm Poppy Silk. I remember you. You came to our hut with that nasty policeman.'

'He was nasty, wasn't he? I thought he was most rude. Have you heard from your father? I wondered if he was all right.'

'We ain't heard nothing. We've got no idea where he might have gone.'

'Well, he evidently hasn't been caught. If he had, you'd have heard.'

'Do you think so?' Poppy said, her eyes brightening at the realisation.

'It's a certainty. Anyway, it's so obvious he'd done nothing wrong. I, for one, don't blame him in the least for scooting off out of the way until the hubbub's died down.' There was a sincerity, an earnestness in his soft brown eyes that Poppy found attractive.

She smiled again at the agreeable things Mr Crawford was saying and shifted her basket to her other arm. His smile was a pleasure to behold, the way his smooth lips formed a soft crescent around beautifully even teeth – not a bit like Luke's.

'He did handle a necklace, you know,' Poppy said confidentially, as if she'd known and trusted this young man for ages. 'He was going to buy it for me, but then somebody snatched it off him and he don't know who it was.'

'That's how I understand it, Miss Silk.'

He'd called her 'Miss Silk' . . . *Her* . . . Nobody had ever called her 'Miss Silk' before. It made her feel ladylike and important. To hide her face – that seemed to be suddenly burning – she looked down at her clogs peering from beneath her skirt. No man had ever made her blush before.

'Thank you for calling me "Miss Silk",' she said quietly, uncertain how she should react. 'Nobody ever called me that before. But you can call me Poppy if you like. Everybody calls me Poppy.'

He laughed good-naturedly. 'A pretty name for a pretty girl. Very well, Poppy. So I shall. And thank you for allowing it. Anyway, your father – I imagine he'll be back soon. Now that Treadwell's have agreed to pay for the damage the men caused to the police station, I doubt if any further action will be taken. Especially for such a small item as a necklace.'

'Oh, that's grand news,' Poppy said happily. 'Does that mean he can come home safely, do you think?'

'With impunity.' He smiled that tasty smile again. 'I would certainly think so.'

A lull followed in their conversation while Poppy tried to work out who 'Impunity' was. She considered asking him, but had no wish to belittle herself by showing her ignorance.

'Is this hobby horse new?' she asked conversationally.

The frame was made of wood, as were the wheels, but each wheel was furnished with an iron rim. The handlebars and front forks were forged from wrought iron, as were the treadles for his feet at the side of the front wheel.

'Not quite,' Mr Crawford answered, and let go of the handlebars to sit back against the pad that shielded him from the larger rear wheel. 'Actually, it's not strictly a hobby horse – I don't know what I should call it. You scoot a hobby horse along with your feet, which is dashed hard on the shoes. This has treadles at the front wheel, as you can see, with connecting rods to these crank arms that drive the back wheel.' He diligently pointed them out to her. 'So you don't have to drag your feel along the ground like you would if you were astride an old hobby horse. Once you've got going, you can keep up the motion, just by working the treadles with your feet.'

'I bet it cost a mint of money,' Poppy commented.

'I lost track, to tell you the truth. I built it myself, you see. All except the wheels, which were made for me by a wheelwright. I didn't really keep a tally of how much it all cost.'

'Where did you get the idea from?'

'Well, I was living in Scotland a year or so ago and I saw some chap riding one. I thought, what a brilliant idea. So I made a few sketches and determined to build one just like it. This is the result.'

'It looks as if it might be fun, Mr Crawford. Is it?'

'Great fun! It's cheaper than a horse and it doesn't get tired or thirsty. You don't have to find a stable either, nor buy feed . . . Look, since you're allowing me to call you Poppy, please call me Robert,' he said as an afterthought. 'There's really no need to call me Mister Crawford.'

Poppy smiled again. 'Thank you . . . Robert.' Savouring the feel of his name in her mouth and on her lips, she said his name again, quietly to herself.

He pulled his watch out from his fob and checked the time. 'I really must go, Poppy. I'm glad I've seen you and had the chance to talk to you. I hope your father will soon return.' He shoved off with his feet, travelled a few yards and stopped again near the entrance to the workings. 'Look, if you'd like to try riding this machine of mine, you can meet me sometime, if you like.'

'To ride it, you mean?' Poppy queried.

'Yes. You said it looked like fun, and it is.'

'Oh, I don't know,' she remarked hesitantly. 'I mean, I

don't think it would be seemly . . . . the sight of me on a hobby horse.' She was thinking about her skirt having to be hitched up. 'Not very ladylike.'

He laughed, somewhat melted by this prepossessing young girl as he realised her predicament. Even to the uncultured young daughter of a navvy, modesty was still evidently a consideration. 'You could sit side-saddle on the crossbar with me, while I rode.'

'All right, I will,' she agreed, with a shy smile and a nod. 'When?'

'Tomorrow? . . . No, not tomorrow, unfortunately. I have to take some measurements on the Brierley Hill section . . . Wednesday. I have my dinner at about one o'clock. I could meet you here, if you like. We could whizz down the rest of Shaw Road as fast as a steam locomotive. And beyond if we wanted to.'

She chuckled with delight. 'All right. Wednesday.'

He waved, turning his machine into the compound, and she watched him dreamily as he leaned it against the wall of the hut the foremen used as an office.

Chapter 4

The womenfolk of the navvies tended to be as sober as their men were drunken. Many were navvy-born, spending their whole lives tramping from town to town, from one huddle of shanties to another. A few had been seduced into following some strapping, carefree, well-paid and handsome navvy who entertained them royally in an effort to impress as he was passing through their town or village. Navvy-born girls, who knew no other life, grew up early and adopted the habits and attitudes of the older women when as young as twelve or thirteen. They worked hard from early morning and into the night, cleaning huts and boots that were forever dirty by virtue of the work the men did. They bore the navvies' children, nurtured them and brought them up as best they could, fretting over their health and well-being. Their particular kind of self-respect seldom extended to matrimony, however, save for their own version of it, which was solemnised by the couple jumping over a broomstick, and then consummating their union in front of as many drunken spectators as could be crammed into the room that housed their bed. Because Lightning Jack was a ganger, he was entitled to take lodgers into the hut he rented from the contractor. Sheba was therefore expected to keep the fire going, darn endless pairs of socks, do the washing, the mending, and the cooking for those paying lodgers.

Poppy and Minnie lived in similar circumstances in different huts that were essentially alike. They were obliged to help their mothers and did so, reliably and willingly. But like their mothers, they were no more than unpaid skivvies. Their rough way of life gave them insights into the goings-on between men and women from which girls in different circumstances would be thoroughly protected. These goings-on affected some more than others, although nothing ever shocked them for they were immune. Minnie, for one, was exhilarated by the sights and sounds of others engaged in sexual intercourse – sights and sounds that she often encountered – and these antics influenced her own lax attitude to sex. Sex was no remarkable phenomenon; it was a commonplace, everyday occurrence to which she attached no greater reverence than she did her other natural bodily functions, except that sex was mightily more pleasurable. Consequently, you might go out of your way to enjoy it.

Poppy, on the other hand, was somewhat differently affected. She preferred to postpone the fateful day or night when she would, for the first time, be expected to similarly indulge. And she had been remarkably adept in pursuing that goal. The thought of doing it on her 'wedding night' in front of a drunken, unruly mob did not suffuse her with either joyful or eager anticipation.

When they had finished their work that evening, Poppy brushed her fair hair, put on her coat and went out into the rain to call for Minnie. Already the ground of the encampment, which had been dry and dusty for weeks, was suddenly a quagmire and her clogs squelched in the mud as she picked her way through it. She reached Ma Catchpole's hut, tapped on the door, opened it and put her head round. Minnie's father, known as 'Tipton Ted', was supping a tankard of beer through his unkempt beard and sucking on his gum-bucket

48

alternately as he sat soaking his feet in a bowl of hot water, his moleskin trousers rolled up to just below his knees. He greeted Poppy amiably and asked if she had any news of her father. She replied that she hadn't.

Minnie then appeared from the little bedroom. She had made a special effort with herself and looked neat and tidy. Her face glowed shiny from the effects of soap and water and her dark hair hung down in tight ringlets under her bonnet.

'I'm ready,' she said to Poppy, and bid goodnight to her folks.

'Where shall we go?' Poppy asked when they were back outside in the rain.

'Anywhere we can find shelter,' Minnie replied, stepping into a mudbath at their front door. 'Look at me boots already. This front door's a muck wallow. Dog Meat and me dad will be moaning like hell tomorrow. It'll be that hard to get the muck out of the wagons when it's wringing wet and stuck together in a stodge.'

Instinctively, they walked towards the footpath and Shaw Road, stepping over black puddles in the half light.

'Have you seen much of that Jericho since?' Poppy enquired.

'Yes, I took him some dinner on a tray. He's got matey with Dog Meat already. They'm going to the Grin and Bear It together. I fancy going there and seeing 'em.'

'You *mean* you fancy seeing this Jericho.'

Minnie nodded and smiled as she glanced at Poppy.

'*I* met somebody today,' Poppy coyly remarked.

'Oh?'

'An engineer who works for Treadwell's. I reckon he's about twenty-three.'

'An engineer?' Minnie sounded incredulous. 'How did you meet him?'

'When I was walking back from the tommy shop. He came

past me riding a two-wheeled machine like a hobby horse. He recognised me. He's the one I told you about who came to our hut with that vile policeman, when me father jacked off. Any road, he stopped to talk. He asked me if I'd heard from me father. He was ever so friendly, and he seemed kind – as if he really cared.'

'What's he look like?' Minnie asked.

'Ooh, handsome,' Poppy said with a dreamy smile. 'And he's got such lovely, kind eyes. I really liked him, Minnie.'

'You liked him? The likes of you have got no hope of getting off with somebody like an engineer, Poppy. Engineers am educated. Unless he just wants to get you down in the grass and give you one.'

'He didn't strike me as being like that,' Poppy replied defensively. 'He called me "Miss Silk". Can you imagine? Me? Miss Silk?'

'He definitely wants to give you one.'

Poppy shrugged. 'He can if he wants. I'm game. I'm meeting him Wednesday. He's going to give me a ride on his machine.'

'Oh, yes,' Minnie laughed, cynically. 'Then when you both fall off, he'll look into your eyes while you'm both lying there – you with your frock up round your neck – and ask, "Are you all right, Miss Silk?" then climb right on top of you. His little pego will be up you like a shot, like an eel wriggling up a stream.'

Poppy giggled girlishly. 'You've got a vivid imagination, Min. But I don't mind if he does. I told you, I really, really like him. I just hope he kisses me to death. Oh, I'd love to kiss them lips of his.'

Minnie whooped with joy. 'I never thought I'd see the day when you was took with somebody, Poppy Silk.'

'Nor me neither,' Poppy answered. 'But I can't wait for Wednesday.'

The two girls arrived at The Wheatsheaf. On tiptoe, they peered through the window for sight of Dog Meat. The public house was heaving with those navvies who still had money to spend, as well as black-faced miners from the several pits that were dotted about the area, and iron workers with whom they enjoyed a friendly rivalry. Dog Meat spotted Minnie and Poppy, and went outside to fetch them in.

'I'll get yer a glass o' beer apiece,' Dog Meat said. 'Go and talk to Jericho.'

Minnie glanced at Poppy and Poppy saw that Minnie's face was flushed at the prospect of being with Jericho. Oh, that Minnie fancied Jericho all right.

Jericho was sitting at a cast-iron table, twisting a tankard of beer around with his fingers. He grinned when he saw Minnie, then beamed at Poppy.

'Who's this then?' he said, in his strange accent. His eagerness to know Poppy was evident in his expression.

'This is my mate Poppy,' Minnie said.

'I never seen so many pretty wenches on a job,' Jericho said with a broad grin. 'Rare beauties all of ye, and that's the truth, so 'tis.'

'Where are you from?' Poppy asked, also fascinated by his piercing blue eyes.

'From Chippenham. A good few days' tramp. Ever been to Chippenham, Poppy?'

'Not unless the railway runs through it.'

'The Great Western runs right through it. I'll take you to Chippenham some fine day. I'll hire a carriage to take us from the station. A pretty girl like you should be treated like a lady. Nothing less than a carriage and pair would be good enough.'

Poppy smiled reticently, remembering Robert Crawford; inevitably comparing the two men.

'Have you got a chap, Poppy?' Jericho asked. 'If not, I'm

just the chap for you. We'd make a fine couple, you and me, eh?'

'You're wasting your time trying to butter Poppy up,' Minnie said jealously, trying to dissuade this new resident away from her friend. 'She's already took with one of Treadwell's engineers. What's his name, Poppy, did you say?'

'*I* didn't say I was took with him,' Poppy argued, aware of what Minnie was up to. '*You* said it. Not me.'

'Only 'cause you *am* took with him, Poppy.' Minnie turned to Jericho. 'Less than ten minutes ago she told me she wouldn't mind this engineer giving her one – and how she's meeting him Wednesday and can hardly wait. What did you say his name was?'

Poppy sighed and looked archly at her slender fingers. 'Robert Crawford.'

'And he rides one o' them two-wheeled machines what looks like an 'obby 'orse.'

'What he built himself,' Poppy added with pride. ''Cept for the wheels.'

'Well, I can see I got some competition . . . Still . . .' Jericho grinned with supreme confidence. 'Competition never bothered me afore.'

Later that night, when they had returned to their huts and Poppy was in bed, she heard a commotion outside in the compound. Men's cheering and jeering voices told her it must be a fight. The sounds of fists slapping against flesh and cracking against bone, the earnest grunts of men in a tussle, confirmed it. She sat up in bed, then threw back the blanket and dragged herself out. She found her slippers in the darkness, put her mantle on over her nightgown, and stepped outside to see who it was. The rain had ceased but mud was everywhere. Silhouetted by the feeble light that fell through the open door of Minnie's hut, a group of men had gathered, encouraging the two men who were grappling each other. Poppy crept forward to see who was involved but, in the darkness, she could not be certain. She saw Minnie, who had also come out to watch, her head darting from side to side as she tried to see round the shoulders of big men in front of her.

Poppy tugged Minnie's coat from behind. 'Who's fighting?'

'Jericho and Chimdey Charlie.'

'What are they fighting over?'

'A pillow,' Minnie replied, as if it were the most normal thing in the world. 'And look . . . they'm as naked as the day they was born.' She put her hand over her mouth in mock shock and giggled joyously. 'He's a strapping chap, ain't he, that Jericho?'

Poppy peered through the crowd and tried to catch a glimpse. 'They must be mad,' she uttered, and turned to go.

'He's got a tidy doodle on him and no mistake,' Minnie remarked, her eyes sparkling with the reflected light of oil lamps from the hut. 'Have you seen it?'

'No, neither do I want to,' Poppy answered with pious indignation.

But the fight was taking a decisive turn and Poppy continued watching, her natural curiosity getting the better of her. One of the men was down in the mud, prone, and showed no signs of getting up yet awhile. The victor stood over the loser, the muscles of his back clear and defined like live eels wriggling under his skin. He rubbed his hands together, then gave his victim a final kick between the legs. The men began to disperse, discussing the finer points of the scuffle, acknowledging that the winner was a fine fighter, as strong as an ox. Poppy saw that it was indeed Jericho. She turned her back on

53

him and walked away, but he had seen her and called after her, ignoring Minnie.

'Did you see me beat that vermin?' he asked excitedly, breathing hard as he caught up with her. His face was unmarked by the fray; only his body had a patch or two of caking mud stuck to it, matted in the dark hairs of his broad chest.

'I don't understand what there was to fight about,' Poppy said indifferently and walked on, determined not to look at him.

'That spunkless article had got two pillows and I hadn't got a one,' he said, following her. 'So I lifted it off his bunk and put it on mine. He didn't take kindly to it, so I offered to fight him for it.'

He walked beside her for a while, unabashed by his naked-ness, and grabbed hold of her, twisting her round to face him. 'Kiss me, Poppy,' he said and his eyes were intensely pene-trating, even in the dimness of the night. He thrust his hands inside her mantle and pulled it open. As he drew her to him she could instantly feel the warmth of his body, hot from his exertion, urgently pressing against hers with only the thin cotton of her nightgown between them. As he sought her lips and found them, she felt him harden almost at once, insistent, pressing against her warm belly. For a few seconds she thrilled to the sensation, pleased that she was having such a rousing effect on him.

'You got nothin' on under your coat except your night-dress,' he commented excitedly as he cupped her small bottom in his huge hands. 'Come with me round the back o' the hut.'

Poppy pulled herself away from him and wiped her mouth. 'I will not,' she said fervently. 'Don't think I'm like other navvy wenches, Jericho, 'cause I'm not. Who do you think you are anyway, coming here and thinking I'm going to fall at your feet?'

He looked at her for a few seconds, uncertain how to react, and Poppy was afraid he might strike her for her disaffection. At last he grinned at her. 'Oh, playing hard to get, eh? Saving yourself for that Crawford, are you? Well, I don't mind playing that game. You'll be worth the wait and you'll taste all the sweeter for it . . .' He displayed himself lewdly, cupping himself in both hands . . . 'And so will I . . .'

Poppy turned and ran back to the hut.

She found it difficult to sleep that night, tossing and turning on the feather mattress till it became lumpy. Images of Jericho, naked in the darkness, invaded her mind. Good thing it had been dark. She knew exactly what Minnie saw in him, with his raw good looks, his thick, dark curls and his muscular body that showed not one ounce of fat. But he was arrogant. He knew women fancied him. Women would be there for the taking, wherever he went. But not her. Not Poppy. Oh, he expected her to be like all the others – easy meat. But he had not met anybody like her before. She was not about to be beguiled by the likes of him. Besides, he was just another navvy. Imagine being his devoted woman, sharing his bed at night, bearing his children, yet never sure that he was not bedding some other woman he'd duped with diverting half promises and the prospect of unbounded pleasuring.

So she turned her thoughts to Robert Crawford . . . Robert Crawford, that gentle soul who was not so high and mighty that he would wilfully pass her by and fail to acknowledge her, even though she was only a navvy's daughter. He'd called her 'Miss Silk'. He'd shown her respect and she enjoyed his courtesy. He was so friendly, so easy to talk to. He had no side on him, and yet . . . His eyes were so bright and alert, and they had been warm on her. Maybe he liked her too, but it could never be as much as she liked him. She would be fooling herself if she allowed herself to believe otherwise. But she wished that he would kiss her. Not roughly, like Jericho, who had stolen a hard slobbering kiss, but warmly, lovingly, with a gentle, sensitive, understated passion that would make her toes curl.

Poppy eventually fell asleep with Robert Crawford in her thoughts. Her dream that night was different from any other dream she had ever experienced. It was not the dream of a child, nor even of a young girl, but of a woman – arousing, stimulating, startling and vividly erotic. It involved herself and two men, both naked, one of whom was riding a two-wheeled machine akin to a hobby horse. She was sitting on the crossbar of the machine in the arms of the naked Robert Crawford, her face against his neck as she nestled in his arms, the wind rippling through her hair, the street flashing past in a blur as they sped down it. And then they fell off the machine into soft long grass and tumbled head over heels. Her skirt was up over her bodice and he was crawling towards her, a look of concern on his beautiful face. 'Are you all right, Miss Silk?' he asked, just as Minnie had said he would, but so tenderly. She nodded, smiling as she realised she was naked from the waist down. He scrambled to get on top of her and kissed her lovingly, yet hungrily, and she felt him enter her, so sweetly, so gently, that she hoped the moment would last forever. But in her dream she was also aware of this other naked man, huge, rough and threatening. He came into view and lifted Robert bodily from her and took his place, hurting her, thrashing inside her like some frantic fish caught in a net. She awoke momentarily, tried to exorcise Jericho from her mind and return to Robert . . . But Robert had gone . . .

* * *

Lightning Jack and Bilston Buttercup had reached the sweeping curve of Chipping Campden's High Street on the day they anticipated. They enquired as to the proximity of the railway line and the Mickleton tunnel but the locals, who seemed very respectable, did not seem kindly disposed towards them. Eventually, they were directed out of the village on a north-easterly path. They came to the railway track bed under construction and followed it until it came to a dead end. Lightning Jack speculated that the tunnel workings must be over the hill that lay before them. It was not long before they saw the mountains of spoil, the shaft with its steam engine, and a small shanty town of dilapidated huts. A navvy directed them to a ganger who set them on.

Both men had exhausted their money, mainly on beer, but they were amply fed and watered that evening by the resident navvies, with typical navvy hospitality. Their lodgings were in a hut similar to that which Lightning had left behind at the Blowers Green encampment. The same ganger who had employed them, called 'Swillicking Mick' because of the vast amounts of beer he was reputed to drink, operated it.

They ate that evening in the common living room of the hut with the others, enjoying cuts from a massive piece of beef and mounds of potatoes from a huge pot that hung over the fire. The only windows, each immediately either side of the solitary door, were stuck in the middle of the room's longest wall. The kitchen was located opposite a stack of beer barrels. It was home from home.

Swillicking Mick kept them amply supplied with beer. 'Pay me when you get paid, lads,' he said. 'I'll not rob thee for it. I brew it meself so it works out cheaper than the stuff from the tommy shop.'

'It's decent stuff an' all,' Lightning commented. 'Pour us another if it's cheap.'

Swillicking Mick's woman, wearing a leather belt from which hung the keys to the locked beer barrels, duly poured Lightning another and made a note of it in a little book that she withdrew from the pocket of her apron.

'There's no decent beer shop hereabouts, so a few on us have begun brewing our own,' Mick informed them. 'Course, you can always tramp into Campden. A good many do of a Saturday night. The beer houses want our trade, but the locals ain't too fond o' the rumpus we cause. Already they've put bars up at the windows o' some o' the properties, save 'em getting bost.'

'The contractors don't like you brewing your own beer, I'll warrant,' Buttercup ventured, nodding in the direction of the barrels. ''Specially if they ain't taking a cut.'

'Nor would the exciseman if he knew,' Mick said with a wink. 'The only problem is, I'm more inclined to sell me beer than work on the construction. So would all the others. It earns us a mint o' money.'

Mick's woman, Hannah, began clearing the things away and the men continued talking. There were nine or ten men in the room; it was getting noisier and the humour increasingly boisterous. Then there was a knock at the door; more customers for Swillicking Mick. A group of five or six ruffians entered, one of whom carried a fiddle and a bow. They bought beer, and the chap with the fiddle began playing a lively tune. Several of the men began dancing with each other, their boots hammering on the floorboards. Others were sitting on the floor playing cards, their poaching dogs alongside them, and they complained that the dancing would be understandable if there were women about. At that, the door opened again and half a dozen women and girls squeezed inside.

'The women from the mill,' Swillicking Mick remarked with a wink.

It was beginning to get crowded. The card-players cheered and got up from the dusty floor, to engage in a more interesting sport.

One of the women – she looked about thirty years old but was possibly younger – attached herself to Lightning.

'I've not seen you before, have I, chuck?' she said in her rural drawl.

'Not unless you can see as far as Dudley,' Lightning answered.

'You do talk funny. Is that how they talk in Dudley?'

Lightning grinned inanely; the beer was having its effect. 'They talk even funnier than me in Dudley. I come from Cheshire. But even Dudley folk don't sound so weird as you with your quaint country twang. What's your name, by the way?'

'Jenny Sparrow. What's yours?'

'They call me Lightning Jack.'

'Well, Jack, you look a big, strong chap to me, with your big, drooping moustaches. Spoke for, are ye?'

Lightning took a swig of beer and wiped his moustache with the back of his hand. 'What's it to you? Fancy your chances, do you?'

'I'm not so ugly as to be discounted, am I, Jack?'

'Ugly?' he queried. 'No, you're a fine-looking wench, Jenny . . . And that's a handsome bosom you're flaunting.'

Jenny beamed. 'Maybe you'd like to help yourself to a handful later?'

'It depends what it's gunna cost me.'

'Oh, I don't do it for money, Jack. I do it for love . . .'

Chapter 5

Waiting for Wednesday was, for Poppy, like waiting for her plum pudding at Christmas. As one o'clock approached, she tried hard to remain calm, anxious not to give her mother any hint at all that she was leaving her to do the cooking and the feeding of lodgers, just to meet a young man – and one above her station at that. Sheba would get to hear of it, no doubt. Somebody was bound to see them and report back. Nor would Sheba be pleased. But Poppy would handle that crisis when it arose . . .

She had taken the trouble to wash her hair the night before. She had cleaned her clogs and her fingernails. In the family's overcrowded bedroom she'd stood at the washstand and enjoyed a thorough wash down, feeling fresh and confident after it. She had laundered her stockings, and inspected the clothes she intended wearing, which, to allay any suspicion, would have to be a working frock.

So, at five minutes to one, she took off her pinafore, tidied her hair and looked at herself briefly in the ancient, mildewed mirror that hung by a piece of string from a nail near the door. If only she had a more alluring frock to wear, but to change it and put on her best red one would have been to broadcast her intentions. So she resigned herself to the fact that she must make do. At least the frock she was wearing was clean. Poppy failed to realise that she looked good in whatever she wore. She was blessed with a beautiful face and a complexion as fair as her flaxen hair. She possessed a natural daintiness and elegance of movement which, had she been dressed in silks or velvets, would have been perceived as grace.

She put on her bonnet and slipped out without a word to her mother. The rain of Monday had ceased and the weather had changed for the better again, with sunshine and a gentle breeze. Thankfully, the mud of the encampment was drying out. Poppy walked towards Shaw Road at the intersection with the footpath where she was supposed to meet Robert, her heart thumping in anticipation. While she waited, first looking up Shaw Road for sight of him, then self-consciously at her clogs, she felt conspicuous, certain that the wary eyes of the encampment were on her and suspicious of what she was up to.

Before too long she heard the familiar clack-clack of the iron-rimmed wheels traversing the craggy surface of the road. She turned to see Robert hurtling towards her, a grin on his handsome face, and her heart lurched.

He'd remembered.

'Have you been waiting long?' he asked, when he came to a stop beside her. 'Sorry if I kept you waiting. I was held up by Mr Shafto – you know, the sub-assistant – wanting some information about some measurements I'd taken.'

Poppy smiled at him brightly. 'It don't matter, Robert. I was a bit early . . . but I had to get out when the chance came.'

'I presume, then, that you haven't changed your mind about riding with me?'

She shook her head. 'No, I ain't changed me mind, but I was thinking about what might happen if we fell off,' she said, vividly recalling her dream.

He shrugged. 'We could, of course. It's entirely possible.

But if the fear of it puts you off, I'll be extra careful that we don't. It's not as if you're going to be an enormous weight to carry. You're quite small really. Why don't you get on?'

She stood close to him and turned around so that she could sit on the crossbar of his machine. It felt hard against her rump, like the bar of a gate.

'You need to sit back a little bit further,' Robert said, 'so that the machine balances. And so that I can get my feet on the treadles.'

She pushed herself further on and felt the crossbar under her backside. Robert was steadying the handlebar and his right arm formed a barrier that she could lean against to prevent her toppling over backwards.

'Are you ready? Lift your feet higher . . . no, higher . . . I have to reach the treadles. Don't worry, I'll hold you.'

He scooted off and, after a couple of initial wobbles, they began travelling in a commendably straight trajectory. The road was pitted and bumpy and the frame of the machine transmitted all those bumps to Poppy. Her very bones juddered, but it was exhilarating. The wind was in her hair and against her face as they gathered speed, and she heard herself shrieking with excitement. They hurtled underneath the new railway bridge and approached a grassy mound that vaguely marked the end of Shaw Road and the start of the undulating footpath to Netherton. As they rode over it, Poppy's innards rolled over and seemed to reach her throat in an unbelievable sensation, making her whoop with delight. She was between Robert's arms, holding on to him tightly while he steered the machine, conscious of his left leg rising and falling under her skirt as he controlled their speed with the treadles. The ground over the footpath seemed softer, with no hard bumps to bruise her bottom and the backs of her thighs more. She would not mind falling off now and rolling into the long grass at the side of the footpath with Robert . . .

But they did not fall off. They bowled past tiny cottages in desperate need of repair, past the Old Buffery Iron Works that glowed red at night-time, flaring the dark sky with an eerie crimson glow. They skimmed past the Iron Stone pit with its huffing, clanking steam engine. Robert slowed down the machine as they reached the turnpike road from Netherton to Dudley at Cinder Bank, and carried on over fields. Just before they reached a fishpond, they stopped.

'Well?' Robert said. 'Did you enjoy that?'

Poppy was breathless after the ride. 'Oh, I loved it, Robert.' She hooted with laughter, and with the back of her hand wiped away wind-induced tears that had traced a watery line across her flushed cheeks.

She sat on the crossbar pressed against him, still trapped between his arms, radiant with excitement. Robert looked at the delightful profile of her face. She was close enough for him to steal a kiss if he wanted, although he did not take advantage. Instead, he smiled with satisfaction at the few moments of joy he'd brought to this enigmatic girl, by giving her something as simple as a ride on his rudimentary two-wheeled machine.

Feeling Robert's strong right arm protectively at her back, Poppy was loath to dismount, but she let her feet fall to the ground and eased herself forward. As she stood, her skirt brushing the side of the machine, she hoped Robert would invite her for another ride at some time.

'Well, we have a long walk back,' he commented, himself dismounting. He turned the two-wheeled contraption round and began pushing it in the opposite direction. 'I've been working on a design for another machine,' he said to Poppy as she ambled beside him. 'Similar to this one but with a better means of propelling it forward. I'm convinced that something like it has immense commercial potential.'

She turned to him and smiled with admiration, uncertain of the meaning of the words 'commercial' and 'potential'. If only she was educated. If only she had been given some schooling, she would be more able to talk with him on his level.

'What time do you have to be back at work?' she asked, mundanely.

'Half past one. Mr Lister, the resident engineer, gets rather rattled if I'm late.'

'So what time is it now?'

He took his watch from his fob and checked it. 'Quarter past. We're easy on.'

'Good. I wouldn't want you to get into trouble on my account.'

For the first few yards of their walk back, there was a pause in their conversation. Poppy noticed the wild flowers growing at the edges of the black earth footpath – buttercups, daisies, ragwort, dandelions. Thistles were thriving too, growing tall in the warmth of the May sun and the recent rain, and it struck her how beautiful they were to look at, if not to touch.

'Thank goodness we didn't fall off into those thistles,' she remarked. 'We'd have been scratched to death.'

'Or into nettles,' Robert replied easily.

She nodded. 'Oh, yes, I hate nettles.'

'So do I.'

'Do you like being an engineer, Robert?'

'Actually, yes, I do.' He turned to look at her face, always an entertaining mix of earnestness and gaiety. He was fascinated as well at how easily she could turn from one subject to another. 'It's interesting being an engineer. There's something different to deal with all the time.'

'What sort of things do you have to do?'

'Oh, measuring and marking out, tracing plans, trying to calculate whether the spoil we take from a cutting will be sufficient to build an embankment. I'm handy with a pair of brass dividers, a blacklead and a straight-edge.'

'I've often wondered,' Poppy said, her face suddenly an icon of puzzlement, 'if they start driving a tunnel from more than one place, how they manage to meet exactly in the middle.'

Robert laughed, fired with admiration for her curiosity. 'By candles, usually,' he replied.

'Candles? How do you mean?'

'Well, it's dark inside a tunnel, Poppy. So what you do is to line up the centre line of the tunnel by exactly placing lighted candles at predetermined intervals. When you have three candles exactly in line as you match them up against the cross hairs on your theodolite, then you know your tunnel is straight – or level, if you're taking levels.'

'What about if there's a bend in the tunnel?'

He laughed again, astonished at her grasp of engineering problems. 'Before you start excavating a tunnel, you sink narrow shafts along the way,' he explained. 'These shafts would already have been pinpointed during a survey. The centres of those shafts meet the centre line of the tunnel perpendicularly and, if they're not in direct line – in other words, if they form a bend – you follow the line they form. Do you understand?'

Poppy nodded and emitted a deep sigh. When Robert looked at her again, her expression was serious, almost grave.

'What's wrong?' he asked, concerned. 'Are you worrying about your father?'

'Oh, no, I was just thinking how lovely it must be to be educated. To be clever enough to do all the things you do.'

'Oh, I'm not particularly clever,' he said modestly. 'But having had a decent education enables me to earn a good living, I admit.'

'I wish I was educated. It'd help me get away from the navvy life. If only I could read and write . . .'

'Don't you like the navvy life?'

'Would *you* like it?'

'Probably not,' he admitted. 'But I work with the navvies, such as your father. I find them agreeable enough, by and large – when they're sober, anyway. Ask them to do a job, explain what you want, and they do it. They work like the devil, shifting hundreds, even thousands of tons of earth in no time. You must have watched an excavation and seen how, in only a few days, they can transform a landscape. They don't mince their words either. If they have something to say, they say it. But living with them? . . . I imagine some of them are inclined to be uncouth.'

'I don't know what that word means, Robert – *uncouth*. I hope you'll excuse my not having been educated.'

'Uncouth?' He smiled kindly. 'It means rough, rude, barbarian.'

Poppy laughed. 'Oh, yes. Most of them are *uncouth* . . . *barbarian* . . . See? I've learnt two new words a'ready. I do wish you could teach me more . . .'

'I'm afraid that what I know is limited to engineering and surveying, and not much use to a young woman,' he said realistically.

He turned to look at her, sympathy manifest in his eyes. This girl was not like the navvies to whom she belonged. She was apart from them, a cut above, bright – extremely bright – thirsting for an education which had eluded her, and thence for knowledge to lift her out of her humdrum existence. It was a worthy aspiration, too. If her life took the normal course one would anticipate of a navvy-born girl, she would be expected at her age, or even younger, to be the compliant bed partner of whichever buck navvy was first to claim her, if not of her own volition then either by buying her, or by fighting somebody else for her. It would be a sin if she were so treated and thus doomed for lack of education. She was worthy of so much better. Her self-respect raised her above the meagre expectations of navvy women. It was truly a wonder she had not already been claimed . . .

'Where the hell d'you think you've been?' Sheba angrily asked Poppy when she re-entered Rose Cottage. 'Fancy sloping off when we was finishing off the dinners. Where've you been? You've been gone nearly an hour.'

Some of the navvies were still in the room, sitting at the round table, their legs sprawling, big boots seeming to take up most of the floor space. The place reeked with an unsavoury mixture of pipe tobacco smoke, beer, sweat, cooking and rotting vegetables.

'I had to go out, Mom,' Poppy replied quietly with a guilty look, turning away from the navvies so that they shouldn't hear.

'Had to?'

'I promised to meet somebody. I couldn't let them down.'

'Bin a-courtin', my wench?' one of the men, called Waxy Boyle, asked through a mouthful of dumpling.

'It'll pay her not to have bin a-courtin',' Sheba railed. 'Not when there's work to be done. Who did you go and meet?'

Poppy blushed. Blushing was becoming a habit which she did not enjoy. 'I'll tell you after, not that it's any of your business.'

'I'll give you none of my business, you cheeky faggot. Get your apron on and do some work, you bone-idle little harridan. Any road, I'll get to know soon enough, whether or no it's any of my business.'

'I ain't been courting, Mom,' Poppy added defensively. She removed her bonnet and hung it up on the back of the door. 'I ain't courting nobody. I just went to meet somebody.'

'A chap or a wench?'

'I'm not saying.'

The assembled navvies laughed raucously. One of them said that it must be a chap, because she'd admit it if she'd only met a wench.

'It's time her had a chap,' Tweedle Beak said to Sheba as he cut a slice of tobacco with his pocketknife from a stick of twist. 'A fine-lookin' wench like young Poppy. By the living jingo, I wish I was ten or fifteen years younger.'

'She can have a chap – I couldn't give tuppence who he was – and he'd be welcome to her,' Sheba replied. 'But when she's supposed to be helping me she'll stay here and work.' She turned to Poppy. 'So get cracking, and knuckle down to it.'

Two more weeks passed and Lightning Jack had not returned. In that time, Chimdey Charlie, whom Jericho had fought and beaten over a pillow that wet and muddy night, had sloped off, owing money to Ma Catchpole for his lodgings. Many speculated that he must have left feeling ashamed at being belittled by Jericho in front of his mates. Ashamed or not, he obviously felt vengeful, because he took with him the pillow he had lost to Jericho. Jericho, however, had gained much respect from winning that fight. Few men were prepared to challenge him, having seen the ruthless efficiency and strength with which he had quickly overcome and downed Chimdey Charlie.

Jericho had not bothered Poppy since, either. She noticed

his ignoring her, but she was steeped in thoughts of Robert Crawford. It did seem odd, though, that Jericho should suddenly fail to pay her any attention at all after the fuss he made over her at first. Evidently he was just another of the faithless type she'd heard about, the type that blows hot and cold, fickle, unpredictable. For all that, she was a little intrigued. How could somebody show such an obvious interest one day, then turn away from her the next? Maybe she had expressed a little too strongly that she was not like the other girls he'd met, that she was not easy meat. Yet he'd said he rose to such a challenge. Well, he hadn't risen to this one – and thank goodness.

Another person who had not been near Poppy, although he had not been entirely avoiding her, was Robert Crawford. Actually, he found her totally disarming, which began to worry him seriously. He was torn between leaving her be, because of her lowly upbringing and complete lack of any station in life, and the desire to gaze upon her striking countenance once more. If he could find a plausible excuse to see her again he would. He had considered offering her some help in overcoming the same lowliness that was manifestly dividing them. But how could he help? It would hardly be seemly to give her money, even if he could afford it. He could hardly whisk her away from the encampment and set her up in a lodging house without the world accusing him of keeping a very young mistress, when that was not his intention. Such an accusation would not do his situation any good at all, with all the responsibilities it entailed.

So he didn't go out of his way to see Poppy. He lacked the excuse. In any case, he didn't want her to get the wrong idea and think he harboured a romantic interest. How could he possibly be interested in the illegitimate daughter of some navvy who'd had to flee the site to avoid prosecution and likely transportation? Just because her face was angelically beautiful and he couldn't keep his eyes off her . . . Just because there was this undeniable grace and elegance behind the rags and tatters and hideous clogs that she wore . . . He would be a laughing stock. All the same, it was a great sin that that same undeniable grace and elegance would never have the chance to surface and decorate the world. It was a greater sin that her natural intelligence would never have the opportunity to shine through. Could it not be nurtured somehow and put to good use, at least for the benefit of the navvy community, if not for society in general?

If only he could devise some way of helping her without compromising either of them. She was worthy of help, that Poppy Silk. She deserved better than the unremitting mediocrity of the life she led. She warranted something more uplifting than constant exposure to the crushing, unrestrainable coarseness and brutality of the navvies' encampment to which she was shackled. But what? How could he, a mere engineer, possibly help *her*?

And then he had an idea.

On the first Saturday of June, as it was approaching yo-ho – the time when navvies finished their work – Sheba and Poppy were sweating over the copper. Lottie and Rose, Sheba's younger daughters, were outside in the sunshine. Her son, Little Lightning, was still at work. Each man's dinner was wrapped in a linen cloth and boiled in the copper, tied to a stick from which it hung. Because the women could not read, each stick bore identifying notches. If a stick had five notches cut into it, it belonged to Tweedle Beak. If it had three notches it was Waxy Boyle's, and so on.

They chatted as they worked, speculating on how much Crabface Lijah had paid for his bit of beef and a few spuds, how much Brummagem Joe's lamb shank had cost, which he was intending having with a cabbage that was also netted in the copper.

Poppy looked up at the clock over the outside door and saw that it was five minutes to one. 'I expect we shall be trampled underfoot in a few minutes,' she said, anticipating the hungry navvies.

'Here,' said Sheba. 'Have this key and unlock the barrel ready. They'll be red mad for their beer as well.'

Poppy took the key and unlocked the barrel. No sooner had she done it than the door opened and Tweedle Beak stepped inside, carrying a dead rabbit.

'Cop ote o' this and skin and gut it, young Poppy, wut? I'll have it for me dinner with a few taters. And doh forget to tek the yed off.'

Poppy looked at the sad, limp thing with distaste. Drawing and skinning dead animals was not her favourite pastime, but she took it from Tweedle and dropped it into the stone sink.

'All right if I help meself to a jar o' beer?' Tweedle enquired.

'So long as you give me the money first,' Poppy replied.

He lifted a mug from a hook that was screwed into a beam above his head and began to fill it from the barrel. 'Yo'll have yer money, have no fear. I'll tot up how many I'n had and pay your mother after. Eh, Sheba?'

Sheba turned around from her copper. 'I'd rather I totted it up meself.'

'Never let yer down yet, have I?'

'No. You'm one of the decent ones, Tweedle. Any road, the first time you don't pay will be the last.'

Tweedle uttered a rumble of laughter. 'Yo'm a fine, spirited wench and no two ways, Sheba,' he said, stepping up to her from the barrel and slapping her backside. 'And yo've got a fine arse an' all, eh?'

'My arse is my own business,' Sheba proclaimed, feigning indignation at his familiarity. 'So just you keep your hands to yourself.'

Poppy noticed with surprise that her mother had blushed, and pondered its significance. Tweedle laughed again, and the facial movement seemed to make his long nose even more pointed.

He swigged at his beer eagerly then looked over to Poppy. 'Hast skinned me bit o' rabbit yet?'

Poppy said that she had, and reached for a chopper that was hanging on a nail, to sever its head. Already, there was blood and entrails on her hands.

Tweedle refilled his mug. 'Yo'm a decent wench an' all, young Poppy . . . 'Cept for yer damned cheek,' he said with a matey grin.

Poppy placed the skinned rabbit on the wooden table and hacked its head off. Then she picked up the head and threw it into a pail that was standing on the floor beside her to collect the rest of the kitchen debris. She drew the innards like an experienced butcher and cleaned inside the carcass while Tweedle watched.

'Yo'd mek somebody a lovely wife, young Poppy, and that's the truth. Her's got the mekins, Sheba, wouldn't yer say?'

'Oh, she's got the makings and no two ways.'

'Her'd be a heap of fun in bed an' all, I'll wager. Bist thou a-courtin' yet, Poppy?'

'No.'

'Has nobody tried to bed thee? Nobody fought over thee?'

'No.' She looked up at Tweedle with a steady gaze that belied her years, to add emphasis to her response.

'What a mortal bloody waste—'

There was a knock on the door and it opened. Dandy Punch, the timekeeper, thrust his head round the jamb. 'Rent day,' he called officiously. 'Have you got some money for me this week, Sheba?'

Sheba had not been looking forward to this visit. Resignedly, she dried her hands on her apron and went to the door. 'You can come inside if you want to.'

Dandy Punch stepped inside. At once his eyes fell on Poppy, who was wrapping the skinned rabbit in the linen, ready to hang it in the copper with Tweedle Beak's potatoes.

'It's three weeks since Lightning Jack sloped off,' Dandy Punch said. 'Now you owe rent to the company for five weeks. Unless you pay me today, Sheba, I have to tell you you'm to be evicted.'

Evicted . . . Sheba sighed heavily, well aware that if she was evicted she would have no alternative but to go on tramp, taking her children with her. They would have to sleep rough under the stars. If they failed to locate Lightning Jack – a likely situation – they would be picked up in some town or village as vagrants and shipped off to the nearest workhouse. Almost certainly she would be separated from her children, and they would all have to wear workhouse clothes to set them apart from everybody else. But this was what it had come to, and she could not afford to wait for Lightning any longer. Why hadn't he come back? Didn't he realise the predicament his absence would put her in?

'Your young son earns money, don't he?' Dandy Punch said. 'Can't you pay me what you owe with that?'

'What he earns don't keep us in victuals, let alone rent,' Sheba said ruefully.

'Well, there's the money you get from selling the beer . . .'

'The beer has to be paid for. They don't dole it out to us out of the kindness of their hearts.'

'But you make a profit on it.'

'Otherwise there'd be no point in selling it,' Sheba agreed.

'But 'tis a small profit, and not enough to keep us. Besides meself and the one who's at work, I got four children to keep.'

'The other problem you got, Sheba, is that with Lightning Jack gone, you got no entitlement to stop in this hut. Lightning Jack was the tenant, and only somebody employed by the company is entitled to a tenancy. He ain't a company employee any more, Sheba. And neither are you.'

Sheba sighed, and Poppy looked on with heartfelt dismay at her mother's impossible situation.

'What about my son, Little Lightning?' Sheba suggested. 'Couldn't he be the tenant?'

'Is he twenty-one?'

Sheba shook her head ruefully. 'He's twelve . . .'

'Then there's no alternative. Eviction's the only answer. It's a problem you'll have to face, Sheba . . . Unless . . .' His eyes met hers intently and Sheba could tell he had a proposition to make.

'Unless what, Dandy Punch?' She looked at him with renewed hope.

'Unless I can have your daughter . . .'

'Me daughter?' Sheba looked at him in bewilderment. 'What do you mean exactly?'

'Let me have your daughter and I'll pay off the rent you owe. *And* I'll let you stop in the hut till Lightning comes back. He'll have to pay the rent he starts owing from this week, though.'

Sheba was still bewildered by the offer. 'What do you mean exactly, when you say you want me daughter?'

Dandy Punch scoffed at her apparent naivety. 'You don't strike me as being that daft, Sheba. I want her for me woman. I want her to keep me bed warm.'

'I ain't going with *him*,' Poppy shrieked in panic from the stone sink where she was scraping potatoes. 'Don't let him,

Mom. I'd rather go on tramp. I'd rather end up in the workhouse.'

'But, Poppy, it'd mean we could stop here, me and the kids, till your daddy came home,' Sheba reasoned. 'I wouldn't have the worry o' going on tramp and missing him coming the other way. We might never see him again. We could end up in the workhouse.'

'No, I won't,' Poppy insisted. 'I'd rather go in the workhouse. I'd rather die.' The thought of Dandy Punch mauling her in his stinking bed and slobbering all over her filled Poppy with a sickening revulsion. 'And you should be ashamed, Mother – prepared to let me go to him just to save yourself.'

Sheba quickly weighed up her daughter's comments. She caught the eyes of Dandy Punch and could not resist a defiant smile. 'She's right, you know. I should be ashamed. I don't think she fancies you that much, by the sound of it, Dandy Punch. I ain't got the right to sacrifice her. She's got notions of her own.'

Dandy Punch looked somewhat embarrassed. 'Well, it's your last chance,' he said, trying to recover his composure. 'And if your daughter can't see the benefit to her as well as to yourself, then she needs a good talking to, and a clip round the ear to boot, for being so stupid.'

'Oh, I don't think she's stupid,' Sheba said. 'Just particular.'

'In that case . . .' He coughed importantly in an effort to redeem some of his ebbing prestige. 'In that case, I'll be along this afternoon with the bailiffs—'

'Hang on, Dandy bloody Punch . . .' Tweedle Beak spoke. He arose from his chair and walked over to Sheba's side. 'I'm glad as I waited and listened, and watched you mek a bloody fool o' yerself, Dandy Punch, lusting after this innocent young wench here. D'yer really think as a young madam like that is likely to be enticed by some dirty, pot-bellied ode bugger like thee? An' any road, I'm an employee o' the company and there's nothing in the rules what says as I cor be the tenant, if I've a mind.' He felt in his trouser pocket and drew out a handful of gold sovereigns which he handed to the timekeeper. 'Pick the bones out o' that lot and gi' me the change I'm due. *I* pay the rent here from now on. *I'm* the tenant in this hut, so write *my* name in your blasted book . . . And Sheba here is *my* woman, if anybody wants to know.' He put his arm around her shoulders proprietorially. 'Does anybody say different?'

Tweedle Beak looked at Sheba and their eyes met. It seemed to Poppy that her mother's silence was consent enough.

Poppy went out that afternoon. She avoided Dudley town and its hordes of people; she avoided The Wheatsheaf with its navvies on their Saturday afternoon randy. She wanted to be alone, to think over just what her mother had let herself in for. Deep in thought, she headed towards Cinder Bank, walking the route she and Robert Crawford had taken on their ride. The hot June sun was on her face, but it did not warm her. She sat on a stile and, with her head in her hands, pondered the prospect of lying in the bed next to her mother and hook-nosed Tweedle Beak. For, despite her tender years, Poppy was canny enough to realise that Tweedle had not done what he had done out of charity; he would claim his rights over her mother that night. Sheba must have known, too. She must have been well aware. Poppy tried not to think about the grunting antics that would be performed with a vengeance as Tweedle drunkenly asserted his manhood and his possession of her mother, but mental images of them invaded her mind. The disturbing reality would arrive soon enough.

She reached out and snatched a stalk of twitch grass.

Absently, she split the stem with her fingernail and felt the moist sap oozing between her finger and thumb. Poppy had imagined that her mother was grieving over the absent Lightning Jack, but perhaps she wasn't. Perhaps she, too, was just yet another woman of easy virtue. Perhaps even she was hungry for a man by this time. Poppy's respect for her mother was under siege. What sort of example was the woman setting? Would it be easy for her to submit so readily to such a man? Was virtue so easily corrupted? Was Sheba really so corruptible that she could rashly sell her own body to Tweedle Beak for the price of a few weeks' rent, and Lightning Jack due back at any moment? Poppy was confusing herself with all these questions which she could not answer. Maybe Sheba had sacrificed herself to protect her from the clutches of Dandy Punch.

Her thoughts turned to Minnie. Minnie was easy; her skirt would be up in a trice for no more than a manly smile and a glass of beer. Why were some women like that? Why did they lack self-respect? Why did they cheapen themselves so? It made no sense. They were no better than the men. They were just as bad, just as depraved.

It then occurred to Poppy that maybe her father wasn't coming back. Maybe he'd used the threatened appearance before the beak and the prospect of transportation as an excuse to get away from a woman he'd been itching to leave for some time. Maybe his promise to return was just empty words. Maybe he'd already found a woman before he left and had sloped off with her. Men did that sort of thing. Maybe Sheba realised it. Even Poppy had known of several who had absconded, never to be heard of again.

So Lightning Jack could surely expect no better from Sheba. He knew the system. He was aware Sheba could not remain in a hut without him. He must also have known her sexual appetite; after all, she was not particularly old – only thirty-one – even though she looked older. Lightning must have known that some other hungry, healthy navvy would seize the opportunity to bed his woman in his absence. The trouble was, his absence suggested he did not care.

Chapter 6

After an hour or so of trying to make sense of this latest disturbing conundrum, Poppy ambled dejectedly back to the conglomeration of miserable huts that were a blight, even on the ravaged, slag-heaped, chimney-bestrewn landscape around Blowers Green. The sun was hiding behind a bank of grey clouds, depriving the scene even of the joy of colour. As she entered the compound, hungry, for she had not felt like eating after what had occurred, she caught sight of Robert Crawford's boneshaker leaning against the side of the hut that the foremen used as an office. She turned away, disappointed with Robert over his failure to seek her out after their dinner-time ride, which seemed ages ago. He must be avoiding her, so why give him the satisfaction of thinking that she wanted to see him?

But as she was about to enter her own hut, he came out of the foremen's and espied her. He called her name and she lost her resolve. His smile, to her delight, did not give the impression that he was sorry to see her – rather that he was decidedly pleased to. They walked towards each other, her smiling eyes glued on his, and they met in the open space at the centre of the encampment.

'Poppy, how grand to see you,' Robert greeted. He was wearing his usual top hat and frock coat, and his watch chain hung impressively across his waistcoat. 'Have you heard from your father yet?'

Poppy shook her head, saddened to be reminded. 'No, Robert, and I've got the feeling he ain't coming back.'

'Oh? Why on earth would you think that?'

'Well, 'cause he ain't shown up yet. He's had plenty time now.'

'But I'm certain he will, Poppy,' he said, trying intently to reassure her. 'Any number of things might have conspired to delay him. Maybe he's found lucrative employment and wants to make the most of it.'

'Lucrative?' she queried wearily. 'You don't half use some funny words, Robert.'

He smiled his apology, feeling mildly chastised for using words that he should have realised were beyond her knowledge. 'It means well-paid, gainful.'

'Gainful or not, he ain't come back.'

'Maybe he'll send for you soon.'

'Well, it won't be soon enough,' Poppy said wistfully. 'He's too late already.'

'Too late? What do you mean?'

Poppy shook her head and averted her eyes. 'Oh, nothing . . .' She felt too ashamed to tell him what had transpired between her mother and Tweedle Beak and the certain consequences of it.

'You must miss him, Poppy,' Robert said kindly.

She nodded and tried to push back tears that were welling up in her eyes. 'Yes, I miss him, Robert. I love him.'

'There, there . . .' He took her hand in consolation but held it discreetly at her side, so that such intimate contact was hidden from view by the folds of her skirt. 'Please don't cry, Poppy. I have such a vivid recollection of you laughing and being so happy that I can't bear to see you crying with sadness.'

'Oh, I'm sorry.' She sighed and wiped an errant tear from her cheek with the back of her hand. She forced a smile and Robert gazed into her watery eyes.

'You have such a lovely smile,' he said sincerely. He squeezed her hand before he let go of it. 'Your smile is your fortune, believe me. I remember how you flashed me a smile the very first time I saw you. I asked myself then, why was I so rewarded with such a lovely smile when I was accompanying such an unpleasant policeman on such a thoroughly unpleasant task?'

'Oh, I could tell you wasn't like the bobby,' Poppy said. 'Besides, you had the good manners to take your hat off when you came in our hut. Even *I* know it's good manners for a man to doff his hat in somebody's house.'

'I'm happy that it pleased you . . . that you even noticed.'

'There's not much I miss, Robert . . .'

He laughed at that. 'And I believe you. But I'm glad I've seen you, Poppy. I've been meaning to seek you out. There's something I wanted to suggest . . .'

'What?' she asked, and felt her heart beating faster.

'Well . . . Last time we met, you told me that you regret not having had the opportunity of an education . . .'

'It's true,' she agreed, puzzled.

'Well . . . Poppy . . .' He fidgeted uneasily, not sure how to word what he wanted to say without her reading into it more than he meant. And then he found the simple words. 'How would you react, if I offered to give you lessons in reading and writing?'

'In reading and writing?' she repeated incredulously, surprise manifest in her face.

'Yes. I think I could easily teach you to read and write. If you wanted to, that is.'

Her tears were quickly forgotten and she chuckled with

delight at the thought. 'Robert, I don't know what to say, honest I don't . . . . D'you really mean it? I mean, d'you know what you're letting yourself in for? I mean, what if I'm too stupid?'

He laughed dismissively at that, partly because he was amused that she should harbour such an absurd notion, partly because he wished to disguise this illogical lack of poise he sometimes felt when he was with her, even though she was way below his station. 'Oh, you're very bright, Poppy,' he reassured her. 'You'd learn very quickly. So what do you say? Do you agree?'

'Oh, yes, I agree, Robert. And thank you. There's nothing I'd like more. But when would we start?'

'Well, why don't we start tomorrow?'

'That soon?'

'Yes, why not? Can you meet me tomorrow?'

'When I'm through with me work. But where would we go?'

'Ah! I haven't quite worked that out yet. But if you could meet me somewhere, we could find a quiet spot where I could first teach you your alphabet.'

Poppy looked up at the sky unsurely. 'Even if it's raining?'

'Yes. Even if it's raining.'

'So where should I meet you?'

'Perhaps as far away from this encampment as possible,' he suggested. 'To protect your reputation, of course.'

'My reputation?' she scoffed. 'Yours, more like.'

He was not surprised by the astuteness of her remark, but he let it go. 'Do you know the ruins of the Old Priory?'

Poppy shook her head.

'Do you know St Edmund's church at the far end of the town, past the town hall and the market?'

She nodded.

'Meet me there.'

'All right. Will three o'clock be all right?'

'Three o'clock will be fine.'

Poppy smiled excitedly. 'I'll bring a writing pad and a blacklead.'

That encounter, and the prospect of another meeting tomorrow, lifted Poppy from her depression. She felt honoured that Robert Crawford was prepared to spend time with her, teaching her to become literate. Did it mean he was interested in her, that he wanted to woo her? The possibility excited her. He must like her, anyway. That much was obvious. Else he wouldn't have offered to do it. Now, she had to scrounge some money from her mother again, to enable her to go into Dudley to buy a writing pad and her own blacklead.

Some of the black spoil that had been excavated from the Dudley Tunnel at the northern end had been deposited over an area known as Porter's Field. The sloping elevation that ensued, having been duly compacted, was considered a suitable site for a fair. That Saturday evening in June, Minnie Catchpole decided that the fair that was being held there might provide her and Poppy Silk with some interesting diversions while Dog Meat and his new friend Jericho proceeded to get drunk.

The two girls entered the fair, looked about them excitedly and drank in the lively atmosphere. Traders had set out their stalls on both sides of the broad corridor of the entrance, and misspelled notices advertised their wares. Everything was available, from the finest leather saddlery and boots, through chamber pots, to sealing wax. An apothecary was telling a crowd around him about the benefits of using his balsam of horehound and aniseed for the treatment of coughs and colds, and of Atkinson's Infants' Preservative, recommended for those children liable to diarrhoea or looseness of the bowels, flatulence and wind. A herbalist was evidently doing good business in blood mixtures, sarsaparilla compound, piles ointments, healing salve, toothache cure, pills for gout and diuretic pills. A little further on, if you were hungry, you could enjoy a bowl of groaty pudding for tuppence, made from kiln-dried oats, shin of beef and leeks. If that didn't suit, liver faggots and grey peas were a tasty alternative, as was the bread pudding known as 'fill-bally', made from stale bread, suet and eggs, and sweetened with brown sugar and dried fruit.

Poppy's curiosity inclined her to spend a halfpenny to see a woman who was supposed to be the fattest woman on earth, until a miner emerged from the tent and declared, 'There's one a sight fatter 'n 'er up Kates Hill.' Elsewhere, a man was grinding a barrel organ; his monkey, on a long lead, was jumping from one person to another collecting small change in a tin mug. A crowd had gathered around a stall where they were invited to part with money to 'find the lady'. Poppy was astounded that she herself never got it right, confident that she had followed the card diligently as it was switched from one place to another in an effort to confound.

In a large tent a company of actors was performing, and not far from that stood a beer booth around which men were gathered in various states of inebriation. A couple of young men in rough clothing called to Poppy and Minnie to join them and, predictably, Minnie couldn't help but be drawn. Poppy had little alternative but to follow. These lads were the worse for drink, but Minnie played up to them and they plied both girls with a mug of beer each. Poppy, to Minnie's eternal frustration, was reticent about getting too involved, but Minnie showed no such inhibitions as she willingly accepted another mug of beer and giggled at their lewdness.

Inevitably, Poppy was showing little interest in the attention and bawdy suggestions from the lad with whom she seemed to be stuck. She was not impressed with anybody who did not recognise the folly of getting too drunk and, besides, her earlier meeting with Robert Crawford was still fresh in her mind. Compared to Robert Crawford, this buffoon, who remained doggedly at her side as she was trying to make her escape, was as nothing.

'Come with me over the fields,' he slurred, unwilling to concede defeat.

'I don't want to,' Poppy replied earnestly, looking behind to check whether Minnie was following.

'But I bought yer a mug o' beer.'

'It don't mean you bought *me*.'

'Oh? Come more expensive than that, do yer?'

Poppy remained sullenly silent, wishing fervently that the young man would go away.

'Got a bob on yerself, ain't yer, for a navvy's wench?' he said scornfully.

'What makes you think you're any better than me?' she asked, indignant at his insinuation.

'What's up wi' yer?' he goaded. 'Yer mate's game. Come on, let's goo over the fields an' have some fun.'

Thinking that intimate bodily contact might render him irresistible, he put his arm around her waist and drew her to him. When Poppy wriggled in an effort to get away, he held on to her tightly, causing her to wriggle more.

'Leave me be,' she said angrily.

'Poppy! Is this chap bothering you?' To Poppy's utter surprise, it was Jericho who spoke.

'Jericho! Where did you spring from?'

'Me and Dog Meat just got here. I watched you walking down here. Is this chap bothering you?'

'Why do chaps always think you're keen to go off with them?' she complained.

Even as she spoke, Jericho had the young man by the lapels of his jacket and flung him to the floor. He dived on him, hurling abuse, fists flying, while the poor victim tried in vain to protect his face from Jericho's vicious blows. Soon, a crowd gathered round and their vocal encouragement added fuel to Jericho's ardour. There was nothing better than a fight to inflame the passions of a crowd, especially when most had been drinking. To his credit, Dog Meat could see which way this fight was going and, fearing a murder, he grabbed hold of Jericho and managed to pull him away.

'You'll kill the little bastard.'

'That's what I'm trying to do,' Jericho rasped, resisting Dog Meat's restraining hold.

'No! You've hurt him enough. Use your brains. Leave him be. Leave him *be*.'

Jericho calmed down and the youth, with a swollen eye and his face smeared with blood, struggled to his feet and slipped into the crowd, out of reach. 'Next time, I'll marmalise yer,' Jericho yelled, shaking his fists. He turned to Poppy, who had turned pale with apprehension. 'Are you all right, my pet?'

'You didn't have to hurt the poor chap like that,' Poppy responded. 'I could've handled him all right.'

'Jesus! Is that all the thanks I get? I could see you was trying to get away from him. I could see he was being a bloody pest. Who knows what might have happened? You should be grateful I was there.'

Poppy smiled reservedly, unsure how to react to Jericho's violent gallantry.

Minnie appeared, having seen the wisdom in breaking free of the lad she had been promising so much to. She smiled at Dog Meat and took his arm. 'I'm glad you come, Dog Meat,' she cooed. 'We was just going to the Grin and Bear It to find you, till that chap tried to get Poppy. But you can buy us a drink here, if you've a mind.'

'Nah,' Dog Meat replied. 'If that chap fetches a bobby we could be in trouble. Let's clear off and have a drink somewhere else. There's plenty places.'

So the foursome left the fair. Dog Meat and Minnie walked arm-in-arm, with Poppy and Jericho behind. They stopped at a public house called The Woolpack in the town and drank outside in the warm summer evening air till closing time. Jericho was successful in occupying Poppy entirely and she told him of her father and how he had been forced by circumstances to leave the encampment. Jericho listened attentively and uttered sympathetic comments.

'And now if he comes back Lord knows what will happen,' Poppy said.

'Oh?' Jericho queried. 'What makes you say so?'

'Oh, because Tweedle Beak has wormed his way into my mother's bed.' She saw no harm in mentioning it. He would know tomorrow anyhow, when the wheels of encampment gossip began turning. And besides, she felt the need to talk to somebody, to get it off her chest and gain another opinion.

''Tis nothing out o' the ordinary,' Jericho said consolingly. ''Tis likely anyhow that Lightning Jack has bunked up with some woman, wherever 'tis he's got to.'

'But he's my dad,' Poppy argued. 'And I don't like the thought of him being done the dirty on. Oh, I know me mother was worried about being turned out and having to go on tramp, but I would've rather gone on tramp if I'd been her. I wouldn't have sold meself for the price of a few weeks' rent, 'specially to the likes of hook-nosed Tweedle Beak. I don't admire what she's done, Jericho.'

'Well, like as not, they ain't been to bed yet, eh? Like as not, Tweedle Beak's still swilling beer down his throat.'

'Like as not,' Poppy agreed. 'But when he gets back, my mother's gunna be lying with him.' She shuddered at the thought.

'Jesus, you're a sensitive soul, Poppy,' Jericho said. 'I ain't never knowed anybody like you afore.'

She smiled up at him. 'I told you that already. I told you I ain't like the others.'

'Nor you ain't. But what does it matter? Life's life. Men are men and women are women, and they'll never be no different.'

'I don't know what it is.' She shrugged and sipped her beer. 'Maybe it's 'cause I see too many women giving themselves to men who ain't worthy to lick their boots. And what do they get for their trouble? A belly full of babby that they've got no alternative but to rear. And do the men care? No. The more babbies, the better. "Keep the women babbied," they say. It keeps 'em out of harm's way, and shows their mates how fertile they are. Men are like kids, Jericho. I never met one yet who's grown up . . . Save for one, maybe . . .'

'You mean me?' he said.

She smiled but didn't answer him.

'Oh, you mean that engineer chap who you'm took with?'

'I never said as I'm took with him . . . Any road, he ain't ever likely to be took with me, is he? A navvy's daughter?'

'But you like him . . .'

She shrugged. 'What girl wouldn't? He's a gentleman, good and proper. He's got good manners and he's polite. There's nothing wrong with that.'

'What's polite? In this world you gotta take what you want while it's going, and never mind being polite. When folks are polite to me, I might start being polite to them. But there ain't much fear on't.'

'I hope you'll always be polite to me, Jericho,' she said earnestly.

Jericho guffawed. 'Oh, you don't half fancy yourself as the lady . . . I'll treat you like a woman, Poppy, and no different. Either way, I'll bed you. And when I do, you won't be putting on airs and graces . . .'

Minnie was only half listening to what Dog Meat was saying. She was standing a couple of yards from Poppy and Jericho and she had an ear cocked towards them, trying to catch their conversation. She was feeling peeved that Jericho seemed absorbed in Poppy. Minnie's face, to anybody who could read it, manifested her jealousy.

After they had left The Woolpack, the four made their way back to the encampment. Jericho continued to monopolise Poppy and walked with his arm around her waist, to Minnie's annoyance. Drink had made him talkative and Poppy even found him amusing.

'Am yer comin' in with us now, Jericho?' Minnie asked as they stopped close to Rose Cottage, anxious to part him and Poppy before it was too late. They had been far too friendly for her liking.

'In a bit,' Jericho replied. 'When I've said goodnight to Poppy.'

'We'll wait, if you like.'

'He don't want us to wait,' Dog Meat scoffed. 'He wants his ten minutes wi' Poppy. Come on, let's have you in bed.'

Minnie turned away sullenly and went with Dog Meat.

'I 'spect you don't wanna go in yet,' Jericho suggested. 'On account o' Tweedle Beak and your mother, I mean.'

Poppy sighed. 'What if I do and they're . . . you know?'

'Then don't go in. Come and sleep with me at Hawthorn Villa.'

'I'm not sleeping with *you*.'

'You will sooner or later. Why not now? The offer's there . . . Come a little walk wi' me then, eh? To pass the time.'

Rather than go into Rose Cottage too soon, Poppy felt it was better to take advantage of Jericho's company and let him keep her out late. She did not want to be faced with the awful truth of her mother and Tweedle Beak cavorting in bed. It was inevitable, of course it was, but she wanted to delay for as long as possible the dreadful, disgusting moment when she would have to witness it. If luck was with her, she would be able to keep Jericho at bay and return home between Sheba's and Tweedle's unspeakable love sessions . . . and fall asleep before they recommenced. As they started walking again, Jericho reached for her hand and she gave it compliantly.

A three-quarter moon emerged from behind clouds of smoke that issued out of the clutter of chimney stacks, and lent an eerie silver glow to the unnatural landscape. Then all at once the sky glowed red and angry, reflecting the blaze and searing heat from furnaces spewing out white-hot iron, and from cupolas vomiting flame. Set against this bloodshot firmament, those same chimney stacks stood out stark and black, like sentries guarding the headgear of the adjacent coal pits, whose turning cranks and wheels rumbled and clanked, while the steam engines that powered them hissed and sighed in their endless toil. The air was filled too with the penetrating roar of blast furnaces, a sound which was constant, however distant.

Jericho led Poppy down the path towards Cinder Bank, the same path she had ridden along as a passenger on Robert Crawford's two-wheeled bone-judderer. Poppy thought about Robert, and wondered what he was doing at that very minute. She had no idea of the time; perhaps he was asleep in bed, perhaps he was reading a book on engineering.

Reading . . . Oh, soon, she would be able to read . . . but not soon enough.

They stopped walking when they reached the bridge under the railway, and Jericho pressed her against the wall.

'I don't half fancy you, Poppy,' he whispered. 'I want you to be my wench.'

'I don't want to be anybody's wench, Jericho.'

'I'll make you change your mind,' he murmured. 'Just give us a kiss.'

She felt obliged to let him, since he had saved her from that overbearing lad at the fair and had seemed sympathetic to her anxiety over her mother. She tilted her head back and tentatively offered her lips. Jericho was upon her like a hog at a sweetmeat and Poppy did not particularly enjoy the experience. His kiss was too wet, his lips slack and slavering through too much alcohol, and his rough tongue, which she imagined as some unutterable, eyeless water vole crazy for entry, invaded her mouth. Without wanting to seem too ungrateful, she tolerated it for a second or two, then had to break off, turning her face away.

'Don't you like the way I kiss?' Jericho asked.

'It's not that . . .'

'What then?'

'It's as if you're trying to rush me into something, Jericho. I don't want to rush into anything,' she said beseechingly. 'Not with anybody. You'll just have to give me time . . .'

'Time?' he scoffed. 'I ain't got time. I might be dead tomorrow. You know how many men get killed digging cuttings and blowing tunnels. What about if some bastard knocks the legs too soon from under an overhang and a hundred ton of earth and rocks come tumbling down on me and bury me? What then? No, I ain't got time, Poppy. Don't ask for time. I want you now.'

He bent his head to kiss her again and she allowed it. Certain that she had submitted, he put his hands to her backside and began hitching up her skirt. At once, she pulled away from him.

'No, Jericho! Please have some respect for me. You have to respect my feelings.'

'Respect you?' he gibed. 'Bugger me, Poppy, anybody'd think you was that Lady Ward, whose husband owns the Pensnett Railway back there – him as has got the ironworks and the collieries all over the place . . .'

'I need time, Jericho,' she pleaded. 'Let me get used to the idea first.' Thoughts of Robert Crawford and her meeting with him tomorrow were more important. What if *he* wanted her to be *his* girl? She had to stall Jericho, even though she knew that he was stronger than her and could easily take her by force if he felt so inclined. 'I need to know you better before I can do what you want.' She took his hand gently, gambling that she could ensure her safe conduct by seeming helpless; humouring him and promising him all in the future, but delivering nothing. 'It could be worth the wait, Jericho,' she whispered tantalisingly, as she led him away. 'I just ain't ready yet . . .'

'Ain't you ever been with anybody afore?'

'No. Never.'

'Bloody hell . . . You're a virgin . . .'

'Course I am. Come on, Jericho. Take me back to the encampment.'

'But what about your mother and Tweedle Beak?'

'I think I can cope with that now,' she said, with an assurance she certainly did not feel.

Chapter 7

Poppy waited beneath the old red-brick tower of St Edmund's church, scanning Castle Street for signs of Robert Crawford and his boneshaker, her head full of the events of last night. Jericho and his amorous advances had set her thinking more about him. There were things about him she liked, but also things she didn't. She liked his sympathetic nature, and the fact that he was easy to talk to; he had a lusty sort of charm and she could understand why he'd had success with girls. What she didn't like was his heavy drinking and the readiness for violence manifested in his fighting, which suggested a short temper and instability. Neither did she like his kisses, but maybe she could get him to alter how he kissed if she became his wench.

A string of children all holding hands and dressed in their Sunday best were being shepherded to Sunday school. Some of them looked with curiosity at Poppy, but she smiled back at their innocent faces and stood back to let them pass.

When Poppy had returned to the hut last night all was quiet, but her mother and Tweedle Beak woke her twice with their vigorous antics in that squeaky bed they were now sharing. Poppy had tried her usual trick of pulling her pillow over her head, but she had not been able to shut out the shaking of her own bed, transmitted from theirs. Maybe when the novelty had worn off a bit she might get an undisturbed night's sleep, but the Lord knew how long that might be.

There was also Robert, of course. Oh, she liked him more than anybody, but she realised she was wasting her time and emotions if she thought he was going to stoop to her level. Yet of all the men she had come into contact with in her limited social world, he was the one with whom she felt she had a true bond. They did not know each other that well, but there was an undeniable rapport, an understanding between them. As yet it remained unspoken – maybe it always would – but it existed. Perhaps it was best left unspoken; the consequences of acknowledging it might present too many insurmountable difficulties, as well as a broken heart.

She scanned Castle Street again and saw him. Today he was without his two-wheeled contraption. He walked towards her with a smile on his face, as usual, and her heart flipped over in a somersault.

'Have you been waiting long?' he asked, looking her up and down.

'No, I only just got here. I got my paper and blacklead, look.'

'Excellent.'

He tried to hide his disenchantment with her red flannel frock. Not only was it a mighty step down from the pinnacle of fashion and inelegant, but it did not fit her particularly well. It was too big at the waist and the bodice rendered her chest shapeless and ambiguous. It was also too short and revealed the ungainly clogs and rough stockings that clearly signalled her background for all to see. She looked infinitely better in those plain working frocks; at least they fitted her, gave some form to her young figure, which he knew to be alluring enough. Why had he now put himself in a position where he would be seen accompanying this uncultured wench, who to any bystander would appear as nothing more than a whore he'd just picked up? Yet her face was as angelic as ever. Her beautiful eyes were clear and blue and exuded such a look of gentleness and honesty. Her hair beneath her bonnet framed her rounded cheekbones with untamed yellow curls, and her lips looked so gloriously tempting. In different circumstances he might fall head over heels in love with this girl; she had the makings. In their present circumstances – and her in that awful dress – that was impossible. Still, he could not help being drawn. She was truly something of an enigma.

'Where shall we go?' Poppy asked.

He wanted to save himself any embarrassment and get as far from the eyes of passers-by as possible. The castle grounds, the entrance to which lay just across the road, would be heaving with strollers in their Sunday best and well-to-do families out in their carriages on a fine afternoon such as this was.

'I mentioned the Old Priory. I think it would be pleasant in any case to sit among the ruins and begin your lesson there.'

'Is it far?'

'No. A six and a half minute walk from here.'

She laughed at his preciseness as they began the short trek. 'Six and a half minutes? Not five, or ten?'

'What do you mean?' he asked, surprised that she should have the temerity to mock him.

'I suppose it comes of being an engineer,' she suggested compassionately, at once taking the sting out of his umbrage. 'You being so exact about the time it takes to walk there.'

'Ah. I see.' He laughed at himself when he understood. 'You have remarkable perception, Poppy. Yes, I suppose it must be comical, put in that context – my engineering back-ground.'

As ever, the town was littered with inebriates tumbling out of the public houses, staggering homewards. Here and there arguments flared over nothing, and Robert took Poppy's arm as they hurried past The Hen and Chickens on the corner of Castle Street and New Street's narrow confines, into which they turned. Several rough-looking men eyed them suspiciously as they went by, commenting lewdly on the obvious incongruity that existed between the couple. Soon, however, Poppy and Robert were away from the rabble and the bustle of the area. In less than half a minute they were surrounded by gardens and fields. Over to their right, the keep of the old Norman castle loomed high on its wooded hill.

'What did you do last night?' Poppy asked Robert.

'Last night? Oh . . . I was invited to dinner. In fact, there was a fair at Porter's Field I had intended visiting, but in the end I was invited to dinner, as I say.'

'Did you enjoy it?'

'Yes, very much. It was a very convivial evening.'

Convivial. What on earth did that mean? 'I went to the fair,' Poppy admitted. 'Pity you didn't go, Robert. I bet I would've seen you there.'

'Who did you go with?' Robert asked.

'With my friend, Minnie Catchpole. You don't know her, do you?'

'Is her father on the OWWR workings?'

'Yes, Tipton Ted,' Poppy told him. 'I bet you know Tipton Ted.'

'Yes, I know Tipton Ted.'

'Minnie is Dog Meat's girl. Do you know *him* as well?'

'Dog Meat? Yes, I know Dog Meat. Drunken lout. And your friend is his . . . his bed partner, I suppose?'

'Yes, course.'

'How old is she?'

'Same as me. Sixteen. She's been sleeping with him since she was fifteen.'

'And Tipton Ted allows that?' Robert asked, hardly hiding his disapproval.

Poppy shrugged. It was not her concern.

'Good Lord! I wonder she's not become pregnant before now. And she so young.'

'Oh, Minnie says she knows how to stop getting pregnant. She goes off with other men as well.'

'Good Lord!' Robert said again. 'Goodness, Poppy, I do hope you have more sense than to do things like that yourself. You do strike me as having a lot more sense.' He looked at her questioningly, for reassurance.

'Me? Oh, you got me to rights there. I wouldn't do nothing like that. Mind you, I ain't been short of offers lately.'

Over to their right they could see the grey ruins of the Old Priory, some ivy-clad walls were still standing but dilapidated, and arched windows still remained, if devoid of glass for a few centuries.

'How old is this place?' queried Poppy as they walked across a field of long grass towards it.

'It was founded around 1160 by Gervase Paganel,' Robert said, 'though it never amounted to much ecclesiastically.'

Poppy looked at him sideways because of that big mysterious word, but did not ask its meaning. She imagined it might have something to do with religion, so it held little interest. In any case, Robert did not bother to enlighten her.

'So it's nearly seven hundred years old?'

Robert looked at her in astonishment. 'You worked that out rather swiftly for somebody who can't read and write.'

'I can work out sums in my head. You have to when you're handing money over in the tommy shop, or one of the shops in the town. If they think you can't count they fleece you rotten.'

He laughed at that. 'I never thought about it, but yes, I see that. All the men do count their money knowingly, even though they can't all read.'

'I know my numbers, Robert. My mother taught me. I can count shillings and pence, and I can tell the time as well.'

'Good. I wondered about teaching you your numbers. Well, that won't be necessary, at least.'

'Oh, but that's a shame,' she said, disappointed. 'It means I shan't have to see you so often. I like being with you, Robert.'

He smiled, a little embarrassed by her innocent admission that proclaimed so much. 'I like being with you, too, Poppy.'

'Honest?'

'I've never met anybody quite like you before.'

They had reached what remained of the large west window. Robert sat down on an outcrop of fallen masonry and gestured for Poppy to sit beside him.

'Somebody else told me that,' she said with a broad smile of satisfaction as she smoothed the creases out of her skirt, about to sit.

'Oh, who?'

'One of the new navvies, called Jericho. Have you come across him?'

'I know who he is. A big, strapping young man.'

'And handsome with it,' Poppy added teasingly.

'You think he's handsome, do you?' Robert tried to stifle the illogical pang of jealousy that seared through him. 'So what's his interest in you, Poppy?'

Poppy felt herself blush and sheepishly cast her eyes down, looking at the grass and moss sprouting between the limestone masonry. 'Oh,' she uttered with as much disdain as she could muster. 'He asked me to be his woman . . .'

'He did? Good Lord! And what did you say?' Robert's heart seemed to stand still while he waited what seemed like an age for her answer

'I told him I didn't want to be anybody's woman, Robert.'

He breathed a sigh of relief. 'So when did you tell him that?'

'After he kissed me.'

Robert felt the breath leave his body and a hammer hit him hard where his heart was. 'No . . . I . . . I meant – how long ago?'

'Oh . . . Last night. After we'd been to the fair. He saved me from some lad who was trying to get off with me.'

'How very gallant.'

'Well, I thought the least I could do was let him kiss me after, for his trouble.'

It pained Robert that the great brute had had such intimate knowledge of Poppy, but the more significant knowledge that she had willingly allowed it disturbed him even more. She was so vulnerable, exposed to all the lechery and immorality of her kind – especially handsome buck-navvies with pockets full of money, muscles flexing and relaxing visibly beneath their rough clothing. Nothing was taboo in that grim society of theirs. There was never any shame. No wonder she spoke so openly, so frankly, about such things; she didn't know any better, she saw no wrong in it.

'Shall we begin your lesson?' he said, wishing to change the subject which was causing him so much concern.

She nodded keenly and looked into his eyes with frank adulation.

'Let me have your writing pad and blacklead pencil and I'll begin by jotting down the letters of the alphabet for you.'

She handed them to him and he began setting down a list of lower case letters in his precise engineer's hand. 'First is *a* . . . then *b* . . . *c* . . .' He wrote them all down from a to z. 'There's a good way of remembering them and the order they always come in. Do you know the tune to "Baa-baa Black Sheep"? Well, you can sing these letters to that.'

He began singing and it made her laugh to hear the sound of a string of letters put to a tune. It sounded so strange, like some foreign language.

'No, it's not to be mocked, Poppy,' he said, indignant at being interrupted. 'This trick will enable you to learn the alphabet very quickly. Just don't laugh. Listen instead to me . . .' He began singing again and once more she giggled, partly at the incongruity of the tune and the letters, and partly at the earnest look on his face and his pleasant voice. Despite her mirth, he carried on to the end. 'Now you sing it along with me, Poppy . . . and stop your giggling, else we won't get anywhere.'

'I can't sing,' she protested playfully.

'Yes, you can. You know the tune. After three . . . One, two, three . . . "Ay, bee, cee, dee" . . .'

Poppy stumbled many times, not knowing which letters were which, but, as they sang it over and over, it started to etch itself into her mind.

'To help you know what sound each letter represents, I'll write a word beginning with that letter alongside it. "A" is for apple . . . you see. "B" is for bonnet, like the one you're wearing . . . "C" is for cutting, like the navvies dig . . . "D" is for . . . drainage . . . No, that's not a very good example. "D" is for door . . .'

When he'd finished, he said, 'I want you to take this home and learn your letters. Practise writing them yourself, copying what I've written. When you've learnt them by heart, I'll show you how to write capital letters and then we'll go on to when to use them.'

'I will,' Poppy promised. 'Thank you, Robert, for taking the trouble to teach me. I shall owe you so much.'

'Tell me, Poppy,' Robert said, still somewhat preoccupied by the disturbing revelations about her personal activities. 'This Jericho . . . Did you give him any inkling at all that you might agree to be his . . . his *woman*?'

'I told him I'd think about it if he gave me time,' she said frankly.

'So you like him then?'

'He's all right. He makes me laugh. I don't know whether I really fancy him that much though . . . Still, what's fancying got to do with it? Minnie says that in the dark you can always make-believe it's somebody you do fancy.'

'I think this Minnie's a parlously bad influence on you, Poppy. Promise me you won't agree to becoming Jericho's woman.'

'But what's it to you, Robert?' she asked, for the first time really convinced of his interest in her.

'Well . . .' He shrugged. 'It's just that . . . I think you're worthy of so much better. Save yourself for somebody more fitting . . .'

'Some duke or earl, you mean?' she said mischievously.

'Who knows? Stranger things have happened.'

'Not to me, Robert. Never to me.'

'All the same, promise me . . .'

She was surprised at the intensity in his eyes. Well, maybe she could use a little guile here. 'I'll tell you the same as I told Jericho. I'll make nobody no promises yet.'

The Oxford, Worcester and Wolverhampton Railway received Royal Assent on 4 August 1845, backed by the Great Western Railway who wished to promote another broad-gauge line. By 1846, work on tunnelling had begun at Dudley, Worcester and Mickleton, near Chipping Campden. By 1849, the Dudley tunnel, for which the contractors were Buxton & Clark of Sheffield, had been finished. The actual railway track had not yet been laid, for there was some political argument about whether broad gauge or narrow gauge was to prosper. The contract for the southern section beyond the Dudley tunnel had been awarded to Treadwell's. Work at the Mickleton tunnel, however, operated by an unfortunate succession of inept contractors, had been beset by problems and was far from complete.

At Mickleton, where Lightning Jack and Buttercup were working, the exact line of the tunnel had been set out and pegged over the surface, as had the rest of the route. Sinkers then dropped trial shafts along the path of the proposed tunnel to investigate the strata and water content of the rock. Standard practice was to sink a shaft at every furlong, but more if considered necessary by the engineer. Having reached the proper depth, some of those vertical shafts would be widened and lined so that men, horses, tools and materials could be lowered into and raised from the workings on platforms or in huge tubs, hauled by stationary steam engines or horse gins. Headings went out on the correct alignment from the bottom of each shaft in opposite directions until the tunnel was driven through the hill.

At the end of June, Lightning Jack arose from his bunk in the shack he shared with the other men, dressed and went outside into the early morning sunshine. He breathed in the fresh morning air of the Cotswolds and looked across at the gently rolling hills around him, the patchwork of fields like a far-flung quilt of yellow and green and gold. This was a far cry from the squalid landscape of the Black Country . . . except for the brown spoil from the tunnel which was turning the top of the hill where they lived and worked into a slag heap of monumental proportions. Soil and rock was ripped from the bowels of the earth beneath his feet and tipped randomly over the hill in separate mounds. One day, perhaps nature would clothe it in trees, in grass and fern, and it would surreptitiously blend into the countryside and leave no clue as to its man-made origin. But now it was an angry boil marring a beautiful face.

Lightning Jack stood, his hands on his hips, morose despite nature's unsullied beauty stretched out beyond the dingy heaps of spoil. He likened himself to that spoil; dirty, unkempt, unwashed, undisciplined. He was unshaven too, except for those nights he had been out carrying on with Jenny Sparrow. How he wished he'd never set eyes on the woman. Oh, they'd had their fun. She had lived up to her sensual promise. She could take her share of drink as well, and seem unmarked by it. Sometimes she would even pay her turn. But she was no good for Lightning, and he had discovered it too late.

Now he yearned for Sheba. He longed to see his children; to ruffle Poppy's restless yellow curls, to hug his younger daughters Lottie and Rose, to put his arms around his son Little Lightning, to see his youngest child Nathaniel at Sheba's breast. How were they faring without him, without his protection? Had Sheba managed somehow to engineer a continued sojourn at the encampment at Blowers Green? If not, where might they be now? Well, there was no point in worrying about it. It did not matter any more. It did not matter where they were or how they were faring.

Lightning Jack heard Buttercup calling him and turned round to look. Buttercup and a score of other tunnellers filed out of the hut, swearing and muttering as navvies did, and headed for the shaft nearby, which was their entrance to the workings. Lightning joined them and fell into step beside Buttercup, behind the others. They reached the head of the shaft, where a steam engine, a great heap of coal penned beside it, chugged and rasped, primed and ready to lower the men into the earth's cool heart. One by one, they stepped onto the platform and Lightning was the last. As they descended, the familiar sulphurous smell made him cough. The platform began to spin and Lightning began to feel giddy. He braced himself against the twisting motion and focused his eyes on Buttercup.

'Bist thee all right?' Buttercup asked his chum, grabbing hold of him. He had noticed a decline in Lightning's demeanour lately.

'Aye, fit as a fiddle, me.'

'Mind as you don't get giddy.'

'I'm all right.'

The temperature inside the shaft became cooler the further they descended, and the air felt damp on Lightning's skin. The light from the open shaft above diminished and the encircling wall grew eerily dark. The rate of descent decreased and the platform halted with a hard bump, which made Lightning's knees buckle. They had touched the level.

In the workings of the tunnel the atmosphere was oppressive, for want of free circulation of clean air. The smell and smoke of gunpowder from the night shift's blasts lingered. Lightning and Buttercup made their way in a single file with the others towards their base. There, each lit a candle. The feeble light exaggerated the dimness of the vault and the thick, foggy atmosphere. They took such tools as they needed and, unspeaking, picked their way through pools of inky black water that plopped with incessant dripping from above. They tramped over the temporary rails laid for the tip trucks, which would collect the spoil and be hoisted up the shaft to be emptied over the once picturesque hill above. In the uncertain light they picked their way past huge blocks of stone, planks of wood, scaffolding, and piles of bricks which were manufactured and employed by the million to line the tunnel. Tiny points of flickering light showed where the navvies were working. The sounds of picks, shovels and sledgehammers echoed, mingling with the shouts, hacking coughs and guffaws of the men, and became louder the closer they got to the work face. An army of bricklayers toiled behind them, working like ants to install the vital brick encasement. The tunnel, which up until that point had been cut and lined to its full dimensions, suddenly narrowed. The level floor began to rise steeply and the gang, with Lightning Jack and Buttercup, were at the face and relieving the other workers who had been there all night.

'Let's get off our steam packets and get stuck in then,' Buttercup declared in their recognised slang, 'else the bloody ganger will be docking us our sugar and honey.'

They took off their jackets and got stuck in, working at a pace that an ordinary mortal would have found back-breaking, by the light of the candles fixed to their hats. Buttercup tightly gripped a six-foot bar of steel, holding it firm against the rock face while Lightning Jack swung a sledgehammer in a great arc with the rhythm of a machine. He aimed it at the end of the steel rod, a drill, and his accuracy was such that he never missed, drunk or sober. Had he missed, he could easily have killed his mate. Slowly, surely, he drove the drill into the rock face. When the hole was deep enough, about five feet, he would pack it with explosive.

Come one o'clock, the ganger blew his whistle and shouted, 'Yo-ho, yo-ho!' It was the signal to stop work and take a break. The men tramped back to where the tunnel was level, set a few planks across small stacks of bricks and sat down. One of the navvies, Frying Pan, called one of the nippers to drum up the tea. The nipper, a lad of about ten or eleven, had already set light to a gob of tallow that had been collected in a round tin box, at once doubling the amount of light in the vicinity. He had then placed an iron bucket containing water on an iron tripod astride the flame. Now he added the mashings of tea and sugar which he took from each of the men, and emptied them into the bucket. While it came to the boil, the men wiped the sweat from their brows, ate their tommy and talked.

It began as a noisy meal, liberally laced with ferocious swearing, bravado and laughter, which echoed and re-echoed around the cavern of the tunnel.

'Still poking that Jenny Sparrow, Lightning?' Frying Pan asked when talk had reverted to women, as it generally did.

'Not any more,' Lightning replied tersely, for it was a sore subject. 'Not that it's any o' your business.'

'Gone off it, have ye? Had your fill?'

'Why are you so bloody interested? Fancy it yourself, do you?'

'I might.' Frying Pan took a huge bite out of his bread. 'If every other bugger in the world hadn't already been there afore me.'

'Well, I can recommend her,' Lightning said coldly. 'Her knows how to draw out the best in a man . . . if you get me meaning.'

'Her's had plenty experience,' another, Long Daddy, put in.

'Piss off, the lot o' yer,' Lightning rasped, and touchily moved away from the ensemble.

He ambled over to the other side of the wide tunnel with his tommy box and settled himself on a remote pile of bricks. He had no wish to air his private problems with the rest of the encampment. If they wanted to discuss their amorous adventures that was up to them, but he didn't want to share his.

Buttercup came over to him and sat beside him.

'What's up wi' thee, Lightning?' he asked quietly. 'Thou hasn't been theeself for a week or two. Bist thee upset about summat? That Jenny Sparrow, for instance? I never realised th' was a-pining for her?'

'The only one I'm a-pining for is my Sheba,' Lightning confessed sullenly.

'For Sheba? Then that's easy remedied. Collect your money tonight and go off on tramp, back to Dudley and the – what? The Blowers Green workings, did'st thou say?'

'Aye, Buttercup,' Lightning said with scorn. 'But that's easier said than done.'

'Why? What's to stop thee?'

'Listen, Buttercup,' Lightning said, and his tone was morbid. 'You've been a good mate to me in the weeks we've been together, and I've appreciated it – more'n you realise, very like. I want you to promise me summat . . .'

'Anything, me old mucker. Just name it.'

'Well . . . if anything was to happen to me, an accident like, would you be good enough to go and let my Sheba know? It'd mean going off on tramp for a few days, but it'd mean a lot to me if you'd undertake to do it.'

'Don't be so damned gloomy,' Buttercup said. 'Tell her theeself. Take theeself home and tell her how much you've missed her. All right, so yo'n had a little diversion with that Jenny Sparrow along the way. So what? Sheba ain't to know that, is she? And any road, yo'll have gone back to her. She'll welcome thee with open arms . . . and open thighs, I'd venture to say.'

Lightning threw a piece of bread down on the ground in

frustration. 'That's just it, Buttercup . . . I can't go back. Not for anything. Not now.'

'Why not, dammit?' He looked at his friend, puzzled.

'Well, Frying Pan's right. Jenny Sparrow has had plenty experience. Too much of it. She's gi'd me a dose o' the rap-tap-tap, and Lord knows what else. I'm even afeared to have a piddle any more, 'cause it's like pissing broken glass. I 'spect I got a dose o' the Durham ox as well, just to round it off nice, like. How the hell can I go back to Sheba when I'm afflicted wi' that? What sort of bloke would knowingly pass on the pox to his woman?'

'Christ! Well, they reckon there's plenty of it about.'

'Aye, but you never think it's gunna get you, do yer, eh, Buttercup?'

'I thought you seemed miserable lately,' Buttercup sympathised.

'Miserable? I tell you, Buttercup, I'm at me wits' end. I never felt so bloody wretched in me whole life. I've messed things up good and bloody proper. I've ruined a perfectly good life wi' Sheba and me kids. I should be hanged for being so bloody stupid.'

'So what yer gunna do, me old china plate?'

Lightning shrugged. 'What the hell can I do?'

'Come on.' Buttercup stood up wearily and stretched. 'Tea'll be drummed up in a minute or two. I got a little tipple o' whisky in me bottle. Me and thee can share it. Things won't seem half so bad after a tipple o' whisky.'

Lightning Jack and Buttercup shared the whisky, finished their dinners and their tots of tea, and then went back to work. It was time to pack explosive into the hole they had drilled and blow the face of the tunnel to bring down more rock for clearing, more clay for making the bricks. From a sturdy wooden box, Jack picked up a linen bag that had already been filled with gunpowder and packed it deep in the hole, with a length of fuse attached, carefully bunging up the hole with clay.

'Ready to blow,' he said to the ganger who was at Lightning's side inspecting the work.

'Ready to blow, it is,' the ganger replied. He cupped his hands like a megaphone around his mouth. 'Clear the area!' he called, then blew his whistle. 'Clear the area!' He looked around for flickering candles in the darkness, which would tell him where the nearest men were working. 'I'll just get that lot to move back,' he said, turning to Lightning who was waiting to light the fuse. 'Give me a minute afore you light it. I'll make sure the way's clear for you to get away.'

Lightning watched as the ganger's shadow became more indistinct. He gave him his minute and duly lit the fuse.

'About to blow!' he yelled at the top of his voice. 'Blowin' up!'

Beneath the shaft, where the men had collected, Buttercup asked for silence.

'What's up?' asked the ganger.

'Listen . . . I can't hear Lightning walking back.'

'You ain't about to with all the racket going on down here. Dripping bloody water, the clatter o' bricks, the squeal o' them there wheels on the damn trucks, blokes chuntering.'

'Look. The fuse is lit. Thou canst see it flaring. But where the hell's Lightning?'

'Give him a chance. The fuse'll be at least a minute fizzling afore it sets off the gunpowder. Get your hands over your ears ready.'

'Nah. I'm going to fetch him. He ain't come away. Look, I can see his candle. He's still there, the damned fool, by the fuse.'

At that, Buttercup hurtled off, running towards the fuse that was still fizzing bright and crackling as it burned its way towards the compacted gunpowder. 'Lightning!' he yelled. 'Move theeself! Get back here!'

'Stay where you are, you bloody fool,' came the reply echoing towards him through the gloom. 'Get back and save yourself. You've got a bloody errand to run for me, remember?'

'You arsehole!' Buttercup bawled angrily as the final, awful realisation of what Lightning was up to struck him. 'Thee bisn't doing *that*. I'm coming to fetch thee. Stamp on the fuse or pull the bugger out. Quick!'

'Get back, Buttercup,' Lightning shouted urgently. 'You're too late. Save yourself.'

There was a blinding flash of light and Buttercup was thrown to the floor of the tunnel as the wave of the blast reached him. He had the distinct impression that his head had imploded. The deafening sound was palpable as it reverberated along the walls and roof of the tunnel section. The ground beneath him and above him shook and shuddered and he fancied he must be dead already and in the midst of a thundercloud with heaven's artillery booming. He lay with his hands over his head, fearing a fall of bricks and debris from the roof, but none fell. He looked up but all was black. He could feel the stench of burnt gunpowder in his nostrils, the dense smoke billowing around him making his eyes run.

'Lightning!' he called out, knowing it to be hopeless. 'Lightning! Where bist thee? Answer me!'

But there was no answer. The smoke deadened even the echo of his calls.

His candle had been blown out in the blast. All was darkness. Never in his whole life had he experienced such complete and utter blackness. The pressure of the darkness on his optic nerves was unbearable. He began choking on the smoke. He could taste it. He was swallowing it. He raised himself to his feet, felt in his pocket for his box of matches and tried to light one. As it flared pathetically, all he could see was the dense miasma of black smoke wheeling all around him. If it would stay alight long enough to light a candle, he could look for Lightning Jack.

It was some time before the smoke had billowed and eddied slowly towards the shaft and had been drawn up it. Had the tunnel been open at either end, or even connected to another vertical shaft further along, the natural draught would have drawn it out comparatively quickly, but it took an age with only one shaft open. The rest of the gang had made their way towards him, and the ganger, fearing he had lost two men, was relieved to see that at least Buttercup was still alive.

'Come on,' Buttercup said. 'We'd best see if we can find what's left o' the daft old bugger.'

Chapter 8

'I'd like us to concentrate on double vowel sounds tonight, Poppy,' Robert Crawford said.

They were sitting in his office, on the first floor of an old house in Abberley Street, off Vicar Street, which the contractors had acquired because it was near the workings. It suited Robert's purpose admirably. Poppy could learn undisturbed, and Robert would not be compromised by being seen in public with a low-class navvy girl. There was seldom anybody who used the offices after about six o'clock of an evening. And he was privy to a key.

The evening rays of an early July sun streamed through the deep sash window, which was open an inch or two at the top, and fell obliquely onto his huge desk, that was covered in drawings and maps. Poppy sat next to Robert at the desk. They were so close that he was aware of Poppy's soft warmth as his thigh gently nudged hers as if by accident in the desk's kneehole.

Robert was hopelessly torn. For two weeks he had contrived to meet Poppy there to give her lessons in reading and writing and, in that respect, both were experiencing singular success. Poppy could already recognise scores of simple words, and write them down in an awkward scrawl. But he had not yet mustered the audacity to suggest anything more than being merely her teacher. He was certain that he had fallen in love with her. If it was not love, it was some other destructive yet utterly overwhelming attraction that he seemed powerless to resist. Whatever it was, he was painfully aware that it could do neither him, nor anybody else, one iota of good. Still, he could not help wanting to touch her, to feel her girlish softness and gentleness. He ached to run his fingers through that tangle of fair curls and feel her delicious-looking lips on his. He was forever trying to glean information as to her likely relationship with that savage they called Jericho, and whether any relationship was flourishing. Always, however, she dismissed it as something trivial. Well, he hoped with all his heart and soul that it was trivial and would remain so.

'If we have two "*o*"s together,' he began to explain, 'they make the sound you get in the word *look*.' He wrote the string of letters down.

'*Look*,' she repeated, forming the word deliberately, and with a delectable pursing of her lips, which gave Robert the renewed and urgent desire to kiss her.

'And this word – *book*.' He wrote that down quickly as well.

'*Book*.'

'*Tooth* . . .'

'*Tooth*,' she repeated seriously, oblivious to the effect she was having on him.

Next, he wrote down the word *hook*. 'So what do you think this word says?'

She studied the word for no more than a second. '*"Ook*.'

He smiled, acknowledging her ability to work it out quickly. '*Hook*,' he corrected. 'You must sound the "*h*" . . .'

'*Hook*,' she said exaggeratedly.

'That's better. So do you understand the sound a double *o* makes?'

'Yes,' she said, with a certainty that was unassailable. 'It's easy.'

'Good . . . Ah! You see there's another . . . the word *good* . . . You're doing well, Poppy. Extremely well. Now, let's look at the vowels *o* and *u* together . . . as in *house* . . .'

''*Ouse.*'

'Pronounce the *h*, Poppy.'

'Sorry, Robert. *House.*'

'Now . . . *mouse.*'

'*Mouse,*' she said, looking very serious.

'*Mouth* . . .' He looked at her lips again. He was fascinated by the way they moved so deliciously as she pronounced the words.

'*Your* mouth, Poppy . . .'

She looked up at him and saw the flame of ardour in his eyes. 'What about my mouth?'

'You have such a lovely mouth. I'm sorry, but I want to kiss you. Would you be terribly offended?'

'No, why should I be?' she answered with neither hesitation nor inhibition, and felt her heart instantly beating faster at the unexpected enticement.

She leaned towards him and pursed her lips and he could have kicked himself for not having asked before. Her lips were cool and slightly moist, like petals unfurling from the bud. He was all at once aware of her chastity and her sexuality, existing together symbiotically.

'That was nice,' she said with wide-eyed sincerity. 'Hey, you don't half kiss nice.'

'Then I'll kiss you again . . . But why not close your eyes this time?'

'I will, if you'll close yours as well. You didn't then, so it's no good telling me to, if you don't.'

'I was merely looking to see if you *had* closed your eyes.'

'I'll close 'em then.'

Their lips met again. Poppy peeped to see whether he had closed his eyes and found him peeping at her once more.

'See?' she complained, breaking off with a girlish giggle. 'You're watching me.'

He laughed self-consciously. 'I was just checking.'

'No checking, Robert. If you want me to kiss you and keep my eyes closed, you have to trust me. Don't keep peeping.'

'I won't peep again. On my honour.'

'Right . . .'

They kissed once more, and neither dared to open their eyes any more to see if the other's were shut. The kiss lingered, each savouring the sensation, and she felt his arm come around her and give her an attentive, affectionate hug, which she enjoyed a great deal.

'I like it when you do that,' she said.

'Then why don't you sit on my lap?' he suggested. 'I'll be able to kiss you more easily and hold you properly, rather than us stretching over.'

Compliantly, she got off her chair and slid into his lap with an appealing saucy smile. She curled up in his arms like a kitten and submitted willingly to his kisses, which she found mesmerising. She stayed like that for half an hour, though it seemed significantly less, enjoying his warm affection, wringing as much innocent pleasure out of it as she was able. Poppy felt herself tingling in the most surprising places. She was peeved at being robbed of the intensifying pleasure when he stopped and said that maybe they should get on with more work.

'Oh, sod the work,' she carped.

'No, Poppy.' It was the most difficult thing in the world to say *no* right then, to deny himself, let alone Poppy, this intimacy he'd secretly yearned for. 'Lord knows what might happen if we lose control of ourselves.'

'What can happen that neither of us don't want to happen?' she asked, baffled at this shattering and unaccountable self-denial of his. 'Don't you want me?'

'Oh, yes,' he said and there was no mistaking the truth of it. 'I want you.'

'So, am I your girl now?'

He laughed ruefully. 'Just a few short weeks ago you told me you weren't prepared to devote yourself to anybody.'

'But you never asked me to be *your* girl, Robert. I would have been, gladly . . . If you'd asked.'

He emitted a profound sigh. 'I'm afraid it's not as cut and dried as that.'

'But you like me, don't you? You must do. You asked to kiss me.'

'Poppy . . .' He looked down into the folds of her skirt as she sat in his lap, her warm weight a pleasure. 'I do like you. I like you much more than I care to admit. But there are other considerations. I don't just want to take advantage of you.'

'You wouldn't be.'

'Yes, I would, and it wouldn't be fair . . . Oh, Poppy . . . I could so easily—'

'So easily what?' she interrupted emotionally, tears filling her eyes. 'Take advantage of me, you mean?'

He shook his head. 'No, not take advantage. Didn't I just say that's the last thing I want to do? No – I mean, I could *so easily* fall in love with you.'

'Then why don't you?' she answered with her young girl's logic. 'I'd fall in love with you, then you could take advantage of me all you liked. I'd want you to.'

He groaned inwardly. Here, unexpectedly before him, was the promise of heavenly bliss with this girl, and he must surrender it, ignore it as if it wasn't there. 'I don't think you understand, Poppy.'

'Oh, I think I do,' said she, as the light of realisation hit her. She got up from his lap and slumped down in the chair she had occupied before. 'You're a clever engineer, a real swell, and invited out to slap-up dinners, you say, whereas I'm just a common navvy's daughter who could never be anything but that.'

'No, Poppy.'

'Oh, yes, Robert,' she sighed. 'I admit I've harboured feelings for you ever since I met you, but I'm daft, aren't I, to have thought I could ever be anything other than a navvy's wench?'

'You can be whatever you want to be, Poppy,' he said sincerely.

'But not your girl . . .'

He did not answer.

She took a rag out of the pocket of her skirt and wiped her tears. 'Unless I suddenly become a lady, eh? I stand no chance unless I suddenly become a lady with airs and graces, and can look down my nose at everybody beneath me. Well, I'll never be like that, Robert. I could never be. It ain't in me. You have to take me as I am or not at all.'

'I would rather take you as you are, Poppy, believe me . . .' He hated to see tears in her eyes. She was hurt and he was responsible. He was sorry and all he wanted right then was to hold her, to comfort her.

She stood up, agitated. 'No, there's too much of a gap between you and me. Everywhere you went you'd be ashamed of me. Oh, I understand your difficulty, Robert, but I could never be content neither, thinking I was never good enough for you.'

'You must never belittle yourself, Poppy.' He stood up and moved towards her, compelled to put his hands to her slender waist. 'I think you're the kindest, most sensitive, prettiest soul

I've ever met.' His tone was a taut thread of emotion. 'I can't get you out of my mind. That's the trouble. And it's driving me mad, Poppy. What am I to do?'

She rested her head against his shoulder as if all the troubles of the world had come to roost on hers. Her eyes were still watery at this unexpected admission of love that had exploded between them all of a sudden, like gelignite going off.

'I don't know,' she answered. 'But why should there be such a big to-do about it? I don't get it. If two people like each other enough . . .'

'Dear God . . .' he said quietly, his heart heavy. 'The problem is, you see, Poppy, it's not that there is a social divide between us. I'm sure that would be bridgeable, for the will to either bridge it or ignore it would indeed be there. It's just that . . .' He hesitated, unsure as to whether to confess his predicament . . . but, hang it all, he had to, otherwise he was being dishonest . . . 'It's just that I'm already engaged to be married. Yet how I wish I weren't . . .'

'You're engaged already?' The possibility had never crossed her mind before. 'Who to? No, don't tell me. I don't want to know who she is.'

'She's a very respectable girl. I imagine you'd like her.'

'I'm sure I wouldn't.'

'No, maybe you wouldn't.'

'I know I wouldn't. I'd like to punch her nose.'

'Oh, Poppy, please don't talk like a navvy.'

'Well, if you're engaged, you shouldn't see me again,' she said resignedly. 'Maybe it'd be best to stop my lessons.'

'Do you want to stop your lessons?' He was sorry that he had put her unorthodox education in jeopardy by his amorous behaviour.

'No, why should I?' she answered defiantly. 'You're teaching me to read and write and I'm learning well. I know I am. Why should I stop now just because you're engaged, just because there's another girl you're fond of? I'll just have to stop liking you like that. Did you know all along how much I liked you?'

He could have hugged her for her kittenish simplicity, her lack of guile, her direct use of simple words. 'From the outset I hoped you did. I hoped with all my heart that you did.'

'So why don't you just give up this girl you're engaged to, if you'd rather have me? It's seems the best thing to do.'

'But I'm promised, Poppy. I knew her long before I met you. Her family and mine are close friends. We are due to be married next year. A man can't renege on a promise to marry. It's a question of honour. The girl has to release him from his promise. Otherwise the consequences for him could be very serious.'

'But if you told her about me . . . Maybe she would release you.'

He shook his head. The thought of confessing to his bride-to-be and her family that he was in love with the daughter of a navvy filled him with dread. Neither they – nor his own family either, for that matter – would regard him as stable. He would be a laughing stock. They might even try to have him certified to protect the integrity of his fiancée. The difficulties were not too hard to foresee.

'It's not as simple as that,' he said.

'I'd better stop having me lessons then,' Poppy said flatly. 'I'd only want us to start kissing again. And if I can't have you in the end, I don't want to start anything in the beginning.'

'Poppy,' he sighed. 'You must continue with your lessons. You said so yourself. It's vitally important for you that you do. I'll be on my honour. I promise not to take advantage.'

'No,' she said assertively. 'It's best we don't see each other. There's no point. I don't want to get worked up into a lather when I'm with you, knowing that you'll never be mine. No, I might as well start seeing Jericho serious.'

'Oh, *Poppy*,' he groaned. '*Must* you?'

Poppy returned to Rose Cottage in a state of bewilderment. She was so exhilarated at kissing Robert Crawford for so long and his confession that she was always on his mind. Yet she was also deeply frustrated that nothing could come of it. It was as she had always suspected; he liked her, but he was not about to lower himself and become involved with her, especially since he was already engaged to some girl whose family might be wealthy and important. It was hardly worth competing for him because, in her position, she could never have him. Why was life so unfair? Why was it tilted so much in favour of the swells who already had everything?

She entered the hut carrying her writing pad and blacklead and flopped them on the table among the dirty crockery that still littered it. Her mother was sewing patches and buttons onto shirts.

'It's quiet in here for once,' Poppy commented.

'Well, the babby's asleep in his crib,' Sheba replied, pulling a needle on a length of thread. 'Lottie and Rose am playing in the cutting and Jenkin's out somewhere with his mates, up to no good, I daresay.'

'So where's Tweedle?' There was a hint of scorn in Poppy's tone, but Sheba could not be sure of it.

'Out drinking, with the rest o' the lodgers . . . Where've you been?'

'Having a lesson. I've been learning words like *look*, and *tooth*, and *mouth* and *house*.' She had sounded her *h*.

'Hark at you. Sounding all swank. 'Tis to be hoped it gets you somewhere.'

'I was learning quick. Robert said so.'

'Was?' Sheba queried.

'Yes . . . was. I'm having no more lessons. I don't see the point. I can read now.' She was grossly overstating her ability, but had no wish to enlighten Sheba as to the real reason.

'That chap Jericho called round after you.'

'What for?'

'How the hell should I know? But I can guess. He's a handsome buck, and no mistake.'

'If only looks was everything.'

Sheba smiled to herself. 'Oh, and what would you know about that?'

'Well, I wouldn't say as Tweedle Beak was handsome,' Poppy replied, with a shrug. 'Would you?'

'It might help if he was . . .'

Poppy laughed. There was a pause in their conversation while she put her writing pad in her drawer to save getting it mucked up. 'What yer gunna do about Tweedle when me father comes home?'

'Tweedle will just be one o' the lodgers again.'

'Providing me dad can get his old job back, you mean.'

'Even if he can't, it wouldn't make any difference. We'd just go on tramp till he found another.'

'So it is me father you love, and not Tweedle?' She regarded her mother earnestly. 'Oh, tell me it is, Mother.'

'Aye, it's your father I love.'

'But what about if he comes back and finds you already pregnant wi' Tweedle's brat?'

Sheba bit the thread she was sewing with, severing it, and rested the crumpled shirt in her lap. 'Oh, well,' she said, looking intently into Poppy's eyes, 'I'm already pregnant. But it's with your dad's child. I knew I was carrying afore he went away.'

Poppy smiled happily. It was the best news she'd had in ages. 'Does Tweedle know?'

Sheba shook her head. 'Neither does your father.'

'But you let Tweedle Beak into your bed just the same?'

'To save us going on tramp and missing your father. As well as all the other reasons. It was the only thing I could do.'

'But that makes you no better than a whore, Mother,' Poppy said, more with concern than with any disrespect.

'All women are whores, our Poppy. We sell that soft place we've got between our legs for whatever we want back in return, be it money, protection or just pleasure. It's a ticket for whatever we want, whatever we need.'

'What about love?'

Sheba smiled knowingly. 'Aye, it's a ticket for love as well. But there's a difference. You don't *sell* it for love, our Poppy. You give it away free. But always be aware of the likely consequences.'

Poppy went to bed that night before her mother and Tweedle, with a great deal on her mind. She was relieved to hear her mother's confession that it was Lightning Jack she loved, and not Tweedle Beak. Poppy could forgive Sheba her horizontal exploits now that she knew that it was merely an expedient device to protect them all. She was pleased also to learn that she was carrying a child, especially that there was no question but that it was her own father's child. It was a sort of insurance that when Lightning Jack returned – which, pray God, would be soon – Tweedle would simply fade into the background of navvies from whence he came, and things would revert to normal. No doubt Lightning Jack would thank

Tweedle Beak for looking after his woman while he had been away. It was the way of the navvies.

Inevitably, Poppy's thoughts turned to Robert Crawford and she relived that delectable half-hour in his arms, feeling his lips upon hers. She compared his gentleness and consideration to Jericho's ill-bred roughness, recalling the time when Jericho had been fighting naked and, naked, took her in his arms afterwards, rubbed himself lustfully against her and expected her to go willingly behind the hut with him. Did she really want Jericho's violent, slobbering kisses, his clumsy fondling, now she had tasted Robert's succulent lips?

Poppy recalled how wet she had felt between her legs while she and Robert were in each other's arms. She was wet now thinking about him. She pulled up her nightgown carefully so as not to disturb her sisters asleep in the same bed, and stroked herself to actually feel it on her fingers. It was wickedly pleasant to rub yourself there. Gently she continued, lying with her eyes shut, her mouth open receiving Robert's luscious kisses. With the other hand she fondled her breasts, arousing her small pink nipples, and imagined him to be doing it. She hugged herself, making believe it was Robert's warm, affectionate embrace that was making her hot, before rotating her thoughts to imagine she was actually feeling his smooth, firm flesh. 'Oh, I love you, Robert,' she mouthed silently. 'I love you, I love you, I love you.' As the pleasurable sensations intensified in her groin, she turned her face into the pillow, sure that her insides were melting, disintegrating, but with such toe-curling intensity. The urge to cry out was strong, but she merely took a gasp of air and sighed with disbelief at the extraordinary wild sensation that had come to overwhelm her.

The door opened. Tweedle Beak and her mother appeared, silhouetted against the light of an oil lamp, with Little

Lightning hovering in the background holding it. Little Lightning spoke and his mother told him to hush and dowt the flame, lest he wake the others. In the darkness, they all undressed and clambered into bed as silently as they could. It was not long before Poppy heard the faint rustle of sheets yielding to movement and the gentle creak of the iron bedstead, as Tweedle settled with unaccustomed restraint into what had become his regular nightly exercise.

Poppy smiled to herself.

Chapter 9

During the weeks that she got to know Robert Crawford, Poppy had become acquainted with the regularity of his comings and goings on the construction site. But work was moving along the trackbed away from the encampment towards Brierley Hill, and she could not always be certain lately that he would be where she thought he might be. In an endeavour to 'accidentally' bump into him as he left his office one dinner time, she tarried between the foreman's hut and Shaw Road, then between the tommy shop and the road. It was the first Thursday in July and the weather had turned, so that you could have been forgiven for thinking it was April, with all the showers alternating with the sunshine that shimmered blindingly off the wet mud.

While she drifted from one point to another, scanning the area for sight of Robert, she saw another man walking towards her. He was unmistakably a navvy, with a bright yellow waistcoat, a moleskin jacket, a quirky cap, and well-worn moleskin trousers with knee-straps to stop the rats running up his legs. He wore odd boots as well, one the colour of dried blood, the other a light tan. Poppy did not know him, so assumed he had been on tramp and was seeking work. As he entered the encampment he touched his cap and smiled amiably. He reminded her strangely of her father, except that he looked older.

She heard the sound of wheels chattering over the road surface and Robert appeared from the top of the hill, riding his machine. Her heart went into her mouth, for she had not the slightest idea what she might say to him. She just wanted to see him, to talk with him, to try and glean whether this unfulfilled love was as painful for him as it was for her. Robert had been on her mind so much these last few days and nights that she was becoming preoccupied. If only he hadn't told her how he felt. If only he had kept his feelings and his hands – and his kisses – to himself, they could have gone on as they had hitherto, teacher and pupil, friends who merely harboured admiration and respect for each other at arm's length, who kept their ardour unspoken and under control. But his confession that he was taken with her, and then his frustrating but tantalising self-restraint, had only fuelled her interest and desire the more. She was hooked, yet she understood that hooking her was not what he had intended. What she did not know was that Robert Crawford had also of late adopted the habit of either perambulating or riding – ostensibly in connection with his work – Poppy's likely routes.

As he approached, she thought she detected a blush from him as he drew to a halt, though it could have been the exertion of riding, even if it was downhill.

'Oh, hello, Robert,' she said, endeavouring to show a decorous amount of astonishment at finding him in the very place she had come to look for him.

'Hello, Poppy,' he greeted with equal surprise, uncertain how he stood now with this perplexing girl.

'Fancy seeing you here. I was just on me way to the tommy shop.' She ignored the pertinent reality that it took twice as long to get to the tommy shop by way of Shaw Road than her usual route of walking through the cutting.

'And I was just on my way to find my colleague Slingsby

Shafto,' he felt compelled to explain, ignoring the equally pertinent reality that he was travelling in precisely the wrong direction. 'Are you well?' he asked awkwardly.

'Oh, yes. I'm very well, thank you. Are you?'

He nodded. 'Yes, yes. I'm not altogether enamoured of this change in the weather, though. Rain makes everywhere so muddy and slows down the work.'

'Oh, I know,' she said. 'All the men moan like whores when the rain comes.'

'Poppy!' Robert exclaimed, unwittingly slipping into the role of tutor. 'You really must temper your similes.'

'I haven't a clue what you're on about.'

'What you just said . . . the men moaning like . . . like *whores*. You would never say that in polite conversation.'

'Sorry, *I* didn't know,' she replied defensively, disappointed at her little blunder, which highlighted once again the class difference between them. 'It's what the men say, Robert. I didn't know it was a . . . what?'

'A simile.'

'A simile?'

'Yes. Of course, it's perfectly normal to use similes, but yours is too inappropriate for polite conversation.'

Oh, yes, we're having polite conversation, more's the pity, she thought, as she regarded his mouth and yearned for him to kiss her. Why couldn't she make it less formal and tell him bluntly that she loved him, that her emotions were all upside down because of him? 'So, what's a simile?' she said instead.

'A simile is when you compare something to something else to enhance its meaning,' he answered, unaware of the turmoil inside her. 'Such as saying the full moon hangs *like* a silver disc, or . . . or . . . your eyes are *like* limpid pools . . . for example. Any such phrase using the word *like* or *as* is often a simile.'

'I'll try and remember, Robert. I'll try and use good, respectable similes in polite conversations in future,' Poppy said obligingly.

He smiled. 'I hope you will.'

'But what about Albert in the tommy shop?' she said, with an impish twinkle in her eyes.

'What about Albert?' he replied, with the feeling he was being led into some tender trap or other.

'Well, will he be offended if I tell him the place stinks like a midden?'

Robert laughed. 'I doubt it. With Albert it'll be like . . . *like* water off a duck's back.'

'Oh, you're sharp today.' She looked at him mischievously. 'You're sharper than a pig's jimmy.'

'Now, I'm not certain whether that's a simile or a metaphor,' he said, and went on his way amused.

Poppy was not really going to the tommy shop even though she ambled towards it. When she could see that Robert had gone inside the foreman's hut, she turned around, acting as if she'd forgotten something, and headed wistfully back to Rose Cottage. She so missed him already. She ached for the opportunity to be alone with him again, to try and win his love. She imagined she had been so close to being his, yet the possibility was all but lost. The pain of unrequited first love increased inexorably and jostled at her heart.

As she approached the hut she became aware of the navvy on tramp whom she'd seen a few minutes earlier walking alongside her as she neared the hut.

'Howdo, Miss,' he greeted. 'Bist heading for Lightning Jack's by any chance?'

'Yes,' she said, instantly throwing off her preoccupation at hearing her father's name. 'I'm his eldest daughter, Poppy.'

'Well, is that the truth? Nor should I be surprised. Just look at thee . . . He said th'art a fine-looking wench. He told me thou tek'st after thy mother in looks. Is thy mother about, young Poppy?'

'She's in the hut, mister. Have you got some news o' me father?'

'Aye, I come bearing news o' thy fairther.'

Poppy looked with apprehension at his grave expression and opened the door of the hut to let him in. The men, who had just finished their dinners, were about to go back to work, leaving their mess to be cleared up by Sheba and Poppy, and her sister Lottie. They trooped outside as Buttercup entered.

'Mother, this man's on tramp and he says he's got news o' me father.'

Sheba looked up and beheld the man with interest as she wiped her hands on her apron. 'You've got news o' Lightning Jack?'

'I have that, missus. Lightning Jack and meself met up on our way to the Mickleton tunnel, and we've bin muckers ever since—'

'Is that where he's gone? The Mickleton tunnel?'

'Aye, that's where he got to. That's where we both bin a-working – side by side.'

'So what have you come to tell me that he wouldn't come and tell me himself, mister?

'Buttercup, missus. Folk call me Buttercup . . . And it ain't that he wouldn't come himself . . . He couldn't.'

'Couldn't?' Sheba said.

'Nah.' Buttercup shook his head solemnly. ''Cause the daft bugger blowed himself up.'

Sheba slumped into a chair, the use suddenly draining out of her legs. 'What exactly d'you mean, Buttercup? What d'you mean, blowed himself up?'

'It was an accident, Sheba. I'll call thee Sheba if th'ast got no objection. It was a tragic accident.'

'So he's dead? . . . Or is he still alive?'

'He's dead, poor bugger. I'm sorry to say.'

There was a wail of anguish from Poppy, as piercing as the cry of a vixen that has lost a cub. At once she went to her mother for mutual consolation and threw her arms about her. 'Me dad's dead!' she keened. 'Oh, no. Please God, don't let him be dead.'

Sheba threw her arms around her daughter. Tears filled her own eyes and she began to tremble at the awful revelation. 'How did it happen? When did it happen?'

'Last Thursday,' Buttercup said. 'He'd packed gunpowder into the face of the rock to blow it and lit the fuse. He hivvered and hovered – I could see his candle in the darkness, not shiftin' – and I called him to come away quick. "I'm a-coming," he called back. But then he fell, Sheba, and I reckon as he twisted his ankle or summat, 'cause he dain't shift no more. It's dark in them tunnels, Sheba – night from dawn till dawn – and it's my guess as he couldn't mek out where he was a-walking, 'specially as he must've had the bright light o' the fuse still flickering in his eyes, making all else seem darker by comparison. I rushed out to fetch him, but I was too late. The gunpowder exploded well afore I could get to him, and I reckon it was the blast what killed him. He was showered wi' great lumps o' rock any road. If he'd lived he'd most likely have ended up a cripple.'

'My poor, poor Jack,' Sheba moaned.

'Aye. Poor Jack, and no two ways about it. Ye was all most dear to his heart, Sheba.'

In her state of already heightened emotions, Poppy released another great howl of lamentation at these powerful but simple reminders of his affection for them, and Sheba hugged her tight. Not only had she lost Robert, but now her father was gone also. Forever. Never would she be able to take his hand and tell him things that she longed to tell him now; feelings she had never thought necessary to divulge to him when he was alive.

'And what about his burial?' Sheba asked.

'He was buried Tuesday. I set off on tramp to let thee know as soon as 'twas over.'

'I can't get over it, Buttercup.'

'Nor me, Sheba. It seems unbelievable. I liked Lightning Jack. We was good muckers . . . Here, I brought thee his things, look.' Buttercup picked up the bundle that he'd laid on the floor between his feet and put it on the table in front of Sheba. 'Summat to remember him by.'

Sheba let go of her grieving daughter and opened up the bundle. She took out Jack's metal tea bottle, the tin in which he kept his mashings, the pouch in which he kept his tobacco, his gum-bucket still reeking of the stuff. There was a razor, a shaving brush that had seen better days, and the remains of a bar of soap. Sheba saw these things and wept.

'Well, Buttercup,' she said eventually, drying her eyes and sniffing as she remembered her duties as regards hospitality. 'How long since you've eaten?'

'Oh, I had a bit o' breffus somewhere round Halesowen.'

'Then you'll be clammed. I'll rustle you summat up. Our Poppy, unlock the barrel and serve Mr Buttercup a quart.'

'That's real decent o' thee, Sheba,' Buttercup said. 'Thou know'st what it's like on tramp.'

'That I do,' Sheba replied.

'Tell me, Sheba . . . Dost think there'll be work here for me?'

'You can but ask. See Billygoat Bob. But the tunnel here's finished, 'cept for want o' the permanent way being laid. I daresay there's other work, though. Folk am coming and going all the time. It's a different contractor now.'

'Well, when I've had that bite I'll seek out this Billygoat Bob. I see as thou tek'st in lodgers, Sheba. Cost find a bunk for me?'

'Oh, I'll organise you a bunk, Buttercup. Have no fear . . . only fourpence a night.'

Word spread around the encampment about Lightning Jack's death like a straw fire fanned by hot wind. A steady flow of navvies and a few women came to see Sheba to pay their respects. Poppy, however, her emotions already running high, took to her bed and sobbed the whole afternoon. If only she'd known, when he'd left that Saturday morning in May, that it would be the last time she would ever cast eyes on her father. She would have prevented him going somehow, hidden him somewhere close by till the fuss and palaver had died down. Even a spell in prison would have been infinitely preferable to his needless death. Such a horrible, sudden death at that. Now he was gone, there was so much she wanted to say to him, so much she wanted to hear.

Poppy refused food when Sheba asked if she was ready to eat late that afternoon, and took only a mug of hot tea. As she lay, her eyes puffy from her constant tears, the door to the bedroom opened and Sheba announced that Poppy had a visitor. The girl sat upright, knowing it could only be Robert Crawford and instantly sorry that he was about to see her at her ugliest, with red puffy eyes. But he might feel sorry for her. Her tears might elicit more tenderness from him; tenderness she craved. Through the haze of tears he was indistinct, but it did not look like the Robert Crawford she knew and loved, and her heart sank. She wiped her eyes, and was surprised to see Jericho standing there holding a posy of flowers.

'I din't know what to get you,' he said clumsily. 'So I brought you these. I'm that sorry to hear about your dad.'

Poppy forced a smile, touched by his unexpected consideration. She took the flowers from him and held on to them. 'That's kind,' she said, realising the barracking he would have got from his fellow navvies for doing something as unmanly as taking flowers to a girl. 'Thank you, Jericho.'

'Folk have told me how you thought the world o' your dad. O' course, I din't know Lightning Jack, but folk have told me all about him. He sounds like the sort I woulda liked having a drink with – and working with, o' course.'

Jericho's voice was surprisingly soothing. He was not saying all the right things, but it seemed he understood. He was giving support in his own limited way. Poppy's eyes flooded with tears again at his compassion and he squatted on the roughed-up bed beside her.

'Would you like a mug of tea?' she asked, remembering her hospitality and wiping her tears again. 'I'll make you one.'

'Nay, my wench,' Jericho answered. 'I'll not bother you in your grief. But I've a mind to call and see how you are later, if you've no objection . . . Maybe you'll feel a bit brighter later.'

She nodded. 'That's very kind, Jericho,' she answered sincerely.

Jericho did call later. Poppy did not feel any less grief-stricken but she was pleased he had shown an interest and had taken the trouble to see how she was. She walked out with him later down the footpath to Cinder Bank and into Netherton. He chatted easily, talking about this and that, and she believed he was trying to take her mind off her grief. They stopped at a public house in Netherton. The flagged floor of the public bar was strewn with sawdust; a few rickety tables and stools were the only furniture. Two men kept nudging each other and eyeing up Poppy with lustful looks. Jericho tolerated it for a while then approached them.

'Have you had an eyeful yet?' he asked them collectively.

'Well, her's a comely enough wench but for the queer frock,' one of them answered, calm, confident, grinning, defiant. 'Yo' cor blame we for lookin', though. Why? Dun yer want to mek summat of it?'

'If you like,' Jericho replied. 'Would you like to take a wander outside, eh?'

'No, Jericho,' Poppy pleaded. 'Don't fight again on my account.' She knew she would feel even more beholden to him.

'I'll not stand by and hear them insult you, Poppy,' he said, handing her his jacket. 'I'll gouge their guts out.'

He led them all outside. The man Jericho had addressed handed his jacket to his mate and stood poised with his fists up.

'Just the one of you, eh?' Jericho taunted. 'I'll fight the pair o' you together if you've a mind.'

'It'll on'y tek one to bump yo' off, you cocky bastard,' goaded the local man.

Jericho hitched up his trousers and grinned, and his opponent lunged out at his head. Jericho deftly sidestepped the punch, intercepting it with an upward sweep of the arm, then struck the local man hard on the jaw with a sickening crunch. The man put his hand to his mouth and looked at it to see if blood had been drawn. Seeing the man's guard was down, Jericho hit him again and the poor fellow slumped to the ground with a lip that was oozing blood.

A crowd was gathering, murmuring, watching intently,

inexorably drawn to the fight. 'Who's this big bugger who's just downed Billy Webb?' somebody asked, obviously surprised that somebody should.

Billy Webb struggled to his feet and his arms shot out at Jericho like the lashes of a whip. But few jabs made contact and they only succeeded in angering Jericho the more. Jericho struck out again at Billy Webb and missed, whereupon Billy landed a telling punch into the stomach that made Jericho wince. Jericho leered in defiance, looking for an opening to drive home a blow. He fought to win and there were no rules. Everything was fair: punching, kicking, kneeing and clinching. Both men were masters of scrapping, a hard-learned craft born of too many cruel fights, too many split lips, blackened eyes and aching limbs, but Jericho was the younger man and the bigger. In a short time his advantage began to tell, while his opponent began to lose confidence.

The growing crowd watched in stunned silence. Their local champion was about to be beaten. After one more blow to the mouth, Billy Webb went down . . . and stayed down.

'Now you, my friend,' Jericho said, offering Billy's mate the opportunity to avenge the defeat of his friend.

The mate put his hands up defensively. 'I'm no fighter, my mon. I'm a drinker. Let me buy you a drink and we'll part friends.'

'I'd see to me mate first, if I were you,' Jericho said. 'Meanwhile, I'll buy me own beer.'

He turned to Poppy for his jacket. Embarrassed, she handed it to him.

'Shall we go now?' she suggested, uncomfortable, feeling that hostile eyes were on her for being the cause of this Billy Webb's downfall.

'Shall we buggery! I'm having a few more drinks yet, my flower. It's thirsty work fighting.' He inspected one of his fists that had become grazed in the scrap, licked it and wiped it on his jacket.

Poppy watched him, disconcerted by the wild, glazed look in his eyes. It was obvious that Jericho enjoyed fighting. Clearly he derived some strange sensual satisfaction from the physical exertion, the exhilaration of danger, or at gaining physical superiority over another.

'Why do you have to fight?' she asked as he sat down, having bought himself a fresh tankard of beer.

''Cause that's how I argue – with me fists.'

'But you hurt folk, Jericho.'

'I ain't hurt you, have I?'

'No . . .'

'So why are you harping on about it?'

'But that's twice you've fought over me. I don't desire it, Jericho.'

'But it's a measure of how much I think o' yer.'

'So is that how you let somebody know how much you like 'em? By fighting?'

'Can you think of a better way?'

Poppy didn't answer. Of course there were better ways. Her thoughts turned to Robert Crawford and his gentleness. There was a world of difference between the two men. Jericho was typical of all navvies – he argued with his fists, his aggression justified by the twisted logic for which an excess of alcohol was responsible. Conversely, was Robert Crawford typical of all men who purported to be gentlemen?

She finished what was left of her drink and looked intently at Jericho. 'I want to go now. I'm going anyway, whether you come with me or not. I ain't gunna stay here any longer.'

'Go then,' he said sullenly. 'I'll find me another wench.'

But then she remembered how considerate he had been, how sympathetic. 'Oh, come on, Jericho,' she pleaded.

'You're not going to let me walk that path all by myself, are you? What if one of these here follows me? What if I get set on?'

He drained his beer and stood up. 'I'd *kill* anybody who touched you, Poppy. Come on, then. Let's went.'

The low sun threw long shadows as they walked hand in hand along the footpath back towards the encampment. Tall grasses and thistles waved lazily in the summery breeze and a white butterfly settled on a cluster of shepherd's purse. The rain that had half threatened all day had not fallen, but bags of dark cloud still chased each other ominously across the sky.

Poppy and Jericho spoke little on the way back. He was reliving, in a silent, very personal exhilaration, every blow he had cast and received. A good hard fight energised him, set the blood coursing through his veins. And after every good hard fight he felt the insistent need for a woman. The one was a counterbalance to the other. The brutal punches and kicks, clenched fists striking the sturdy flesh and bone of some other man in desperate anger, could only be neutralised by the soft caress and accommodating smoothness of a woman's willing body.

'I want you, Poppy Silk. Let's lie down in the grass.'

She looked at him apprehensively, seeing the lust in his narrowed eyes. He had been taken like this each time she had seen him fight. The first time, after he'd fought naked, he'd wanted her to go behind the hut with him. The second time, after the fair, he'd tried to seduce her under the bridge that they were approaching again now.

'I won't rest till you're my bed wench,' he said earnestly. 'I had a word with Dog Meat. He reckons it'll be all right if you and me sleep together in Tipton Ted's hut. We could hang a sheet round the bunk for a bit o' privacy.'

He was going far too fast, taking far too much for granted.

'I don't know if I want to do that, Jericho. I don't want to be anybody's bed wench.'

'Don't you love me?' he asked, as if there were no earthly reason why she shouldn't.

'I like you,' she replied. 'Course I like you. You've been kind to me.'

'But you don't love me.'

'I can't say as I do.'

'I'll make you love me.'

She shrugged. 'I don't see how—'

He took her in his arms with a roughness she did not enjoy and searched hungrily for her lips. Poppy was in two minds whether to submit but, in the same instant that she felt Jericho's ungainly kisses, she remembered Robert Crawford's sweet, stimulating caresses, and had to turn her face away.

'What's up wi' yer?' Jericho asked, impatient. 'Are you still hankering for that bloody chickenshit of an engineer? That Crawford?'

'No, course not,' she answered, averting her eyes away from his.

'Christ almighty, I'll kill the little bastard. I swear, I'll swing for him if ever you are.'

'I'm not, Jericho,' she protested with a vehemence that was sham but convincing. 'Course I'm not.'

'So what's up wi' yer then? Why d'yer keep saying no to me all the time?'

'Jericho . . .' She uttered his name softly, soothingly. 'It's not that I don't like you . . . I *do*. But I don't want to be anybody's bed wench, woman, whore, wife, or whatever else you want to call it. Not even yours, Jericho . . . Don't you understand? I want to be Poppy Silk, owned by nobody but

139

meself. I don't want to have to sleep with somebody every night of my life and end up having a babby every ten months, like some o' the women I know.'

'You're a bloody icicle,' Jericho proclaimed angrily. 'Christ, there's more warmth in a dead nun than there is in you. I'd throw you to the ground and take you here and now, but I'd most likely skin me dick to shreds trying to shove it up your stone-cold cleft.'

'And what do you expect from somebody who's just had news of her father's death?' Her eyes filled with tears as another wave of grief subdued her. 'Don't you understand that I got other things on me mind than lying with you, Jericho. Leave me be. Just leave me be . . .'

So it was not late when Poppy returned to Rose Cottage that evening. The hut was quiet. All of the men had gone out drinking. Sheba was subdued and Poppy could tell that her mother had been crying.

'Did you tell Tweedle Beak about me dad?'

'Yes, I told him,' Sheba replied.

'And what did he say?'

'Not much. He said as he was sorry, but I think he was a bit relieved.'

'You mean because he won't have to face me dad now?'

Sheba nodded. 'I reckon that's why.'

'Did you tell him that you're carrying me father's child?'

Sheba shook her head dejectedly. 'Not yet. I'll tell him when I'm ready . . . If I think it's worth telling him at all.'

'You'll have to tell him sooner or later.'

'Or let him think the child is his . . .'

'Mother, you wouldn't . . . Would you?'

'What else can I do, our Poppy? If he knows the child is Lightning Jack's he'll disown me. He wouldn't stand to be

140

ridiculed. We would all be back where we started when your father went on tramp. We'd all end up in the workhouse.'

'Oh, Mother . . .' Poppy sighed. 'What are we going to do?'

'Lord knows . . . Oh, there's a note here . . .' Sheba fished in the pocket of her apron and pulled out a cream-coloured envelope, which she handed to Poppy. 'It was pushed under the door o' the hut after you'd gone out. I hoped as you might be able to read it.'

Poppy took the envelope and recognised her own name written clearly on the front. Her heart went to her mouth as she tore it open. She withdrew the notepaper inside and scanned it for words that she could recognise. Some words were immediately recognisable, some she had to build up, but it was written in a precise hand that was easily legible.

'What does it say?' Sheba enquired fretfully.

'Mother, I'm trying to read it . . .'

It was hard to construct the words, many of which she had not learned, but she built them up logically from the letter sounds she knew, and it all made sense.

'It's from Robert,' Poppy said softly, her heart beating fast.

'Read it to me, our Poppy.'

'It says, "Dear Poppy, I heard today of the sad death of your father. The news came as a shock to me, so it must be an even greater shock to you and your family. I want you to know how distressed I am to hear of it. I can only begin to imagine how you must feel. Please pass on my . . . con-dol-en-ces" . . . I think that's the word . . . "to your mother. If there is anything I can do please let me know. Your friend . . . Robert Crawford."'

'Well, that's decent of him,' Sheba remarked. 'Thank him for me when you see him.'

'I will, if I see him . . .'

Chapter 10

That same evening, after Jericho had left Poppy near Rose Cottage, he made his way to The Wheatsheaf in a state of high exhilaration and frustrated lust. Fighting did this to him. It was the reason he sought to fight. But each emotion was only one half of the equation, and the lust was an encumbrance unless it could be satisfied, hence his frustration. He honourably forbore to take advantage of Poppy due to her grief over Lightning Jack, but he was desperate for a woman to mollify this virility that burned so ferociously within him.

Dog Meat was sitting in the public house accompanied by a tankard of beer and a ragbag of other navvies bent on getting drunk. He gestured to Jericho to join them. Jericho stood first at the bar and ordered a tankard for himself and one for Dog Meat.

'I'd have got up and bought you one if I'd got any money left,' Dog Meat remarked, taking the beer from Jericho gratefully and turning his back on his other mates. 'I didn't expect to see you in here. I reckoned you'd be too busy rogering young Poppy.'

'Huh! There's more chance o' being struck by lightning in that bloody tunnel over there. I'm desperate for a jump, Dog Meat. I could roger me own mother.'

'How much you willing to pay?'

'Pay? I wouldn't pay to roger me mother, Dog Meat, you daft bugger.'

'I don't mean your mother, you fool. I mean how much would you pay to have a woman?'

'Why the hell should I pay? Wenches are normally willing enough.'

'But it's finding one, eh, Jericho? And there's nothing spare in here tonight.'

'Come a walk with me into the town then, eh?'

'I told yer, I got no money.'

'I'll pay for your beer. I bet there's plenty spare knocking about Dudley.'

'I can't be bothered. I'm stopping here. How much you willing to pay for a woman, Jericho? Just tell me.'

'Why? What's it to you?'

'Well . . . I'm skint, see. Give me the price of a gallon o' beer and you can borrow Minnie. That way we help each other out.'

'Are yer serious?'

'Course I'm serious.' Dog Meat raised his forefinger in warning. 'Only one jump, though. And don't let on to her as we've got this arrangement. Just pretend you want to seduce her.'

'And what if she won't let me? What if she's as tight with it as that Poppy Silk?'

Dog Meat grinned. 'Well, I can make you no promises, Jericho. It's a risk you'll have to take. But it's the best offer you'll get this side of tomorrow morning. She was always game enough with me.'

'And it don't bother yer, her going with me?'

'Bother me? Why should it bother me? It only bothers me if I can't get a damned drink. Have her. Just so long as she don't know as I've had beer money off you for the privilege.'

'So what you gunna do while I'm getting stuck up your wench, eh?'

'I'm gunna stop here and get bloody soused. It's a good scheme, eh, Jericho? This way we both get our fill.'

'Fair enough,' Jericho said. 'So where is she?'

'At Hawthorn Villa, as far as I know.'

Jericho dug in the pocket of his trousers and pulled out a handful of coins. He counted them and handed them over to Dog Meat. 'I'll let you know what I think of her,' he said with a leer. 'If you're interested, that is.' He finished his drink calmly and went out.

Minnie Catchpole was standing on the front doorstep shaking a rug as Jericho approached Hawthorn Villa. A cloud of dust and debris was instantly taken by the breeze, which blew much of it back over her. Minnie pulled a face and cursed as she spat out some of the pieces and picked bits out of her hair. When she saw Jericho striding towards her, she gave an embarrassed smile.

'Minnie! How are you?'

'Covered in dust, Jericho. Seen Poppy, have yer?' She rolled up the rug ready to take inside.

'Don't talk to me about Poppy. She's full of herself, feeling sorry for herself, thinking the world revolves around her.'

'Well, she has lost her father,' Minnie reminded him.

Jericho shrugged. 'Aye, I know all about that. But it ain't just that, Minnie. She only ever thinks of herself. Now you . . .' He looked at her admiringly.

'What about me?'

'I get the feeling as you're easier to get along with.'

Minnie smiled coyly. 'I might be, Jericho. Who knows?'

'I do. And what's more, you'm pretty with it. I don't know why I waste me time on Poppy bloody Silk when there's lovely wenches like you around . . . Pity Dog Meat's already bagged yer for himself, eh?'

'I know,' Minnie replied ruefully, desperate for a way to tell him that Dog Meat wouldn't stop her doing what she wanted to do. Already her heart was beating faster at what Jericho was implying. 'But Jericho, I'm always open to offers, you know. I mean, Dog Meat does what he wants to do, and I do what I want. It ain't as if we'm proper wed. I on'y sleep with him.'

Jericho shrugged, overtly feigning resignation of the circumstances, but inwardly heartened by her response. 'Fancy a walk, do yer? It's a grand evening.'

'I don't mind. Where to?'

He shrugged again. 'Anywhere. I dunno. In the opposite direction to The Wheatsheaf, eh?' There was a gleam in his eye. 'We could talk some more, if you like . . .'

'All right. But maybe we shouldn't be seen together. Folk might get the wrong end o' the stick.'

'That's a point,' said Jericho. He looked up at the sky. It was dusk and would soon be dark. 'Tell you what, Minnie . . . Meet me just inside the tunnel . . . In five minutes.'

'Shall I bring this rug wi' me? It'd be something for us to sit on while we talk . . .'

He nodded and couldn't help but grin. 'Good idea. I'll wait just inside the tunnel, like I say.'

Jericho stalked away from the encampment to the cutting and the entrance to the tunnel, hunching up in his moleskin jacket in an effort to make himself look smaller. He turned his head and looked furtively behind him towards the untidy shanty of huts two hundred yards away. Not a soul stirred. Already an old moon, reddish and low, was hiding behind black-fleeced clouds that were tinged with its eerie glow. Across the landscape, plumes of factory smoke bent like the tails of a hundred furry dogs. Here and there a feeble light glimmered.

Jericho breathed deeply, drawing in the cool night air. His exhilaration was matched now by his anticipation. He moved a further twenty yards inside the tunnel and waited. Within a few minutes, he could make out the figure of Minnie in the dimness as she walked briskly towards him; the rug she had been shaking was rolled up under her arm. The blood started coursing through his veins once more.

'Psst! Over here,' he said in a hoarse whisper and Minnie headed towards him.

'I don't think anybody saw me,' she breathed.

'There's nobody about. But we'll go a bit further into the tunnel, for fear.'

Stumbling here and there over loose stones in the darkness, their noisy footfalls through the gravel bed echoed along the tunnel in the hundred and fifty yards or so that they put between themselves and the entrance. It was as dark as a crypt in there. Outside, the mean backsliding dusk allowed no light to enter.

'Here?' Minnie queried.

'Aye, here will do.'

Unable to see what she was doing due to the extreme darkness, Minnie carefully laid out the rug on the gravel, made sure it was level, and they sat down, each blind to the exact position of the other. She reached out a hand and felt his arm. She hitched herself closer to him and was reassured by the warmth of his body as they made contact.

'It's so dark in here,' she whispered. 'You can't see your hand in front of your face.'

'Are you frit?'

'A bit,' she admitted.

'Don't be. Here, let me put me arm around you to keep you safe . . . There . . . How's that?'

'Better . . .'

'Good.'

A pause developed when neither could think of anything suitable to say because of the curious circumstances. Minnie broke the silence.

'It seems funny, me being here with you like this.'

'I don't mislike it. Do you?'

'No. I din't say as I mislike it . . . I like being with you, Jericho.'

'You know I fancy you, don't you, Minnie? I've always fancied you.'

'I've always fancied you, Jericho. But I thought you was struck on Poppy.'

'I still fancy Poppy,' he admitted shrewdly. 'But she's a bit slow to let go of it.'

'You ain't had her then?'

'Not much chance o' that, Minnie.'

'More fool her, I'd say.' Minnie giggled girlishly. 'Anyway, what would you say if Dog Meat found out we'd bin in the tunnel together?'

'Christ, we mustn't let him know, Minnie. It must be our secret.'

Jericho felt Minnie's arms come about him and he sought her lips urgently. When their mouths connected, they leaned backwards and lay on the rug. At once, Jericho reached out and took a handful of the hem of her skirt and hoisted it up to her waist as she raised her backside to aid him. She was wearing no stockings and the smooth flesh of her bare legs, slightly moist with the day's perspiration, was a tonic to goad him on.

'Oh, Jericho,' she sighed as his large but skilful fingers gently caressed between her thighs. She reached down to the front of his trousers, unfastened the buttons of his fly and probed inside.

'Christ, he feels lovely and hard, Jericho . . . And big.'

'Oh, he's big all right. And you feel lovely and soft, ready and waiting for him, by the feel o' yer.'

Minnie unfastened the rest of his buttons and eased his trousers over his buttocks. He manoeuvred himself between her legs and, without further ado, she guided him in. As she gasped with the pleasure of his movements, she pictured him naked on the night he fought Chimdey Charlie, remembering well how the sight of him excited her. Well, now she was enjoying him to the full as he thrust lusciously inside her. She pulled him hard into her by his buttocks and raised her legs so he could fill her up the more.

'Christ, Jericho,' she uttered ardently. 'Jesus Christ . . .'

'Am I hurting you?'

'No, you do it really lovely. Ooh, ever so lovely . . . I could stand this all night . . .'

They settled into a steady rhythm that too soon was interrupted by groans from Jericho.

'Don't stop, Jericho . . . What have you stopped for? You ain't finished already, have yer?'

'Christ, I'm done,' he groaned, spent.

'Well I ain't. I hope you'm gunna finish me off . . .'

'Course I will. There's no rush . . .'

'You could've fooled me.'

'Well, I wanted you so bad, Minnie.'

They lay a while longer, still joined, till a drip of water from the roof splattered on him and dribbled coldly down the cleft of his bare behind. He rolled off Minnie, lay beside her, then fondled her again with his dextrous fingers till she began wriggling more insistently. She let out shrieks of ecstasy that diminished into a series of little moans, then sighs, but the smile on her face remained fixed, although invisible in the darkness.

'Better now?' he asked.

'Oh, Christ, yes,' she responded, with breathless enthusiasm.

'I needed that, Minnie.'

'And me, Jericho.'

'We'll come here again, eh?'

'Tomorrow night, if you like,' she suggested. 'When Dog Meat's gone out on the beer.'

'Let's hope somebody can lend him some money,' Jericho remarked, the irony in his voice beyond Minnie. 'You won't tell him, will you?'

'Am yer mad? He'd kill me.'

'And don't tell Poppy neither. If you tell Poppy, I'll tell Dog Meat . . .'

'Don't worry. I won't tell your precious Poppy.'

They lay still and silent for a while, each privately reliving the pleasure. A few feet away, they heard a scuffling and Minnie thought it must be a rat. She froze and clutched Jericho's arm tightly. Somebody tried to stifle a cough . . . or was it a laugh?

Jericho sat bolt upright. 'Who's there?' he challenged. 'Who's there?'

'Tweedle Beak,' came the amused reply.

'Tweedle Beak? What you doing here?'

'Daft bugger. What d'yer think? Same as you, Jericho, old son.'

'Oh? So who'm you with?'

Tweedle mumbled to his unseen companion. 'What did you say your name was, love?'

'Eliza,' a little voice replied.

'I'm with somebody called Eliza, Jericho.'

Jericho realised there was a glimmer of hope. 'I take it as you want me to keep me trap shut, eh?'

'It'd be as well.'

'Then you'd better keep yours shut about me and Minnie Catchpole.'

Tweedle Beak grunted. 'Well, I ain't sid yer in here, have I, you dirty bloody ram? Not in this darkness.'

'Then I ain't seen you neither, Tweedle.'

Minnie and Jericho stood up, and Minnie felt round for her rug in the blackness while he hitched up his trousers and fastened his fly buttons. She found the rug and rolled it up, felt for Jericho, and held his arm as they made their way back to the tunnel's mouth, followed close behind by Tweedle Beak and the woman he had picked up from one of the local public houses.

Two minutes later, Buttercup left the tunnel. He had entered it earlier with a lantern to inspect the standard of workmanship required by Treadwell's. When he saw two other people about to enter, he blew out his light and waited patiently while they got on with what they had come for. When another couple entered and revealed their identities, his interest intensified. When they made their exit, he followed them unseen to the edge of the encampment, where they all went their silent, separate ways . . .

Next morning, after a fitful night's sleep, Poppy awoke to the sound of her mother vomiting into the jerry that lurked under her bed.

'What's up wi' thee, wench?' Tweedle muttered from under the blanket.

'Something I ate,' Sheba replied economically, and heaved

150

again into the jerry that she held in her lap as she sat on the bed.

'Well, mek sure as yo' doh ate it again. What time is it?'

'Time to get up, I reckon.' She put down the pot and wiped her mouth with the hem of her cotton nightgown. As she stood up and stretched, she ran her fingers through her long hair. Poppy peered over her bedclothes watching her mother, wondering how much she was pining for Lightning Jack. She knew her mother's expressions; they were a signal of her innermost feelings, and thus she could read her anguish. If only Jack were here; he would be proud as punch to know she was carrying another child.

The rest of the household began to stir. The dog belonging to one of the navvies in the next room yapped at being disturbed, and a disgruntled voice suggested the animal must be hankering for a kick up the bollocks. Tweedle Beak rose from his side of the bed and scratched first his beard and then his backside before a succession of ripping farts diminished all other sounds to incidental background noise. Poppy judiciously held her blanket to her nose and waited till Tweedle got dressed and was gone before she ventured out of bed. She washed and dressed and brushed her teeth, a habit she had acquired some time ago when she realised that such things as toothbrushes and tooth cleaning powder were available at modest cost and made your breath smell sweet. (She had been grateful for it when the opportunity to kiss Robert Crawford had presented itself.) That done, she took out the jerry, holding her breath while she carried it outside to the midden heap.

Poppy wished to contrive another casual meeting with Robert Crawford when she had finished her jobs. She wanted to thank him for his note and for his kind consideration. So, when the time was appropriate, she tied on her bonnet, took off her apron and stepped outside into the warm midday sunshine. The area around the encampment was quiet now that the workings were concentrated towards Netherton and Pensnett. Poppy did not know that Robert Crawford was once more also contriving to meet her. They coincided close to where they had met the last time.

'Oh, Poppy, I'm so glad I've seen you—'

'Thank you for your note, Robert. It was very thoughtful.'

'You were able to read it?'

'Oh, yes. It was kind of you to send it.'

'But I want to tell you face to face how sorry I am to hear of your father's death. You must be distraught.'

'I don't know about that, Robert, but it's upset me a lot. I thought the world of my dad.'

'I distinctly gained that impression. And how is your mother?'

She shook her head and tears glimmered in her blue eyes. 'My mother misses him as well . . . We all do.' She did not want to expand on her mother's situation. He might know about her and Tweedle Beak already for all she knew, but just in case he did not, she had no desire to mention it.

'Please pass on to your mother my sincerest condolences, Poppy. He was a good man, your father. Hard working, decent, down-to-earth. Very likeable. I'm sure all his workmates will miss him.'

Poppy broke down in a flood of tears. 'I'm sorry, Robert,' she blubbered, taking a rag from the pocket of her skirt and drying her eyes. 'I can't help crying over him. I can't believe that I'll never see him again. I keep thinking any minute he'll come walking round the corner with his pickaxe and shovel over his shoulder. If only I'd known what was going to happen to him when he left us, I'd have stopped him going somehow.'

'You could never have known, Poppy,' Robert said gently and drew her to him consolingly. 'It's not your fault that he's dead, and you mustn't blame yourself . . .'

Poppy leaned her head against his chest and sobbed. It was so good to feel his arms about her again. Maybe this was all she needed – to be in Robert's arms. Maybe it was Robert she was really grieving for. But how could she tell when her emotions were so agonised? It was difficult to separate them. Was the grief she felt for Lightning Jack any more acute than that which she felt over losing Robert, however brief their affair? But being back in Robert's embrace only made her weep the more. No doubt he would think her a complete fool.

Robert looked over his shoulder to see if they were being watched and self-consciously, but reluctantly, let go of her. 'Listen, Poppy, walk with me a little way. Talk about your father all you want. My own father always reckons that talking about your problems with somebody lessens them, and I'm certain it's true.'

She nodded tearfully, content to walk at his side. Rather than walk towards the town, they ambled down the path towards Netherton.

'So,' Robert said. 'Tell me more about Lightning Jack.'

Poppy wiped her eyes and sighed profoundly. 'What is there to tell? He was a good man at heart. You said so yourself. He cared for us, his children. He cared for my mother in his way, although he drank like a fish and would spend most of his money on drink when he got paid.'

'In that, he was no different to any of the others,' Robert suggested. 'But I sense he was more considerate than most.'

'He was,' she agreed. 'He was a decent man although he wasn't religious. He used to take the mickey out of anybody from the billycock gang who came to preach to the men—'

'Poppy, what's the billycock gang, for goodness sake?' Robert asked.

'Preachers. Those who used to come every so often to try and change the men in their ways and convert them to Christianity.'

'There's nothing wrong with Christianity, Poppy,' Robert said, turning to look at her. 'And in times of grief such as yours, I believe it can be a great comfort.'

'Honest?' She regarded him earnestly. 'How?'

'Well, I'm not particularly religious myself. I've had religion forced down my throat far too long for it to have any appeal now. But I do believe it helps to pray sometimes.'

'I don't know how to pray. I wouldn't know what to say. I don't reckon there's much to all that claptrap anyhow.'

'Well, you could try it. Why not give it a try and reserve judgement until you have.'

'Would you teach me how to pray, Robert?'

'I'm not qualified, Poppy. I'm not a priest.'

'But you can give me an idea what to do and what to say. If you go to church regular, you must have an idea.'

It was a God-given opportunity to see her again. Of course he must grasp it. He was emotionally torn, of course he was, but he could not just dismiss this delightful waif, who looked up to him for help and guidance with those exquisite blue eyes. As well as being drawn to her irrevocably, he felt obliged to help her, obliged to guide her. Continuing to plague himself in the doing might well end in disaster, but it was a course he had no choice but to pursue. There was something about this girl that he could not abandon. She had got under his skin and was proving impossible to remove.

'Then why don't you meet me tomorrow at the church and we'll go inside and I'll try and teach you,' he suggested.

'But tomorrow's Saturday. Not Sunday?'

'You don't want to go when all the regular churchgoers are about, do you?'

'No, I s'pose not,' she answered with a shrug.

'Tomorrow then. One o'clock outside St Thomas's.'

'The one with the spire?'

'Yes, the one with the spire, at the top of the hill there.' He stopped walking. 'Are you feeling better now, Poppy?'

'A bit, thank you.'

'Good. Maybe we should head back now.'

She nodded her agreement and looked at him longingly. 'And thank you again for your note, Robert. It was a lovely thought.'

'I'm just happy you were able to read it.'

She smiled self-consciously. 'Oh, every word.'

'That shows how well and how easily you learned.'

Poppy blushed at his compliment that meant so much to her. 'I liked learning to read and write. But I still have such a lot more to learn, don't I?'

'If you really wanted to, perhaps we could resume your lessons.'

'Oh, I'd really like to, Robert . . . as long as you . . . if you don't mind, I mean . . . If I wouldn't be taking up too much of your time.'

'I've rather missed teaching you, Poppy,' he said candidly and smiled. 'You're a model pupil, you know. Not that I'm any great shakes as a teacher . . .'

'Oh, I think you're a good teacher, Robert. I wouldn't have anybody else teach me.'

He smiled again and looked into her eyes. 'You seem much brighter now. I told you it helps to get things off your chest by sharing your problems. Do you still want to meet me tomorrow?'

'Oh, yes,' she reassured him, not about to let such an opportunity pass. 'I ain't never been in a church before.'

'Never? Well, I hope you don't grow too fond of it. I'd hate it to change you. I like you fine the way you are.'

Chapter 11

The silence inside St Thomas's church overwhelmed Poppy. The clack of her clogs on the hard tiled floor rang off the walls and around the huge stone pillars that supported the gallery and the high, vaulted roof as she followed Robert up the centre aisle and into a front pew facing the choir stalls. She sat down beside him and looked in wonder at the painting on glass that filled the east window above the altar.

'What's that picture?' she asked in a whisper, for to speak in her normal voice would be an unwarranted intrusion on the church's cool tranquillity. 'It's beautiful.'

'The Ascension,' Robert answered. 'Christ risen.'

'Oh,' she said and nodded.

Robert had picked up a copy of the *Book of Common Prayer* from the rear of the church as they entered. He opened it up and handed it to her with an affectionate smile.

'See if you can make sense of this, Poppy.' He pointed to a block of text that looked inordinately daunting to her eyes. 'Read it out to me.'

She studied the text for a few seconds, then, garnering her confidence to try, she began reading very slowly, building up the words as best she could, '*Our Father . . . which – art – in – heeven . . .*'

'Heaven,' Robert corrected.

'Oh. *Heaven* . . . But I thought an *e* and an *a* together said *ee*, like in *bean*.'

'Not always, Poppy. There's no rule.'

She tutted diffidently. 'So what's that next word?'

'Hallowed.'

'What's it mean?'

'Revered . . . Respected . . . Admired.'

'Oh . . . Hallowed – be – thy – name – Thy k – kin – king – dom – come – Thy – will – be – done – on . . . What's that word, Robert? It's a hard one.'

'Earth,' he said, with unending patience.

She looked at him intensely and nodded, then returned to the book. She read it through to the end, taking her time, meticulously trying to construct the words from the letters and combinations she had already learnt.

'What's this word, Robert?'

'*Amen*. It means "so be it".'

'Then why don't it just say "so be it", instead of "Amen"?'

'Because it's either a Latin or Greek or Hebrew word that means *so be it*. When you say a prayer you generally start it with the words "Our Father", and end it with "Amen".'

'So it's a sort of rule, then?'

'Yes. Or rather, a sort of convention . . . I must say, you read that very well. I know it was slow, but speed comes with practice. The more you read, the easier you'll recognise words, and the faster you'll become. You'll also learn a great deal from reading. It's the gateway to all knowledge.'

'Is that all there is to praying then?'

'You are supposed to word your prayer to suit whatever it is you're praying for.'

'So if I wanted to pray to God to send me some new boots, what would I say?'

Robert smiled to himself. 'That would depend on what size you took.'

'Size four, I think.'

'God needs to know, you see. So you would say a prayer to God asking for some boots and tell him what colour, size, et cetera . . . It's normal to kneel while praying to demonstrate our humility, but we won't bother with that rigmarole. Humility is such an aggravating attribute. It's just as easy to pray sitting down . . . And a sight easier on the knees. Now put your hands together and close your eyes – like this . . .'

She did as he bid.

'Ready to say your prayer?'

'Yes,' she said and took a deep breath. 'Our Father, please let me have a pair of dainty black boots with 'lastic sides . . . size four should do it . . . Amen.' She opened her eyes and turned to Robert. 'Do you think it'll work?' she asked eagerly.

'Oh, I doubt it. It's not considered good practice to pray for material things. Only spiritual. For instance, why don't you say a prayer for your father and perhaps your mother?'

'How? Will you say a prayer to show me how?'

'I'll try. But please remember, Poppy, I'm not an ordained priest and I haven't the command of religious language like priests have. But I will try, and hope it doesn't sound trite. Here goes . . . Hands together now, eyes closed . . .' Poppy peeped at him and thought how very solemn but how very handsome he looked. 'Our Father . . . we commend the soul of the dearly departed Jack Silk unto Thy care and protection. Please receive him, Lord, into the bosom of Thy tender mercy and forgive him his trespasses. We pray also for Sheba Silk and Poppy Silk and the rest of his family left behind, who grieve over his passing. Comfort them and nurture them with Thy eternal strength and goodness . . . Amen.'

Poppy was moved. A tear trembled on her eyelash and rolled down her cheek, but she checked herself from weeping. 'That was beautiful, Robert,' she breathed. 'I shall never forget what you said. It was beautiful.'

He turned to her and smiled with all his affection manifest in his eyes. 'Does it make you feel a little uplifted?'

'Oh . . .' She pondered the question for a second or two. 'In a funny way, yes. I don't feel half so sad as what I did before. I s'pose it's knowing that our Father which art in heaven will look after me dad now . . . Oh, I don't feel half so sad, Robert. Thank you.'

He could have hugged her. He wanted to hug her. He wanted to take her in his arms and never let her go. But he was in God's House and such shenanigans would only be frowned on and ultimately punished by that good and bounteous God who totally disapproved of bodily contact between man and woman unless they were bound in matrimony.

Poppy turned her face to him and pursed her lips without inhibition. Without thinking, he met them with his own and they kissed. It was not a lingering kiss, little more than a peck, but it was so natural, so unpretentiously given, that it quite took his breath away. Never had he known such unstinting warmth from another person.

'What are you going to do now?' he asked. 'When you leave here, I mean?'

She shrugged girlishly. 'Go home, I 'spect. I got some work to do yet. That new chap who come – you know, my dad's mate, Buttercup – he wants me to wash his shirt and things. I promised I would.'

'Have you had much to do with him?'

'Not yet. But I like him. He seems like me dad . . . kind and easy to get along with. I hope he stays with us awhile.'

'I . . . er . . . I bought you this, Poppy . . .' Robert felt in his pocket and fished out a little parcel. 'I thought it appropriate. I do hope you like it.'

'What is it?'

'Open it, and you'll see.'

'Robert, thank you, whatever it is. I don't get presents very often.' She opened the parcel. 'Oh, it's a book,' she said, delighted.

'Written by a young woman,' he said. 'It's called *Pride and Prejudice*. My aunt, who used to be a teacher – I told her about you, by the way – informs me that it gives a good insight into English life and manners. You might find it difficult reading at first, so don't be disheartened. Persevere and it should be worth it. You'll soon be reading quite quickly.'

'Oh, I'll try and read some tonight and I'll let you know how I get on.'

'Good . . .' He smiled. 'You know, Poppy, I think we ought to go now. Would you still like to resume your reading and writing lessons, then?'

'Yes . . . Course.'

'So shall we meet on Monday at my office, after the works have finished?'

'Oh, yes, please, Robert.'

Meanwhile, Sheba was in the living room working alone. The children were out playing, and Tweedle Beak was at The Wheatsheaf grinning and bearing it, as were the rest of the hut's usual contingent. Except for Buttercup. He left the dormitory where he had been fiddling and entered the living room, where he believed Sheba was on her own.

'Still hard at it, Sheba?'

'Is it ever any different?'

'I reckon not. Where's young Poppy? Has she gone out to play and left her mother to do all the work?'

'I don't begrudge the wench some enjoyment, Buttercup. It's my guess as she's gone to meet that engineer what's learning her to read. She's got a soft spot for him, and no two ways. Trouble is, she's gunna be let down with such a bang. She's set her sights way too high.'

Buttercup pulled a chair from under the table and sat down. 'Fill we a tankard o' beer, eh, Sheba?'

'Oh? Ain't you going to The Wheatsheaf with the others?' She took the key from her pocket and unlocked the barrel.

'I can goo theer anytime. Besides, there's no sense in getting lagged out o' thy mind on beer all the time. I'd rather tek the time to talk . . . if yo've a mind to talk to me, Sheba.'

'I'm content enough to stop and talk.' Sheba filled a tankard and handed it to him.

'Ta, my wench. Bist havin' one theeself? I'll treat thee.'

'That's decent of you, Buttercup. Thanks, I will.' She took a tumbler from a cupboard and filled it with beer. 'Here's to you.'

'Here's to thee . . . And here's to Poppy an' all, whether or no her's set her sights beyond her.'

Sheba sat down at the opposite side of the table. 'The trouble with our Poppy, Buttercup, is that she'll have no truck with any o' the young navvies. She's made it plain she don't want to end up a navvy's woman.'

'The wench has got some sense,' Buttercup remarked. He took a slurp of beer and wiped his chin.

'But that Jericho keeps on coming round after her. Maybe you've noticed. He seems decent enough, but our Poppy's heart's set elsewhere, I can see that.'

'Jericho, eh?' Buttercup rubbed his whiskers thoughtfully, reminded of the incident in the tunnel. 'I bain't altogether sure as that Jericho deserves her, any road, Sheba. He's a bit wayward that one, wun't thee say so?'

'Always up to fighting, they reckon. But then, so am a good many. They fight over the daftest things. All of 'em.'

Buttercup nodded. He took another quaff of beer and wiped his mouth on the back of his hand. 'Then let's hope Poppy keeps him at a distance . . . And theeself, Sheba?'

'Me?'

'Aye . . . And Tweedle Beak? How dost thou fare together?'

'Me and Tweedle?' Sheba shrugged. 'He ain't no Lightning Jack, but . . .'

'But what?'

'Well, that's the top and bottom of it, Buttercup. He ain't Lightning Jack Silk . . .'

'But yo'm content to lie with him?'

'Content? What choice have I got?'

'Oh, I bain't judging thee, Sheba,' Buttercup said kindly. 'Let him as is without sin cast the fust stone, as they say . . .' The stem of Buttercup's clay pipe was sticking out of the pocket of his moleskin jacket. With a sigh, he withdrew it and placed it carefully on the table while he cut a knob of tobacco from a stick he pulled out of another pocket. 'But if thou bistn't content, thou'st got no choice at all if he babbies thee, Sheba, my wench.' He failed to meet her eyes while he rubbed the knob of tobacco between the palms of his hand to break it into shreds. 'No chance at all.'

'Ah . . . Well that's another problem, you see, Buttercup . . .' Their eyes met and Sheba's expression was one of candour. She trusted this man. He had been a good mate of Lightning Jack's, and Jack had always been a good judge of a man's character. She smiled tentatively, and lowered her eyes like a young girl as he tried to read her mind.

While he filled his gum-bucket, it struck Buttercup how little more than a girl Sheba was. Lightning, by his own confession, had taken her as a fourteen-year-old, hardly more

163

than a child. By the time she was fifteen she'd had Poppy. She could be no more than thirty or thirty-one now, he estimated. She was still comely enough, even though she'd had several children, even if the ceaseless grind of navvy life and moving from one encampment to another had taken its toll. No wonder Tweedle Beak had intervened to save her from a life on tramp. She was eminently beddable still.

'Art thou already in the family way with him then?' Buttercup asked, lighting his pipe.

'Not with Tweedle. I'm carrying Jack's child.'

Buttercup grinned, his pipe held horizontal between his teeth. 'Well, I'll be damned. Does Tweedle know?'

Sheba shook her head. 'Soon enough he will . . . when me belly gets bigger.'

'So dost thou intend to let him think it's his?'

Sheba uttered a laugh of derision. 'Do you think he's that daft? He'll work out soon enough that it ain't.'

'And then what?'

Sheba shrugged. 'Aye, then what? You tell me.'

Buttercup sucked on his gum-bucket and blew a cloud of smoke into the room. 'Well, who knows, Sheba? I reckon 'tis a decision thou must make some time soon.'

'Oh, I reckon the decision's made already, Buttercup. I'll not pass off this child as Tweedle Beak's, although it did occur to me to do it. I'm too proud that it's Lightning Jack's.'

Buttercup beamed and his eyes crinkled into creases that Sheba found mightily attractive. 'Good for thee, Sheba,' he said. 'I can't abide that Tweedle Beak meself. Let's have a drink on it, eh? Pour us another, my wench.'

Poppy tripped back to Rose Cottage feeling light and breezy compared to how she felt earlier. So she was going to meet Robert again on Monday. Once more they would be alone together in his office. Would he ask her to sit on his lap again and smother her in those delicious kisses that made her toes curl? The spectre of the girl to whom he was promised rose up and plagued her thoughts. Best not think about *her*. Pretend *she* didn't exist. If only Robert could escape her clutches. Maybe he would, for Poppy sensed his fondness for herself, despite their class difference. And, like he'd said before, class difference was not an insurmountable barrier if you had the will to overcome it.

She saw that Buttercup was seated at the table smoking his gum-bucket and grinning, a full tankard of beer in front of him. Her mother was sitting opposite, also drinking beer and smiling contentedly. Poppy noticed how, at her entrance, they immediately fell silent for an awkward second or two, until Buttercup greeted her cordially.

'Well, talk o' the devil . . . Here her is, that sprightly young filly o' thine, Sheba.'

'What's that you're carrying?' Sheba asked.

Poppy raised the book in her hand. 'Oh . . . a book. Robert gave it me to read.'

'Thou canst read then, eh?'

'Somebody I know is learning me.'

'That young engineer chap I mentioned,' Sheba said.

'Robert Crawford,' Poppy informed her for the umpteenth time.

'Can't say as I know him yet,' Buttercup said. 'But it's a fine thing, bein' able to read an' write. Keep it up. It'll stand thee in good stead. But, tell me, wench . . . in all the excitement of learning to read, hast thou forgot about washing me shirt?'

'No.' Poppy felt herself blushing, not sure if he was mocking. 'That's why I've come back early. To wash your shirt, and anything else that needs a good wash.'

'Good lass.' He stood up, took off the garment and threw it onto another chair close by. 'Thy fairther, God bless him, always said thou was a good little lass. He always said thou would'st mek somebody a splendid wife.'

'Just as long as he ain't a navvyman . . . Is there some hot water, Mother?'

'Should be.' She turned to Buttercup. 'See? I told you as much. She'll have no truck . . . Are you going out tonight, our Poppy?'

Poppy picked up Buttercup's shirt and shrugged as she made her way over to the stone sink. 'I don't know. It depends whether Minnie wants me to. Or even Jericho.'

'What if neither is about?' Buttercup asked.

'Then I'll stop in and start to read me book. It's wrote by a young woman, Robert says. He says I'll like it.'

'Robert says so, eh?' Sheba flashed a knowing look at Buttercup. 'Well, if Robert says so, you can bet you will . . .'

That warm summer's evening, Poppy went to Hawthorn Villa to call for Minnie.

'You've just missed her, my flower,' Ma Catchpole informed her. 'Her went out half hour ago.'

'Is she likely to be long? I mean has she gone out with Dog Meat for the night?'

'That drunken bugger? No, Dog Meat went up the Grin and Bear It as usual. He must be in truck up to his arsehole, the money he spends on beer. Leastwise, I doubt if anybody's saft enough to lend it him.'

'Well, if she comes back soon, send her round for me, would you, Mrs Catchpole?'

'I'll tell her as you've bin after her, young Poppy.'

Poppy ambled back towards Rose Cottage disconsolately, disappointed that her friend had not called for her. Saturday nights they always went out together while Dog Meat went drinking. Maybe Minnie had sloped off to see some young beau she'd met. Maybe even that local lad again, called Tom. Often had she sung Tom's praises. Poppy picked up a stick from the ground and sat on the front step of the hut, scratching letters in the dust.

Then she remembered her book. She could make a start on that. If she could read only the first page she would be mightily proud of herself. She would have achieved something. Back inside the hut she picked up her book and took it into the bedroom. She plumped up her pillow and, still dressed, lay on the bed and opened the book to the first page of the story. Slowly, carefully, she built up each word.

'Chapter One. It is a truth universally acknowledged, that a single man in possession of a good fortune must be in want of a wife . . .' Goodness! Did that apply to Robert as well? He was surely in want of a wife . . . It was wonderful how it all made sense. Already Poppy was spellbound. She could hardly wait to complete the next sentence. She read for ages and fell asleep fully dressed, only to wake fully dressed next morning, her brother and sisters having failed to disturb her when they retired to bed.

On Monday, after the works had shut for the night, Poppy skipped along to the house the company had occupied, which served as offices. Gingerly, she climbed the linoleum-clad stairs to Robert's office and, to her great relief, saw him sitting at his desk, which was, as usual, covered in maps and diagrams. He turned and smiled to greet her when he heard her footsteps.

'Poppy! I thought you weren't coming.'

'Am I late?' she queried. 'I'm not surprised. There was a lot of the men about. I waited till they'd all cleared off, then waited a bit longer.'

'Sensible,' he said. 'We don't want tongues wagging, do we?'

Poppy shrugged. It would make no odds to her if they did. Indeed, too many folk already knew that Robert Crawford was teaching Poppy Silk to read for it to remain a secret for long. But she understood that he wished for greater discretion.

'I brought my book,' she said. 'I've been reading it. I love it.'

He smiled warmly. 'Good. Read some to me. Let me hear how you are faring.'

She sat in the chair beside him and read the first page while he listened and prompted from time to time, watching the wonderfully animated expressions on her face and in her crystal clear eyes. As she spoke the words, he was captivated again by the beautiful sensuous shapes her lips adopted, and he ached inside for her. It struck him then that love can be the most wondrous thing, but it can also be the most torturous if the object of your love is forbidden.

After a few minutes she stopped reading and looked up at him with wide, questioning eyes.

'Your reading has improved immensely, Poppy,' he said. 'Already you are reading faster than you were before. But perhaps we should concentrate on some spelling and punctuation. Do you have your writing book with you?'

She fished in the pocket of her skirt, withdrew it and placed it on the desk.

'Just a few of the more difficult words you've come across . . . *acquaintance* . . .'

'What's an acquaintance, Robert?'

'A friend,' he answered patiently. 'Not necessarily a close friend, but somebody whom you know. Somebody with whom you are *acquainted*.'

She nodded her understanding.

'So write *acquaintance* down, Poppy . . .' He spelled it out for her and she methodically inscribed it in her steadily improving hand. 'Now *daughter . . . extraordinary . . . considerable . . . neighbourhood . . .*'

Poppy wrote down many words, and did it with a zeal for learning that could not fail to impress Robert Crawford. He went on to explain the rudiments of punctuation: full stops, commas, inverted commas, colons, semicolons, question marks. Poppy nodded thoughtfully as each was explained, as she absorbed the knowledge like a sponge absorbs liquid.

'You have done extremely well,' he said. 'You are learning much quicker than I ever imagined you would.'

'Am I?' she replied with a gratified smile that turned into a blush.

'And I have a small gift for you, to mark my recognition of the hard work you have put into your efforts. Efforts which are quite voluntary, and thus the more laudable.'

'Laudable?'

'Praiseworthy, Poppy. Deserving.'

'Then why didn't you say praiseworthy or deserving, instead of lordabubble? Anyway, what sort of gift have you got for me? Another book?'

'No . . .' He leaned forward and stretched out to retrieve a parcel of brown paper and string that lay under his desk near his feet. 'Here . . .' He smiled, eager to see her response. 'I want to watch your expression as you open it . . .'

'What is it?' She looked at him with a mixture of apprehension and delight as she took the parcel from him.

'You'll see.'

Eagerly she undid the knots in the string and discarded it, then set about carefully unwrapping the box. It had a lid, which she lifted it a little and then let fall again to prolong the pleasure of anticipation. Robert watched her, as excited as she was, urging her to reveal the contents. She removed the lid and gasped.

'Robert! Oh, Robert, it's a pair of dainty black boots with 'lastic sides. Oh, thank you, thank you. How can I thank you enough?'

'Well . . . a kiss would suffice.'

'Oh, I'll give you a hundred kisses – a thousand.'

She leaned forward with her typical lack of inhibition and their lips met. Their arms went about each other in tentative desire . . . Tentative, because each was aware of the forbidden nature of their fervour. She withdrew her lips with profound reluctance and regret, and rested her forehead on his chest, unable to quieten the sincere love she felt for him.

'Oh, Robert . . .' she breathed, her voice so strained with emotion that she needed no further words.

He hugged her tight and nuzzled his cheek against her lush, fair hair. Why did he torture himself so? Why indeed did he torture her? It was so obvious even to him that she was head over heels. It must be correspondingly obvious to her that he was equally besotted. Yet what remedy did they possess? How could they possibly satisfy their love?

'Shall I try on the boots?' she said, sensitive to his dilemma and not wishing to augment the pain by prolonging it.

'Of course . . . You see, Poppy . . .' He swallowed hard in his effort to regain his composure. 'Your prayer for a pair of boots has been answered.'

'I know,' she said, sitting down again and slipping her clogs off. She looked him squarely in the eye. 'And when I go to bed tonight, I'm going to say another prayer, if it's that easy to get what you want . . .'

Chapter 12

Robert Crawford set off home with his awkward two-wheeled contraption. The hill ahead of him was daunting in the heat, and too steep to treadle his way up. So he gripped the handlebars, took a deep breath, and began pushing the heavy machine. Workmen turning out of the pits and ironworks made their way home or to the nearest beer shop, sweating in their shirtsleeves, their jackets and waistcoats bent over their arms or tossed over their shoulders. Women struggled with bags and baskets of provisions, irritated by whining children who tugged at their skirts or walked under their feet.

Robert's thoughts were focused on Poppy Silk. Should he take advantage of her love for him and trifle with her, or should he take her devotion seriously? Common sense told him he should do neither. He should steer well clear of her, with or without his two-wheeler. His heart, however, was urging him to do both . . . Well, such was his confusion. Ever since he first became acquainted with Poppy, she had enchanted him. Consequently, he had lost interest in the fine decent girl to whom he was already engaged. To that respectable girl, any interest he showed was pretence.

It was flattering to have two very pretty girls vying for his affection. He was, however, uncompromising in his determination to be fair to both.

Yet he was becoming increasingly aware that the mutual fondness he and Poppy shared was special. He also realised that the effect of its denial was torture on him. How long could he tolerate it? How long was he prepared to? Furthermore, what effect was his warm attention, but ultimate denial, having on Poppy?

To her detriment, Poppy was the daughter of a mere railway navvy, and a product of that ungodly, itinerant sect that were all but outlawed by decent society. She was uncultured, untutored in anything until he himself had shown her the rudiments of reading and writing. She had been raised in that shady circumstance where morality was non-existent, where violence was the norm and thieving was accepted. In her world, life itself was dominated by the subversive lure of beer and whisky, and just how much of it the men could drink before falling over or maiming each other in fights. She wore clothes that were odd, old, unfashionable and sometimes shabby. He had been so dismayed by her poverty-stricken clogs that he had been only too happy to buy her a decent pair of boots. Without some radical change in her, he could not possibly take her home to meet his parents and say, 'This is Poppy Silk, whom I adore and want to marry. This is the woman I prefer over the more refined, more respectable girl you expect me to wed. This is the woman I want to bear my children and bring them up in a clean, respectable home, who will teach them to become model citizens. This is the woman I expect you to admire and take to your hearts, despite her shabbiness and her total ignorance of the niceties of life, despite the rigid social conventions that rule our lives, of which she has no grasp, albeit through no fault of her own.'

They would laugh at him.

They would scorn him and think he had gone utterly mad. If he tutored her from now till doomsday . . . Yet despite her faults, was Poppy Silk not the dearest, the most delightful soul? Her hair was a dishevelled mess much of the time, but was it not lovely for all that, and the most divine shade of wheat that had been sun-ripened to perfection? Was its texture not that of the softest spun silk? Was she not also the girl with more youthful grace and zest than any other he had met? Would her enchanting face not be the envy of the most strikingly beautiful goddess? Did she not possess the clearest, biggest, bluest eyes imaginable? Was her nose not the most exquisitely formed, her neck the most elegant, her lips not the most delicious that ever man kissed? And those were only the parts of her he'd had access to. There lay concealed other, perhaps even more beguiling, attractions. And besides these outward manifestations of beauty, did she not also possess the sweetest nature, the most admirable, intelligent demeanour?

Even so, what could he do? He must be fair to both these young women who had taken over his life, else he would not be able to live with himself. Indecision was his enemy, but he could not decide what to do to be fair, not only to them, but to himself as well. Procrastination could cause him to lose this one enigmatic girl who he was certain would be the love of his life. Hesitancy could induce him, through a reluctance to be cruel to the other, into a marriage that was destined to fail. Indecision, procrastination, hesitancy . . . These were his failings, but at least he was aware of them. Somehow, he must work out a solution.

He had reached the top of the hill and was perspiring in the July heat. In front of him King Street was a downhill run before it levelled out. He could ride from here. The flow of the breeze against him as he rode would cool him. So he cocked his leg over the frame of the two-wheeled machine and shoved off.

A solution of sorts began to take form in his mind, which

could be fair to both girls and to himself. It seemed the only way he could extricate himself from this dilemma and emerge with a clearer understanding of what would ultimately be the best thing to do. He needed time. Only then could he become more rational. Time would enable him to sort himself out, free him from the perplexity of all-consuming emotions, which were intensified in turn by his own refusal to submit to them. Poppy, meanwhile, might fall prey to the foul attentions of one of the roughnecks among whom she existed. He must be aware, therefore, that while in one sense a friend, time might also turn out to be a traitor and rob him of her.

Robert had reached the brow of the hill where Waddams Pool became Dixons Green Road. A little further on, the splendid home of his family stood in its own extensive grounds. He rode his machine into the drive and put it away in one of the stables at the rear, realising he had no recollection of the ride home, save for his thoughts. However, he had made an important decision. Now, he must implement it.

A month passed. A month in which midsummer progressed in a succession of hot and sultry days, when only occasional dark clouds drifted like bruises across a sky that quickly healed. In the distance towards the rolling Clent Hills, in the patchwork of fields beyond the chimney stacks, wheat and barley revelled in the warm breeze and ripened, waiting to be harvested. In some fields, hay had already been cut and stood in stooks, like little huts ready to be occupied by hobgoblins.

Work on the Oxford, Worcester and Wolverhampton was, yard by yard, day by day, shifting further away from the encampment at Blowers Green. Thus it was taking the men longer to get to the workings and longer to return to their lodgings after their toils. The stables were moved so that the mules and horses could be closer to where they were needed. Still there was no sign of the permanent way being laid.

Sheba's morning sickness persisted and her belly, though hardly yet any bigger, was getting firmer. Tweedle Beak had twigged that she was pregnant but, not unnaturally, assumed the child was his. So far, Sheba had not denied it, biding her time for the right moment. Minnie Catchpole and Jericho continued their sensuous liaison clandestinely. Minnie remained ignorant that Dog Meat had prostituted her for the price of a gallon of beer, and so eager was she to make herself available to Jericho that he saw no sense in paying Dog Meat for the subsequent use he made of her. As far as Minnie was concerned, it was a love match. Jericho, however, was tiring of the intrigue. There was still that other finer-looking girl who had not yet succumbed to his charms.

Poppy had noticed that neither Minnie nor Jericho seemed to be available to go out nights. If she had alienated Minnie in some way she was sorry, but could not think how she could have done it. Jericho? Well, he had most likely just grown tired of getting nowhere with her.

Poppy, though, remained preoccupied with Robert Crawford. He continued to give her lessons two or three times a week and was delighted at the progress she was making. He remained equally preoccupied with Poppy but sought not to show it, wishing to give her neither encouragement nor false hopes, for he was minutely aware of her devotion to him. In that month, Robert had laid his plans assiduously and everything was in place.

Poppy also made a decision as she sat on the front step of Rose Cottage playing with the dog that belonged to Waxy Boyle, one of the lodgers. The dog was rolling on its back in the dust, enjoying the ecstasy of having its belly rubbed.

When Poppy ceased, it thrust its cold, damp nose under her hand, selfishly urging her to continue. But she was deep in thought and the dog did not appreciate the fact. She had intended to say a prayer later that night, as Robert had taught her, to ask God to deliver Robert safely, permanently into her heart and her life and to propose marriage. But, when she thought it through, she decided she wanted neither favour nor interference from God. Robert must make any decision himself. He must make his own way to her because he wanted to, without God's prompting. Besides, God would think her as self-centred and as greedy as the young whelp she was teasing now, if she demanded too may favours.

Lately, her ability to reason and think had changed. She saw things – all sorts of things – more clearly than ever she had before. It was because she was allowing her thoughts to meander in the direction of the likely consequences of her actions or words. Perhaps Robert was responsible for that. Not only had he taught her to read, but what she had been reading had given her a tantalising insight into other modes of thought, how different expectations altered your perception of things. This other way of thinking was far removed from the navvy attitude to life. She was beginning to understand that not all life was tawdry and disgusting and impoverished, either materially or spiritually.

The little dog shuffled to its feet and nuzzled its wet nose against her hand again. She playfully pushed it away and it came back again for more. Maybe that was the way to handle a man. It was the way that Robert was handling her. Whether he realised it or not, his pushing her away, his aloofness, was having the opposite effect to that which he evidently sought. Well, maybe that was the way to handle Robert.

The trouble was, she did not have the nerve. If she pushed

him away she might lose him forever. The effect would be to merely thrust him more forcibly into the arms of the girl he was engaged to, her rival. In any case, Poppy trusted her own way of influencing Robert; she sensed correctly that he was responsive to tenderness and high emotions. Maybe she could sway him with a sincere admission of her love. The time had come to lay her cards on the table anyway, to lever him out of his hesitancy. He either loved her or didn't. For too long he had shilly-shallied, tormenting her as she was now tormenting the dog. Did Robert want her or not? It was time he climbed down from the fence he'd straddled for too long. Yes, she would confess her devotion, tell him how she truly felt, admit the effect he was having on her and how much it was hurting. She would tell him how she wanted to grow into his life, how she ached to be his lover. He would not have the resolve to resist. She was aware that whenever he looked at her there was love and desire in his eyes. She was canny enough to recognise it. His eyes always lingered on her. Even when she wasn't looking at him she could feel his eyes on her, and she was glad of it; she did not mind at all. Why shouldn't she exploit the assets she was blessed with? A means to an end. Even then, she had an inkling that where Robert was concerned, her best assets were her simple sincerity and her love for him.

A day or two later, the second Thursday in August, Poppy had arranged to meet Robert at his office after the works had closed down and, when she arrived, was surprised to see him waiting for her outside. He was wearing old working clothes that he used for grubbing about in and looked for all the world like a navvy.

'As it's such a beautiful evening, Poppy, I thought we'd take a stroll.'

'I don't mind,' she readily agreed. 'Which way shall we go?'

He inclined his head in the direction of the town and they began their walk.

'Why are you wearing such scruffy clothes?' she asked.

'They're what I wear when I have to go grubbing about.'

'Are you going grubbing about with me then, as you're wearing them now?'

'Do they offend you?' he said.

She laughed, gratified at his concern. 'No, course not. You still look smarter than any navvy I know . . . Just.'

He smiled enigmatically. The truth was, he did not want to appear the young gentleman with a girl who was obviously of a lower class. He had dressed to match her so they would not look incongruous together. But he could not tell her this. In a way, he was glad of the opportunity to get closer to her level, to feel uninhibited about being seen with her and not have to worry about appearances or making a spectacle of himself. Nobody would look at them twice while they were both apparently working class. Nobody would believe any more that he was a toff who had paid for the services of a street girl.

'You can pretend I'm a navvy if you want,' he said.

'As long as you don't act like one,' she replied astutely. 'So where are you taking me?'

'I thought we might go for a walk in the grounds of the castle. Have you ever been there?'

'Once. When me dad first came to work on the Old Worse and Worse.'

Robert chuckled as they set off. 'Is that what they're calling the Oxford, Worcester and Wolverhampton these days? Because of all the delays and political problems I imagine . . . So, tell me, Poppy. How are you getting on with your book?'

'Oh, I'm working me way through it all right.' She smiled

up at him for approval. 'That Mrs Bennet is a proper dizzy-brain.'

'It is full of intrigue as well, I believe?'

'Ain't you read it?'

'I seldom have time to read novels.'

They walked through the town, chatting about this and that. Poppy felt somehow closer to him than she had been for a while. He seemed more accessible, not as aloof as he had been lately. Maybe it had something to do with the clothes he was wearing. Maybe he had made a decision about her . . .

'You can hold my hand if you want,' she said experimentally. 'I don't bite.'

He laughed at that and took her hand as they walked. 'I didn't want to be so presumptuous.'

'I don't even know what that means, Robert.'

'It means—'

'No . . . Please don't bother to tell me. I can guess what it means. You know very well that you wouldn't be being presumptious—'

'Presumptuous, Poppy,' he corrected. 'Pre–sump–*tu*–ous.'

'As I was saying,' she said feigning haughtiness. 'You wouldn't be being presump*tu*ous. I want you to hold my hand. At least it tells me you think something of me and you're not afeared to show it.'

'Of course I think something of you.'

'You wouldn't know it from the way you've been acting lately. You make me feel as if I've got the plague or something.'

'I'm sorry.'

'Well, I think it's time we laid our cards on the table, Mister Robert Crawford. Don't you?'

They were entering the castle grounds now, at the start of the path that would meander steadily uphill in the shade of high elms and eventually lead them into the ruined castle courtyard. Squirrels played in the rustling trees above while wood pigeons cooed and looked on in unperturbed docility.

'Yes, I think it might be a good night for laying our cards on the table,' he agreed, to her surprise.

'Good. I want to tell you things, Robert. Things that have been in my heart to say for so long now. And this seems a perfect opportunity – you and me together on a lovely evening, in this lovely old place.'

He looked at her apprehensively as they ambled along. But when he saw the earnest look on her face he wanted to take her in his arms. He had a notion of what she wanted to say and he so much needed to hear it.

'Go on,' he said.

'Well . . . We are good friends, aren't we?'

'We are the very best of friends, Poppy,' he answered sincerely. 'I hope we shall remain so, whatever befalls us.'

'But I want us to be more than just friends, Robert. Oh, I know you're engaged and that, but . . . and that's why we ain't been more than just friends, I know. Except for the odd times when we've kissed and cuddled . . . But I kept hoping that you'd get weary of her and pick me . . . Oh, Robert, can't you see I love you so much? You must know how much I love you.'

He nodded, thoughtful. 'Yes, Poppy,' he breathed. 'Dearest, dearest Poppy . . . I'm fully aware of your feelings towards me. I am ever mindful of them—'

'Well, I think you love me as well, Robert. I'm so certain of it, but I think you're afeared of letting yourself go . . . of letting yourself come to me properly. You ain't got no idea how much that upsets me. My poor heart is breaking for you, Robert, yet you keep so . . . so . . . You keep your distance . . . I don't know how else to say it . . . I ain't got the cholera or the plague, you know.'

He stopped and she turned towards him. He looked into her eyes that were so appealing and held his arms out to her. At once she fell into them and savoured his embrace as he tenderly stroked her hair. Others were walking past them, but Poppy and Robert were so preoccupied with the moment that they were oblivious to anybody and anything else.

'Poppy . . .'

She raised her head and looked up at him. His eyes had a troubled look that frightened her.

'What?' she said anxiously.

'Poppy . . . dearest little Poppy . . . You are absolutely right in your estimation of how I feel about you. I do love you. With all my heart and soul I love you—'

'And I'm so glad to hear it, Robert.' She sighed, smiling, hugging him joyously. 'Oh, it makes me so happy to hear it. So you are going to make me your girl and shout it to the world?'

'It's not that simple. As I have told you before . . . Listen . . . I have come to a decision that affects you, me, and the girl to whom I'm engaged—'

'A decision?' Alarm bells were ringing in her head. 'What decision? You just told me you love me.'

'Allow me to speak and you will hear it.'

'I'm allowing you. Tell me. But don't tell me anything I don't want to hear.'

'Well, you may not want to hear it, but I have to tell you anyway . . . I have decided that the only way that you and my fiancée can emerge from this with any integrity is if I go away for a year or so. Given some time we shall all know how we truly feel. It's possible we shall look at things from a totally different perspective.'

'You might see things from a different prospective, Robert, but I won't. I trust my feelings now. I know how I shall feel in a twelvemonth – exactly the same as I do now. Why do you tell me one moment you love me, then the next that you're going away? It's all you ever do . . .'

'Because it's the only answer.' He held her tenderly by her arms as she faced him. He loathed himself for having to put her through this agony, but his resolution to be fair would allow him no other way. He could not trifle with her. 'You are as important to me as anybody else in the whole world. If it were not so, I wouldn't put myself through this pain. I would trifle with you scandalously, take advantage of you and then let you go. I wouldn't feel the need to go away to sort myself out. But I have never taken advantage of you. I esteem you too much for that.'

'Then esteem me less, Robert . . . I want you to. We could have such lovely times together if you stay. If you stay, we shall become lovers . . .'

'No, Poppy. I will not, I cannot. You mean so much more to me. Don't you see? It's because I feel so deeply for you that I have to go away. I'm engaged to be married, as I told you at the outset. Engagement is no trifling thing. I took the decision to marry with a clear mind. At the time, I considered myself in love with my sweetheart and the match was welcomed – even desired – by both our families. I have to be fair to both of you . . . to our respective families as well.'

'Have you told her about me?'

'Yes,' he said quietly. 'I have told her that my feelings have been diverted by another—'

'What have you told her about me?'

'Nothing. Except that my feelings for you are of sufficient strength to warrant my taking some time away to sort my life out. I have asked her to release me from my promise to marry, but she has refused. I want you to understand, Poppy,

182

that it's exactly the same for her as it is for you. She is prepared to wait for me to . . . to come to my senses, as she puts it.'

'Do you love her, Robert?'

'How can I love two girls at once? It's *you* I love, Poppy. But I am responsible. I am engaged to another. It is a question of trying to salvage some honour.'

'Honour?' she scoffed. 'Whose honour? But you'll write to her, won't you? You'll keep in touch with her?'

'That is not my intention. I intend making a complete break of it for a year, with no contact whatsoever. Only without her influence or yours can I become rational again.'

'But in a year the encampment will have moved. We might be anywhere in the country, on any railway. I'll never know if you chose me or not, 'cause you won't know where the hell I am.'

'It's a risk I have to take, Poppy. In any case, in a year you might well feel differently.'

'Never! Never in a thousand years.'

'Oh, in just one year you might well have fallen in love with somebody like Jericho and forgotten all about me.'

She screwed her face up in disgust. 'The likes of Jericho? Never. I don't want the likes of Jericho, Robert, I want *you*.'

'Come on, Poppy. Let's continue our walk.' He took her hand again and she allowed it, walking sullenly beside him.

'Where will you go?' she asked.

'I'm going abroad.'

'Abroad? When?'

'I leave on Saturday.'

'Saturday?' Her heart sank. 'So soon?'

'Yes, Poppy, so soon.'

'But that's the day after tomorrow. I wish you'd told me sooner.'

'I didn't want to tell you sooner . . . oh, for purely selfish reasons. I wanted – I needed – to revel in your devotion for as long as I could. I'm going to miss you, Poppy. I know I'm going to miss you terribly. It will be unbearable, but I'm determined to endure it. Only then can I be sure. Only then will I have been truly fair to both of you.'

'I think you are being truly unfair by leaving me. 'Specially just after you told me you love me. It makes no sense, Robert. It don't make no sense at all.' Her bottom lip began to quiver and she bit it appealingly.

He looked at her and saw how emotional she was. 'You're not going to cry, are you?'

'What d'you expect me to do? So what if I do?' She sniffed defiantly and stemmed her tears, wiping her eyes with her long sleeve. 'But why should I give you the satisfaction?'

'I have cried, Poppy.'

'You? Honest?'

'Why should I not? I feel this just as acutely as you, believe me. I am just as capable of hurting inside as you are. I am just as capable of shedding tears.'

'But you're a man.'

He laughed self-mockingly. 'And men don't shed tears in your world.'

'I never seen nobody.'

'Well . . . perhaps they're all too intent on presenting a very masculine front. I know how tough and nonchalant they all purport to be.'

'Is it because you're ashamed of where I come from that you're leaving, Robert?' she asked pointedly. 'Aren't you just trying to escape from me?'

He shook his head emphatically. 'Escape? From you? The only escape I am trying to effect is from my own ridiculous indecision. As for where you come from, Poppy, that is of no consequence whatsoever. I love *you*. To me, your background doesn't matter.'

'But you'd have trouble introducing me to your family . . .'

He laughed ruefully. 'One or two of them might well have to be convinced. But that would be their problem, not mine.'

'So when will you come back?'

'In about a year. I told you.'

He felt in his pocket and pulled out a folded slip of paper. 'Here . . . Take this. It's the address of my widowed Aunt Phoebe. She used to be a teacher and I've already spoken to her about you. She'll be happy to continue your lessons if you still feel inclined. She can teach you so much more than I could, since she has the right books and many years' experience teaching different subjects. I urge you to present yourself to her at some time.'

She took the slip of paper, opened it and looked at it before she put it in the pocket of her skirt. She would read it later when she returned to Rose Cottage.

'In any case,' he went on, 'it will be to the benefit of both of us if you make contact with her. It is to my Aunt Phoebe's that I will send you a message in a year's time, whether you are still interested in receiving it then or not. Odds are that you won't be, and serve me right. Odds are that you will have forgotten all about me. Nor would I blame you. You're still only sixteen, remember, Poppy, with emotions like quicksilver—'

'My emotions are *not* like quicksilver,' she protested at once. 'They're constant. And another thing – yes, I'm sixteen, like you say. Not a child. A grown woman.'

'I was about to say, Poppy, that it might take me more than a year to be entirely sure of my feelings—'

'Maybe less,' she suggested.

'Maybe. Who knows? Either way, I shall only move when I'm certain.'

'Then you might never move,' Poppy suggested ruefully. 'What if you fall in love with some pretty girl wherever you are and never come back. Then I shall never see you again. Ever.'

'It's not beyond the realms of possibility, I suppose,' Robert replied. 'In which case I shall let you know. But I have my doubts. I know myself too well, Poppy.'

They walked on, hand in hand. Poppy was desperately trying to come to terms with what had happened. She was gratified beyond belief to hear Robert's confession of love, elicited by her own, but her sadness that he was immediately depriving her of it overshadowed that. Now she had to wait another year at least before she would know her fate. A year was a long, long time to a sixteen-year-old, even though she was a grown woman.

Chapter 13

The end of August brought with it a change in the weather. Gone was the humid heat, replaced by cool rain that fell steadily for two days, turning the dust of the Blowers Green encampment into a quagmire. Dog Meat and Jericho squelched through the sludge of the workings near a little community known as Woodside and headed back to the encampment along the gravelled trackbed they had already laid. Other navvies tramped before them and behind them, heads hung low, a weary army.

'Bloody good job it's payday tomorrow,' Jericho remarked. Rain was dripping from his sodden hat and trickling down the back of his thick neck, but what was a mere trickle of water when his clothes were already saturated, not only from the rain but from the hot sweat of his body?

'Payday might be all right for you, old mate,' Dog Meat said, 'but it ain't gunna mek a scrap o' difference to me.'

'What d'ye mean by that, Dog Meat?'

Dog Meat hoicked his pick and shovel onto his shoulder as if they were a pair of rifles. 'I mean I already owe too much in truck to Treadwell's and on me scoresheet at The Wheatsheaf. By the time everybody's had what I owe there'll be sod all left.'

'Don't drink so much,' Jericho advised plainly. 'Don't spend all your money on drink.'

'A man has to have a drink, Jericho. Christ, the work we do, we need a drink after it to numb the aches and pains.'

'I have no bother with aches and pains,' Jericho said.

'Aye, well, maybe you'm a fitter man than me.'

'I like a glass or two of ale, but I don't drink so much as you, Dog Meat . . . Tell me, do you get any succour from the Catchpoles? Apart from sleeping with their daughter, I mean . . .'

'For all the use she is lately.' Dog Meat emitted a scornful laugh. 'For a wench o' sixteen you might expect her to be a bit more lively in bed. Lately she's like a log . . .'

Jericho gave him a sideways glance that conveyed no hint of guilt. 'Aye, well, maybe it's you, Dog Meat. Mebbe you're too fuddled at night to do anything. Mebbe you're going at it too much like a pig at a tater. Mebbe you need to hone your skills a bit.' He was aware of the truth of it from Minnie.

'D'you want to borrow Minnie again, Jericho?' Dog Meat enquired sincerely. 'Maybe you could rekindle some flame in her for me.'

'I reckon not, Dog Meat. Oh, I don't mean she ain't worthy. She's a fine-looking wench and plenty to grab hold of, I grant ye. But I had me fill—'

'I could do with the money, Jericho . . .'

'And couldn't we all?' Jericho pulled up his collar. The drips down his neck were cold now to his skin, which was already cooling.

'Any fear of a loan then?'

'I never loan money, Dog Meat. Don't believe in it. Ask Tipton Ted Catchpole for a sub if you're that desperate.'

'Tipton Ted? He wouldn't give me the drippings off his nose. I even have to provide me own vittles. Which reminds me . . . I got sod all to eat for me dinner tonight.'

'Well, steal something.'

'If you'll help me, Jericho . . .'

Jericho nodded.

They were ambling through a shallow cutting. Just behind them stood the newly erected bridge that carried the road to Pedmore and Lye Waste. Woodside was a smattering of cottages and workshops, huddled in a warren of short, narrow streets. The two young men turned back to the bridge and scaled the embankment.

'Now what?' said Dog Meat.

'Mebbe there's a corner shop . . . Hark . . . Can you hear what I can hear?'

Dog Meat cocked an ear. The raucous cackle of a hen elicited a grin as he imagined tender plump chicken for his dinner that night with a mound of boiled potatoes. The sound originated some distance from the top of the cutting, so they followed it. It led them along a bending narrow lane at the end of which lay a fenced field that housed a pig sty, a hen house and, at its furthest point, a cottage. The pigs evidently enjoyed having the run of the field, judging by the black mud they had churned up where they had been rooting. A score of hens pecked at the ground, overseen by a proud, strutting cock.

Jericho looked about him for signs of human life. All seemed quiet, save for the snorts of the pigs and the clucking of the hens.

'I'll nip across and pick up one o' them chickens,' Dog Meat said.

'And how many dinners will yer get off that?'

'Tonight's.'

'Well, think on, Dog Meat.' Jericho tapped his temple with his forefinger. 'If you could pick up a young pig it'd feed you for a few nights.'

Dog Meat looked at his workmate and grinned. 'Roast pork. D'yer think Ma Catchpole would roast it for me?'

'Aye, especially if you promised her a bit for herself. And if you gave some to Minnie, it might put you back in her good books.'

Dog Meat was convinced. 'Help me catch that little bugger, eh, Jericho?' He pointed to a small pig that was rooting in the mud, remote from the rest of its family.

'Mebbe we should wait till it's dark,' Jericho suggested. 'Somebody might see us and tell the police.'

'That's all well and good, Jericho, but if it's dark I won't be able to see the bloody pig. Any road, there's nobody about, look.'

'Suit yourself.'

They clambered over the picket fence that was lined with chicken wire and, in the rain, crept stealthily up behind the young pig. When both men were within two yards of it, the pig turned around with a squeal and scampered off, turning away from them.

'Bugger!' Dog Meat cried, and turned to follow it.

The pig began rooting again in a fresh spot and seemed to settle down. Once more, Dog Meat and Jericho inched towards it, a step at a time. Once more, the pig turned and scarpered.

'Stun it with a brick,' Jericho advocated, and himself picked up a half house-brick that lay close by. The pig found another spot where he hoped for some uninterrupted rooting, and Jericho hurled the brick. He missed, merely succeeding in splattering the animal with mud, provoking it to move on again.

'Dive on it, Jericho,' Dog Meat urged in a hoarse whisper. 'It's the only way.'

'You dive on it,' Jericho replied. 'It's you as wants it.'

'Might as well dive on a sunbeam. Tricky little bugger this, eh? Why don't I just get a fowl?'

'Nay, go for the big prize,' Jericho encouraged. 'It'll be worth it. Just dive on it.'

Dog Meat dived. Just as he was about to smother the pig it let out a frightened shriek, wriggled free and scurried smartly away. Dog Meat was face down in the sticky black mud where the pig had been standing. Jericho laughed aloud as Dog Meat, recovering from his prone position, sat covered in treacly goo and reached down for his boot, which he took off and hurled at the pig resentfully, missing the animal again.

The commotion had, by this time, alerted the occupiers of the cottage that stood at the far end of the field that something was amiss. A window opened and a man's voice called, 'What the bloody hell d'yer think yo'm up to?'

'Christ! Get me boot, Jericho!'

'Well, you ain't about to get the pig now,' Jericho responded.

'Bloody, buggering, brilliant idea o' yourn,' Dog Meat moaned, standing on one leg in the mud. 'Fetch me me boot quick, afore that bloke gets here. He might have a gun.'

A huge pig, that Jericho estimated must be at least a quarter of a ton in weight, trotted towards them from the far end of the field, splattering dabs of mud behind him.

'Aye up!' Jericho yelled. 'Sod the bloke and his gun. The biggest bloody pig you've ever seen in your life has spotted us. Quick, Dog Meat, run – else that's what you'll end up as – bloody dog meat.'

Dog Meat turned to look and saw the great, grotesque animal bearing down on him, great swathes of fat shuddering around him as he ran. The navvy struggled to upright himself and began hopping desperately through the mud. 'Where's me bloody boot? Get it for me, Jericho.'

But Jericho was striding through the mud towards the

sturdy fence over which they had climbed in the first place to get into the field. When he reached it he turned to look at Dog Meat lurching towards him on one leg, the vast pig angrily looming ever closer.

'Run, Dog Meat, you daft bugger,' Jericho shouted. 'Never mind bloody hopping. You'll never make it.'

Dog Meat heeded the advice and threw himself headlong over the fence just as the pig got its snout to his damp rump. He rolled over and shook his head, taking a second to get his bearings and to decide whether or not he was hurt. He sat up then, his hat skew-whiff, a disgruntled expression on his mud-bespattered face. The sight of him amused Jericho and he guffawed.

'Remind me never to heed any of your damned advice again, Jericho,' Dog Meat muttered truculently. 'Christ, you coulda got me killed. And I've still got no dinner.'

'Aye, and you've thrown a shoe, into the bargain.'

'And a new pair is gunna cost me even more money.'

The next evening, Dandy Punch and two others ambled over to The Wheatsheaf with the men's wages, as they did at the end of every month. Two hundred men awaited them outside, each tormented by a raging thirst that none but a few were able to satisfy before the money was doled out. As each envelope was handed over, the recipient inspected it, counted it and generally muttered his irritation at how much had been deducted as owing.

'This ain't right,' Tweedle Beak complained to Waxy Boyle as he counted his wages. 'But how the hell am I to prove it? Now I got me score to settle with Toby Watson. Trouble is, I'm never sober when he gets me to put me mark on it.'

'Neither is anybody else,' Waxy said. 'He fiddles everybody blind. Come on, let's slake our thirsts.'

As the first of the newly but temporarily enriched navvies trickled into The Wheatsheaf, Toby Watson, the landlord, handed the scores to each man that owed him money and they settled. Then they were entitled to take a tankard of beer from the dozens that had already been poured, and which lined the top of the counter in anticipation of the rush.

Tweedle Beak and Waxy sat on abutting wooden settles in the corner of the room at an iron-legged table. Many other navvies would cram in with them, complain about their lot and get drunk. Sure enough, they were soon joined by Windy Bags and Crabface Lijah. Crabface carried a cribbage board and a box of dominoes as well as his frothing tankard. Windy Bags counted his wages and slipped the money into one of his pockets before shuffling the dominoes that he had laid face down on the table. Brummagem Joe appeared, sat beside him and asked if he could join in the game.

'We need another,' Crabface declared. 'D'you want to play, Tweedle?'

'Count me in,' Tweedle responded.

They settled into the first game and were joined at the table by Jericho and Dog Meat. Next to arrive was Buttercup. He drew up a stool, filled his gum-bucket, lit it and watched the game of dominoes with interest, occasionally needling Tweedle Beak with sharp comments. Already there were eight men sitting around the table. The room was filling up, not only with men but with tobacco smoke, and it was growing noisy. Soon it would become rowdy. A further group from Hawthorn Villa occupied the adjacent table, including Tipton Ted, and others with names like Masher, Green Gilbert, and Fatbuck. Dandy Punch, who had done his job of paying everybody, soon joined them.

Jericho went to the bar and appropriated two more drinks for himself and Dog Meat. When he returned he narrated the story of their encounter the day before with the oversized boar. The men found it funny and the story was passed on to the next table and the next, and Dog Meat became the butt of several jokes, to his annoyance and humiliation. The room was so crowded by this time that men were standing around between the stools and tables. Jericho thrust past them to get to the bar again, and once more returned with beer for himself and Dog Meat.

'He's a good mate to thee, Dog Meat,' Buttercup remarked sarcastically. 'He keeps getting up and fetching thy beer, and I ain't sid thy hand in thy pocket yet.'

'All me wages have gone in what I owe, Buttercup,' Dog Meat replied ruefully. 'I had a bit left over but that's gone now I've settled me score with Toby. It's why I was trying to steal me dinner afore we met that bloody great pig.'

'Nipped thy arse, did it?'

'Would've, if I hadn't got over the fence in time.'

Jericho, seeing Dog Meat and Buttercup in conversation, turned to Tweedle Beak. 'I could do with a word, Tweedle. Just the two of us.'

'You'd best say what you've got to say here, lad. I ain't shifting from here whilst I'm in the middle of a game o' dominoes. I'll lose me seat. What's up?'

'I, er . . . I've been meaning to ask for a while now, but . . .'

'But what? Spit it out, lad.' He scanned the dominoes he held secretively in both hands

'I, er . . . Well, the truth is . . . I want young Poppy. Now as you're the breadwinner o' that family and seeing as how Sheba's carrying your bab, I look to you, Tweedle, to tell me what you'll take for the wench.'

'Money, you mean?'

'Aye,' Jericho replied assertively. 'To jump the broomstick. Ever since I clapped eyes on her, I knew as she was the one for me, the one I been waiting for. How much would you want for me to take her off your hands?'

Tweedle Beak placed a domino at the end of the line that zigzagged across the table and chuckled. 'Yo'm a dark hoss,' he said with a knowing look. 'I know yo' was sniffin' round the wench a while ago, but then I reckoned as your interests was diverted elsewhere.' He winked at Jericho. 'Who'd have thought it, eh?'

'Well, what do you say, Tweedle? How much? If it ain't an unreasonable amount, you can have the money tonight. I ain't short. How about thirty bob?'

'Thirty bob?' Tweedle scoffed. 'No, the wench is worth more than thirty bob. At least twice that much.'

'Three pounds?' Jericho queried. 'That's a bit steep. There ain't much of her, you know.'

'Yo' either want her or yo' don't.'

Ears pricked up at this conversation and one nudged another to draw attention to it.

'I bet there's many a single chap here who'd willingly gi' me three pounds for Poppy Silk.'

'Hear that?' Windy Bags said, looking up from his dominoes and nudging Crabface Lijah. 'Tweedle's about to sell young Poppy.'

Those at the next table also looked expectantly at Tweedle.

'What's the bidding?' Dandy Punch asked, with sudden interest.

'The wench is on offer at three pounds,' Buttercup said nonchalantly. 'Any advance?'

'I'll give yer three pounds ten, Tweedle,' Dandy Punch responded. 'Aye, and more.'

'Will you bollocks!' Jericho protested. 'The wench is mine.

I asked first . . . All right, Tweedle . . . Four pounds. Four pounds and she's mine, eh?'

'I'd give you five pounds if I thought I could have her,' the Masher said, a quiet young navvy who dressed almost as flamboyantly as Dandy Punch.

Jericho rummaged in his pocket for money. 'Here, Tweedle . . . Here's a sovereign. Have this as a down payment. I'll pay you the other four pounds later.'

'Nay, lad,' Tweedle said, refusing to accept the money. His enterprising brain could see the potential here for making a handsome kill. 'Nay, lad, there's many an interested party here. Poppy Silk goes to the highest bidder . . .' He pondered a moment. 'Better still, let's have a lottery . . . Let every man interested pay me a couple of quid, say, and I'll put his name into a hat. But first let's spread the word around. I want as many as possible to take part. Fair chances for everybody who's interested.'

Buttercup drew on his pipe looking unconcerned, but he was seething inside. He resented Tweedle Beak anyway, but encouraging the men to draw lots for poor Poppy Silk was despicable. He nudged Jericho. 'I would have thought Tweedle Beak would've offered thee a bit more consideration,' he said loudly for all within earshot to hear. 'Especially in view o' the circumstances.'

'What circumstances, Buttercup?'

'Well, I mean, in view o' the fact that he was in the tunnel giving that young Eliza a good seeing to who he picked up from The Bush at the top o' Bumble Hole Road, at the same time as thou was in there giving young Minnie Catchpole the benefit. I'd have thought he'd want it kept quiet.'

Jericho and Tweedle Beak were both shocked into silence, a hush that rapidly spread as the implications were noted. They looked at each other suspiciously while the others looked expectantly towards Dog Meat, expecting a fight to flare up. But there was no sign of a fight, not between Dog Meat and Jericho at least.

Tweedle Beak stared with burning animosity at Buttercup. 'What's it got to do with you?' he rasped, wagging his finger animatedly at Buttercup. 'You'm a bloody troublemaker, you. I knew you was sodding trouble the minute I cast eyes on yer.' He turned angrily to Jericho. 'And you, Jericho, you young bastard. I thought we agreed not to tell anybody about that. Now you've told bloody Buttercup. Now the bloody world knows.'

'I ain't told nobody,' Jericho protested, his face reddening. 'I ain't breathed a word to nobody. I wouldn't, would I, if I intended asking you for Poppy.'

'Well, it must've come from thee, Tweedle,' Buttercup suggested mischievously. 'Thou wast the only bugger who knew about it. Typical of a man in his cups.'

'What's this about him being in the tunnel wi' my daughter?' Tipton Ted said with rising indignation, thumbing at Jericho. 'Dog Meat, do you know aught about this?'

'Nothing, Ted,' Dog Meat lied. 'But I'll get to the bottom of it when I see Minnie.'

'You ought to bost his yed,' Tipton Ted goaded. 'Bost his yed in. Goo on . . . What's wrong wi' yer?'

Tweedle raised his hands and called for order. 'Listen, lads, listen. We'm veering off the point here,' he said, perceiving that his chance to make money from Poppy was slipping away. 'Let's get back to the business in hand. Who wants to buy a lottery ticket for young Poppy Silk?'

'The way I see it,' Buttercup calmly interjected, 'nobody's got the right to set up a lottery to draw for young Poppy. Least of all thee, Tweedle Beak, seeing as how her rightful father's dead and buried.'

'I'll say again, Buttercup,' Tweedle Beak retorted acidly. 'What's it got to do with you? Keep your nose out of my business . . . or risk having it spread across your face.'

Buttercup smiled. Unperturbed, he picked stray crumbs of tobacco from his waistcoat pocket and stuffed them into the bowl of his gum-bucket that had since gone out. 'That snout on thy ugly fizzog would be a tidy sight bent about a bit, an' all, Tweedle, eh? Just don't push thy luck wi' me, you parrot-faced wreck.' He emptied his tankard and stood up. 'Go on, fix thy lottery. I wouldn't expect a louse like thee to pay any mind to what the young wench herself wanted, 'cause that's the sort of vile shit thou bist. But, if yo' insist it's thy business and nobody else's, then get on with it and we'll see how much good it does thee.' He left, to seek a less polluted atmosphere.

Undaunted, Tweedle Beak pressed on with his plan. 'Right. A lottery it is then. Two pounds a ticket. Dog Meat, get some paper and a blacklead from Toby's daughter and ask her to come and write the names down.'

Dog Meat did as he was bid. He returned with young Selina Watson, a girl so plain that the navvies seldom harassed her.

'Jericho, how many tickets do you want?' Tweedle asked.

'I want five,' he answered. 'But I can't pay you ten pounds right away. I'll have to owe you.'

Tweedle shook his head. 'I'll only have tickets wrote what can be paid for.'

'Then I can't give you no money tonight, Tweedle.'

'Aye, same for me,' said the Masher.

'And me,' said Dandy Punch. 'Why don't you give us till this time next week to raise the money, them as wants to?'

'Better still, next month's payday,' suggested the Masher. 'By that time, we'll all have more money. We can save more in the meantime to buy an extra ticket, borrow some even. That way we get a better chance o' winning.'

Tweedle looked about him and saw the earnest expressions on the faces of those around him keen to win Poppy Silk. Had he realised she was such a prize, he would have organised a lottery for her long ago. Minute by minute the scheme was gathering momentum and he could see the financial advantage in waiting; more contenders might well be keen to buy tickets as word spread through the encampment. There was also an advantage to be gained by lowering the price to one pound each. More would be inclined to part with a pound, and those fools whose deprived dicks were ruling their heads would buy several tickets each.

'Right,' said Tweedle. 'Here's what I'm gunna do. Tickets'll be a quid each. The last day for staking your claim is next payday at the end o' September. Everybody can buy as many tickets as they can afford, depending on how much you want the wench . . . But there's a condition . . .'

The navvies looked at him expectantly, wondering what condition he could possibly lay down.

'I have to protect me own interests in this. So any one of you young bucks who tries to sweep young Poppy off her feet in the meantime to try and beat the lottery will have his tickets withdrawn . . . and no refund. Is that clear?'

The navvies looked from one to the other and nodded.

'I reckon that's fair,' the Masher said. 'It puts paid to any ideas of trying to put her in the family way meanwhile. Do yer agree, Jericho?'

'Why look at me?' Jericho asked resentfully.

''Cause you've bin sniffing round already, and am likely to sniff round again unless there's a rule agin' it . . . So, do you agree?'

'I reckon so,' Jericho said with reluctance. He could see his chance slipping away. He had been so close to buying Poppy, but that chance was all but gone now. Now he would have to consolidate his resources and buy as many tickets as he could to boost the odds.

Chapter 14

Dandy Punch, the stocky timekeeper, called at Rose Cottage after work had finished on Saturday to collect the rent. Poppy answered the door to him and was gratified to see him drenched to the skin as he hunched under his hat as if it might afford adequate shelter from the rain.

He bid her an obsequious good morning, which made her flesh creep. 'You look a picture today, young Poppy,' he said with a slavering leer, his voice as smooth as lard. 'But then, you always do.'

'I'll fetch me mother,' she said offhandedly, at once turning her back on him.

'Is Tweedle Beak about yet?' he called after her. 'I'd like a word if he is.'

Having heard, Tweedle rose from a chair and, in his shirt-sleeves, went to the door. His hand was in his pocket delving for the money to pay the rent in anticipation of Dandy Punch's asking for it. He counted out the exact amount then handed it over to the timekeeper who, in turn, made a mark in his collection book.

'A word, if you please, Tweedle . . .'

Dandy Punch turned away from the door and from the hut, signifying to Tweedle that the conversation should not be overheard. Tweedle followed him, closing the door behind him.

'What can I do for you, Dandy?' he said, eyeing resentfully the dark clouds above that were spilling their contents over him.

'Quite a bit, I fancy, Tweedle. They say as how one good turn deserves another . . .'

'Oh?'

'You remember after Lightning Jack left . . . I turned a blind eye to you paying the rent on this hut . . .'

'Turned a blind eye?'

'Well, it was all done unofficial, Tweedle. Strictly speaking, Treadwell's like to have gangers renting the huts, not ordinary navvies. Gangers have a bit more sway with the lads who lodge, you understand.' He turned up the collar of his coat. 'But since I knew you was trying to protect poor Sheba and her brood, I had to admire you for it. It was a noble thing to do, Tweedle. Very noble. There was no fear of me turning round and saying you couldn't do it, neither to you nor any of the gaffers.'

'What am yer after, Dandy Punch?'

'Well . . . the time's come when I reckon it behoves me to ask a favour in return . . . And not just a favour for meself, Tweedle, 'cause I'll be doing you one as well.'

'What is it you want?' Tweedle asked pointedly. 'Come on, mek it quick. I'm getting bloody drenched.' He did not take kindly to having it identified that he owed a favour to anybody. That which Dandy Punch had done he had not perceived as a favour, more in the line of duty.

'Well . . . this lottery as you'm about to run . . . I reckon as you'll be wanting somebody to write out the lottery tickets, putting the names on, and keeping an account of the money you collect.'

'Listen, Dandy, I can keep an account o' the money meself without any help from you or anybody else. But yo' could write the names on the tickets, if yo've a mind, 'cause I can't. Already I've took a pound each off the Masher, off Fatbuck, off Waxy Boyle and Windy Bags.'

'Hang on . . . Let me write 'em down . . .' Dandy Punch fumbled between the pages of his dog-eared rent book for his blacklead. He licked the lead and began to write, hunched over his book to keep it dry. 'Masher . . . Fatbuck . . . Waxy . . . Who was the last one you mentioned?'

'Windy.'

Dandy wrote it down. 'Let me know who they are when you take their pounds and I'll see to it as there's a ticket wrote for every pound took, eh?'

'Fair enough, Dandy.'

'Now look, Tweedle . . .' Dandy tucked his book under his arm and felt in the pocket of his trousers. He drew out a handful of coins and counted them into Tweedle's hand. 'That's five pounds, Tweedle . . . Now what you can do for me in return is to let me have two tickets for each of me pounds, so as I have ten tickets for five pounds. That's my discount, like, for helping you to operate the lottery, and for turning a blind eye to your tenancy.'

Tweedle shook his head. 'It ain't enough,' he said, seeing an opportunity to profit further. 'It ain't enough to warrant that sort o' discount. Look, Dandy, it strikes me as yo'm keen to win this Poppy, eh?'

'That, I am. Right keen. She's a fine madam.'

'And that's why you want to boost your chances, I can see that. Well, all I can say is boost 'em good and proper by paying for ten tickets and write yourself twenty. Yo'd be almost certain to win the wench. I can't say fairer than that.'

Dandy Punch hesitated and sucked on his lips. 'Ten pounds is a lot o' money, Tweedle . . . I'd invest it without a second thought if you could guarantee as *my* name would be picked out o' the hat . . . Nobody else need know, o' course.' He tapped his nose and winked. 'It'd be just between us two. You could still collect the money off the other chaps and make a tidy profit.'

Tweedle Beak considered it for no more than two seconds. 'Give me twelve quid, Dandy, and I'll guarantee it. But so sure as yo' breathe a word o' this to anybody, I'll skin thee alive.'

'Have no fear. It's just between you and me, Tweedle. And I'm a man of me word. I knew we'd understand one another. Just let me know who's paid and I'll write out their tickets as well.'

Tweedle leered. 'Not that they'll see the light o' day, eh, Dandy?'

'Oh, they'll have to be put in the hat, Tweedle. But mine'll be a different colour. Whoever does the draw will have to know what colour to pick out.'

'Oh, that's easy fixed,' Tweedle said. 'Leave that to me.'

Poppy's elusive dream of winning Robert Crawford lay ravaged. The first couple of days without seeing him was not in itself so bad, for she could imagine his being there still, perhaps in his office, but too busy to see her while he attended to problems on his section of the railway. The truth, however, was irrevocably registering that she might never see him again, inducing the severely acute pains of adolescent emotion, for which she had no antidote as yet. Never had she known such feelings of desolation and hopelessness. His departure could only be interpreted as rejection; and it hurt. By God, it hurt.

On the Sunday morning, she awoke early, disturbed by a gnawing inner awareness of her heartache, for there was no respite in sleep. Tweedle Beak lay alongside Sheba, his hooked nose the sail of a coal barge heaving on the erratic swell of his raucous snores. Her brothers and sisters were contained in their sound, juvenile slumbers, their faces the epitome of innocence. Poppy got out of bed and crept barefooted into the communal living room, leaving the creaking door ajar behind her to prevent the mechanical clack of the latch waking anybody. She stood shivering, peering out of the cracked windowpane that overlooked the chaotic squalor of shanties. Another damp dawn was breaking. Out of habit, she raked the ashes out of the fire, shovelled them into an iron bucket ready to heap onto the midden, and laid a new one. Her thoughts, though devoid of hope, were only of Robert Crawford. She'd had no time to come to terms with the torture his going away had wrought. Her desires, her goals, lay in ashes. Life was no longer worth the living.

She lit the fire and knelt before it, little more than a child but with all the high-strung emotions of a woman. With a match, she lit the paper at the base of the fire and watched as it ignited the strips of wood in turn. These newly kindled sticks represented her first encounter with Robert; the flame of fondness had caught, tentatively at first, then more surely, just as it had with the sticks. It was never a sudden thing, more a growing realisation that she needed to be near him as often as she could, to feed off his intellect, his sincerity and his kind attention. Always, there was that initial warmth that drew her to him, like the warmth now that induced her to huddle over the yet ineffectual flames.

Robert's going was a bereavement. She felt it more acutely than the grief following her father's death. It was all the more painful and tormenting because Robert had admitted that he loved her heart and soul, and because she had not tried hard enough to detain him. What inner turmoil was he suffering now that he had gone? It could be no harder to bear than her own.

The pieces of wood beneath the coals were burning brighter

now, like her love had burned bright during her early infatuation. Soon it would change, transfer its glory to the lumps of coal that were already glimmering at the sharp edges where the yellow flames lapped around them. So was her love transmuted to a higher plane, the better she got to know him. The pure fire of her passion would burn even brighter and for a long, long time, rooted as it was in the less volatile but more substantial substructure of admiration and respect that she had always harboured for Robert. This was the fuel of her emotions, like the coals were the fuel of a long-burning fire. Hers would last her lifetime, young as she was, inexperienced as she was. Instinctively, she knew it.

'What are you doing up so early?' a voice said quietly.

Poppy turned around and saw her mother standing at the bedroom door in her nightgown. 'I woke up early.'

Sheba ran her fingers through her bedraggled hair and yawned. 'Is it worrying you then, our Poppy?'

'Is what worrying me?' She was uncertain as to whether her mother was referring to Robert's departure.

'This scheme of Tweedle's?'

'What scheme?'

'You haven't heard?'

'Heard what?'

Sheba pulled a chair from under the rickety table and sat down. 'I thought you must have heard from somebody. Everybody's talking about it.'

'Nobody's told me anything.'

'He's running a lottery. A pound a ticket. You're the prize, our Poppy.'

'Me?' Poppy laughed with incredulity. 'What a cheek. Who does he think he is?'

'Well, he's the breadwinner.' Sheba, unsmiling, hunched her shoulders and pressed her hands together between her thighs for warmth and Poppy perceived from her mannerisms that it was not a joke. 'I reckon he must think that keeping us gives him the right.'

'The right? What sort of prize am I supposed to be? Does whoever wins the lottery expect a kiss or something?' she asked naively.

'Oh, more than a kiss, our Poppy. The deal is that you jump the broomstick with the winner.'

'What! I'll kill meself first. What if it's somebody like Crabface Lijah or Fatbuck?'

'On the other hand, what about if it's Jericho or the Masher?'

'The Masher's all right. But I wouldn't want to *sleep* with him.'

'Well, as I see it, you've got no say in the matter, our Poppy. And I don't see as it matters any road, now your Robert Crawford's gone. One chap's much like another in the dark, our Poppy, when you'm a-lying under him. And it was no good setting your cap at him any road. He would never have stooped to a navvy's daughter.'

'Yes, he would,' Poppy protested. 'He loves me.'

'Ah . . .' Sheba nodded mockingly. 'That must be why he's buggered off . . .' She rolled her eyes at what she perceived as Poppy's naivety. 'Listen, our Poppy, I want you to go along with this scheme of Tweedle's, 'cause it'll bring in a heap o' money at the end o' the month, he reckons. I'm hoping as I'll be able to have me a new coat and a new pair o' boots for the winter out of the proceeds. And I daresay as he'll treat you as well.'

Her mother's attitude implied far more than mere profit to Poppy. 'So, you'm letting him believe he's the father of the child you'm carrying then?'

'I might as well,' Sheba admitted with a shrug. 'There's no

sense in upsetting the apple cart now. Who else would look after us and keep us on the outside of the workhouse?'

Poppy appreciated her mother's dilemma but made no comment. That she should be a sacrifice to her mother's wellbeing, however, did not fill her with joy. On the other hand, she could be neither the instrument of her downfall, nor the downfall of her brothers and sisters. There seemed little alternative but to go along with Tweedle's scheme, however abhorrent. Whatever fate awaited her, she could accept it passively; it would be as nothing compared to her losing Robert. Then what if Robert returned in a year and wanted to tell her he wished her to be his bride after all? Well, she would not have the opportunity to discover it. She would be none the wiser; therefore, nor would he be. By then she might be miles away, living on some far distant railway construction site, already the bed partner of another man. By then she might be carrying a child or have one at her breast. So better to believe he would never come back for her.

'I don't see as I've got much choice, Mother,' Poppy said.

If Robert were still here it *would* be different. She would go to him, tell him what had been planned for her and take his advice. But he had gone. He could give her no advice, offer no help. She was at the mercy of Tweedle Beak, who only wanted to exploit her. There was nobody to talk to. Least of all the men, who must surely condone the scheme without exception. She was at a dead end.

'Well, the fire's caught nice, our Poppy,' Sheba remarked. 'Let's get the kettle on.'

The fire . . .

The fire symbolised her love for Robert. Whatever happened, whoever she was expected to live with and lie by, that flame of love would never extinguish. So she resigned herself to the necessity of tolerating the unwanted fumblings of a man she did not love, found repulsive and had no respect for, while her poor heart forever ached for Robert Crawford.

Dog Meat's financial difficulties were made worse by the need to obtain a new pair of work boots from the tommy shop. Having tried them on for size and comfort, he signed for them, then trudged out into the clinging mud of that first Monday in September. His mates mocked him when they saw him, some asking whether they were made of pig skin, others whether he had made a pig of himself with Minnie on his day off. He suffered ribald and insensitive comments about Jericho and Minnie. His standing in the community had diminished, he had lost whatever esteem he had previously earned, and he was painfully aware of it. Nor was Minnie sympathetic. It reflected badly on her that she was still associated with him after her apparent conquest of Jericho had been made common knowledge. Dog Meat clung to her, however, like a man drowning in a river clings to a tuft of overhanging grass as the current tries to pull him under.

The new Parkhead Viaduct straddled three prongs of a watery fork that was the junction of three canals. It was built entirely of wood. Sturdy trestles supported the thick planking above, which drummed beneath the abrasive scrunch of two hundred pairs of leather boots, stomping out of step across the span. Dog Meat was one of the men traversing the viaduct on his way to the cutting, avoiding the company of other navvies. Suddenly, he was aware of another person walking alongside him and he turned his head with resentment to see who.

'Morning, Dog Meat. Smart new boots th'ast got there.'

'Buttercup! Don't *you* start! I'm pig-sick o' folk taunting.'

'*Pig*-sick, eh?' Buttercup smiled at Dog Meat's unwitting self-mockery. 'Well, I bain't about to needle thee, lad. I had it in mind to ask what thou thought about Tweedle Beak holding a lottery for young Poppy Silk.'

'You wanted to ask me?' Dog Meat queried, looking at Buttercup with an unbelieving eye.

'Aye, thee. Th'ast got an opinion on it, I tek it.'

'Huh. I just wish I could afford to buy a ticket. She'd be a good woman, would Poppy.'

'Better than yon Minnie Catchpole?'

'Yes. Even though there's talk of Poppy and that young engineer—'

'The engineer? Aye, but sod all will ever come o' that, Dog Meat. The lad's buggered off. Abroad, I heard. Any road, he was on'y learnin' her to read and write.'

'And I wonder what else,' Dog Meat suggested cynically. 'Why else would he bugger off?'

'He wouldn't need to bugger off if he'd got young Poppy into trouble. She's on'y a navvy's daughter. Who from his class cares about such as her? Now . . . if it was some daughter o' the gentry . . .'

'It's a useful skill to have in a woman, reading and writing,' Dog Meat said after a thoughtful pause. ''Specially when you can't read and write yourself. If I won Poppy in the lottery I could be done with Minnie.'

'Or has Minnie already done with thee, Dog Meat?' Buttercup asked pointedly. 'I mean to say, she's had Jericho ferreting up her frock regular, by all accounts.'

Dog Meat shook his head resolutely. 'Just the once.'

'Oh, just the once, eh? Yo' sound as if yo' know all about it after all.'

Dog Meat frowned with puzzlement at Buttercup. 'Aye, just the once,' he affirmed. 'He only paid me for the once any road.'

'Paid thee?' Buttercup grinned. 'Yo' mean you sold him the wench?'

'He gi'd me the price of a gallon o' beer. It was only for one jump, though.'

The older man guffawed. 'Methinks you sold her too cheap, Dog Meat.'

'You do?'

'He's bin cheating thee, that Jericho. He's been seen going in and coming out of the tunnel a few times with that Minnie o' thine.'

'The bastard!' Dog Meat exclaimed at the realisation. 'How many times?'

'The Lord only knows, Dog Meat. How many times a night could thou manage it?'

'Christ! He must owe me a fortune,' Dog Meat cried, at once sorting his priorities. 'I'll part him from his money one road or another.'

Later that day, as Buttercup strutted towards Rose Cottage after his day's work, he espied Poppy Silk scolding Rose, the younger of her two sisters. He slowed down, waiting for the argument to die, then called Poppy's name. She halted and straightened her apron when she saw him, then smiled with embarrassment at having been thus seen.

'Hello, Buttercup,' she greeted, looking up at him expectantly.

'Poppy. I'm glad as I've caught thee. There's summat as I wanted to talk to thee about. Can you meet me after? It ain't summat as I want to discuss where other folks can hear.'

She looked at him mystified. 'If you want. What time? Where?'

'When the others am in the alehouse getting fuddled. Meet me by the bridge where the road ends and the footpath starts – towards Netherton.'

'I know it,' she answered. 'About eight?'

'Eight'll do. It'll be getting dark by then. Don't let on to anybody as you'm meeting me.'

She nodded, wondering what on earth he wanted to see her about. Back inside the hut she continued with her work, cooking the meals that the lodgers had left with her, that were wrapped in linen and steeping in the boiling copper. One by one she drained them and plated them before she handed them out to their respective owners.

Most men took beer with their meals, a taster before the serious drinking that would ensue later. After they had eaten, the men would linger, talking, putting the world to rights, before they dispersed to change into their more flamboyant clothes.

'You'll make somebody a grand wife,' was a common compliment in anticipation of the fate that was to befall her.

'Somebody? I wonder who?' she would reply, irrespective. To another she added, 'Just as long as it ain't you. So please don't buy a lottery ticket.'

When the work was done, Poppy glanced at the clock. It was almost eight and she was aware that Buttercup had left the hut. She took off her apron, teased her hair and slipped out without saying a word. She hurried to Shaw Road and walked hurriedly downhill, looking behind her to see if anybody was watching. It was still slippery with mud underfoot, but the rain had ceased and the sky was clear. Buttercup was already waiting by the bridge, smoking his clay pipe.

'Sorry if I kept you waiting, Buttercup.'

'It meks no odds, young Poppy,' he said kindly.

'What did you want to see me about?'

'I wanted to know how thou feels, wench,' he replied. 'Having known thy father as well as any man, being privy to his hopes and dreams and taking to him the way I did, I feel a mite responsible for thee, young Poppy. I sort of feel entrusted to be thy guardian.'

She smiled up at him gratefully. 'What do you want to know? How I feel about men drawing lots for me?'

'Aye. That sort o' thing.'

'What do you think about it, Buttercup?'

'I think it's a scandal.'

'Do you think my father would've sold lottery tickets to get shut of me, or to profit from me?'

Buttercup shook his head. 'Never in a million years. It was one of the big regrets in me life that I dain't have the privilege of knowing thy father longer, Poppy. But I know well enough that he would never have sacrificed thee to the gamble of a lottery. Lord knows who's likely to have the winning ticket. It's just as like to be somebody you detest as one of them handsome bucks.'

'I don't want to be drawn by anybody, Buttercup, handsome or not,' she said. 'I always swore I'd never end up with a navvy . . .'

'Don't none of 'em appeal?'

She shook her head.

'What about Dog Meat?'

She pulled a face. ''Specially not Dog Meat. He ain't got the brains of a gnat.'

'Who then?'

'Why? Are you going to fix it somehow?'

'Me fix it? Nay, wench. Tweedle Beak'll let me nowhere near him nor his lottery to meddle with it.'

'Are you going to buy a ticket for me, Buttercup?'

He laughed at the thought. 'Nay, wench.'

'Please, Buttercup,' she pleaded softly. 'I wouldn't mind if you won me. At least I know you'm kind. I know you'd be gentle.'

'Nay, wench,' he said again, flattered that she had the nerve to say it. 'Thou wouldn't want an old bugger like me. Now, thy mother . . . Now that'd be a different kettle o' fish. I'm nearer thy mother's age . . .'

'Do you like my mother, Buttercup?'

'Oh, I think she's a fine, plucky woman, Poppy. I can't say as I'm enamoured o' the shit heap she sleeps with, though.'

She giggled. 'Nor me . . . But why did you mention Dog Meat?'

'Oh . . . It's nothing to do with me really . . .'

'Tell me . . .'

'Well, it's just that he admitted to me this morning how he'd let Jericho have young Minnie Catchpole for the price of a gallon o' beer.'

'*Have* her?'

'Aye. *Have* her. To do as he wanted with her for one night. Dog Meat was desperate for money and Jericho was desperate for a woman. Dog Meat's always desperate for money, from what I can see of it.'

'And did he? Jericho? *Have* her, I mean.'

'Oh, aye. The trouble was, the bastard was having her most every other night after it, but not letting on to Dog Meat. They used to go in the tunnel regular for their shenanigans.'

Poppy was unable to say anything for some seconds, so startled was she by this news. There were so many questions to ask, and she didn't know which to ask first.

'But it was Jericho wanting to buy thee off Tweedle who started this whole business of the men drawing lots for thee,' Buttercup explained.

'If Dog Meat took money for Minnie's favours, Buttercup, that means he sold her for a common whore.'

'Aye, that's the way I see it, Poppy.'

'Poor Minnie . . .'

'And yo' ain't sore with Minnie for having Jericho?' he asked. 'One or two say as how you was sweet on Jericho.'

'I never was, Buttercup. I was only ever sweet on Robert Crawford, the engineer who was teaching me to read and write.'

Buttercup smiled and his eyes creased in that way which always seemed to enhance his likeableness. 'I knowed it! And now he's buggered off, eh? Never mind. Maybe he'll come back for thee, young Poppy.'

'I'm sure he will. He told me he loved me . . . For all the good it'll do me once I'm carrying somebody else's child.'

'So did he ever tek advantage of thee, young Poppy, this engineer?'

'No, he never took advantage of me, Buttercup, more's the pity. Robert is too much of a gentleman for that. He said he esteemed me too much.'

'Christ, then he must be a gentleman. He must have meant what he said. I'd stick out for him, if I was thee.'

'Except that with no prospect of escaping that lottery, my future is already sealed.'

'Aye, it'd seem that way,' Buttercup agreed.

When she returned to the encampment, Poppy called at Hawthorn Villa hoping to see Minnie. For once, Minnie was in, and Poppy said she wanted to talk to her. The full moon tinselled the dew that settled on the shepherd's purse, on the thistles, and on the spiders' webs so intricately engineered in between. Poppy related to Minnie what Buttercup had told her of Dog Meat's arrangement with Jericho.

'And I thought it was 'cause Jericho loved me,' Minnie declared ruefully. 'Lord, what a fool I've been.'

'He don't love anybody but himself, Minnie,' Poppy consoled. 'And I wouldn't have no truck with him any more after that, if I was you.'

'I won't, I won't. But it means Dog Meat sold me, Poppy.' Minnie was visibly annoyed. 'He sold me for money, as if I was a whore.'

'It's true.'

'Well, why should he have the money, Poppy, if it's me what's doing the work? Oh, I'll show him. As sure as day's day, I'll show him . . .'

Chapter 15

As soon as Tweedle Beak finished work on the day of his lottery draw, 28 September, he changed into his better outfit, reserved for drinking and womanising, and hurried to The Wheatsheaf. Final and important arrangements had to be made. The only patrons there at the time were four miners, blackened with coal dust, who were evidently on their way home from their pit. They paid little attention to Tweedle Beak as he strode up to the bar.

'You'm early,' Selina, the landlord's daughter, commented.

'I've come to see you, Selina,' Tweedle replied and raised his eyebrows as if to suggest he was interested in her. 'Before the others get here.'

Selina blushed at the implied flattery and became flustered. She was not used to the attention of navvies, except for one lad once when they first became a blight on the area; he'd had a bet with his mates as to who could suffer to seduce the ugliest wench in Dudley one Saturday night.

'Can I pour you a drink?' she asked.

'A quart o' your best, Selina,' he said. 'And have one yourself.'

'That's very kind, sir,' she replied, unable to use his name because she was not sure of it. She picked up a pewter tankard and, while he watched, drew beer into it and placed it before him on the counter.

Tweedle handed her a sixpence. 'No, you can keep the change,' he said, amiably, when she offered him some coppers. 'I wanted to ask you to do summat for me, young Selina, if you would.'

'If I can, I'll be happy to oblige.'

He felt in his trouser pocket and pulled out a half sovereign. 'This is yourn, Selina, if you'll do a little task for me, secret like. It's just between you and me . . . Understand?'

'I ain't no blab-mouth,' Selina said defensively, looking covetously at the half sovereign held between his fingers and noticing his grubby, broken nails. 'I can keep a secret.'

'That's partitly what I wanted to hear . . .' He grinned at her affably and his long nose drooped in consequence. 'Later on, when the men have been paid, we'm having a lottery draw—'

'Oh, I heard summat about it. One o' the navvy wenches is being raffled off, in't her?'

He nodded and grinned again, placed the coin on the counter tauntingly, then supped his beer. 'Word gets around . . . Any road, this is where you can help, Selina. I want to call on you to come and draw the tickets out o' the hat.'

'Yes, all right,' she willingly agreed. 'I don't mind.'

Looking around furtively, he felt in another pocket, showed her a piece of folded paper and leaned towards her. 'This is the winning ticket. I want you to keep it safe till I ask you to come and do the draw. Then, you must have it hid in your hand, ready. When I ask you to dip your hand in the hat, I want you to pretend as you've just pulled out this very piece o' paper. Understand?'

Selina nodded uncertainly. 'So it's a cheat. The draw is already fixed.'

'Let's say the winner has already been decided by other means. O' course, the money's all going to charity, you know.

We just need to make the draw look real to them lads who've bought tickets who'm unsuitable and unworthy o' the wench being raffled. You understand, eh? I mean *you* wouldn't want to end up with any Tom, Dick or Harry, if it was yourself, would you?'

Confused, she said no and nodded. Once more she glanced at the half sovereign. She could buy loads with that; it was a handsome bribe. She hesitated a second. She could try her luck and stall for a whole pound . . . but then this man might withdraw the offer and ask somebody else. 'All right,' she said at last, and held her hand out for the lottery ticket.

'But it's just between you and me, Selina.' He pressed the ticket into her hand but did not release it while he held eye contact with her.

'It's just between you and me,' Selina agreed.

Tweedle Beak let go her hand. 'Just be sure to come to me as soon as I call you.'

She took the half sovereign and he winked knowingly. 'Have no fear . . . sir . . .'

He finished his beer and ordered another.

Legal wrangles continued over the implementation of Brunel's broad gauge in preference to the more widely used narrow-gauge track. Coupled with inordinately slow progress, due to a string of inefficient contractors that had slowed down the job intolerably, it was decided that all work on the Oxford, Worcester and Wolverhampton Railway was to be wound down and suspended by the end of next month. The friendly and helpful alliance with the Great Western Railway had proved to be neither friendly nor helpful after all. The encampment at Blowers Green would consequently disband, and the navvies who had lived and worked there for months, with a common purpose, would up sticks and set off on tramp to seek employment on other civil engineering projects. Men who had become firm friends, or even sworn enemies, would part company and possibly never meet again, for better or for worse.

The men were advised of this as they lined up to collect their pay. A letter was included in each pay packet, but since all but a couple could not read, it had to be explained to them by a representative of the company. Those who wanted to seek alternative employment could leave at once. Those who wished to stay would be kept on only until the end of October.

There had been rumours for ages that the company was in financial straits, but it all made little sense to the men. As far as they were concerned, the section from Worcester to Dudley was all but complete, save for a mile or two of cuttings and embankments, the laying of the track and the building of stations. Between Worcester and Oxford, however, it was a different story. The Mickleton tunnel, for instance, was nowhere near finished and Mr Brunel was said to be livid about the spiralling costs and his plummeting reputation.

The women that dwelt in the encampment were oblivious to the commercial turmoil that would affect all their lives. In anticipation of Tweedle Beak's lottery, they had collected switches of gorse, which they had tied together and fastened to a broomstick for the ceremonial jumping over it later that evening. Another had made a chaplet of flowers for Poppy's hair. They were excited, and took great trouble to tease Poppy whenever she appeared, particularly Ma Catchpole. She not only considered it a golden opportunity for Poppy, but declared it was about time the girl settled down with a man and had some babbies. Poppy, however, was not so enthusiastic.

Tweedle had collected forty-seven pounds in lottery contributions, a sum he had stored in a leather pouch in his locker in the main room of Rose Cottage. Dandy Punch had duly written the names of contenders on squares of white paper, which had all been neatly folded and which accompanied him to The Wheatsheaf for the draw that evening. Despite the news that all work was to be held in abeyance, Tweedle Beak was still hopeful that payday might induce a few others to speculate on the enticing possibility of winning an exceedingly bonny, industrious and highly desirable young bed partner. His hopes were well founded. Several men had been waiting for payday so that they could afford tickets, and he collected a further fifteen pounds. Dandy Punch wrote those names on tickets.

The atmosphere in The Wheatsheaf that evening was buzzing with a heady mixture of despair and anticipation. Some men were openly devastated that work was being shelved, others could not have cared less. Nonetheless, it was a major topic of discussion as they slaked their thirsts with excesses of foaming beer. The air of anticipation, however, was stirred by the impending lottery draw. The usual gathering sat in front of their tankards and speculated on the outcome, while Tweedle Beak excitedly pocketed his latest booty and Dandy Punch wrote out the final ticket, inscribing the words 'Dog Meat' upon it.

'How many tickets hast thou bought, Dog Meat, me old mate?' Buttercup asked, rubbing his fingers through his whiskers.

'Just the one,' Dog Meat replied. 'Tipton Ted lent me the money after all.'

'Aye, well, p'raps he wants to get shut of thee. Did you have any luck wheedling any more out of Jericho?'

Dog Meat shook his head. 'No, and I wasn't about to argue with him either. He gets nasty when he's offended. I din't fancy a broken mush.'

Buttercup looked at Jericho. 'How many tickets has thou bought, Jericho?'

'Enough to put me in the reckoning.'

'Dandy Punch has bought ten, I hear.' Buttercup turned to Tweedle Beak whose nose was in his tankard. 'Is that right, Tweedle? Has Dandy Punch bought ten tickets?'

'Ask Dandy Punch, why don't you?' Tweedle replied off-handedly. 'It's his business how many tickets he's paid for. It ain't for me to tell you his business.'

Buttercup looked at Tweedle with distrust. 'I reckon we need a scrutineer to check the tickets in that hat o' thine there. Seeing as how I got no interest in the matter, I reckon it should be me.'

'Sod off, Buttercup,' Tweedle Beak rasped, piqued as always by Buttercup's goading. He took the floppy hat, which was occupying pride of place on his lap, and closed it up protectively. 'There's no need for e'er a scrutineer. This lottery's being run fair and square.'

'So how long have we gotta wait afore *we* know who's won it?'

'We'll be doing the draw in ten minutes.'

'And who's gunna draw it?'

'Selina, the gaffer's daughter.'

'I bet if you'd put Selina up as a prize, you wouldn't have sold many tickets, eh, Tweedle?' Jericho suggested.

Tweedle looked Jericho squarely in the eye. 'Say what you like about Selina, she's a decent wench.'

'Tell me, Tweedle,' Buttercup interjected. 'How is this stopping o' the work likely to affect thee? D'you intend to stop on through October, or bugger off early?'

'What's it got to do with you?' Tweedle asked defensively.

'I was just trying to be friendly. Either road, it'll be a tidy tramp for Sheba and her kids, wherever you go, Tweedle.'

'What's it to you?'

'I'm just commenting, me old mate. You mustn't forget as she's a-carrying.'

'It's in the forefront o' me mind, Buttercup.'

Jericho nudged Dandy Punch who was sitting on the stool next to Tweedle. 'How many tickets have you bought for young Poppy, Dandy?'

'None o' your business, lad. Who says I've bought any?'

'Buttercup reckons so. Any road, I've bought six. Tell me how many you've bought,' he persisted.

'All right . . . I bought six. Same as you. So me and you have got equal chances.'

'Well, if I win I shall take her to live in Chippenham, now as the work here is shutting down. I shall go back to being a farm worker. I'll rent a cottage and who knows, I might even have me own smallholding someday.'

'Noble ambitions, Jericho. Who'd have thought it from you?'

'And what about you, Dandy? What'll you do if you win the wench?'

'I'm assured of work with Treadwell's, Jericho. Next job, wherever that might be, I shall rent a house. Me and Poppy will have a proper wedding and we'll settle down and raise a family. I always wanted a family.' He smiled to himself with satisfaction at the certain prospect. 'I've got it all planned out.'

Their attention was drawn to Tweedle Beak, who was beckoning Selina.

'Lads!' he cried, and stood up. 'Can I have your attention . . . ?'

He looked about him at the unsightly collection of expectant faces. Selina meanwhile shuffled through the crush of navvies who were all intent on watching the proceedings. As she approached, she felt in the pocket of her apron for the ticket that was to win.

'We've all had a month to ponder the prospect o' winning the beautiful young Poppy Silk in this raffle,' Tweedle Beak was saying, enjoying the moment. 'Well, now's the time to make the draw . . .'

Selina was standing close to Tweedle Beak now, but was still fumbling in her pocket, suddenly hot with panic. She pulled out a rag and pretended to wipe her nose with it while she felt about with her other hand. But the ticket had attached itself to the rag and fluttered to the floor at the feet of Buttercup, who leaned forward and picked it up. Tweedle Beak viciously tried to snatch it away, but Buttercup had it in his closed fist. He opened it.

'Well, now . . . What's this?' he exclaimed to all, holding the ticket aloft. 'Here, Dandy Punch . . .' He showed Dandy the ticket, keeping Tweedle Beak at arm's length. 'What name does it say?'

Dandy adjusted his spectacles and peered through them. 'It says "Tweedle Beak".'

'Is that so? Tweedle Beak, eh?' He looked at Tweedle accusingly, then at Selina. 'Was this a fix, Selina? Was thou supposed to pretend to pick this ticket out o' the perishing hat?'

'No . . . I never seed it afore.'

'Fancy that . . . And yet I just watched it fall out o' thy pocket. If thou never seed it afore, wench, how come it was in thy pocket? Well, let me hazard a guess . . . That weasel, Tweedle bloody Beak, gave it thee. Hear that, lads?' All eyes were on Buttercup as he stood up and addressed the rest of the navvies. 'Tweedle Beak has tried to fix this draw so as he wins young Poppy himself . . . And him already sleeping with the wench's mother . . .' Buttercup's derision and loathing was amply manifest, not only in the way he prodded his forefinger at Tweedle, but in his scowl.

''Tis a lie,' Tweedle protested. He glanced at Dandy Punch apprehensively. 'I did no such thing. I wouldn't . . . For the very reason Buttercup mentioned . . . Because o' Sheba.'

'It looks mighty suspicious to me, Tweedle,' Dandy Punch said with bitter resentment, seeing his cherished plans doomed, but unable to further his complaint for fear of being perceived as the perpetrator of another fiddle, as yet uncovered.

'Suspicious?' Buttercup hissed. 'I'll say it's bloody suspicious. Thou bist a shit heap, Tweedle bloody Beak.'

'Aye, and more,' Dandy Punch exclaimed, seizing the first chance to vent his anger and disappointment on Tweedle Beak. 'You tried to fix this draw and run off with the daughter o' the woman who's already expecting your child? You're worse than any shit heap. You're lower than any slime that ever slopped about in a millpond.'

Buttercup then saw his opportunity to inflict the ultimate humiliation on Tweedle Beak and could not resist it. He took a deep breath and his chest swelled in anticipation. 'Well, now,' he said, addressing everybody. 'I've got some information about the babby yon Sheba's a-carrying . . . And I can tell ye all that it ain't Tweedle Beak's . . .' A deathly hush fell among the men who had been jeering. 'No, sir . . . It's Lightning Jack's child . . .'

There were cheers and guffaws from everybody. Tweedle Beak had gone suddenly pale. Never in his life had he looked such a fool. He had tried to cheat his fellow workers and had been exposed. He had tried to cheat Dandy Punch, who in turn had tried to cheat everybody else, and the plot had faltered due to Selina's carelessness. Now he had been belittled beyond redemption. He was a laughing stock. Even if it was a lie about Lightning Jack being the father of Sheba's child, he could never be sure and he would be forever taunted about it. He wanted the ground to open up and swallow him, to relieve him of his absolute embarrassment and shame. He saw only one possible way out . . .

He raised his hands, begging to be heard. 'Lads, lads . . . All right, I admit I tried to fix this draw in me own favour, and it ain't no fault o' Selina's. A good many of yer have paid good money for the chance to win Poppy, I realise that and I'm sorry. I reckon as we should mek the draw any road.' He looked at Dandy Punch, seeking his acknowledgement of his desperate attempt to make amends. 'So I'm asking Selina to mek the draw proper.'

'Look in her hands fust to mek sure as her's carrying ne'er another ticket,' somebody yelled.

Selina, also acutely embarrassed at being seen as part of the treachery, held up her empty palms for all to see. Tweedle held up the hat and she thrust her hand into it, drawing out a white ticket. She opened it up slowly, fumbling a little in her nervousness. The men, especially Dandy and those others that had invested heavily, watched Selina with an angry intensity.

'Whose ticket is it?' Buttercup asked. 'Thou canst read, eh?'

'It says "Dog Meat",' Selina uttered quietly.

'Dog Meat!'

The former enthusiasm, the avid interest, the intrigue was dead. Nobody cared about the draw after the sham of Tweedle Beak's cheating. The lottery had lost its credibility. For all they knew, even the drawing of Dog Meat's ticket could have been a fix. And so much hard-earned money invested as well.

'You damned Judas!' hissed Dandy Punch through the

hubbub. He had been sitting next to Tweedle Beak. 'I want my money back.'

Jericho overheard the comment. 'Aye, and if he gets his money back, I want my money back as well.'

'We all want our money back,' several others shouted.

'Nobody gets their money back,' Tweedle scoffed. 'The draw was made. As agreed.'

Buttercup had been studying Tweedle Beak and his reaction to the events and accusations. He regarded him through despising, narrowed eyes, with an increasing sense of satisfaction at having humiliated him. But still he felt like killing the blackguard. He lunged at him, fists flying. 'Thou shit heap! Thou doesn't deserve to lick the boots of Sheba and Poppy, nor Lightning Jack. Any road, what gives thee the right to have a lottery for a decent innocent like Poppy Silk? Thou bisn't her father. Thou bisn't anything, other than a great heap o' shit. As far as I'm concerned thy lottery's a sham, and I'll kill thee.' Buttercup was about to land a second punch when Jericho pulled him away.

'He's mine, Buttercup.'

'Nay, lad. I've been itching to do this vile bastard some damage. Take your turn.'

'But he took six quid off me. Six quid!'

Glasses, bottles and tankards began flying. Beer was swilling over tables, spilling onto the sawdust-sprinkled floor. Men struggled one with another as the fighting instantly spread. Tweedle Beak, free of Buttercup's unwanted attention for a second, saw his chance to escape. He turned round to pick up his hat, which contained further evidence of bias in the number of tickets bearing the name of Dandy Punch.

The hat had gone.

So had Dandy Punch, though nobody made the connection,

for Dandy was not thought likely to get mixed up in any fighting.

'What are you looking for, Tweedle?' Jericho screamed at Tweedle. 'The hat with the tickets in? Just when I want to see if my tickets was ever put in there.'

'They was in there,' Tweedle tried to reassure him.

'I've only got your word, and that don't count for much any more. You're a sly, sneaky bastard. Now, if you can't show me me tickets, I want me money back.'

'That you won't have, Jericho.'

'Then outside.'

'Aye, I'll go outside with yer, you cocky young bastard.' Tweedle had got nothing more to lose. He had lost his credibility and what friends he'd had. He might regain some respect if he could beat Jericho in a fistfight. If he couldn't, he might win some sympathy as the loser.

The room full of angry men became quiet as the dispute between Jericho and Tweedle Beak flared. Those closest stood back to let the two men pass, then they all finished what beer still remained in their tankards and followed them outside. At once, Selina and her father set about clearing up the debris.

Buttercup felt robbed that he was not about to get a crack at breaking Tweedle's jaw, but he was sufficiently content to let the swine suffer at the hands of Jericho, since there was no doubting the outcome of that fight. A trickle of blood appeared from Tweedle's mouth as they fought. Buttercup turned his back on the struggle. There was a more important task in hand.

As Buttercup reached the encampment, the women were standing in the centre, gossiping and laughing with expectation. When they saw him strutting towards them looking agitated they fell silent.

'Who's the lucky chap then?' Ma Catchpole enquired. 'We'n got the broomstick ready and Poppy's all dressed up, a-waiting.'

'Good,' he said and walked past them.

The women looked from one to the other with puzzled expressions.

'Is it you, Buttercup?' one asked. 'Shall you be jumping the broomstick wi' young Poppy?'

'Not me,' he called, and went inside Rose Cottage, slamming the door behind him.

Sheba, Poppy, and the other children were all waiting apprehensively for the result of the draw. Poppy was in her best red flannel frock and the boots that Robert Crawford had bought her. She was pale and trembling as she looked anxiously at Buttercup.

'What happened?' Sheba asked.

'I'll tell thee in a minute. I want a crowbar.'

Buttercup entered the navvies' sleeping quarters and came out bearing one. At once he strode over to the line of lockers.

'Which is Tweedle's?'

'This one.' Sheba pointed it out.

'He tried to fix it so as *he* won,' Buttercup informed them as he shoved the end of the crowbar between the door and its stout frame. 'That means as he was planning to leave thee, Sheba.'

'Does he know as it ain't his child I'm a-carrying then?' She showed little emotion.

'He does now. But I reckon it meks no odds to him either way. The fact as thee bist a-carrying, whether or no 'tis his, meks no odds to him. He's a bad un, Sheba. Yo'm well rid of the bastard.'

'Does that mean as I ain't got to jump the broomstick with anybody?' Poppy asked.

'When the lottery got drawn proper, Dog Meat's name came out o' the hat.'

'Dog Meat!' Poppy groaned. 'I can't stand him. Oh, tell me this is a vile nightmare I'm having.'

'It's a vile nightmare,' Sheba agreed.

'Fret thee not,' Buttercup declared earnestly. 'It was a fiddle from start to finish. Nobody's having thee, Poppy. Not Dog Meat, nor Jericho, nor Dandy Punch. Least of all Tweedle bloody Beak. There'll be nothing left of him any road once Jericho's finished with him.'

'Honest, Buttercup? You mean I'm free to do as I please?'

'I'd never let anybody take thee as thou didn't want, wench,' he said resolutely. 'Tweedle Beak had no right to do as he did. He wasn't thy father. He was nothin' to do with thee.'

'But what about Dog Meat? He'll come and claim me before long.'

'Don't worry about Dog Meat. I'll sort him out.' Buttercup had managed to break the lock and the door swung open. He reached inside and took the leather pouch that he knew contained most of the money Tweedle Beak had collected. He tossed it to Poppy. 'Here . . . The money's thine, Poppy.'

'But that Tweedle Beak,' Sheba said, the news impacting on her. 'He was intending to run off with me own daughter and spared not a thought for me, or even the child I'm carrying.'

'Aye, and he's took money off a good many besides, knowing full well as he was gunna fix it for himself to win. But he was never clever enough to see it through proper. Well, he'll be leaving tonight any road, if he can still stand. But not with his money.' He turned to Poppy. 'Take the money, my flower. Tomorrow, get theeself away from this camp and navvydom. There's enough there to see thee through many a month. Even a twelvemonth. Tek theeself off and wait for that young engineer thou'st got thy eye on.'

Poppy looked enquiringly at Sheba, then at Buttercup. 'If Tweedle Beak intended to cheat everybody, don't you think we should give the money back to the men who've been cheated?'

Buttercup took his clay pipe out of the top pocket of his waistcoat and put it in his mouth. 'If we could be sure who's paid what,' he said, taking a stick of twist tobacco from his pocket and cutting a piece off it. 'Somebody else must've been in on it besides, 'cause the hat suddenly went missing with all the damned tickets. And if we ask who paid money, every bugger will say he paid for two tickets when he only bought one. Nay, wench, have the money thyself and let it do thee some good. Besides . . .' He tapped the side of his nose. 'Everybody'll think as Tweedle himself has sloped off with it. When word gets round, he'll not be able to find work navvying anywhere. But that's his own saft fault.'

Poppy looked at her mother again. 'I don't know what to do, Mother. What should I do?'

'Before your mother says anything, Poppy,' Buttercup said, stuffing strands of tobacco into his gum-bucket, 'you should both know that work on the railway is being stopped. Some of the men am leaving right away to find other work. Them who'm stopping have on'y got till the end of October. Then we'll all be on tramp.'

'All the more reason for the men to have their money,' Poppy said. 'And for me to come with you.'

Buttercup reached down to the fire with a spill, ignited it and lit his pipe with it. 'Nay, don't worry about thy mother, young Poppy.'

'What do you mean?' Sheba asked.

'I'll look after thee, Sheba . . . And thy brood.' He sucked on his pipe and blew out a cloud of sweet-smelling smoke. 'No strings attached, if that's the way thou wouldst rather have it. On the other hand, I'd be honoured to be husband to thee, and father to thy nippers.'

Sheba and Poppy looked at each other and laughed with joy.

'How did you know that's exactly what she'd want?' Poppy said, looking at her mother with love in her eyes.

'I didn't.'

'I did. She never said a word, but I knew.'

'I should just hate to see her go to waste, put in the work-house and separated from her children. Besides, Lightning Jack would've wanted me to look after thee, Sheba. It's what I want to do . . . if you'll have me . . .'

Tears trembled on Sheba's eyelashes and she wiped them with the backs of her hands. 'You are the most . . . surprising man, Buttercup,' Sheba said quietly, sincerely. 'Oh, I've always had this admiration for you, from that first day I set eyes on you. I'll not deny it. But I never thought . . . Oh, I'd be privileged to be your woman . . . Just as long as you can forgive me my dallying with Tweedle Beak.'

'Don't give it a thought,' Buttercup said kindly. ''Tis a certain fact as you had no choice. You have a choice this time, though. Go with Poppy and live comfortable on Tweedle's ill-gotten money, or settle with me and let Poppy follow her heart.'

'What do you want to do, our Poppy?'

'I love Robert Crawford, Mother,' she said without hesitation. 'I have to follow the path that might bring him and me together. Before tonight, I thought he was lost to me forever.'

'Then that's settled . . . Buttercup, you've got yourself a family.'

Buttercup beamed. 'Capital! Just hang on here while I go and have a word with Dog Meat. Poppy, pass me a sovereign so's I can give the poor bugger his stake back. He even borrowed it off Tipton Ted Catchpole.'

Outside the hut they heard the sound of raucous singing and shouting. Poppy went to the door and opened it. A crowd of navvies had gathered in the centre of the encampment, and the women who had been earlier hanging around had evidently joined them. Among them was Minnie. Poppy could see the tall, muscular frame of Jericho, unmistakable in the gloaming. Just then he looked up and saw Poppy silhouetted in the door frame by the feeble light of the oil lamp. He strode over to her intently.

'Poppy, I could've killed the swine.' Jericho's eyes were ablaze with the after-effects of his fight. 'To think as he could pull a trick like that to get his dirty maulers on you.'

'I suppose you mean Tweedle Beak.'

'Aye, Tweedle Beak. You'll not see him again. Nor would you want to, I fancy. I paid six quid for lottery tickets to win you and the bastard tried to fix it so as he'd win himself. If Buttercup hadn't noticed the rogue ticket lying on the floor . . .'

'We heard,' she answered. 'Buttercup told us.'

'Aye, well, I got my money back. I knocked it out of him. He'll not pull a trick like that again.'

'Where is he? Tweedle, I mean.'

'Gone. He skulked off with a black eye and a fat lip.'

'Gone already? Good . . . I'm glad . . .'

'Poppy . . .' His look was intent, hungry, and typical of the way he always was after a fight.

'What?'

'Fancy coming a walk with me? There's things I want to

233

say to you. Things I thought I'd never have the chance to say after tonight's episode.'

'No, Jericho,' she said quietly. 'I've had enough excitement for one night. And I've decided, I'm leaving here in the morning.'

'Leaving? Where will you go?'

She shrugged, aware that for such a big solid man he seemed emotionally tormented, childishly unstable. 'I don't know yet. I can read and write a bit now. I might try my luck applying for a position in service in Dudley somewhere. I'd make a good maid, I reckon.'

'Aye, you would at that. But I want to look after you, Poppy.' He scratched his head under his hat. 'I had such grand plans for me and you, if I'd won you in that lottery.'

She smiled sympathetically. 'It wouldn't have worked, Jericho. I have my own dreams . . .'

'Here . . .' He felt in his pocket and pulled out a handful of sovereigns that glinted in the half-light. 'Have this money. It's what I took off Tweedle. Keep it . . . or give it your mother.'

Poppy shook her head. 'No, give it back to the men who paid Tweedle. Give it to Dog Meat, if you like – you cheated him out of money, by all accounts . . .'

'Dog Meat? You heard about that?'

'Yes, I heard.'

'Is that why you won't come with me now? Because of me and Minnie?'

She giggled at the thought. 'No. It's got nothing to do with that. I've told you why.'

'I should've known from the first time that I'd never do any good with you, Poppy. You only ever turn me down.'

'I'm sorry.'

'No more than I am.' He took a step backwards. 'I'll leave

you in peace then. I might never see you again. I wish you health and happiness.'

'Thank you, Jericho. I wish you the same.'

He turned and went.

Jericho went straight to Minnie. She was gossiping with the women about what had happened that night and speculating over the likely consequences. He drew her aside, at which the other women flashed knowing glances at each other.

'Come into the tunnel with me, Minnie,' he said in a whisper.

'You've got a cheek,' Minnie responded acidly. 'First you give money to Dog Meat for me, and I was daft enough to believe you took me 'cause you liked me. Then you cheat on him by not paying him what you agreed. You'm a rat, Jericho.'

'I ain't no rat, Minnie. I really like you. I like doing it with you. I always intended to pay him, but then I thought it might put you in Queer Street with him. I was trying to protect you. He'd have known something was going on if I'd paid him money out of the blue.'

Minnie smiled too easily, forgiving him. 'Shall I get me rug then?'

'Yes,' he grinned. 'I'll go first. I'll make me way there now. You come as soon as you can.'

'There's just one thing, Jericho . . .'

'What?'

'You was prepared to pay Dog Meat to have me. Well, I resent him selling me. I work for nobody but meself. From now on, you'll have to pay me.'

'Pay you?'

'If you want me, you'll have to pay me.'

'How much?'

'Well . . . you was prepared to pay a pound a ticket for Poppy, I suppose. I reckon I must be worth ten shillings.'

'That's ridiculous,' said Jericho. 'I'll give you a shilling.'

She turned to go.

'One and a tanner then?'

'Five shillings,' she said.

'Two.'

'Three.'

'Two and a tanner.'

'All right,' agreed Minnie, with a sparkle in her eye. 'Two and a tanner. But I want the money now. Afore we start.'

Chapter 16

Poppy Silk woke up frowsy-eyed and blinked at the soft, hazy light encroaching into the spartan bedroom through grimy panes. In a flutter of anxiety, she turned her head to see who was lying beside her, having experienced a vivid, disturbing dream. She sighed with relief. Only her mother was at her side. Well, thank the Lord. It had been just a dream and she was safe. Poppy had decided to share her mother's bed after Tweedle Beak had sloped off; Buttercup, although he had promised to protect Sheba and her children, had chosen to remain in the lodgers' dormitory . . . for the time being, at any rate.

Sheba opened her eyes, roused by Poppy's nervous fidgeting.

'You're awake, our Poppy. Are you getting up?'

Poppy stretched, her slender arms poking out of flannelette sleeves and thrust out over the bedclothes. 'I'll light the fire.' She pushed back the blankets and swung her pale legs out, but remained sitting on the edge of the bed.

'I had a vile dream, Mom.'

'Oh?' She sat up and puffed up the lumpy pillow behind her.

'I'd jumped the broomstick with Dog Meat, and Minnie came chasing after me with the same broom I'd jumped over, except that it had grown to twice the size. Then we was bundled into bed by everybody . . . with Minnie and Jericho laughing their heads off and watching. Dog Meat was horrible as well. I couldn't stand him kissing me. His breath stunk horrible.'

Sheba chuckled. 'Well, you don't have to kiss him. It was only a dream.'

'But it could have been real – if Buttercup hadn't stepped in . . .'

'Thank God for Buttercup . . .' Sheba mused.

They were silent for a second or two, contemplating the happenings of last night in the light of the fresh perspectives that a decent night's sleep affords. Poppy was first to resume the conversation.

'I meant what I said last night, Mom – I love you all, but I can't go on tramp with you and Buttercup.'

Sheba pushed away the bedclothes and began picking at a fragment of loose skin around her bunion. 'You're a grown woman now, our Poppy. You have your own life to lead, and I won't stand in your way if you want to get out of this rut we're all in. So what d'you intend doing?'

'I just don't belong here,' Poppy said, combing her fingers through her tangle of yellow hair. 'I don't belong on any navvy encampment. I've always felt it, for as long as I can remember. I want to find work in service. I want to see how other folk live in their big red-brick houses. I want to sleep in clean sheets, work in clean clothes. I want to live in a warm house, and polish fine furniture and silverware. I want to be where there's spotless clean floors with no filthy mud, where smelly men don't swear and spit all the time, where there's a lock on the privy and I can have a pee and that without having to keep my foot pressed against the door. I wouldn't mind washing dishes, turning a mangle and pegging somebody else's washing out. It'd be luxury compared to this.'

'So when will you go?'

'Today. I might as well. I've got that money Buttercup gave me . . . But I still think it ought to go back to them as paid Tweedle.'

'Keep it, our Poppy. That's my advice. If they was prepared to hand over money to win you, when you was supposed to suffer the consequences and have no say in the matter, then they don't deserve any money. They're as bad as Tweedle Beak. They're all thieves and liars anyway, as likely to pinch off their own grandmothers as off anybody. Like Buttercup says, everybody will think Tweedle's sloped off with the money anyway. If you intend making a new life for yourself, that money will come in useful.'

Poppy smiled. 'Yes, it'll come in useful all right.' She stood up and the hem of her nightdress fell around her calves. In her bare feet she padded out into the main room and lit the fire as usual.

Poppy left the hut for the last time that same dinner time. She kissed her mother, her two sisters and two brothers a tearful goodbye, and went to say farewell to Minnie.

'Where are you going?' Minnie asked, with a sudden avid interest.

'I'm off to make me own way in the world.' Poppy smiled bravely. 'I've had enough of the navvy life. And now that me mother and the kids are going on tramp with Buttercup, I thought it was as good a chance as any to get away.'

'What will you do, Poppy?'

'I'll try for work in service.' She shrugged. 'It might be a risk, but it's a risk I want to take.'

'I'm coming with you.'

Poppy's eyes sparkled with affection for her friend. 'Honest? You want to come? What will your mother and father say?'

'Good riddance, I wouldn't be surprised. Who cares? Hang on. I'll just get me things and say ta-ra to 'em.'

While Poppy waited for Minnie she pondered that at best it might be a long, long time before she ever saw her family again, perhaps years; at worst, never. Yet life was like that. Nothing was ever certain. Her father had gone away, forced to do so by circumstances, and all she had of him now were her memories. Robert Crawford had gone, and while he said he would be back, it did not necessarily mean that she would see him again either. But she was surviving, despite these enormous emotional setbacks. It was painful to think of losing her father and Robert, and in such short order, but she would come through it. It was amazing how other events occurred to occupy your mind and keep you from pining for all those absent folk you loved so well. Well, so it would doubtless always be. Life went on . . .

'I'm ready,' Minnie said, as she closed the door of the shanty they called Hawthorn Villa for the last time, carrying a bundle wrapped in a pillowcase. 'Where shall we go?'

'Into Dudley,' Poppy said, as if there could be any question about it. 'Have you got some money? We'll have to find somewhere to sleep tonight.'

'I got two and six.' Minnie looked at Poppy with an expression first of sheepishness and then triumph. 'I went with Jericho again last night and I made him pay me.'

'Minnie! You never.'

'It was lovely enough, without being paid for it as well.' She giggled as she recalled it.

'Minnie, you're the limit.'

They walked on, speculating on when they might next see their families, and on what they might expect from the great big burgeoning world into which they were about to launch themselves.

The clock on St Thomas's church struck three.

'Let's look in the shops, Minnie,' Poppy said as they walked down Dudley's Georgian high street. 'Buttercup gave me some money. I think I'll buy me some new clothes. I can't stand these I'm wearing any longer. I feel like a navvy's wench in them. I'm determined to get rid of all traces. Lord knows what I must look like to other folk.'

They walked past elegant dwellings with their porticoes and mullioned windows, past alehouses and hardware shops, haberdashers, milliners, a barbershop. As usual among the shoppers, there was a contingency of drunks stumbling from one tavern to another. A street hawker passed them coming in the opposite direction pushing a handcart. He was selling candles and the two girls avoided him. Horses clopped over the cobblestones, and the wheels of the vehicles they hauled rattled as they rolled over the uneven surface. Near the town hall Poppy and Minnie tarried outside a ladies' outfitters, gazing at the tempting display in the window. Eager to see what else was on offer, Poppy pulled Minnie inside.

'Can I help you?' a young woman asked hesitantly, inhibited by their rough appearance.

Poppy guessed the girl was about eighteen or nineteen. She had a pleasant face with large eyes, and was wearing a plum-coloured muslin skirt flounced and edged with embroidery, and a blouse to match.

'I'm looking for something like what you'm wearing,' Poppy said brightly.

'I can have something made for you, miss. It could be ready in about a week. Would you like me to take your measurements?'

'Ain't you got something I can wear now?'

'Only second-hand, I'm afraid.'

'Can I see?'

The girl eyed Poppy up and down estimating her size, then turned to a rack of clothes. She rummaged through it, hesitating at an indigo garment before moving on to another.

'That blue one,' Poppy said. 'Can I see it?'

'I thought about that, but I thought it too old for you, miss. But try it on if you like. It's about your size, I think.' She took it from the rail and held it in front of herself for Poppy to inspect.

'It's a lot nicer than the one I'm wearing. Can I try it on?'

'Yes. You can change through there . . .' The girl pointed to a door.

Both Poppy and Minnie entered the musty changing room and Poppy slipped off her red flannel frock, of which she had become very self-conscious. She saw too how shabby her shift looked in the long mirror before her. She slipped the blue dress on and noticed that it had an underskirt sewn in at the waist. When she had adjusted the fall to her satisfaction, Minnie fastened the eyelets at the back of the bodice. Poppy looked at herself in the mirror, and turned sideways to gain a view of the dress in profile. It all fitted perfectly, emphasising her narrow waist and pert bosom. She smiled with pleasure and, without hesitation, left the changing room and went back to the assistant, with Minnie in tow.

'It fits perfect, look.'

The girl inspected it, rearranging the fall of the skirt and its flounces. 'It fits you very well, miss,' she said sincerely. 'And you carry it off nicely . . . But then you have that sort of face and figure.'

'What sort of face and figure d'you mean?'

'Well . . .' The assistant smiled reservedly. 'I think you could wear anything and look right in it. Some girls can. I envy you.'

Poppy smiled at the compliment. 'How much is it?'

'Half a guinea.'

'I'll give you eight shillings.'

The girl shook her head. 'I daren't, miss. I'd get the sack.'

'Nine and six, then. Or I'll go somewhere else.'

'All right . . . But even at half a guinea it would be a very prudent purchase, miss. It would have cost seventeen shillings and sixpence new. And it looks so well on you.'

'I'll take it,' Poppy said. 'But I need some other things as well.'

'Oh? Whatever help I can give . . .' The girl smiled more confidently now.

Poppy, still conscious of her origins, said, 'I need a new shift, chemise, stockings, garters . . . Oh, and a mantle for the winter. Our fathers were navvies, and we've just left the railway encampment at Blowers Green.' She felt sure that an explanation was appropriate. 'It's closing down and we've decided we want to make our own way in the world. So we need to look neat and tidy if anybody's going to give us work. If you've got any tips you can give us on what to wear for the best, miss, we'd be glad of 'em.'

'Of course. I'd be only too pleased.' The girl smiled amenably now. These were not only down-to-earth girls and sociable, but they even looked up to her, a mere shop girl. There was also a shilling or two to be made here.

'And when you've done me, Minnie wants new clothes as well.'

'But I've only got two and sixpence, Poppy,' she protested.

'Oh, don't worry, Minnie. I've got enough for both of us.'

* * *

243

'You didn't have to buy me a whole new wardrobe, Poppy,' Minnie said, as they left the shop feeling like real ladies, having decided to wear their new purchases. 'How much did you spend?'

'Less than four pounds. I told you, Buttercup gave me some money before I left. What use is it unless you spend it?'

'I don't know how to thank you, Poppy . . .'

'You're my friend, Minnie. You'd do the same for me. Anyway, I might want a favour myself some day. And that frock looks like it was made for you.'

'And yours. It matches your eyes beautiful.'

They walked on, carrying their old clothes in bags the shop girl had supplied.

'Did you notice that girl's hair, Minnie?' Poppy asked.

'Course.'

'I'd like mine done like that, pinned up all neat and tidy. I'll try and do it later, when we've found somewhere to sleep tonight.'

'Where are we gunna sleep, Poppy?'

'An inn, I reckon, eh? Then we can look for cheaper lodgings that'll do us till we find work.'

Poppy and Minnie found a room at the Old Bush Inn in the middle of Dudley town, about a hundred yards from the old town hall. The landlord was reticent about letting them have it at first. He looked at them suspiciously, for he could not quite place them in the social scale, and asked them why girls so young wished to take such a room when they were clearly unchaperoned. But, when he saw Poppy's money and took a deposit, he was left in no doubt of her ability and willingness to pay. He warned them that they must not have men in their room; he would not tolerate that sort of thing going on. His was a respectable coaching house and he had to maintain its reputation, with respectable visitors from London and other faraway places coming and going all the time.

Poppy nudged Minnie and grinned at the absolute novelty of being shown to their room by a serving maid, however untidy. Her hair was awry under her mob cap, and her finger-nails still showed signs of a visit to the coal cellar. At the top of the stairs, she unlocked a door and allowed the young guests to enter.

'This is yer room. I hope you'll be comfitubble.'

'Thank you,' Poppy said with an indulgent smile, enjoying the novelty of feeling sublimely superior and ladylike in her new blue outfit and stockings and the fashionable boots Robert Crawford had bought her.

'I'll be back in a bit to light yer a fire. It goes chilly this side o' th'ouse.'

'Thank you,' Poppy said again, unfastening the ribbons of her new bonnet.

After the maid had lit the promised fire, the girls settled in, giggling and pampering themselves, all too aware that for the time being they were free from the drudgery of work. Poppy placed a chair in front of the window and peered onto the heads and hats of passers-by in the street below, while Minnie dressed her hair for her, in an effort to copy the shop girl's style. A coach halted outside and there were calls from the driver and the ostler as passengers disembarked and its cargo of luggage was unloaded. A horse whinnied, a cart clattered past. There was so much going on down there, noise and an endless movement of people and traffic.

'Did you notice the maid?' Poppy said. 'She must've thought us proper ladies in our new clothes.'

Minnie chuckled delightedly. 'I know. I thought that. It's nice to be looked on as somebody important, in't it?'

'For once.'

'What shall we do tonight, Poppy?'

Poppy shrugged. 'We could go for a walk in the town and show off our new clothes.'

'Yes,' Minnie replied with enthusiasm. 'Who knows? We might even meet a couple of dandies.'

'You've got men on the brain, Minnie. Am I done yet?'

'Just about.' Minnie patted Poppy's hair a last time. 'Turn your head. Let's have a look . . . Yikes! Now you really do look a somebody . . .'

'Let me see.' Poppy stood up and walked across the room to the wardrobe that had a long mirror on one door. She looked at herself, turning her head this way and that to view the creation from all angles. The set of her head looked different with her hair up. There was an elegance about her that she did not realise she possessed, and it delighted her. 'I'll have to make sure my neck's clean in future, Minnie,' she giggled.

Minnie laughed too. 'Not just your neck. Ladies have a bath regular, I bet. I never bin in a bath in me life.'

Poppy pinched her cheeks and bit her lips to redden them. 'Oh, I don't see as you need to go in a bath if you have a good wash down regular.'

'Well, we can have a good wash down here all right, with no navvies to come a-spying . . . So you like your hair then?'

'I love it,' Poppy replied. She turned away from the mirror. 'I'll do yours now, shall I, Minnie?'

'I doubt if it'll look as good as yours.'

'Are you saying I won't be as good as you at this hair-doing lark?'

Minnie chuckled happily. 'I mean my hair, not your fiddling with it . . .' She sighed contentedly. 'You know, I'd love a cup of tea, Poppy. Shall we ask that scruffy little wench to bring us a pot? I'll pay . . .'

*   *   *

Dudley Town Hall was a looming two-storey affair built of brick and stone. The civic business of the Town Commissioners was conducted in the rooms on the upper floor, where tall, rectangular, Tudor-style windows afforded views towards St Thomas's church at the top end of the town, and the old St Edmund's, dwarfed by the castle, at the bottom. It was crowned by a small tower, from which tolled the original bell, taken from the Old Priory, when the marking of civic occasions and calamities was required. The lower part of the building was open to the elements, being nothing more than a series of arches that supported the upper floor. It provided accommodation for traders who set up stalls there on market days and shelter from the rain for everybody else.

It was providing shelter that Saturday evening for a miscellany of folk, including Poppy and Minnie, who had been taking their stroll when the rain came down, threatening to spoil their new clothes and bonnets.

Minnie tapped her foot impatiently on the stone flags beneath her feet, gazing with longing at The Seven Stars Inn across the road in High Street. 'That's where Tom and that Luke have a drink.' She nodded her head in its direction. 'We ought to go over when it's stopped raining and see if they'm in there.'

'I doubt if they'd recognise us now,' Poppy answered indifferently. 'Anyway, I don't want to see Luke. He's got black teeth. Nor should you want to see Tom.'

'I like Tom,' Minnie asserted. 'I'd like him to see me in me new outfit.'

'Anyway, I doubt if you'd find respectable girls going into a public house without a man to go in with.'

The rain started to ease and many of the people sheltering left and made a dash for it. Minnie walked over to the high wrought-iron railing set in one of the arches and, with her face pressed between two bars, peered through optimistically. A black clarence was being driven past just then, and Minnie caught sight of a middle-aged man looking at her from within. At once he hailed the driver to stop and opened the door. He opened the door, leaned out and beckoned. Minnie glanced at Poppy to see if she had noticed the exchange, but she evidently had not. The man beckoned again and Minnie went towards him, alerting Poppy to this unexpected arrival.

'What d'you want?' Minnie asked, smiling with curiosity.

'What do you do?' came the reply.

'What do I do?' Minnie queried. 'I think you mean how do you do.'

The man grinned. 'I know what I mean, young miss. I ain't seen you around here before. What's your name?'

'Minnie. What's yours?'

'Minnie!' he repeated, ignoring her question. 'A pretty name. But then, you're a very pretty girl. Are you going to come with me? Out of the rain?'

'Where to?'

'Well, we don't have to go anywhere special. I have a couple of bottles of champagne right here. You look the sort of girl who might appreciate champagne.'

'What's he on about?' Poppy asked, on hearing the exchange.

'He's got summat he calls champagne,' Minnie whispered out of the side of her mouth. 'It's a drink o' some sort, in't it?'

'Is it?'

'He wants me to go with him.' Minnie turned to the man in the clarence. 'I got me friend wi' me. Can she come as well?'

'The more the merrier. What's she like? Is she as pretty as you?'

'Here she is . . . Show yourself, Poppy. The gentleman wants to see you.'

Poppy stepped forward and stood by Minnie.

'God's truth, she's a dazzler. I'll give you a shilling each if you'll come with me.'

Polly tugged at Minnie's sleeve with the intention of pulling her away. 'He thinks we're street wenches, Min,' she warned in a hoarse whisper. 'Come away from him.'

'He's a toff, Poppy,' Minnie hissed impatiently. 'Come on, we can get blathered and it won't cost we a penny.'

'I don't want to get blathered.'

'Oh, Poppy . . . You never want to do anything. You'm never no fun. Come on. You'm coming with me for once.' Minnie took Poppy's arm and coaxed her along to the clarence.

The man smiled and pushed the door wide open for them to enter, then took their hands in turn as he helped them up the iron steps of the carriage.

'So you are Minnie. So, who is your friend?'

'Poppy,' Minnie answered, settling herself on the plush leather seat, facing the man.

'Minnie and Poppy. Well . . . How come I've never seen either of you two little beauties before?'

'Because we don't come up the town regular,' Poppy replied. 'We're not street wenches.'

'I'm very relieved to hear it. So . . . let's take a little ride out into the countryside and open that bottle of whisky.' He tapped the roof of the carriage with his cane and they lurched forwards.

'I thought you said champagne.'

'Did I say that? Slip of the tongue.'

'Where are you taking us?' Poppy enquired. 'I don't think I want to go to the countryside.'

'Oh, it's not far. Don't worry, Poppy, a little trip to the Oakham Fields will only take us ten minutes at a trot.'

They did a circuit of the town hall and turned into a narrow road called Hall Street. There was just enough width to drive a carriage through, but folk walking the street had to press themselves against the windows of the shops and public houses that lined both sides to prevent the wheels splashing them in the gutter. Poppy was inclined to ask that they drop her off, but she could not forsake Minnie alone with this stranger, however respectable he seemed. Minnie had to be protected, if only from herself. They drove on, leaving the huddle of Hall Street behind, and pressed on to where the road became wider at Waddams Pool. It was uphill here and the driver allowed the horse to haul the clarence at its own lumbering pace. The rows of shops and little houses petered out and Poppy could see open fields and a flat stretch of road, where the horse then broke into a trot.

They passed a magnificent house set in its own grounds . . . then another . . . and another . . . For a few moments Poppy was oblivious to the banter already going on between Minnie and this well-dressed man, lost in her own dream world. She was a conscientious maid, dressed in a clean, crisp uniform, employed in one of these fine houses. Of course, she could not have known that one of these fine houses, the one she especially liked the look of, was the home of Robert Crawford.

They stopped briefly at a toll gate, then pressed on. The horse slowed to a rolling walk once more as it pulled them up Oakham Road's steady incline. Here it was a grotto over-hung with trees, and the drops of rain dripping off the leaves was like gravel falling on the carriage's roof. Fields, bare and harvested, lay on both sides, with only the occasional fine house now. The driver seemed to know where he was going, and climbed down from his box to open a gate to a field that lay behind a tall hedge, well hidden from the road. Poppy looked at the middle-aged man uncertainly and, as the driver put on the brake, it struck her that this opening of the gate and entering the field was done with the practised slickness that regularity affords. To her surprise, the driver took off his cloak, shook the water off it and entered the carriage.

'So, who have we here, Alfred?'

'Minnie and Poppy. Lovely little popsies too, don't you think? Minnie and I seem to have a rapport already, James. If you have no objection I'll stick with her. We can always swap later. Come and sit by me, Minnie . . .'

James regarded Poppy with a lascivious interest, looking her up and down. 'Oh, I think this one'll do me fine.' He leered at her. 'Come here, my flower, and sit close to me. Let me get the feel of you.'

Poppy obstinately remained where she was while Minnie compliantly crossed to the opposite seat and shuffled close to Alfred with an expectant smile.

'How old are you, little popsy?' James enquired.

'Sixteen. How old are you?' There was scorn in her voice.

He laughed, but there was no mirth in it. 'It's of no consequence, little popsy. I'm the one paying the money, so I'll ask the questions.'

'You're old enough to be my dad.'

'He might be your dad,' Alfred quipped. 'Here, James . . .' He handed him the bottle of whisky. 'I do believe yours needs a slug or two of this to loosen her up.'

James took the bottle, uncorked it and offered it to Poppy. She turned her face away sullenly.

'Have some whisky, little popsy . . . No? I bet your friend would like some.'

He handed the bottle to Minnie who took a slug as if she had been drinking the stuff regularly for years, then offered it to Poppy once more.

'Go on, Poppy,' she urged, wiping her lips. 'Have a drop. A drop won't hurt you.'

Poppy shook her head with defiance and Minnie thought she detected a shudder of fear in her friend.

'She don't drink,' she said in her defence.

'Does she screw?'

'No, I do not,' Poppy shrieked and reached for the door handle, burning with indignation.

James caught her arm and yanked her back, pulling her against him. 'Then I think it's time you did, little popsy.' He reached down and took a handful of skirt and petticoat, which he pulled up, exposing her legs. 'Well, you've got a fine pair of legs, little popsy. I can't wait to get between 'em.'

He raised his knee and thrust it between hers, at the same time pinning her down on the seat while she struggled to free herself. He fingered the buttons of his fly.

'You're hurting me!' she screamed. 'Don't you *dare* touch me.'

'Easy, easy,' James said in a calm, soothing voice, a grin on his thin face. 'It's so much better if you don't struggle. For both of us. You'll get your money afterwards. I'm not going to hurt you. Besides, if I like you, I shall see you again. That's the way it should be. Not this senseless resistance. You could do well out of me if you play the game . . .'

Poppy had not lived on a navvy encampment most of her life without picking up a few tips in self-defence. She clenched her tiny fist and whacked James on the temple. As he reeled from the unexpected clout, she brought her knee up hard and rammed it, with all the velocity she could muster, into his testicles. He winced with pain, clutching his crotch, unable to catch his breath to utter any curse. Poppy took the opportunity to grab hold of the door handle and shove the door open. Disentangling herself completely, while the others watched stupefied, she leapt down from the carriage, stepped into a pool of mud and ran towards the gate in the pouring rain.

Chapter 17

As she fled down Oakham Road, Poppy kept looking anxiously behind her to see whether James was following, with or without his friend to aid him or the carriage to expedite him. It was dark now and she looked continually for places to hide if need be. She searched for lights, for signs of habitation, but there were only dark fields and ragged hedges, spooky with the sound of cows lowing in the distance at the miserable weather. She had no idea how far they had travelled from the town. The journey had seemed like ages. Nor had she any notion of the time, but it could surely not be late.

She felt guilty at leaving Minnie at the mercy of the two men. But Minnie had shown no sign of fear, only eager anticipation at what must inevitably come to pass. Why was there such a difference between them when it came to men and what you could be getting up to with them? It was as if Minnie could not help herself. Poppy wondered whether there was something lacking in herself, since she patently did not feel the same. She would happily give herself for love, but she would never sell herself. She would have willingly, eagerly, lain with Robert Crawford if he'd asked her to. Tonight he would have been proud of her, applauded the way she halted that rat James with a deft knee into his privates.

Thoughts of Robert stirred up again the familiar ache of

longing. So acutely did she yearn for him, especially now when she needed him. Without him she was a flower without sunshine, a wilderness without rain. Damned rain . . . She pulled up the collar of her mantle and adjusted her bonnet. Thank goodness for the mantle. At least it would protect her lovely blue dress. She hurried on in the darkness, picking her way through puddles and mud, holding her skirt up a little to protect it from the splashes her scurrying feet kicked up. There was no footpath on either side of this lane, only the rough, uneven track lined with shepherd's purse, thistles, nettles and blackberry brambles all weeping and soggy and snagging on her skirt if she passed too close. At a bend in the lane, a dead tree loomed, its bare gnarled branches dripping black against the sky, poised unstirring, like some gothic spectre determined to leap out and grab her. Poppy shuddered and quickened her pace, unaware that this was a hangman's tree, used in times past as a gallows to hang felons. Next to it stood a cottage, dilapidated but still inhabited, according to the waft of smoke that curled sparsely from the leaning chimney. It did not look welcoming.

As she rounded the bend, the lane descended and she could just discern its lie, which was straight for as far distant as she could determine through the dim tunnel of trees. The lights from a house flickered with a feeble warmth some distance away. If she heard the rumble of the carriage now she could always run, hammer on the door and ask for protection until they had gone past. Somebody would surely shelter her.

That Alfred . . . He must be married. She would bet any money on it. A married menace. James too. No doubt, they had sons and daughters of a similar age to herself. And yet Minnie was all too ready to go with them. No reluctance, no apprehension, no aversion, no fear. It was hardly bravery. Rather, it was stupidity, naivety. And yet Poppy felt little anxiety over her friend. Whatever else she was, Minnie was artful, knowing and confident with men . . . She knew how to take care of herself. No doubt they would all be swigging whisky now, laughing at Poppy's dissent and reluctance to engage in whatever shameless antics Minnie was content to go along with. Well, if Minnie wanted to be like that, it was up to her.

Poppy hastened on, listening for the sound of the carriage and the horse's hoofs. All was quiet. She was quite alone. The only sound was the squelch of her own footsteps on the sopping ground. *Follow this lane* . . . She hoped nobody else was abroad to induce her heart to leap into her throat.

After hurrying for about ten minutes she came to a sort of crossroads where the toll gate stood. Signs of life. She tried to remember from which direction they had come in the carriage. Facing her was a squalid-looking alehouse with a crooked railing in front of it. She recalled seeing it when she had travelled, uneasy but dry, in the carriage. Of course she must take the road to the right. What if she took the wrong turning and found her way back to the Blowers Green encampment? No, that would never do. Everybody would think she was incapable of making the break. She would never go back. Not now she had come this far.

That big house again on the right-hand side . . . the one she had noticed during the drive . . . Such an imposing place, set well back from the road as it was, with a sweeping in and out drive. It was well lit inside, if the light spilling from the windows was anything to go by. At each side of the front door lamps burned, throwing a dancing yellow light onto a pair of horses and a black carriage that glistened with wetness. The front door opened . . . Poppy hesitated, curious. She watched a young woman step out wearing a dark mantle and bonnet. It was difficult to ascertain her age in this light, or what she looked like, but she was probably about twenty years of age, judging from her bearing. With audible farewells, the girl waved goodbye to the middle-aged couple who remained inside, while a footman opened the door to the carriage. Poppy watched as the girl stepped up into it and the footman closed the door. Then, as it was driven round the circular drive towards the front gate, she turned so as not to be seen and went on her way.

Such an elegant life some girls lived . . .

Poppy found her way back to Dudley town. She decided to walk in the middle of the road where she could be seen, with less chance of being accosted by drunken youths, and eventually returned to The Old Bush Inn soaked through, a little wiser, but none the worse for her adventure.

She found a maid and asked for a candle to light her way to her room. There, she undressed and put her new clothes to dry over the back of a chair, which she placed in front of the fire. She unpinned her hair, brushed it and put on her nightdress. Then she took the candle, along with the book Robert Crawford had given her, and continued reading from where she had left off a few days ago. If only he were still here she could ask him what some of these long words meant that were so difficult to build up. But she could read more fluently now, as Robert promised she would.

Reading, she fell asleep . . .

She had no idea what time she was awakened, but the candle had burned down a couple of inches. Minnie was taking off her dress in front of the fire, casting large, swooping shadows on the opposite wall.

'Minnie . . . You're back. Are you all right? What happened? I'm sorry I left you like that, but I was frit to death of what that man was going to do to me.'

'Who, James? Oh, he was all right.'

'So what happened after I'd gone? I thought they might come after me.'

'You kneed him in the taters good and proper.' Minnie laughed as she recalled it. 'He couldn't move for ages, cursing after you he was. By the time he could move, he'd decided he wasn't gunna waste his time and money on somebody what wasn't interested. So we drank that bottle of whisky between us . . .'

'And then what?'

'I made another two shillings out of 'em.' Minnie chuckled contentedly. 'Both of 'em. Honest, Poppy, this doing it for money is a lark. I'll be rich in no time. Men are such fools – dead keen to part with their money for a quick poke.'

Poppy sat up. 'But you're not going to do it regular, are you, Min?' she asked apprehensively, concerned more for her friend's morals than for her safety.

'It's easy money, Poppy. You should think about doing it as well. We could make a fortune on the game, you and me. There's plenty of men about daft enough to pay. And you know me, Poppy . . . I love it anyway . . .'

'You'll catch something, Minnie, I swear. If not a baby, then something you *can't* get rid of.'

Minnie shrugged. 'It's a chance you take. If I *do* catch anything it won't kill me. Not right away any road. I'll have had me fun by the time it does.'

'Well, I want something better out of life,' Poppy declared. 'I don't want to go flitting from one man to another. What if they knock you about?'

'I'd hit 'em back.'

'It's your concern, Minnie . . .' Poppy lay back on the plump pillow again and sighed. 'Night-night, I'm going to sleep now. I'm glad you're back all right.'

Poppy was dozing when Minnie slipped into bed beside her.

'Are you still awake, Poppy?'

'No.'

'I've bin thinking. If I'm gunna go on the game regular I'd better find me some lodgings. Somewhere I can take men back to. Shall you want to come with me?'

'To look at lodgings, you mean, or to live with you?'

'Both.'

'I'll *look* at lodging houses with you, if you want, but you'll need money to pay rent in advance. That's the way landlords work.'

'Oh, I'll soon get money, Poppy. Believe me.'

On the Monday morning, Poppy and Minnie went to look at a back-to-back house Minnie had been told about. It was in Gatehouse Fold, a development of terraces which had been built for the influx of workers from the countryside to fill the jobs in the pits and ironworks. A miserable huddle of dwellings, it lay physically, but by no means spiritually, close to the church of St Edmund. A channel of slurry, that stunk like the open sewer it was, bisected a squalid courtyard. Poverty-stricken garb fluttered faded and dingy in the chill October breeze, strung out across a propped line that spanned the fold. Barefoot children with running noses and faces as dirty as their feet played, oblivious to the squalor, while others skulked, blatantly scheming. Poppy shuddered. It was no better, and in some ways worse, than the Blowers Green encampment.

It had been arranged that the landlord's agent should meet them there, a weasel of a man with unkempt curls strategically trained to cover his balding pate. Inside, the only downstairs room was bare. The unplastered walls needed a fresh coat of whitewash and the quarry-tiled floor needed a scrub. Several windowpanes were cracked. A door next to the fire grate led upstairs via a steep, narrow staircase. In the solitary bedroom the floorboards needed a sweep and a coat of woodstain, and the windows a clean. Cobwebs hung in tacky threads from the ceiling, and Poppy noticed a pair of woodlice sneaking into a crack under the window frame.

'All we need is a mattress to sleep on,' Minnie said, undaunted. 'A mattress shouldn't cost much.'

'What about furniture downstairs?' Poppy prompted. 'A table, a couple of chairs, a settle . . .'

They descended the stairs. Poppy noticed another door and asked where it led.

'To the cellar,' the landlord's agent informed them.

'It's not much of a place, is it?' Poppy said, unimpressed.

'What do you expect for the money? Buckingham Palace?'

'I don't mind it,' Minnie proclaimed. 'It's handy for the town . . . And as it's me what'll be paying the rent, I'm the one to decide. I'll take it, mister.'

'Three months' rent in advance, if you please.'

'Three months? Lord! How much is that?'

'Nineteen shillings and sixpence.'

Minnie looked at Poppy beseechingly. 'Poppy, I ain't got that much on me . . . Can you lend it me? I'll pay you back as soon as I can.'

Poppy looked around the walls with distaste. 'Are you sure you want this place?'

'Yes. Like I said, it's handy for me work. Anyway, it's a start. I can always get somewhere better later.'

'All right, Minnie, I'll lend you the money.' Poppy fished out of her pocket the small soft leather bag that Buttercup had handed to her and counted out nineteen shillings and sixpence into the man's hand. 'Can I have a receipt or something, please? To say you've had the money.'

The man smiled. 'That, you can, miss.' As he wrote it out, she said, 'How soon can she move in here?'

'The place is vacant. She can move in today.'

Minnie grinned with pleasure. 'Oh, Poppy, we'll have to go and buy a mattress straight way.'

The man left them with a key and went on his way.

'There's tons of things we'll need,' Minnie said, looking around her with pride at this dubious acquisition. 'We'll need bedclothes, candles, pots to cook in, cups to drink out of, plates to eat off, curtains up at the windows, as well as new furniture. We'd better go to the shops.'

Poppy nodded, but without enthusiasm. It was curious how Minnie had already assumed that Poppy was going to share the house, when Poppy herself was reticent. Certainly, it would mean that Poppy would be paying for everything, since she was the one with the money.

'Let me make one thing plain, Minnie,' she said, in an effort to set the record straight. 'This is your house and you're the tenant. I'll stay here with you till I find work, then I'll go. I don't mind lending you the money for things to help you get started, but you'll have to pay me back as soon as you can afford to.'

'Course,' Minnie agreed. 'I'll be able to pay you back in no time. I know I will.'

'Well, my money won't last for ever.'

The two girls walked the town for things they needed. Items that were too big to carry, such as the mattress and furniture, were to be delivered the following afternoon. The rest of the stuff, things that were easy to carry, they took themselves. They would sleep at the Old Bush that evening, settle up their bill, and move to the house in Gatehouse Fold tomorrow.

261

That night Minnie decided she was going out to ply her new trade. When she returned to the inn she recounted her experiences.

'I only had one chap,' she said, taking her bonnet off for the second time that evening. 'He said his name was Jack. He took me to this big house where you could rent a room by the hour – a bawdyhouse, I think he called it. It was lovely and warm in there, with nice furniture and velvet curtains and things. The toffs there seemed to know this Jack. We had a lovely soft feather bed and we drunk brandy together. I got ever so tiddly.'

'How much did you charge him?' Poppy asked, disapprovingly.

'Two shillings. It was a fair price, considering how quick it was all over – the first time any road . . . It just goes to show again how easy it is to make money on the game. You ought to try it, Poppy. Anyway, he wants to see me again, this Jack.'

'Minnie, I really wish you wouldn't do this whoring lark. It can only lead to trouble.'

'No. Not trouble, Poppy. The life of a lady. That's what it'll lead to. You'll see.'

The next day saw the pair move into the little house in Gatehouse Fold. Minnie trudged to the nearest coal yard and three-hundredweight was later delivered by a young man whose features were unidentifiable because of the black dust on his face. That was but a minor impediment to Minnie, who gave him sufficient encouragement to visit that same evening, cleaned up. His name was Arthur. The couple went out walking, but Poppy tactfully went upstairs to bed when they returned.

The next night, Minnie came back to the house with the same Jack who had previously taken her to the bawdyhouse but, seeing the opportunity to save himself the price of a room, suggested they use hers. Poppy was disgruntled; she had to stay downstairs looking at the burning coals in the fire grate, her chin resting in her hands, glumly listening to the grunts and antics of Minnie and this Jack as they cavorted in the bed *she* was supposed to sleep in. When he came down, Jack looked at Poppy covetously and asked what she charged. With glinting, hostile eyes, she told him he would never be able to afford her.

These events were typical of the pattern that was developing over the week, and Poppy resented it intensely. Even though she was not participating, she felt tainted and degraded by it all. She had the feeling that neighbours were looking at her disparagingly, and it was obvious to her that they imagined she was also involved in prostitution with Minnie. She just had to get away and leave Minnie to her own fate. Minnie, in her wild abandon, was already beyond redemption.

Poppy had seen no news-sheets advertising jobs, so she didn't know where to start looking for work. Oh, she could go and knock on the front doors of some of the grand houses, and even those not so grand, and enquire within if there were any situations vacant, but she feared the prospect of rejection.

Then, the following Sunday morning, while sorting through her things, she found the note that Robert Crawford had given her just before they parted, bearing the name and address of his Aunt Phoebe at Cawneybank House, Rowley Road. He'd urged her to present herself soon to this lady. That was more than six weeks ago. She peered out of the window. Gatehouse Fold was quiet for once, save for the peal of bells calling the believers to worship at St Edmund's. Well, this afternoon she would make her way to the address and introduce herself. She had little to lose and, even though she had little to gain either, it was an exercise she felt compelled to undertake, if only out of respect for Robert. It was just possible that Aunt Phoebe might know of a vacancy for a maid. In any case, she had to make contact in time for next year when Robert returned. She had to have somewhere to collect his message.

Poppy explained to Minnie what she was intent on doing. Minnie said she would walk with her. So, Poppy spruced herself up, pinned her hair up neatly and made sure her prized blue dress was presentable before they set off. At the end of Hall Street, she asked a kindly-looking woman if she knew where Rowley Road was.

It was a fair walk and Poppy found herself retracing steps. Once again she passed the fine house she'd admired on Dixons Green Road and commented to Minnie on how she'd seen a young woman get into a carriage on the night she excruciatingly quelled the ardour of that scoundrel James. This time she noticed there was an iron plaque adorning one of the stone pillars of the front gate and read it aloud: 'Tansley House'.

The woman who had given her directions told her she was to take the right fork at the toll house. After that, she should take the left one, if she didn't want to find herself among the brickyards, the clay pits and the Old Buffery Iron Works in the smoky hollow of Bumble Hole Road.

Cawneybank House was less than a quarter of a mile down Rowley Road. It looked nowhere near as grand as Tansley House, modest indeed by comparison, but it stood in its own neatly manicured grounds.

Poppy glanced at Minnie apprehensively. 'Wish me luck, Min.'

Minnie smiled her encouragement and affection. 'I wish you luck, Poppy. I'll hang around here somewhere till you come out.'

Poppy took a deep breath, summoning as much poise as she could while she wandered up the drive to the house trying to summon some confidence. She checked her mantle and her skirt, pinched her cheeks, and knocked hesitantly on the door. A maid little older than herself answered it.

'I've called to see Mrs Newton. My name is Poppy Silk.'

The girl looked at Poppy dubiously. 'Is Mrs Newton expecting you?'

Poppy shook her head. 'I doubt it. But I've got a sort of invitation . . . from her nephew, Robert Crawford . . . Here . . .' She handed the girl the note bearing the name and address.

The maid took it. 'Wait there, miss.'

She closed the door unceremoniously, and Poppy stood in front of it, perplexed and a little disgruntled at being treated so off-handedly by a mere maid. Self-consciously, she looked over her shoulder to see if Minnie was watching, but there was no sign of her. Poppy had a fine view of a range of green hills, however, beyond the pit head gear and the brickworks' chimneys that smoked profusely in the valley before her.

The door opened again.

'Mrs Newton will see you, miss. Come in.'

Poppy summoned a smile for the girl and said thank you. She was ushered through an elaborately tiled hallway with an ornate cast-iron hatstand, a grandfather clock, and a tall table bearing a plant of some sort, which Poppy did not recognise. In a small sitting room to the right, a warm and welcoming fire blazed in a pristine tiled and blackened grate set low in its hearth. The mantelpiece was adorned with strange vases and a crucifix, and a huge mirror hung over it. On the floor was a thick green carpet.

At the fireside a neatly turned out woman of middle age

sat, her hair taken back and set off with a mob cap, her bespectacled eyes curiously intent on Poppy. Phoebe Newton was plump, with a round and charitable face that exuded warmth and compassion as she stood up to greet her unexpected guest.

'So you are Miss Silk. My nephew has told me something about you.' She spoke in a kindly way, and at once Poppy was at ease. 'Please sit down, Miss Silk.' The older lady looked beyond Poppy at the maid who was hovering intrusively at her back. 'Perhaps Miss Silk would like tea. Would you be so kind, Esther?'

'Yes, ma'am.' Esther duly disappeared.

'I tremble to think what Mr Crawford has told you about me, Mrs Newton,' Poppy ventured.

'Very little, Miss Silk, yet, in a way, sufficient. He told me he had a young friend whom he had been teaching reading and writing. I gleaned, from the mere fact that my nephew mentioned you, that he must hold you in some regard, but especially so when he asked me if I would be prepared to advance your education.'

Poppy looked into the fire to avoid Mrs Newton's gaze, and smiled, thrilled at this more than adequate reference that Robert had given her.

'Evidently, he thinks you are worth it. I presume, therefore, that you have had no formal schooling.'

'None, Mrs Newton.'

'But it has been some weeks now since the request was made, and I'd more or less given up hope of you ever arriving.'

'Oh . . . There's been a lot going on, Mrs Newton . . . This is the first chance I've had. I hope it's not a funny time for you, me coming today . . . Have you heard from Robert, by the way, since he went away to work?'

'Oh, I wouldn't expect him to write to me. He has enough work to do, I'm sure . . . and enough letters to write. Do tell me how you both came to know each other.'

'Well . . . me dad was working for Treadwell's, the contractors for the section of the Oxford, Worcester and Wolverhampton Railway what runs to Dudley, what Robert was working on,' Poppy began. 'He got killed last summer in an accident . . . me dad, that is. I think Robert sort of took pity on me. Anyway, he seemed to go out of his way to be a friend to me—'

'I don't wonder at it, Miss Silk,' Mrs Newton said with a knowing smile. 'You are an exceedingly pretty girl.'

'Thank you.' Poppy smiled graciously.

'Robert did mention the death of your father. I was so sorry to learn about it. Wasn't your father a navvy?'

'A ganger.' Ganger sounded so much more elevated than navvy. 'He was in charge of a gang o' navvies.'

'Of course, we hear so many horrific tales about navvies and their antics. The newspapers are full of their criminal acts up and down the land. I can only hope such reports are exaggerated.'

'Well, they ain't all rogues and vagabonds,' Poppy replied, trying to stifle the defensive edge in her voice. 'Some have the kindest hearts . . .'

'Of that I'm sure. To my mind, there are good and bad in all walks of life . . .' She adjusted the lie of her spectacles. 'You were telling me how you got to know my nephew. How did your friendship progress?'

'Oh, yes . . . Well . . . we used to stop and talk a lot, Robert and me. We would bump into each other as I went to the tommy shop and he went about his business. Once, he took me for a ride on that two-wheeled machine he'd made.' Poppy laughed as she recalled it.

'That infernal hobby horse . . .' Mrs Newton rolled her eyes good-naturedly.

'Oh, but it was a lot o' fun, Mrs Newton. We seemed to have fun together whenever we met, Robert and me.'

'I take it you met unchaperoned?'

'Well, yes, but—'

'You realise, of course, that he is engaged to be married?'

'Yes, I do know . . .' Poppy felt reprimanded. Maybe she had said too much, appeared too enthusiastic about her meetings with Robert.

'So how old are you, Miss Silk?'

'Sixteen. I'll be seventeen next April.'

'A lovely age, to my mind . . . So tell me – are you keen to resume your learning?'

'Yes. If you have time, Mrs Newton. Depending on how much you charge.'

'Oh, I don't intend to charge, Miss Silk. The privilege would be mine. I used to be a teacher, as Robert must have told you. I continued to teach long after Mr Newton and I were married. I didn't need to, of course, and Mr Newton would have preferred it if I hadn't. But I wanted to. I felt I was doing some good. Regrettably, my husband died four years ago. He owned a metalworking company, you know, which has prospered over the years. It fell to me to maintain the business. It's still functioning, run by a manager now. I have no family – children, I mean – much to my regret. It was always my dearest wish that I would have a daughter, but it was not to be. I tended to regard my pupils as my children . . .' Poppy detected a wistful look in Aunt Phoebe's eyes. 'So . . . as you can imagine, Miss Silk, nowadays I have plenty of time on my hands. I rather miss teaching. I enjoyed it, and I was rather good at it, although I say so myself.'

'I can imagine you was,' Poppy said with a smile.

'My nephew did tell me that you are a very quick learner. He said you have *"limitless potential"*. His very words. He felt it would be a great sacrifice if your abilities were never developed. Praise indeed, you know, Miss Silk.'

They heard the chink of crockery on a tray and the click of footsteps on the hall floor. The maid tapped on the door, and Mrs Newton bade her enter. Esther gently laid the tray on the occasional table that stood between host and guest.

'Thank you, Esther, I'll pour . . . Milk and sugar, Miss Silk?'

'Please . . .'

When the maid left them, Mrs Newton said, as she poured the tea, 'So tell me, my dear, when will it be convenient for you to come for lessons?'

'The way things am at the moment, I could come any time. But I intend to find work in service as soon as I can. Work on the railway has been stopped till they sort out all the problems, you see. So me family have moved on, and I left them so as I could make me own way in the world. I want to earn me a decent, honest living, Mrs Newton . . . I don't want to end up a street wench if I can help it . . .' She said it as though prostitution were the most natural progression. 'So me intention was to ask you if you knew anybody what needed a maid. I'm a good worker. I can do most things.'

'I didn't realise,' Mrs Newton said pensively as she handed Poppy a cup and saucer.

'Thank you, Mrs Newton . . .'

'So if you've already left the bosom of your family, where are you living?'

'At a place called Gatehouse Fold . . . with me friend who just rented a house there. It's not the best place for a young woman trying to make her way decently in the world.'

A look of apprehension clouded the older woman's face. 'I take it you are not living with a man.'

'Oh, no, Mrs Newton. With Minnie Catchpole. We've known each other years.'

'Gatehouse Fold . . .' Mrs Newton ruminated earnestly over the name. 'Yes, I recall . . . Gatehouse Fold is certainly not an ideal place for any decent young woman. It's surrounded by some awful public houses. Dens of iniquity.'

'There's nothing I can do about it till I find a job as a live-in maid, Mrs Newton.' Poppy shuffled self-consciously and spilled some tea into her saucer, which she tipped back into her cup.

Mrs Newton suffered the impropriety and smiled tolerantly. 'May I be frank with you, Miss Silk?'

'Oh, yes, o' course. I always think it's better to be honest, and say what you think.'

'Well, when my nephew mentioned you I did not know what to expect. When he said he had met you on the navvies' encampment, I was horrified at whom he might be associating with. However, I feel bound to say you are not in the least what I expected. I see before me an intelligent girl, polite, decently dressed. In all honesty – and you must not take offence at this – I see some rough edges too, but nothing that could not be smoothed out with a little more education and regular lessons in etiquette and elocution. I would consider it my crowning achievement to render you a respectable young lady fit to grace any company. To my mind, you certainly have looks and demeanour in your favour.'

Poppy smiled demurely, uncertain how to respond to this assessment.

'So come tomorrow morning and I'll assess your reading and writing. We'll take it from there. It will also give us a chance to get to know each other a little better, don't you think so, Miss Silk?'

Poppy grinned happily. 'Yes, Mrs Newton. And thank you.'

Chapter 18

Poppy attended her lesson, and several more besides, over the days that followed. During that time, she and Mrs Newton did get to know each other better and their easy accord was confirmed. But it was not only Mrs Newton that appealed. Poppy was fascinated with the library where she took her lessons. Because she had seen nothing like it before, it provoked no memories, only discoveries. There were books galore. She looked at the rows neatly lined up on shelves, and craned her neck to read the titles on the spines. She ran her fingers across them with a touch that was almost sensual, occasionally pulling one out, opening it with extreme care and reading a few lines before replacing it exactly as she had found it. On a chest of drawers a globe of the world stood, curiously tilted, Poppy thought. She put her fingers to it and gently turned it, wondering what the oddly shaped blobs of colour represented. On one shelf stood the alabaster bust of a man. She liked his face, whoever he was, and traced the carved features with her fingers, enjoying the surprising smoothness of the cool stone.

Under the window that looked out onto the back garden was a highly polished desk, on top of which lay a writing pad, a blotter and an ornate glass inkwell. A robust wooden chair upholstered in dark green leather accompanied the desk. In one corner a grandfather clock chimed the hours and steadily ticked away the years, and on the chimney breast hung a watercolour painting of men and women gathering in a harvest. Poppy looked at it intently and marvelled at the way the artist could produce something as lifelike on paper, using only ink and a few splodges of watery paint.

Poppy was actually invited to lunch on the Sunday. She sat primly at the dining table opposite Mrs Newton, taking her lead from her when it came to eating. Dining in a house like this was obviously a more genteel affair than gobbling food down in the hut on the Blowers Green encampment to the accompaniment of navvies belching and farting.

'My dear, I have come to a decision,' the older lady said as she pushed her plate away. 'It is unthinkable that you should continue to live in Gatehouse Fold. It is a midden of down-and-outs, unless I am mistaken. Half the strumpets of Christendom live there.'

Poppy regarded her with interest.

'So, if you have no objection, Miss Silk, I have a proposition to put to you that should benefit both of us . . .'

'Oh?'

'Yes. I would like you to consider the prospect of taking up employment here in this house?'

'As a maid, you mean?'

'No, not as a maid.' Mrs Newton smiled indulgently. 'I mean as my paid and kept companion. It would be my intention to make a lady of you, and you cannot be a maid and a lady. You would continue your learning, of course.'

'Oh, Mrs Newton . . .' Poppy sighed, touched by Mrs Newton's extreme charity. 'I don't know what to say . . . I'm a bit took aback to tell you the truth . . .' She put her hands to her face to hide her tears, a gesture that conveyed to the older lady the depth of Poppy's astonishment. 'I didn't think I deserved such kindness . . .'

'I want you to think about it carefully, my dear. You don't have to make a decision now.'

Poppy smiled self-consciously. She needed no time to think it over, no second asking. This would be infinitely preferable to working as a maid, beyond any dreams she'd ever harboured.

'Oh, Mrs Newton,' she replied. 'If you'm sure, I'd like nothing better.'

'Capital!' The old lady laughed with joy. 'Marvellous! Well, that's soon settled.'

'I just hope you can put up with me and me quaint ways, that's all.'

'I think quaint ways are more in my domain,' Mrs Newton said kindly. 'Not yours, my dear.'

'So when would you want me to come?'

'Just as soon as you like.'

'Can I come today then?'

Mrs Newton beamed. 'Of course. Why not? I have a very comfortable spare bedroom. I can get Esther to light a fire in there straight away to air it. You are quite sure that your mother wouldn't mind?'

'Oh, I think my mother would be relieved if she knew.'

'Miss Silk, I am so pleased and delighted. I am, in some ways, a selfish old woman, always determined to get my own way. But you will be comfortable here, and I certainly hope you will be happy as well. Anyway, I see no reason why you should not be. I try to be fair, as my staff will attest, and you will learn that I am not ungenerous.'

'So will you please call me Poppy, Mrs Newton? Everybody else does.'

Mrs Newton laughed contentedly and her eyes twinkled as

they reflected the firelight. 'Very well, Poppy. Then why don't you call me Aunt Phoebe?'

'All right, I will. Thank you . . . Aunt Phoebe.'

'Will it take you long to get your things?'

'I ain't got much. I can be there and back in an hour.'

'You've fell on your feet and no mistake,' Minnie said, when Poppy returned to Gatehouse Fold for her things. 'I never met anybody in my life as lucky as you. I bet I'll never see you again, living the life of a lady.'

'Oh, I'll come and see you, Min. Just 'cause I'll be living in a big house, you'll still be me friend. You're me only friend, remember. I shan't forget you. Ever.'

'Come and see me from time to time so's I know you'm all right. Anyway, I have to pay you back what I owe you.'

Poppy's new bedroom was large and pleasant, clean, tidy, and luxurious compared to the jumble and scatter of Rose Cottage and the damp austerity of Gatehouse Fold. The bow window, hung with cream calico curtains printed with pink flowers, looked out onto the front garden and Rowley Road. Against the wall furthest from the window stood a wardrobe and, next to that, a tallboy with a glass vase and crocheted doily sitting upon it. There was a dressing table with mirrors that were adjustable so you could see the side of your head. On it stood a trinket box, also made of cut glass, a silver-backed hand mirror and hairbrush, and more crocheted doilies. There was a washstand with a bowl and ewer in a floral pattern. But the bed . . . Poppy sat on it, bouncing up and down like an excited child, making the bedstead creak, it was so soft and springy and inviting.

Aunt Phoebe came in after allowing her time to get to know the room a little. She was carrying a bundle of towels.

'I thought you might enjoy a hot bath.'

'Yes, I don't mind.' Poppy had never been in a bath and the prospect was daunting, but she decided it was best to accept it gratefully.

'Is the room to your liking, my dear?'

'Oh, it's lovely, Aunt Phoebe,' she replied with a broad smile. 'And this bed is so soft. I think I shall be very comfortable.'

'Good. While you were fetching your things I asked Esther to change the bed linen. To my mind, clean bed linen is essential once you've had a hot bath. Oh, and if it's too warm, you can open the sash, you know.'

'Oh, no, it's just right.' Poppy went to the window. The front garden below seemed more formally laid out than she had noticed when she had first arrived. The roses were colourful against the monochromatic lawn and the foliage of shrubs. The idea of tending to plants on a warm summer's day had a sudden appeal; it conjured up images of contentment, of being civilised, of serenity. Then there was the view . . . 'What's that line of hills on the horizon?'

'They are the Clent Hills, my dear. If you see it raining on the Clent Hills, you can be sure it will rain here within a few minutes . . . Well, Poppy . . . shall we put your things away?' Aunt Phoebe opened the wardrobe door. 'I'll help you, while Esther fills the bath for you.'

Esther poured another bucket of hot water into the tin bath that had been taken to Poppy's room and set in the ample space between the foot of the bed and the dressing table. Poppy smiled at the maid apologetically for being the cause of so much extra work.

'I ain't got much to put away, Aunt Phoebe . . .' She pulled out her old red flannel dress, one of her cotton working frocks, stockings and a chemise.

'But my dear . . .' Aunt Phoebe looked at them aghast. She picked up the stockings between her thumb and forefinger and let them drop to the floor with distaste. 'I don't think you'll be wearing those again . . .'

'That only leaves me with the dress I'm wearing.'

'Then tomorrow we shall visit my dressmaker and have you measured.'

Poppy smiled appreciatively. 'Honest? But how much will it cost? I might not have enough money.'

'You are not expected to pay, Poppy.'

'You're ever so kind, Aunt Phoebe, but I've managed for ages with just two working frocks . . . and this flannel one was me best till I got me blue one.'

'Your blue one is certainly quite presentable.' Aunt Phoebe smiled kindly. 'But one good dress is not enough. You need more. You cannot continue to wear the same dress all the time when you are visiting people, or when we are being visited.'

Aunt Phoebe and Esther left Poppy to enjoy the bath with some privacy. She revelled in the warm, sudsy water, the sensation of lather caressing her skin. She liked how the thin film of soapy water made her skin look so glossy and feel so smooth. She sensually soaped her shoulders, the silky mounds of her breasts, the soft dimple of her belly button and the drift of downy hair below. Even the splashing sound was a novelty. She bent her knees up and lay back in the tin bath, basking in the water's all-enveloping embrace. It ran in her ears, strangely deadening all sounds, seeped through her mop of fair curls to her scalp, and she shook her head gently to saturate every strand. She rolled onto her stomach and dipped her face in the water, screwing up her eyes. Surfacing again, she puffed out her cheeks and blew the bubbles away, stroking away the long tresses of hair that clung to her smiling face.

Oh, yes, she was smiling. How lovely it was to take a bath, to experience the pleasantness of cleansing, to sense the stickiness and grime being magically lifted from you. It was a whole new set of sensations.

Being taken in and cared for by a kindly lady, who obviously had her well-being at heart, was a new and unanticipated development, which Poppy had not yet fully grasped. Oh, these new permanent surroundings were different and entirely novel, the spectacular cleanliness of the place was astonishing, as was the cosseting warmth and cosiness. But the extent of her good fortune, and the changes that must inevitably ensue, she had yet not had time yet to speculate on, nor understand.

Poppy began to wonder what life would be like in this comfortable house among these people. She liked Aunt Phoebe. She had liked her from the moment she saw her; her plump homeliness, and her unassailable wisdom. She possessed also a sort of benign pomposity that seemed comical to Poppy and which might be fun to provoke from time to time. Aunt Phoebe exuded a reassuring confidence that told Poppy she would be safe, even protected, from the seedy side of life that Minnie was being drawn into. Poppy ought even to make a friend of Esther. After all, she was no better than Esther. She'd even aspired to being a maid, like Esther. And if these were the sort of comfortable surroundings a maid was privy to, then maybe it was not such a bad life.

Poppy lay down again and stretched contentedly, watching the warm water make a little pool in the dimple of her belly button. This was how other people lived, those more privileged, who did not have the transitory and uncertain life of living in navvy encampments, with the breadwinner hired and fired at the whim of the contractor. However, this home, she could already appreciate, was above and beyond what the average working family might enjoy, even those with settled roots. Routines here seemed sedate. There was no rush, no fuss. Nothing, it appeared, was too much trouble. She was certain she would be able to settle down happily here. For her part, she would try her best to fit in, to belong. She was already missing her mother, her brothers and sisters, but this offer of shelter from Aunt Phoebe – and in such a place – was a godsend she could never have foretold, and neither could she have refused it.

The bath water was cooling down and she stood up, feeling the simple pleasure of it trickling down over her body and her legs, seeing how her skin glistened in the fading daylight from the window. She reached for the towel that Esther had draped over a chair back and rubbed herself dry, delighted by the firm roughness of the towel over her skin. She stepped out of the bath onto the edge of another towel Esther had thoughtfully laid there, and dried her feet. Then she rubbed up her hair and looked at herself in the mirror . . . tousled, naked and comical. She laughed contentedly.

There was a tap-tap at the door.

'Come in.' She had not the slightest thought for her naked-ness.

Esther opened the door and peered around it. 'Oh! Pardon me, miss . . .'

'Come in, Esther,' Poppy chirped.

Esther looked with embarrassment at Poppy. 'Ma'am said I was to try and do something with your hair. I'll get you a dressing gown first, miss. You don't want to catch a chill.'

Poppy felt a little guilty that Esther was running round doing things for her, things that she could easily do herself. The girl never stopped. To-ing and fro-ing. Fetching and carrying. She returned with a white dressing gown and helped Poppy into it.

'If you'd like to sit at the dressing table, miss . . .'

Poppy stepped towards it and sat astride the quilted stool. 'Esther, why don't you call me Poppy?'

''Cause I'm supposed to call you "miss", miss. I'm gunna dry your hair a bit more now, miss.'

Esther had brought with her another clean dry towel, and she began vigorously rubbing, shaking Poppy's head from side to side, then forwards and backwards. But Poppy did not protest. When the maid had finished, Poppy looked again at her tousled mane that seemed more yellow than she had ever known it.

'Your hair's a lovely colour, miss.'

'D'you think so, Esther? Honest?'

'I wish mine was that colour.'

'It generally goes a bit lighter in the summer. Now winter's nearly here it's goin' darker again. But it always looks the brighter for a good wash.'

Esther picked up the brush with the silver handle and began gently brushing. 'Mine always looks so dull.'

'It's funny how we always want something we ain't got. Don't you think so, Esther? But your hair's nice. And a nice colour. I wun't mind it.'

Esther smiled, grateful for the reassurance. 'How long you stopping here for, miss?'

The relevance of the question suddenly struck Poppy. 'A long time, I think. I hope so, any road . . .' She was looking at Esther in the mirror as she spoke. 'For as long as Aunt Phoebe wants me to stay, I s'ppose. However long it is, I hope you and me'll be friends, Esther.'

Esther smiled again, evidently flattered. 'Am yer her niece, then?'

'No. I ain't no relation. But I know her nephew.'

Poppy's hair was taking on a well brushed, sleek look, her curls non-existent now.

'Which one?'

'Oh . . . Mr Robert Crawford.' Poppy caught Esther's eye in the mirror and at once felt herself blushing. A glance at her own reflection confirmed it. 'Robert's me friend.'

'I thought he was engaged.'

'Oh, he is . . .' Poppy affirmed.

'To you?'

'No, not to me. Worse luck!' She uttered a little laugh that held traces of sadness and embarrassment.

'You fancy him then, miss?'

Poppy looked up from under a fringe of hair. 'Wouldn't you, Esther?'

'Me? Oh, I got no chance of ever getting off with the likes o' Robert Crawford. I ain't pretty enough. I got a face like a turnip and figure like a bolster, and no two ways. He's a likely enough lad for any wench to fancy. But not me. I got no time for all that fallalery, what with helping Dolly in the kitchen, keeping the furniture and household goods looking summat like, sweeping and cleaning. I'm glad there's no men living in this house, spitting in the grates, walking on the carpets wi' mucky boots and crumpling up the antimacassars with their greasy hair. Men in the house make too much mess.'

'I don't think all men am the same, Esther.'

'Me own father's worse than a dog. Maybe not your Robert Crawford, though,' Esther conceded. 'He seems betterer'n most.'

'Did he used to come here a lot?'

'From time to time.' She bent forward to Poppy's ear and whispered, 'They reckon as his family's one o' the richest for miles.'

'Honest?'

'That's what they say. But I expect you knew that already.' Esther lifted Poppy's hair away from her neck, holding it up to ascertain the effect. 'Shall I try and pin it up afore it dries out, miss?'

'If you like.' She recalled Minnie's efforts to do likewise.

'I reckon it suits yer pinned up . . .' Esther sighed. 'I do wish I had hair this colour, miss.'

'You could always dye it.'

'Dye it?' Esther chortled at the very notion. 'Lor! Me mother'd kill me when she sid it. I daresn't dye it.'

'You could always keep your bonnet on.'

'Or borry a wig,' Esther quipped with a chuckle.

Poppy changed the subject. 'How old is Dolly, the other maid?'

'Twenty-five.'

'I ain't had the chance to talk to her much.'

'It's her afternoon off. Gone a-courting, I 'spect. She'll be back tonight. Dolly does most o' the cookin' and looks after the kitchen. I do the housework . . . and the donkey work . . . Oh, and then there's Clay. You must've seen Clay afore. He does the gardening and anything to do with outside—'

Poppy grinned. 'Clay? That's a good name for a gardener.'

Esther laughed again, revealing the gap between her two front teeth. 'I hadn't thought about it, but you'm right. Any road, I think Clay used to work for Mr Newton afore he died, driving him about in his carriage. He still drives Mrs Newton about from time to time.'

'But he don't live in the house?'

'No, thank the Lord. He lives over the stables. He cleans up his own mess.'

The hair was done, to the satisfaction of Poppy and Esther, and Poppy put on her one and only dress. She went downstairs to Aunt Phoebe who was laying the dining-room table for tea herself. Poppy had never seen a tablecloth so white.

'My goodness, your face is glowing, Poppy my dear,' Aunt

Phoebe remarked. 'It must be the hot bath. Do you feel refreshed?'

'Yes, thank you. D'you like the way Esther's done me hair, look?' She swivelled her head from side to side, seeking Aunt Phoebe's approval.

'Very elegant, my dear. Very elegant. Would you like to take tea now, or would you prefer to wait?'

'Now, if you want. I'm hungry after me bath.'

'Good. I prefer to take tea even earlier than this on a Sunday on account of going to church. But we shall have to forego church this Sunday – it's been quite hectic, your moving in . . . Esther, would you make us a pot of tea? Poppy, would you be so kind as to go with Esther and slice and butter the bread, on account of it being Dolly's afternoon off? Then bring it to the table with the jam and the cakes, if you please. I'll lay out the crockery and find the serviettes.'

So Aunt Phoebe and Poppy sat down to tea together. Although she was hungry, she did not want to disgrace herself, and was restrained when it came to filling her plate with sandwiches. Eclairs and custard pies also sat invitingly on the crystal glass cake stand before her. But she first took a sandwich and began munching it.

'How old is Robert, Aunt Phoebe? He never told me.'

'Robert is twenty-four. He will be twenty-five next May. He is now the black sheep as far as his family is concerned, you know,' Aunt Phoebe declared conversationally. 'However, he just happens to be my favourite nephew.'

'Why is he the black sheep?'

'Because he was expected to join the family firm. His going away has delayed that. He went much against his father's wishes. However, he has always wanted to be independent of his father, and that has always been in his favour as far as I'm concerned. From a small boy, he had his heart set on becoming an engineer, though, like Mr Stephenson and Mr Brunel, whose work he has followed and studied assiduously. Of course, he has had the privilege of meeting Mr Brunel himself and working with him on the Oxford, Worcester and Wolverhampton project.'

Poppy listened with wide-eyed interest as she ate. Robert had never discussed his family.

'So he applied himself to civil engineering and, when he was nineteen, he dashed off to Edinburgh, with his father's blessing, to study the subject at the university there. Would you like another sandwich, Poppy?'

'Can I have one of those as well?' She pointed to a custard pie.

'Of course. Help yourself.'

Poppy reached over and put one on her plate. 'Where's Edinburgh, Aunt Phoebe?'

'Why, Scotland, my dear.'

'Oh, Scotland . . .' She nodded thoughtfully, at the same time eyeing up her custard pie. 'That's when he must've had the idea to build that funny two-wheeled machine he rides everywhere. He said he had the idea in Scotland . . .' Poppy was pleased she'd made the connection between his education in Scotland and his machine. But there was still plenty more she wanted to know. 'So when did he meet that girl he's engaged to?'

'Her family have been involved with Crawford's for many a long year, I understand. I suspect she and Robert have known each other a long time. But their engagement was announced, oh . . . less than a year ago.'

'Do you know this girl, Aunt Phoebe?' She took a bite from the custard pie.

'I know of her. I have been acquainted with her family. They are respectable and very affluent—'

'Affluent? What does affluent mean? Robert was always teaching me the meaning of words.'

'Affluent means wealthy. It stems from the Latin word *affluere*, to flow to. So, when money flows to you, you are considered *affluent*.' Aunt Phoebe smiled indulgently, pleased that her new protégée was not inhibited about asking such questions.

Poppy returned the smile, still munching, grateful in turn for the explanation. She had so much to learn in this world and she was a late starter. Another word kept cropping up as well, and it seemed these people of quality were preoccupied with it.

'Why does everybody make such a fuss about being *respectable*, Aunt Phoebe?'

'Oh, my dear!' Aunt Phoebe picked up her napkin and dabbed at her mouth. 'To my mind, respectability is all. To my mind, unless you earn the respect of people you are nothing.'

'So how do you go about earning it?'

'Initially, by not speaking when your mouth is full, Poppy.'

'Oh . . . Sorry.'

'One earns respectability simply by conforming to the standards of behaviour and etiquette expected of decent people. If you are deemed respectable you merit *esteem*. You do not merit *esteem* if you behave in a manner likely to cause offence or nuisance, if you behave immorally, dishonestly, or deceitfully, with no regard for others. Being respectable is being aware of your obligations and duties, and upholding them conscientiously. Being respectable is not putting a foot wrong. Respectability is an important word – a beautiful word – and I am pleased that you have asked me about it.'

'So, if Robert were to give up this girl he's engaged to and go off with somebody else, he would not be esteemed or seen as respectable?'

Aunt Phoebe looked at Poppy askance. 'I'm sure it would depend on the circumstances. But why would that be of interest to you, Poppy?'

Poppy shrugged, feigning indifference, and popped the last piece of egg custard into her mouth. She made sure she had finished eating it before she spoke again.

'There's something I don't understand, Aunt Phoebe,' she said with a frown of puzzlement. 'If this girl's family are so well known to the Crawfords, how come you don't really know her?'

'You must understand, Poppy, that I am no blood relation. I am only related to the Crawfords because my husband was the brother of Robert's mother, Clarissa. Since my husband died, I have had little to do with any of them . . . or, rather, they have had little to do with me – save for dear Robert, bless his heart, who has not forgotten me.'

'No, Robert wouldn't forget you, Aunt Phoebe. He always struck me as being thoughtful.'

The next day saw Poppy being shown more of the house and gardens, now that she was a resident. The back garden seemed vast once you were in it. The ground rose up from the house so that when you reached its extremity and looked back you could actually see the Clent Hills over the slate roof. Mature trees were in abundance and provided some shade, which would be delightful on a hot summer's day, as would the secluded summer house she saw overhung with climbing roses. Flowerbeds were everywhere, with no formal arrangement to them, but straight borders ran alongside the ancient brick walls that formed the boundary on either side. Poppy was introduced at last to Clay and the smell of his pipe tobacco reminded her poignantly of her father. He told her it was twist and she told him she liked it. It was enough to establish a regard for each other.

A great source of curiosity was the old square piano in the drawing room. The first time Poppy was close enough, she felt compelled to press down a key and was immediately delighted with its musical plink. She beamed an apologetic smile to Aunt Phoebe. Perhaps, when she was alone some day, she could return and plink some more keys, and discover the kinds and combinations of sounds it might be possible to produce.

About halfway through the morning, Poppy sat at the desk in the library with Aunt Phoebe, who was determined to get Poppy to read to her so that she could assess her progress. Poppy read a page from *Pride and Prejudice*, which Robert had given her.

'Have you read that page before, Poppy?'

'No, Aunt Phoebe. I just carried on from where I'd got to.'

'And how long have you been reading?'

Poppy shrugged. 'Not till after me dad died. Less than six months, I s'pose.'

'You read remarkably well. I see you have ploughed some way into the book. Are you enjoying it?'

'Oh, yes,' she enthused. 'It's so funny. I love the bit where—'

'What have you gleaned about manners and etiquette?'

'Etiquette?' Poppy looked unsure.

'*Pride and Prejudice* is full of it. How people behave towards each other in a way that is polite.'

'Oh, yes. That.'

'I suspect it was the reason Robert gave it to you. So that you would learn from it. Well, I shall teach you etiquette along with everything else. We shall make a proper lady of you, I have every confidence.'

Somebody knocked at the door and Aunt Phoebe called for whoever it was to come in. Dolly entered looking agitated.

'What is it, Dolly?'

'The butcher, ma'am. You know we ordered a rabbit to make a stew, but the one he's sent ain't bin skinned and drawn, ma'am. And he knows very well how I can't abide messing with 'em. Should I send Clay back with it so's he can do it for me?'

'Clay's busy, Dolly,' Aunt Phoebe declared. 'If I interrupt him with such trivialities we'll never get the garden tidied for the winter. Is it such an awful task to skin and draw a rabbit?'

'It's still got the yed on,' Dolly added. 'I hate doing it, ma'am. It turns me stomach.'

Poppy looked first at Dolly, then at Aunt Phoebe. 'I can do it,' she said, as if it were the easiest thing in the world. 'I can skin and draw a rabbit. I'll do it for you, Dolly, if you like. Save disturbing Clay.'

Aunt Phoebe huffed disapprovingly. 'Really, Poppy, I don't think *that* is quite the sort of thing I would expect *you* to do . . . And what about your lesson?'

'Oh, I don't mind, honest. I'll gladly do it. I'm used to it.' She got up from the desk and moved towards Dolly.

'Just this once then. To show Dolly and help her overcome her aversion.'

'There's nothing to it,' Poppy said affably, as the maid led her towards the kitchen.

'Well, thank the Lord you can do it, miss. I'm that grateful, honest I am. I hate and detest messing with the things.'

'It don't bother me.'

'So where did you learn how to do such things, miss?'

'Oh, I used to have to help me mother,' she said artlessly. 'I was always having to pluck chickens and ducks. I was always pulling the innards out of something or other. Men was

287

always bringing things for us to cook – things they'd poached or pinched.'

They entered the kitchen, warm with a fire burning in the cast-iron range. A dead rabbit lay limp and fluffy on a wooden workbench, its upturned eye open, looking vacantly at the whitewashed ceiling.

'See what I mean?' Dolly remarked. 'Poor thing. It makes me cringe to have to chop its flipping head off.'

'But it don't matter, Dolly,' Poppy reasoned. 'It's dead. You can't hurt it now.'

'I know, but the smell when you gut it. It's vile.'

'Oh, the smell's nothing. No worse than a privy. Just hold your breath . . .'

'Here, miss . . . put this pinafore over your clean frock.'

'Thank you, Dolly . . . Have you got a cleaver?'

Poppy fastened the strings of the pinafore and pulled up her sleeves, while Dolly reached for the cleaver and handed it to Poppy. Poppy held it poised over the rabbit and, with a single deft action, decapitated the furry corpse.

'There y'are, Dolly.' She took a sharp knife and slit the pelt, then peeled it away. 'At least with the skin on you know you got a rabbit, eh? When it's skinned it could be anything. A cat, even.'

'I know. It wouldn't be the first cat neither that folk have ate, thinking it to be a rabbit, eh, miss?'

'How's your young man, Dolly?' Poppy asked, changing tack. 'Esther tells me you go a-courting on your afternoon and evening off.'

Dolly smiled bashfully. 'He's all right, miss, thank you.'

'What does he do for work?'

'He's a puddler at the Dixons Green Iron Works down Bumble Hole,' Dolly replied.

'Have you been courting long?'

288

'Not that long. Mind you, I've had plenty chaps in me time.'

'But he's the one you liked best, eh?'

'Not really,' Dolly said resignedly. 'He's the ugliest, though. You couldn't punch clay uglier.'

'So why did you take to him over the others?' Poppy asked, her fingers covered in entrails.

''Cause he earns the most . . . And his mother told me he can draw fowl. I hate drawin' fowl and things.' Dolly watched what Poppy was doing with distaste, her mouth turned down at the corners. 'It don't bother you though, does it, miss?'

Poppy smiled, content that she had helped Dolly, happy that this opportunity to befriend the girl had arisen. It was in her nature to be friendly in any case, to want to please. She was anxious to let these servants see that she was no different to them, that she was not likely to look down on them just because she was unexpectedly thrust into the elevated position where she was to be waited on and looked after. She didn't particularly relish the idea of them doing her bidding. She didn't warrant it. No, she would rather help them than find them tasks. Because she was no better than them, how could she reasonably be expected to give them orders? If they sensed that she was no better, how indeed could she expect them to respond if they did not like or respect her? Ah . . . Respect . . . Respectability . . . She washed her hands in the bowl of water that was in the sink.

'I'm that grateful, miss. Honest,' Dolly said again, offering Poppy a towel to dry her hands.

'Oh, I don't mind, Dolly. Anytime I can help, just let me know . . .'

*　　*　　*

Poppy was taken to Aunt Phoebe's seamstress, Mrs Gadd, and measured. Together they chose material and flipped through patterns for everyday dresses, evening dresses, walking out dresses, skirts, blouses, petticoats, chemises, and frilly drawers. Poppy's choice was frequently tempered and guided by Aunt Phoebe. Poppy was to return a week later for her first fitting. The next day, Tuesday, Aunt Phoebe had Clay drive them to town after Poppy's lessons to buy mittens, day gloves, evening gloves, decent stockings, a purse, several bonnets, scarves, another cloak, a crinoline, another pair of dainty boots, and two new nightgowns, and to be measured for a corset.

As Poppy's first week progressed, she had more lessons in reading, writing, elocution and deportment. On her second Sunday, she was taken to church in the carriage, along with Esther and Dolly, who sat in a pew at the rear of St Thomas's church. Although the relatively new St John's was nearer, Aunt Phoebe had always attended St Thomas's. Poppy's second week subsequently included an introduction to the scriptures, learning the Lord's Prayer by heart, and Aunt Phoebe presented her with a map of the British Isles to pore over. First Poppy looked for Dudley, then Edinburgh, and thought about Robert Crawford and his two-wheeler. She found Mickleton, where her father had met with his death, but the map was not sufficiently up to date to show the Oxford, Worcester and Wolverhampton Railway line, although the Great Western from London to Bristol was shown, as was the London and Birmingham.

Poppy went alone to Mrs Gadd, the seamstress, for her first fitting.

'Hold your arms up, young Poppy,' Mrs Gadd said, somehow magically since she was holding a row of pins between her lips. 'I just want to see if the bodice rides up.'

The bodice did not ride up appreciably because it was tight, as was the fashion, but Mrs Gadd found some material to pinch together and inserted a pin.

'My word, you've got a lovely little figure, Poppy.'

'Thank you, Mrs Gadd.'

'You remind me o' me eldest daughter. She's got a figure like you, you know. She's had three kids an' all, but she ain't lost her figure. Gets it from her father's side, I reckon. His mother was like a whippet. Whippets run in that family. She certainly don't get it from me.' Mrs Gadd laughed self-deprecatingly. 'Look at the size o' me. I'm like a Netherton bonk 'oss. But not our Ruth.'

Poppy smiled indulgently, twisting one way then the other while the seamstress made her adjustments.

'How old am yer, Poppy?'

'Sixteen. I'll be seventeen next April.'

'Seventeen? Phew! What I wouldn't give to be seventeen again and know what I know now . . . Stand up straight a bit while I just look at the hem . . .' Mrs Gadd got down on her knees and fiddled with the hem, sticking pins in here and there. 'That other dress . . .' She nodded in its direction as she stood up again. 'The pale blue satin one . . . You'll fetch the ducks off the water wearing that. By God you will. Take a tip from me . . . You'm a young madam yet, and you'll have a fair few handsome young bucks offering theirselves. Keep 'em dangling, that's my advice. It makes 'em all the more interested.'

Poppy smiled, uncertain how to respond.

'But never stop single,' Mrs Gadd went on. 'I don't hold wi' women stopping single. They get funny ideas with ne'er a husband around 'em to drain all the softness out o' their heads. I got an aunt what never wed, and she took it into her head as she was gunna be an invalid. Well, she'd got some new complaint every week, and was drinking laudanum by the bucketful. Sent her yampy, it did. There's ne'er a husband as would've stood for such softness.' Mrs Gadd stood back to admire her work and wiped a bead of sweat off her brow with the back of her hand. 'That one should be all right. Now let's have a look at that blue satin frock . . . eh? Change into it, my flower.'

Poppy released herself from the day dress and slipped on the evening dress. Mrs Gadd rearranged the fall of the skirt and the set of the bodice.

'Course, there'll be no chemise under this when you wear it, eh?' The seamstress winked at Poppy. 'Bare shoulders and arms, eh? And a tempting glimpse o' cleavage. That's what gets the pulses racing.'

Poppy smiled demurely.

'Turn around, my dear.' Mrs Gadd fastened the tiny buttons at the back of the bodice. 'Seen anythin' o' them Crawford lads?'

'No,' Poppy replied.

'The middle one – Robert. I heard as he's gone off to Brazil.'

'Brazil?' Poppy turned round sharply and risked being stuck by a pin. 'Where's Brazil?'

'Where's Brazil? You mean you don't know? My dear, Brazil's on the other side o' the world. A savage, ungodly place, I shouldn't wonder, with neither church nor chapel.'

'Where's Brazil, Aunt Phoebe?' Poppy asked when she returned to Cawneybank House. 'Mrs Gadd's heard that Robert's gone to Brazil to work.'

'I didn't know he was going to Brazil. Goodness, it's in South America. A long way off.'

'Can you show me where it is?'

They trooped to the library. Aunt Phoebe went straight to

the globe on top of the chest of drawers and turned it on its axis.

'There. That's Brazil. That lilac bit. It doesn't look much there, but it's a huge country.'

'And wild?'

'Oh, yes, Poppy. Very wild.'

'How big is it?'

'Well, just compare it to Great Britain . . . There's Great Britain . . .'

'Yes, it's much bigger. I hope he'll be safe there, if it's so wild.'

'Oh, so do I,' Aunt Phoebe agreed.

Chapter 19

The months passed. Winter, along with its attendant snow and icicles, came and went. Poppy had never known anything like Christmas in the way that it was celebrated at Cawneybank House. Many of Aunt Phoebe's friends visited them, bringing gifts that delighted Poppy. Aunt Phoebe was increasingly proud of her young companion and the way she was responding to her coaching. March blew in like the lion it was always expected to emulate but, by the end of that month, the winds had died, the chill had receded and April crept quietly in. The warmer rains encouraged new buds in the garden, fresh green leaves on the trees, and the occasional break in the clouds promised summer just around the corner.

In her improved situation, Poppy had not forgotten Minnie. Indeed, she made an effort to visit her most weeks if she got the chance. The stark contrast between life at Cawneybank House and the back-to-back in Gatehouse Fold became ever clearer the more she visited her friend. The first Friday in April Poppy tapped on Minnie's door. It had been a month since last they had met. She waited in the drizzle, feeling conspicuously well dressed in a new dress, new cloak and bonnet. She tapped again, harder, as a middle-aged man peered at her from The Hare and Hounds on the corner and scowled at her, as if in envy of her obvious well-being. Poppy heard the screech of an upstairs sash and looked up to see Minnie thrust her tousled head out, peering down apprehensively.

'Poppy!' Minnie's face lit up when she saw her friend. 'I'm glad it's you. I thought you was that wench what started to come round trying to get me on the straight and narrow. I'll be right down to let yer in.'

Presently, the door opened and Minnie stood aside. 'Come in out the wet . . . God's truth, look at ya, Poppy. Dressed up like a princess, and no mistake.'

Poppy grinned, delighted as always to see her friend. 'Oh, Aunt Phoebe's looking after me good and proper.'

'I'm still in me nightgown, Poppy,' Minnie said apologetically.

'Oh, I don't mind . . . I swear you're losing weight, Minnie.'

'A bit. I'm glad to see you looking so well, Poppy.' Minnie seemed tentative, on edge, and she shivered in the cold of the room that was cheerless without a fire. 'I love your cloak . . . and your dress.' She felt the material between her fingers. 'Good stuff, in't it?'

'I've come to ask you if you'll come to my birthday party, Min.'

'A party?' Minnie glanced at the stairs' door as if expecting it to open. 'You'm having a party?'

'In the assembly rooms at The Dudley Arms. You know. That big hotel by the town hall. A week on Saturday night. I'd love you to come, Minnie. Have you got a nice dress you can wear?'

'Are there likely to be many chaps there?' Minnie whispered.

'Some real toffs, I would've thought. Aunt Phoebe's arranged the guest list, though. Why are you whispering, Min?'

Minnie pointed to the ceiling. 'Somebody up there,' she whispered.

'Oh, I see . . . I'd better go then. So will you come? A week on Saturday, about eight o'clock?'

'I'll try . . . Listen, do I still owe you any money, Poppy?'

'No, you paid me back.'

'Did I? Good. I'm glad. Hey, I'm making a mint o' money. I told you I would. I can easy afford to buy a dazzling new dress for your party.'

Poppy smiled. 'If you can afford a new dress, buy yourself some fire coal as well, Minnie. You'll catch your death else. Get back to your warm bed and that chap you've got up there, before you freeze.'

Minnie grinned. 'Still the same old Poppy under all that finery, ain't ya?'

The days and evenings at Cawneybank House remained pleasant. Poppy was keen to learn, an eager pupil, and Aunt Phoebe continued to lavish time and trouble on her companion, teaching her, correcting her patiently and with endless devotion. Considering that just a few months earlier they were not only strangers but more than a generation apart, they lived in perfect harmony. In the evenings they sat and talked and exchanged confidences. Poppy made Aunt Phoebe laugh with her down-to-earth comments and her uninhibited sense of humour, which was often a little bawdy for the older lady's taste. But she took it in good part. She was astonished by some of the tales Poppy recounted about navvy life, especially the story of how her mother and Tweedle Beak became entangled in a loveless relationship. When Poppy told her about how Tweedle Beak had tried to raffle her off and fix it so he won her himself, she was outraged that any man could stoop to such absolute dishonour.

'Thank goodness I helped you keep away from all that immorality,' she said, looking up over her spectacles from her embroidery.

'Oh, I know,' Poppy replied, with all the conviction of a socialite. She was knitting as they talked, a skill she was learning, and the white scarf she was attempting had grown to about a foot in length.

'But I hope your poor mother will have settled happily with that man you referred to as Buttercup.'

'Oh, I think she will've, Aunt Phoebe. He'll look after her. He's a good man. He reminded me so much of me dad.'

'*My* dad, Poppy,' Aunt Phoebe gently corrected. 'Not *me* dad. *My* dad. How many times—?'

'Sorry . . . *my* dad . . .'

'Let us hope they will marry and make a legal match of it. If only to stem their incontinence.'

'I hope so as well, Aunt Phoebe,' Poppy replied, clueless as to the meaning of the word incontinence.

'But I can't help thinking *Buttercup* is such a strange name for a man.' Aunt Phoebe pulled a green thread through the taut drum of her work.

'It's a nickname. All the men go by nicknames. Sometimes, you never get to know their real names.' She swapped her needles over and played out a little more wool from the ball in her lap. 'Take Jericho, for instance. Nobody knew his name. I don't think he knew it himself. If he did, he never told nobody.'

'Never told *anybody*, Poppy. You are using a double negative again . . .'

'Oh, damn,' she said with genuine disappointment. 'I must try and think about what I'm saying before I say it, eh, Aunt Phoebe? You're very patient with me . . .'

'I try. And please, never say *damn* either. At least, never in company.'

The composition of her birthday party had been discussed and they agreed that as many people of Poppy's age as possible should attend, chaperoned, of course, by their parents. Such a sprinkling of the young and unmarried would, it was hoped, lend the party some zest.

'It's a splendid opportunity to meet more of my family and friends,' Aunt Phoebe said to Poppy. 'Many have sons and daughters your age. The Crawfords must of course be invited. I haven't seen them for months. They have a daughter a little younger than you, but she is at boarding school, I believe. I seldom see her. However, I shall be interested to learn what you make of Robert's two brothers . . . I would stress, Poppy, that you would be wise to keep to yourself the fact that you were a friend of Robert – that you and I met through him. Such an admission would only invite questions and, if you answered them too candidly – as well you might – your origins will be revealed and all the excellent progress you've made over the months could be negated.'

'What do you mean, Aunt Phoebe?'

'I mean that unless they delved, nobody would know that you are the daughter of a railway navvy, reared on an ungodly encampment. So let us not make it known. Let's maintain the subterfuge that you are employed solely as my companion. You've already surpassed my expectations, my dear. I'm proud of you.' Aunt Phoebe paused, and Poppy waited for the tempering statement that always followed praise. 'That's not to say there are no more rough edges to be rounded off. Indeed, there are, but the fullness of time and greater experience will see to that. In any case, your guests will not notice any flaws. To my mind, they have plenty themselves and will be used to seeing and hearing such faults every day in everybody else. We've still plenty to do yet in the matter of your education.'

'I have to thank you, Aunt Phoebe,' Poppy said sincerely. 'For everything. For giving me a home, a comfortable bed. For being so kind . . .'

Aunt Phoebe looked over her spectacles at Poppy with genuine affection. 'Just as long as you are happy.'

'Happy?' Poppy smiled brightly. 'Oh, I'm happy. I love being here with you, Aunt Phoebe. I feel as if I've lived here all my life. I think about my family a lot and I wonder where they've got to now. I *do* worry about them, you know . . . But I look upon you as my mother nowadays . . .'

Aunt Phoebe reached out and took Poppy's hand, touched by her openness. 'And you have turned out to be the daughter I never had. I'm so glad you're happy. You've made me very happy too, Poppy. It's so fortunate that we were brought together.'

'Esther and Dolly as well,' Poppy said, wide-eyed. 'They're like sisters to me . . . and Clay's like an old uncle . . .' She laughed happily. 'Oh, Aunt Phoebe, I dread to think what would have happened to me if I hadn't dared to come and see you that Sunday . . .'

'What on earth do you mean?'

Poppy looked at her knitting, deliberately avoiding Aunt Phoebe's eyes lest she read too much into them. 'My friend Minnie . . . The one who lives at Gatehouse Fold. She's the daughter of a navvy as well. Did I tell you? She's not been as lucky as me. She's getting into bad ways . . . I suspect I might have done as well after Robert went away . . .' It was not the first time Poppy had admitted, to herself at least, that she might have become drawn into prostitution, especially when the money that Buttercup gave her had run out. 'Anyway, I invited her to my party. I hope you don't mind.'

'Oh, my goodness . . .' Aunt Phoebe sat bolt upright, her expression suddenly grim. 'I'm not sure that's such a good idea, Poppy. I mean to say, however much of a friend she is, do you really want a street girl at your party to lower the tone? There will be some very respectable people there. They will not want their sons and daughters to be mixing with that sort of girl.'

'But Minnie's all right, Aunt Phoebe. Honest. And she'll be all dressed up in nice new clothes. She's really very friendly. Nobody'll know she's that sort of girl, I promise.'

'Are you absolutely sure?'

'Yes, I'm sure. Anyway, I've asked her now . . .'

'Very well then,' Aunt Phoebe grudgingly agreed. 'Will she be escorted?'

'You never know with Minnie.'

A string quartet had been engaged and they sawed their way through the first half hour or so almost unheard, and certainly disregarded, as the guests arrived and engaged in excited chatter. Aunt Phoebe stood in front of the fire that burned brightly in the huge grate. With a roundly smiling face, she introduced Poppy to everybody in turn. Although Poppy was determined to remember all the guests' names, she knew she must inevitably fail . . . but not with the Crawfords . . .

'Clarissa, dear, how lovely to see you.' The two women greeted each other superficially. 'Clarissa, let me introduce you to my friend and companion, Miss Poppy Silk . . . Poppy, Mrs Crawford, my dear sister-in-law . . .'

'How do you do, Mrs Crawford?'

So this was Robert's mother. It was obvious she had once been a fine-looking young woman and the years and bearing of children had not been entirely unkind. She was not tall, but her demeanour, her slenderness and straight back made up for it. She wore a dark green velvet dress and matching stole, and she smiled cordially as she took Poppy's hand, of course unaware of her association with her long-absent son.

'It was such a pleasant surprise to receive an invitation from Mrs Newton to the birthday party of her friend and companion,' Mrs Crawford said to Poppy. 'We had heard that she had a companion living with her, so we just *had* to come and see you for ourselves. It's such a pity that my daughter couldn't be here. She would have enjoyed mixing with people of her own age.'

'Yes, it's a pity, Mrs Crawford. I would have liked to meet her.'

'We see precious little of her ourselves while she's at boarding school.'

'I see. What's her name?'

'Elizabeth.'

'So she must be your youngest?' Poppy deduced.

'She's sixteen. Not much younger than yourself, Miss Silk. Anyway, I do hope our birthday gift to you will be to your liking.'

'Thank you,' said Poppy, taking the small parcel.

'It was actually suggested by the fiancée of my son Robert.'

'Oh, then I'm sure I shall like it a lot.' Well, fancy that – the choice of Robert's fiancée. It felt like a book.

'Now let me introduce my husband, Mr Crawford . . .'

'Delighted to make your acquaintance, Miss Silk.' Ridley Crawford's eyes scanned Poppy up and down assessively. He was a tall man, heavily built. Poppy, still a navvy's daughter beneath her finery, imagined him and his slim wife in bed engaged in awkward copulation, she smothered by his bulk. She smiled to herself, glad that he could not read her saucy thoughts.

Aunt Phoebe turned to a young woman who was waiting to be introduced, the wife of Robert's elder brother. 'Clare. It has been too long since last we met. How well you look.'

'Thank you, Aunt Phoebe. You too. I've never seen you looking better,' Clare Crawford responded.

'And how are the children?'

'Little tinkers,' she giggled. 'But thank you for enquiring.'

Aunt Phoebe laughed with her. 'This is Poppy Silk. We get on so well, Clare, I can't begin to tell you ... Poppy, Mrs Oliver Crawford.'

'So this young lady is your companion these days?' Clare looked at Poppy expectantly and smiled. 'How do you do, Miss Silk?'

'Very well, thank you. And yourself?'

'Well enough. This is my husband, Miss Silk. Mr Oliver Crawford. Oliver, this is Miss Silk whose birthday we are celebrating.'

Poppy looked at him with curiosity, looking for a facial resemblance to Robert. She found none, except for the shape of his mouth when he smiled. 'I'm pleased to meet you, Mr Crawford. I've heard very little about you, but you must be Mr and Mrs Crawford's eldest son.'

Oliver looked her up and down like his father had. 'I am indeed. I hope we shall have the opportunity to speak later, or even dance together, Miss Silk.'

She smiled at him appealingly. 'I'll be sure to keep one dance free in case you come asking.'

Poppy's heart jumped when she saw Bellamy Crawford, the youngest son, Robert's younger brother. There was no mistaking him. He had a distinct and disturbing facial resemblance to Robert.

'This is such a pleasant surprise,' he said, looking directly into Poppy's shining blue eyes. 'You know, I rather expected the new companion of Aunt Phoebe to be a bit of a frump. I hardly expected to see such a vividly beautiful, fair-haired girl who makes the other ladies here pale into total insignificance. Please assure me, Miss Silk, that you are unattached . . .'

Oh dear . . . She nodded and smiled, uncertain what to say at his gushing praise.

'Please may I have the first dance with you? And, indeed, the second?'

'I'll gladly have my first dance with you, Mr Crawford, once I've met all my guests.'

As more people arrived and handed over gifts in that smoke-filled, noisy room with the maroon velvet drapes and flock wallpaper, Poppy graciously met them and seemed to grow in confidence and poise. Aunt Phoebe watched her with increasing pride. Poppy was statuesque in the pale blue satin dress that set off her figure to perfection. Esther had carefully tended her hair and it was piled on top of her head, enhancing the elegant set of her youthful neck. Her bare shoulders glistened like flawless ivory and her breast rose and fell with every excited breath and each peal of laughter. Her face was a picture of spontaneous gaiety and her large blue eyes sparkled with the reflection of the gas lamps that hung from the ceiling.

Aunt Phoebe watched with amused interest the reactions of the young dogs that came sniffing around; and the not so young ones too, who could not prevent their eyes from dwelling on Poppy. She felt a great surge of satisfaction. Oh, this Poppy Silk was going to be the toast of the town.

Another guest stood waiting to be introduced. He was tall and erect with a military bearing, and aged about forty-five, Poppy estimated. Quite old.

'My dear Cecil,' Aunt Phoebe cooed. 'How good of you to come. How is your mother? Is she improving?'

'Mother won't improve,' Cecil replied, his eyes dancing between Aunt Phoebe and Poppy, in anticipation of meeting her. 'It's just a matter of time, I'm afraid.'

'Do give her my love. I must get Clay to drive Poppy and me to see her one of the days . . . You haven't met Poppy yet, have you? Cecil, this is Poppy Silk, my companion. Poppy, Captain Tyler.'

'Miss Silk . . .' He took her hand and held on to it for longer than was necessary. 'Enchanted. So you are the fine young lady who has kept my cousin company through the long dark days of winter?' His voice was deep and masculine and his diction was perfect.

'Cecil was an army man, Poppy,' Aunt Phoebe explained. 'Recently retired, of course.'

'Oh?' Poppy said, wishing to appear interested but drawn by curiosity to seek out Bellamy Crawford in the throng. 'Did you enjoy being a soldier?'

'Loved it. You must allow me to regale you with some of my exploits some day, Miss Silk. You would find them very entertaining, I'm sure.'

Poppy smiled politely.

One or two of the younger people were beginning to dance and the band played with more enthusiasm in consequence. One set of dances finished and, after the couples had returned to their tables for a refresher, the leader announced another. Poppy caught the eye of Bellamy Crawford and, as he smiled, her heart went into her mouth. It was not for him, though, it was for Robert, because he reminded her so much of him. She raised her eyebrows at him and he took it as a signal, making his way towards her at once.

'Excuse me, Miss Silk, you promised me your first dance. May I claim it now?'

Poppy looked apologetically at Captain Tyler. 'If you will excuse me, Captain . . .'

Captain Tyler smiled grudgingly and nodded. He turned to Aunt Phoebe. 'What an enchanting princess you have captured as your companion. Do I have your permission to call on her?'

'You may call on me, Cecil,' Aunt Phoebe replied astutely. 'But I suspect you'll be well down the queue when it comes to calling on Poppy.'

'I hope you're not expecting a brilliant dancer,' Poppy said, as Bellamy led her to the floor.

'I wouldn't know a good dancer from a bad one, Miss Silk,' Bellamy replied. 'But it's a perfect excuse to hold a pretty girl around the waist and get to know her a little.'

As they began waltzing, she smiled up at him, imagining she was looking up at Robert. It was very disturbing being held by a young man so much like him. He was not quite as tall as Robert, but his eyes were similar, the way they crinkled so appealingly when he smiled. The nose was akin, too, as was the shape of his face. But the mouth was different. Oliver, the older brother, was blessed with a mouth more like Robert's. All the same, she could not help wondering if it would be as pleasant to be kissed by this younger brother.

'Where are you from, Miss Silk? We certainly haven't met before.'

'Oh, I've lived in Dudley for a year or two now,' she said ambiguously, gliding across the floor as gracefully as she could. 'Before that I lived all over the place.'

'I see. Ever lived abroad?'

'No.'

'Your family isn't army then?'

'Oh, no.' This was dangerous ground. She desperately

305

needed to sidetrack him. 'I understand you have a younger sister, Mr Crawford, but do you have any other brothers besides Oliver?' It was the first thing that came into her head.

'Indeed I do. Robert. Robert is older than me but younger than Oliver. He's twenty-four. I'm twenty-two.'

'Is he much like you, this Robert?' She became confused over her footwork and they had to start the sequence of steps again. 'Sorry, Mr Crawford. I told you I wasn't much of a dancer.'

He smiled his absolution. 'No matter, Miss Silk. I'm as much to blame . . . People say we are alike, Robert and I, though for the life of me I can't see it meself.'

'Is he here? I haven't met him, I don't think.'

Bellamy laughed. 'Good God, no. Poor devil's in Brazil of all places. He felt the need to visit the wide-open spaces of South America. He'll probably come back with severe malaria or beri-beri, I shouldn't wonder. Always provided he doesn't decide to stay and become a cowboy.'

'Brazil?' Poppy said, feigning ignorance. 'Have you heard from him since he went to Brazil?'

'A short letter to our mother and father every month or so, I think.'

'And is he all right, did he say?'

'I believe so.'

Poppy breathed a discreet sigh of relief. 'What's he doing in Brazil?'

'Surveying for a new railroad. Damn fool. He should join the family firm like Oliver and me instead of trying to make a name for himself. Then there'd be no need to risk life and limb in some godforsaken hole like Brazil. They say there are untold dangers out there. But let's not talk about him. Let's talk about you, Miss Silk.'

'Oh, I'm not that interesting, Mr Crawford.'

'Call me Bellamy, eh?' he said jovially. 'And I'll call you Poppy. Poppy's such a sweet name. It suits you. Tell me, Poppy, do you think Aunt Phoebe would mind if I took you home afterwards?'

'It's very kind of you to offer, but I wouldn't dream of leaving Aunt Phoebe to go home by herself.'

'I daresay she'll have Clay to watch out for her, won't she?'

'But Clay will be sitting outside on the driver's seat. Aunt Phoebe will be inside. No, I couldn't.' She failed to say that Esther and Dolly would also be travelling back with her, since they were at the party too.

'Then may I call on you?'

'Yes . . . If you want to, I suppose . . . If you're married or engaged though, you needn't bother.'

He hooted with laughter. 'Me married? Indeed not. Nor even engaged. Haven't met the right girl, Poppy . . . Till tonight, that is . . .'

The dance finished and Poppy returned to Aunt Phoebe's side. Captain Cecil Tyler was still talking to her, along with another woman who was plainly dressed, but imposing.

'Poppy . . . You remember Mrs Green . . .'

They had met before.

'Mrs Green,' Poppy greeted and offered her hand. 'How lovely to see you again.'

'Mrs Green and I have been discussing you, Poppy. We were schoolteachers together some years ago, as I think I must have surely told you. She is connected with Baylies's Charity School in Tower Street. It's a sort of Ragged School, of course. They need some help in the classroom and Mrs Green wondered if you might be willing.'

'Me?' Poppy looked at Mrs Green for confirmation.

'Yes,' Mrs Green replied. 'Mrs Newton tells me you are an able reader and writer. We have placed advertisements in the *Ten Towns Messenger* for a teacher's help, but to no avail. I am certain your qualities could be put to good use. Of course, a knowledge of singing as well would be indispensable.'

'It would be a wonderful opportunity for you, my dear,' Aunt Phoebe urged.

'But I can't sing. I don't know a thing about singing.'

'I'll teach you to sing,' Aunt Phoebe said, as if it would be the easiest thing in the world. 'Not only would you be continuing to learn in this school, but you would also be gaining invaluable experience. Experience which could possibly lead to a full-blown teaching position somewhere. You would also be earning a little extra money. You should consider it very carefully, my dear.'

'D'you really think so, Aunt Phoebe?'

'My dear, I would not be so keen on you doing it if I did not think so.'

Poppy saw Bellamy Crawford making his way towards her again. 'Very well, Aunt.' It was time to postpone this conversation lest she miss the opportunity to dance with Bellamy again. 'We can talk about it more tomorrow, maybe.'

'Indeed we shall.'

'And thank you, Mrs Green, for thinking about me.'

'You are an obvious candidate, Miss Silk.'

Bellamy arrived at her side. Smiling affably, he acknowledged Aunt Phoebe, Mrs Green and Captain Tyler in turn. 'Would you mind greatly if I robbed you of Miss Silk's company?' he said.

Captain Tyler's expression did not change, but the two women flashed knowing looks at each other and smiled their assent before Bellamy turned to Poppy.

'Poppy, would you care to dance again?'

'Thank you, Bellamy,' she consented graciously, and he led her away.

'This time it's a polka . . .'

'I'm not very good at polkas, Bellamy.'

'No matter. It's just that I can't seem to settle when somebody as beautiful as you is in the same room. Perhaps you would accompany me in to supper afterwards as well?'

'Yes, all right,' she said contentedly.

Chapter 20

Bellamy Crawford would have called at Aunt Phoebe's on the following Monday evening, had he not risked appearing too keen to see Poppy. So he left it till the following evening, the Tuesday, another mucky, drizzly night. He walked from Tansley House with his collar turned up to keep out the damp and cold. Esther opened the front door to him and took his wet coat while he complained about the weather and thanked her for her attention.

'I saw you were at Miss Silk's party, Esther. Did you enjoy it?'

'Oh, yes, sir, thank you, sir. It was a grand night.'

From another room towards the rear of the house he could hear the stilted endeavours of an unpractised pianist, while Esther led him into the drawing room where Aunt Phoebe was sitting, attached to her embroidery.

'Good evening, Aunt.'

'Bellamy! What a pleasant surprise.' Carefully, she put down her work and stood up to welcome her nephew. 'Fancy venturing out on a night like this.'

'Please, don't get up, Aunt . . . Here, I've brought you flowers.'

'Roses. Good gracious!'

'Well, I thought it might behove me to come and say thank

you for the splendid evening on Saturday. I had a glorious time.'

'Thank you, Bellamy. They're beautiful. Are they for me, or for Miss Silk?'

Bellamy grinned sheepishly. 'For both of you, of course.'

'Do sit down . . . I'll lay them on the table and ring for Esther to put them in some water . . . Yes, it seems to have been a very successful evening. At least we achieved its objective of celebrating Poppy's birthday.'

'Isn't she delightful?' Bellamy said. 'I was so pleasantly surprised. I must say I quite took to her.' He felt himself colouring up at the admission.

'Can you take to her piano playing?' Aunt Phoebe said with a bright laugh, cocking an ear. 'That's her, practising her scales.'

'Is she not accomplished already?'

'Not in piano playing. But she's a trier. I believe she has a feeling for the piano, but we're all fingers and thumbs when we begin to learn.'

He gave a polite little laugh. 'Indeed, yes, Aunt.'

'How are your dear mother and father? I trust they enjoyed the party as well?'

'Oh, indeed, Aunt. As did Oliver and Clare. No doubt they will send you a note.'

'No doubt.' Aunt Phoebe wanted to say that no doubt that was all she *would* get. Certainly not a visit. Neither was she fooled by Bellamy's calling tonight with roses. 'Would you like a cup of tea or coffee, Bellamy? Or even something stronger?'

'Do you have chocolate, Aunt?'

'I believe so.'

Esther entered, responding to the bell, and looked enquiringly at her mistress.

'Esther, would you take these roses that Mr Crawford has kindly brought and make an arrangement of them? But first, bring us hot chocolate and Poppy. Mr Bellamy is dying for one or the other.'

Esther smothered her amusement. 'Yes, ma'am.'

'Thank you, Aunt,' Bellamy said when Esther had gone. 'Of course, both will be welcome. But it would be odious of me to declare which will be the more so.'

'Oh, I think I can hazard a guess. As I was saying, it was good to see you all at Poppy's party. I see all too little of the Crawfords these days.'

'I shall try and correct that oversight, Aunt, given your permission.'

Poppy put her head round the door and smiled, wide-eyed, when she saw Bellamy.

'We have a visitor, Poppy,' Aunt Phoebe announced. 'Or more accurately, I think, *you* have a visitor.'

'Poppy . . .' Bellamy looked her up and down admiringly, and a lump came to his throat as he stood for her. 'No, my eyes did not deceive me on Saturday, even though my memory has been playing diabolical tricks. You are just as lovely as I thought you were.'

'Thank you, Bellamy.' She blushed becomingly.

'But, for the life of me, I couldn't remember what you looked like, you know . . . Have you ever experienced that, Aunt? You meet somebody. You know she is divinely lovely, but you can't seem to remember her face. That's how it was with my memory of you, Poppy.'

'Fancy.' Poppy was not sure how to respond to this compliment.

'I've just asked Esther to bring us chocolate, my dear.'

'Oh, thank you, Aunt Phoebe. I love chocolate.' Poppy sat on the sofa opposite Bellamy, wearing one of the many everyday dresses she now possessed, her hands demurely in her lap, her back erect. 'I've just written a note to your mother and father, Bellamy, to thank them for the lovely Bible they gave me for my birthday, which was chosen by Robert's fiancée. If you'll take it with you when you go, it'll save me posting it in the morning.'

'Of course, Poppy. Happy to oblige.'

'I was just about to ask Bellamy, Poppy, what news from Robert?' Aunt Phoebe turned to Bellamy. 'I barely had an opportunity to ask your mother.'

'His last letter told us he was well. He lost one of his colleagues to yellow fever, you know. I think that rather made him wonder at the logic of going to such a backward, disease-ridden country in the first place.'

'Do you think he might catch it as well?' Poppy asked, concerned. 'This yellow fever?'

'Let's hope and pray he returns unscathed, Poppy, and sees the sense in joining the family firm. It seems idiotic not to when there is no doubt that he will wed upon his return.'

Poppy's heart sank. 'Has he said so in any of his letters?'

'Not in so many words. But, reading between the lines, I should say he's anxious to get back. That can only mean he's missing his fiancée. And why not? She's such an angel, and they're such an appropriate match . . . for both our families.'

Aunt Phoebe flashed a concerned glance at Poppy, trying to read her reaction.

'In what way is it such a good match?' asked Poppy, uneasy at this information.

'Because they are both good and kind people. And for no other reason than because our two families are inextricably linked financially.'

'Forgive me a moment,' Aunt Phoebe said, tactfully rising from her seat. 'I'll go and see what Esther is up to. I have an

313

awful feeling she will make a dog's dinner of the roses, unless I show her how it's done. And Poppy hasn't seen them yet, have you, my dear?'

'No, Aunt.'

For a few long seconds after Aunt Phoebe had left the room, Poppy and Bellamy were stuck for words. She smiled at him unsurely, the similarity in his looks poignantly reminding her of Robert. If only it *was* Robert sitting there looking at her so covetously.

'It's a foul night outside,' he said at last, stymied for more stimulating conversation. 'Had it been fine and dry, I would have ventured to ask if you'd care to take a walk with me.'

'I would have to ask Aunt Phoebe's permission first, Bellamy,' she responded.

'Actually, the flowers were intended for you, Poppy, but I could hardly not include Aunt Phoebe.'

'Oh, it's good of you to include her. She's the one who deserves them, not me.'

'I . . . enjoyed your company enormously on Saturday night, Poppy. Our dancing together. Our chat.'

'So did I.'

'There's a refreshing frankness, a candour about you that seems to be lacking in other girls I've met. You have no airs and graces, yet you are all graciousness. Besides which, you're such fun and so easy to talk to.'

'It's good of you to say so.'

'Not at all . . .' He paused, looking self-consciously at the patterns in the burning coals. 'I wrote to you, you know . . .'

'When? I never got a letter.'

He laughed with self-derision. 'I know. I threw the damned thing in the fire. I felt it better to come and ask you face to face.'

'Ask me what?'

'Oh . . . Ask if you would care to accompany me on a drive . . . On Sunday. After dinner, perhaps? Always assuming the weather is not too inclement. It would give me the greatest personal pleasure if you would consent . . .'

'That would be very nice, I'm sure, Bellamy. But I must ask Aunt Phoebe first.'

'No, no, Poppy. If you are agreeable – and it seems you are – then I will ask Aunt Phoebe. It's my place to ask.'

'All right,' she said brightly. 'But where will we go?'

'Anywhere you've a fancy. Do you have a fancy for anywhere in particular?'

'From my bedroom window I can see the Clent Hills. They look ever so green and inviting now spring is just around the corner. So different from the filthy drabness of the slag heaps and the sooty sky. I'd love to go there, just to see what it's like. If it's not too far.'

Aunt Phoebe returned at that, carrying a cut-glass vase containing the arrangement of roses. 'There. Aren't they beautiful, Poppy? Intended primarily for you, I suspect.' She looked benignly but knowingly at Bellamy.

'Aunt Phoebe . . .'

'Yes, Bellamy?'

'Aunt Phoebe . . . Do I have your permission to take Poppy for a drive on Sunday afternoon? She is quite agreeable to the suggestion, so long as you give your permission.'

Aunt Phoebe turned her gaze on Poppy. 'If Poppy is of a mind to accompany you, then I have no objection.'

'Thank you, Aunt Phoebe. Thank you. Shall we say two o'clock on Sunday, then, Poppy?'

Poppy grinned, complimented by his attention. 'Yes. Sunday.'

* * *

The following evening, while Aunt Phoebe was instructing Poppy on the lineage of the Stuarts, another admirer paid a visit.

'My dear Cecil!' Aunt Phoebe greeted when he was shown into her sitting room. 'How lovely of you to call and see us, it being only last Saturday that we saw you last.'

Captain Tyler chose to remain indifferent to his cousin's mild sarcasm, realising what she was implying. 'Good evening, Phoebe. And good evening to you, Miss Silk. I came to thank you both for the wonderful party the other evening. A splendid do.'

'So you enjoyed it. Pray, do sit down, Cecil. Let me offer you a drink. Would you like tea?'

'I'd prefer something stronger if you have it, Phoebe. You know me.'

'Whisky?'

'Whisky's fine. Thank you.'

Aunt Phoebe smiled, glad of the opportunity to get out the whisky bottle a little earlier than she normally would.

'Poppy, would you be so kind as to pour Captain Tyler a glass of whisky, please? And I'll have a small one myself.'

'Of course, Aunt,' Poppy replied biddably, and stepped over to the drinks cabinet.

'Poppy and I were just discussing Charles the Second,' Aunt Phoebe said conversationally.

'Then no doubt she will be glad of some relief,' Captain Tyler replied dryly. 'Shall you partake of a little whisky yourself, Miss Silk?'

Poppy looked up at their guest and smiled politely. 'I seldom drink spirits, Captain Tyler.'

'I don't blame you. Ruins the complexion, drinking spirits. And you, my dear Miss Silk, have a fine complexion that is far too precious to ruin. Has she not, dear Phoebe?'

'I had such a complexion myself when I was younger.'

'Would you like water in that, Captain Tyler?' Poppy asked, holding the glass up to show him.

'Oh, indeed not, thank you, Miss Silk. I'll take it as it comes. Neat whisky doesn't scare me, you know.' He grinned affably. 'Comes from years of drinking gallons of dreadfully dubious liquors, veritable firewaters – especially in Ireland.'

Poppy handed him his glass and he thanked her. She poured a small one for Aunt Phoebe and sat down again primly. Conversation swung between the health of Captain Tyler's ailing mother and the prosperity of the factory which Aunt Phoebe owned. Until Aunt Phoebe saw fit to let him know that Poppy had had a visitor the previous evening, merely to discourage him from thinking he could unreservedly pursue her charge himself. He was much too old for her, after all.

'Young Bellamy Crawford called on Poppy last evening, you know, Cecil. It was such a surprise to see him . . . And yet no surprise at all when you consider the similarity in their ages, don't you think?'

'Indeed,' Captain Tyler replied nobly, picking up the hint. 'I gained the distinct impression that he was full of admiration for Miss Silk . . . May I call you Poppy, Miss Silk? It's so much less formal.'

'Oh, please do, Captain Tyler.'

'Thank you . . . And I was about to say, why shouldn't he admire you if he's so minded? You are a fine-looking young lady, Poppy. If I were him, I would have no scruples in indulging my admiration to the full.'

'Well, he's indulging his on Sunday afternoon, Cecil. Isn't he, Poppy dear?'

Poppy smiled pleasantly and nodded. 'Except that I think maybe Bellamy is always likely to choose the wrong woman for himself.'

'Oh, in what way do you mean?'

'Just that if I were him, I would hardly be so impetuous. Besides, I would be looking for a rich girl . . . If I were him.'

'I must confess,' Captain Tyler replied, 'that money would never enter into it where I was concerned. I consider a person's character a much more important qualifier.'

'You mean irrespective of their standing?' Aunt Phoebe asked.

'Financial or social. It matters not a jot. But things are somewhat different for a man. A woman, on the other hand, is prone to accepting the hand of her wealthiest admirer. If he's handsome to boot, then so much the better for her.'

The doorbell rang again and Aunt Phoebe glanced with puzzlement at Poppy. 'Who could that be? Not Bellamy again, I trust.'

As Esther answered the door, they listened. Besides Esther's voice they heard only the voice of another woman, which Poppy recognised. The door to the sitting room opened and Esther announced that a Miss Catchpole had called to see Poppy.

'Minnie!' Poppy exclaimed and shot up eagerly from her seat to greet her friend. 'Minnie, come in. What brings you here?'

'Well, I got the right house, by the looks o' things. Hello, Poppy. And you must be Aunt Phoebe . . .'

'Miss Catchpole, how nice to meet you at last,' Aunt Phoebe said, surprised at how decently dressed this young woman was for somebody of her background. She was thus more inclined to welcome her into her home. 'I've heard so much about you.'

'And I've heard a lot about you an' all.'

'This is my cousin Captain Tyler, Miss Catchpole . . .

Captain, let me introduce you to Poppy's friend, Miss Minnie Catchpole.'

'Delighted, Miss Catchpole. So, you are a friend of Poppy.'

'Oh, have bin for donkey's years,' Minnie affirmed with a grin. 'I say, Captain, what's that you'm a-drinkin'?'

'Whisky. Do you like whisky, Miss Catchpole?'

'Hey, I love whisky.' She sat on the sofa beside the Captain. 'And call me Min. I ain't one for all this Miss Catchpole malarkey.'

'As you wish, Minnie. And you can call me Cecil.'

'Cecil?' Minnie's distaste for his name showed on her face. 'No, I'd rather call yer Captain, I think. I like the sound o' that better.'

He grinned. 'Then Captain it is.'

'Would you like me to pour you a glass of whisky, Minnie?' Poppy asked.

'Yes, if you can spare a drop.'

Poppy handed her a glass.

'Ta, my wench.' She took a good slurp.

'You didn't come to my party, Minnie. I wondered what had happened to you.'

'I know. I've come to say sorry. I got me a lovely frock an' all.'

'So why didn't you come? You'd have loved it.'

'Well, to tell you the truth, it was 'cause I wun't've knowed nobody else, only you, Poppy. And I knowed all the chaps would be wanting to dance with yer. I din't want to be no wallflower.'

'You'd have been no wallflower, Minnie, I'll be bound,' Captain Tyler remarked amiably. 'We'd have wanted to dance with you as well, us men. No doubt, you would have looked absolutely exquisite in your new dress. You could most certainly have marked your card with my name . . . several times over . . . had it pleased you to do so.'

Minnie smiled interestedly at this man who was charming, a quality that had been missing in other men she'd known. And he was so much older than she was. 'That's kind of yer to say so, Captain. And I don't see why I shouldn't mark me card wi' your name, neither. I bet you'm a good dancer an' all, ain't yer?'

'Tolerably light on my feet, Minnie. I manage to get around the floor without too much stumbling.'

Minnie laughed. ''Cept when you've had a few, eh?' She gave him a friendly nudge.

'Indeed, Minnie.' Now Captain Tyler laughed heartily. 'Except when I've had a few, as you suggest.'

'Poppy, I bought yer a present for your birthday.' Minnie felt in the pocket of her skirt and pulled out a smallish wrapped cube.

'Thank you, Minnie. What is it?'

'Open it and see. I thought it'd be useful.'

All eyes were focused on Poppy as she opened the package. At last she removed all the wrapping and held it up to inspect it.

'An ink stand!' she exclaimed with joy.

'Wi' silver cap and base. Hallmarked, an' all,' Minnie added proudly, and took another swig of whisky.

'Oh, thank you, Min. That's going to be most useful.'

Min licked her lips. 'I reckoned as much, what with all the writing you must be doing these days.'

'A fine gift,' Aunt Phoebe confirmed, realising it must have been expensive. 'It's very good of you, Minnie.'

'She's worth it, Aunt Phoebe, my mate Poppy.'

The four continued with enlivening conversation. Captain Tyler was struck by Minnie's artless chatter and her unpretentious manner. He teased her gently and made her laugh, and she made the others laugh in turn.

After about an hour, he said, 'What o'clock is it, I wonder? I've left my watch at home. I've no wish to drink you clean out of whisky, dear Phoebe, nor outstay my welcome.'

'I got the time,' Minnie said helpfully, and pulled out an old and dented fob watch from another pocket in her skirt. She scrutinised it closely. 'It was me father's, this. Trouble is, it's generally either ten minutes slow or twenty minutes fast.'

'And which is it now?' Aunt Phoebe queried.

'Lord knows, Aunt Phoebe. I can never be sure.'

Captain Tyler chuckled. 'There must be something wrong with its workings.'

'You reckon, Captain? No wonder I'm either a mile too late or two miles too early for everything.'

'Would you like me to have a look at it?' he suggested. 'I have a certain expertise with watches. I could let you have it back in a very serviceable condition in a day or two.'

'Well, that's very good of you, Captain, and no two ways,' Minnie answered, delighted with the offer, for she would get to see him again when he returned it. 'When it really plays up rotten I get a hairpin and give it a real good stir up inside.'

He roared. 'Good Lord. I'm surprised it works at all.'

'No, it don't seem to do it no harm. The thing generally behaves itself all right for a week or two after that, neither losin' nor gainin' more than five minutes either road. But then it falls back to its old ways.'

'Inevitably,' Captain Tyler said. 'Well, Minnie, you've stirred me up, I'm quite prepared to admit. If you are also about to leave the kind hospitality of Mrs Newton and Poppy, I would be happy to convey you home.'

'That's very decent of yer, Captain. Save me poor little legs it would, and no two ways. Not to mention me shoe leather.'

'The pleasure is all mine, Minnie.' He finished his whisky, put his empty glass on the occasional table in front of him and stood up. 'Phoebe, dear, it's been grand to see you again. You, too, Poppy . . . No don't bother the maid. I can see Minnie and myself out . . . If you are ready, Minnie?'

'Yes, I'm all ready, Captain.'

Baylies's Charity School lay set back from the road in Tower Street, next door to a public house called The Lord Wellington and backing onto the glassworks in Downing Street. At each end of the early Georgian façade was a door, and set into the wall above each was an alcove in which stood a painted statue of a schoolboy wearing the uniform of blue coat and cap. The school was established in 1732 for the purpose of teaching and clothing fifty boys, chosen from some families of the town who could not afford to pay for their sons' learning. Poppy, accompanied by Aunt Phoebe, was to meet the superintendent, Reverend James Caulfield Browne, the vicar of St Thomas's.

The school comprised one classroom, which could be divided into two when needed. A blackboard and easel stood in front of a huge fireplace with a brass fender, a wrought-iron fireguard and a voluminous coal scuttle. The windows were vast and let in plenty of light, but you could not see the road outside because they were set so high in the walls. It was Friday, the boys were hard at work, their chalk sticks squeaking across slates as they wrote. Poppy felt self-conscious that their eyes were following her, however, as she glided across the wooden floor of the classroom to the master's study, keeping close behind Aunt Phoebe. They exchanged pleasantries and Reverend Browne, who was already acquainted with Aunt Phoebe since she was one of his congregation, invited them to sit down.

'How old are you, Miss Silk?' Reverend Browne enquired, peering over his spectacles.

'Seventeen, sir.'

He wrote it down. 'Mrs Green, one of our benefactors, has recommended you, Miss Silk. She seems to think you could offer a good and reliable standard of help in our school.'

'I'm sure I could, sir. I can read and write and do arithmetic.'

'You would not be required to teach these things, of course, but merely to assist Mr Tromans, our schoolmaster. I am pleased also to have the endorsement of Mrs Newton with whom you reside. I have known you for – what, Mrs Newton? Four years, is it?'

'Four years it is, Reverend . . . Tell me, do you still live outside Dudley?'

'With the express permission of the Bishop, Mrs Newton.' He put his pen down and leaned back in his chair as if anticipating a lengthy chat. 'And due, as I'm sure you must be aware, to the insanitary condition of the town.'

'To my mind, things are improving, Reverend,' Aunt Phoebe replied, in defence of her home town. 'At least we have had no cholera epidemic for a number of years.'

'Indeed, not since eighteen thirty-five. I am often reminded, however, that the graveyard of our beloved St Thomas's that year was full to overflowing, and the surplus dead of the parish carted to Netherton for burial.'

Aunt Phoebe nodded. 'Indeed, it was as you say, Reverend.'

Reverend Browne placed his fingertips together as he studied Poppy once more, almost in a gesture of pious prayer, she thought. 'To return to the matter in hand . . . Baylies's Charity School was founded for the purpose of educating boys from poor families, Miss Silk, on the principles of the Christian religion, according to the doctrine and discipline of the United Church of England and Ireland. I take it you attend church regularly?'

'Yes, sir,' Poppy confirmed truthfully, though as yet she knew little of the scriptures, and only the Lord's Prayer and the Creed by heart.

'Indeed, I have seen you there, come to think of it . . . I trust you would not be grossly overwhelmed at the prospect of working with so many boys?'

'Oh, no, sir.'

'Tell me, are you able to play the harmonium, Miss Silk?'

'I'm not that good, sir.'

Aunt Phoebe said, 'Miss Silk has only recently begun piano lessons. But I have every confidence that she will progress quickly.'

'So what formal education have you had, Miss Silk?'

'Miss Silk has been having the benefit of private tuition with me for some months, Reverend,' Aunt Phoebe interjected. 'Unfortunately, she began her learning late. She has, however, made remarkable progress and would be a valuable asset here, able to help any of the younger pupils.'

'It is with the younger pupils that we need the extra help, Mrs Newton. A strong academic background is hardly necessary. Merely an ability to read and write, to be trustworthy and reliable, and to understand our Christian discipline.'

'What hours would Miss Silk be expected to work, Reverend?'

'From half-past eight in the morning till four o'clock in the afternoon, Mondays to Fridays, and on Saturdays till one.'

Aunt Phoebe pursed her lips thoughtfully and looked first at Poppy, then at Reverend Browne. 'No, I'm afraid I couldn't allow her to work such hours, Reverend. Miss Silk is my helpmeet and companion and, with the best will in the world, I could only spare her mornings.'

'I see,' the vicar replied, obviously disappointed. He drummed his fingers on the desk in front of him, a pensive look on his face. 'Such a pity . . . Look, allow me to bring in Mr Tromans to meet Miss Silk,' he suggested more brightly. 'I will discuss with him when you have gone the possibility of employing Miss Silk on mornings only. I will let you know the outcome in due course. I presume you would be free to commence duties straight away, Miss Silk?'

'Oh, yes, sir.'

He got up from behind the desk and fetched Mr Tromans.

As they walked back to Rowley Road and Cawneybank House – the clarence was not available since Clay was busy greasing the axles – Poppy and Aunt Phoebe discussed the interview. Aunt Phoebe was of the opinion that Reverend Browne considered Poppy suitable for the position and would try and convince the schoolmaster, Mr Tromans, that he could manage with morning help only.

'That will enable you to continue your learning at home, and still have some time to yourself.'

'I wouldn't have dared suggest it, Aunt Phoebe,' Poppy said. 'I wouldn't have even thought about it. Don't you think it might put them off having me?'

'I think not, my dear. Having been a teacher for many a long year I am aware of the reality of what is desirable compared to what is possible. It is not uncommon to use pupil teachers in classrooms. All too often it is necessary. For you, so many young boys under one roof could be very tiresome if they are not sufficiently well disciplined. I must say, though, Mr Tromans seemed to keep them on a tight rein. He seemed no fool. If you are offered the position, I'm certain he'll be fair and respectful towards you.'

They walked on in silence for a while, up the road known

325

as Waddams Pool, with cottages interspersed between factories on both sides, and dotted with dollops of uncleared horse manure. A horse and cart passed on the other side of the road and the carter raised his hat to them with a cheery smile. The sky, however, was like lead and threatened more rain.

'Maybe we should have taken the omnibus, Poppy.'

'Oh, I don't know. A drop of rain won't hurt us.'

'I wasn't thinking so much of the rain as my poor legs.'

'I remember the men at the railway encampment when they worked in the rain. They always moaned. It made the earth thick with mud and so much heavier to shift, but they shifted it all the same. But the mess they made with their boots after . . .'

Aunt Phoebe smiled indulgently at her. 'Those days are gone for you, Poppy, are they not?'

'Yes, they're gone, but I don't ever regret them. I can't forget them, either. I remember them now with fondness, and the folk who lived and worked there . . . I wouldn't want to go back, though. Not when it was always my intention to get out anyhow . . . I wonder where my poor mother is now, and my sisters and brothers . . . And Buttercup.'

'Buttercup,' Aunt Phoebe mused. 'I hope some day I might meet this Buttercup. I hope some day I might meet your mother too, and the rest of her children. I wonder what she would say if she saw you now, if she saw the change in you.'

'She wouldn't recognise me. Especially not in all these lovely clothes.'

'Oh, she would. Of course she would. Her own daughter.'

They were passing Tansley House, the home of the Crawfords. It started spitting with rain.

'Maybe we should knock on the Crawfords' door and ask if we can shelter from the rain, Aunt Phoebe,' Poppy said, half-serious.

'Oh, I think not, Poppy. Tansley House would be my last choice of refuge without an invitation. But you'll get to see it, no doubt, if you begin to see Bellamy regularly.'

'I'm not sure that I want to see Bellamy regularly,' Poppy replied.

'But such a handsome young man, and with such an assured future. So obviously taken with you. My dear, what girl of seventeen wouldn't want to be seeing Bellamy regularly?'

'This girl.'

'Oh? And why is *this* girl so different from others?'

Poppy hesitated to say.

'Go on . . . There must be a reason . . .'

'Because . . .' She blushed vividly. 'Because *this* girl's in love with Robert.' It was the first time she had admitted it to Aunt Phoebe.

Aunt Phoebe turned to look at Poppy and saw her heightened colour. 'Ah . . . Of course, I suspected it, so I'm hardly surprised. But you must know it's futile, my dear, your holding out any hope of landing Robert.'

'I'm not sure what *futile* means, Aunt Phoebe, but if it means it's a waste of time, then I don't agree. You see, Robert told me he was in love with me as well. And if he *was*, then I reckon he still is. I'm still in love with him anyway. Why should it be any different for him?'

'Are you sure he loves you? This is not just merely some young girl's fancy, is it?'

'No, Aunt, he told me. *And* he meant it. He went to Brazil to get away from that girl he's engaged to, to get away from both of us, so's he could make his mind up about us. I know he wouldn't have married me then – I was just a navvy's daughter – but he loved me all the same. He had to get away to straighten himself out. I do know how hard it is for him having a fiancée already, with his mother and father pressing him to wed her.'

'Mmm . . .' Aunt Phoebe murmured pensively. 'There's a ring of truth in what you tell me. I must say, he gave me no clue when he called to see me before he left, but the fact that he wished me to help you lends it some credence now.'

'It's true, Aunt Phoebe. I don't tell lies.'

'Then, is it fair that you should be going out with Bellamy on Sunday? After all, you could be giving him entirely the wrong impression, falsely raising his hopes, when it's his brother you're really interested in.'

'Oh, I won't give him any wrong impressions. I won't lead him on a bit, I promise. But I do like him. He reminds me of Robert.'

'As I've said before, don't admit to your having known Robert previously. Now . . . Tell me, Poppy – and I apologise if this sounds a little indelicate – but were you and Robert ever . . . ever improper?'

'You mean did we couple, like man and wife?'

Aunt Phoebe gasped. 'My goodness! What a way you have of expressing things.'

'I just say things the way they are, Aunt Phoebe,' Poppy said unapologetically. 'Anyway, no. We never did that. Not that we didn't want to . . . But we never did.'

'I'm glad to hear it.' The older woman uttered a sigh of relief. 'I'm very glad to hear it.'

At about the same time that Aunt Phoebe and Poppy were walking home under the steely sky of a drab April noon, Minnie Catchpole was holding a piece of bread on a toasting fork in front of the fire, when she heard a knock at her door. She was not expecting anybody in particular, but it could have been any one of half a dozen men who had taken to spending a couple of shillings for her charms at odd times during daylight. She pulled the bread from the fire and put it unfinished onto the plate that was on the table, then went to answer the door.

'Oh, it's you, miss.'

'Yes, it's me again, Minnie. Are you going to invite me in?'

'Yes, come in if you want.'

The visitor looked behind her as if checking to see if anybody was watching, and stepped over the threshold with a basket over her arm.

'I've brought you another loaf of bread and some cheese. I managed to get half a dozen oranges as well, and some bananas. There are few decent apples about at the moment, though.'

'It's very kind of you, miss, but there's no need to go to the trouble. How much do I owe you?'

'Nothing, Minnie. They are my gift to you.'

The girl was about twenty, maybe twenty-one, with well-tended raven hair under a plain bonnet. She was slim with an elegance that breeding brought, with classic facial features but not pretty. Her expression seemed perpetually serious but, when she did smile, her eyes softened as they lit up and her lips formed an appealing crescent that revealed two ever so slightly crossed front teeth. Her clothes were plain and unfussy, but their fine quality was undeniable.

'I don't know as I need any help o' that sort,' Minnie answered. 'Not with fittles at any rate. But it's kind o' you all the same. Would yer like a cup o' tea or summat? I got the fire a-goin' today, look, so I can boil a kettle. If you hang on a minute, I'll run to the pump and fill it.'

'If it's no trouble, Minnie,' the girl said, glad of the chance to be detained, for it would prolong the time she could usefully spend with her. 'Aren't you going to put a coat on? It's quite cold outside.'

'Oh, I'm hardy, miss.'

The young woman sat quietly, taking in the awful ambience and squalor of the little house, while Minnie fetched the water. Soon she returned and hung the filled kettle on a gale hook, its base resting on the hot coals.

'It'll soon boil. Would you like a bit o' cheese on toast, miss? That's what I was a-doing for me dinner.'

'Oh, please carry on, Minnie. Don't let me interrupt you having your meal.'

'Right . . . if you got no objection, miss . . .' Minnie pierced the half-toasted piece of bread with the fork again and, leaning forward on her chair, resumed holding it in front of the fire. 'You still reckon I'm a lost soul then, eh?'

'I don't believe you are lost yet, Minnie. I don't believe it's too late to save you from the precipice you're swaying over . . .' Minnie uttered a little laugh of mockery. 'You would soon find forgiveness in Christ—'

'Am yer a Methody, miss?'

'No, I'm not a Methodist, Minnie . . . Don't you ever consider the joy and contentment marriage might bring, Minnie? The love and devotion of one man?'

'That's a joke, miss,' Minnie retorted disparagingly. 'I can see no man ever giving me love and devotion. Leastwise, not the sort you'm on about. Nor me them either, to tell you the truth.'

'I think you could be pleasantly surprised. Holy matrimony was ordained not just for the procreation of children, but as a remedy against sin, to avoid fornication, so that those who are not blessed with the gift of continence might keep themselves undefiled members of Christ's body.'

Minnie turned the piece of bread on the fork to toast the

other side. 'I don't know about all that, miss. Men am ten-a-penny and I fancy having me share of 'em afore I'm done. I like men, and men like me. Why shouldn't I enjoy 'em, and make a shilling or two at the same time? Me only power over 'em is when I got 'em danglin' on a string, wanting me. Once a man gets me in wedlock, then that string'll be round *my* neck, but good and proper. Bearin' kids, cookin', bakin', washin', workin' – mekin' nails up some backyard till all hours, an' all, I shouldn't wonder. I mek me living by lyin' on me back, miss. It's easy work, it comes natural to me and I enjoy it. I don't see as how marryin' some chap's gunna improve *my* lot.'

It was a long speech for Minnie and the toast was done. She cut a few slices off the lump of cheese that was on the table and placed them methodically on the toast. Then she opened the oven door at the side of the grate and popped the toast inside to melt the cheese.

'But Minnie, don't you feel any damnation for your sin?'

Minnie looked candidly at the young woman. 'Only from you, miss.'

The young woman returned the look with caring, sympathetic eyes. 'Why don't you let me help you find repentance in God's love?' she beseeched. 'Would you not prefer the love of God to the arms of Satan? Let me help you find salvation . . . and faith. I beg you to reach out for Christ, and feel His love for you returned a hundredfold. Rejoice in His absolute redemption of your sins. Follow the guidance of the Good Shepherd, Minnie.'

The girl had a soft persuasive lilt in her voice, but Minnie shook her head with a serious look on her face. 'No, miss. It ain't for me, this church lark—' Minnie gave the fire a poke and the kettle sighed as the coals beneath it were disturbed. 'I don't see as why you should want to bother wi' me, miss.'

'You don't have to call me "miss". Let us be friends, Minnie. Please call me Virginia.'

'That your name? Virginia?'

Virginia smiled, her doe eyes exuding a look of gentleness and unending patience. 'I wouldn't ask you to call it me if it wasn't.'

'You know what it means, don't ya? Virgin?' Minnie asked provocatively.

'Yes.' She smiled again, a little embarrassed at Minnie's directness and what she implied. 'I possibly know more about the name than you, but I understand the point you are trying to make. Virginia was originally a Roman family name, but it has a greater significance now as a reference to our great Queen Elizabeth, the Virgin Queen.'

'So, am yer a virgin . . . Virginia? I mean – you *know* as I ain't.'

The rich aroma of cheese cooking permeated the room and Virginia breathed it in. It was a warm, homely smell, incongruous in this spartan den of iniquity in which she now sat.

'I am unmarried, Minnie. But rest assured that I shall remain a virgin until I attain the blessed state of holy matrimony.'

'You don't know what you'm missin', Virginia . . . You don't, honest.'

'No, and I can't begin to imagine, either, Minnie. I'd rather not even try.'

The kettle was starting to bubble and steam profusely, so Minnie lifted it from the fire, holding the handle with a rag. 'I'll mek that tea now.' She reached into the cupboard at the side of the grate and took out a packet of tea.

'I shall not be deterred by your resistance to repentance, you know, Minnie,' Virginia said. 'God's bounteous love is too potent a force to resist for long. So I shall not be despairing of you.'

Minnie smiled appreciatively. 'I know you'm a good person, miss. You'm well meaning an' all that. You'm welcome here any time. We can always enjoy a mug o' tea together, eh? But I ain't gunna promise that I'll ever tek up this church lark . . . Nor give up me whorin'.'

Chapter 21

In his eagerness to see Poppy, Bellamy was a few minutes early collecting her for the drive to the Clent Hills. She was in her bedroom when he arrived, putting the final touches to her hair. Looking in the mirror, she pinched her cheeks and checked her teeth before she ventured down, wearing a walking dress of dark green woollen cloth, a little shorter than the day dresses she wore in the house. As she stepped downstairs she could hear Bellamy and Aunt Phoebe talking in the drawing room. She appeared at the door and smiled affably at him.

'Hello, Bellamy. I just need to put on my mantle and bonnet.'

'If I were you, I'd put on that scarf you've knitted,' Aunt Phoebe advised. 'And take my muff as well. It's chilly today.'

'All right, Aunt.'

Poppy returned after a few minutes, with Dolly behind her.

Bellamy stood up and smiled at Poppy. 'My cart is outside,' he said, denigrating his gig.

'What time do you intend getting back home?' Aunt Phoebe asked, accompanying them to the front door.

'What time d'you want me to be back, Aunt Phoebe?' Poppy asked.

'In time for you to have tea before we go to church. No doubt by then you'll be starving.'

'I'll make sure we're back by then, Aunt,' Bellamy said.

He helped Poppy into the gig before clambering in himself. 'I'm glad the weather's so fine today, Poppy. A beautiful sunny day, even if it is verging a bit on the chilly side. D'you think you'll be warm enough?'

She nodded reassuringly. 'I reckon so.'

'Good.' He clicked to the horse and flicked the reins and they both turned to wave to Aunt Phoebe.

'How far is it to the Clent Hills, Bellamy?'

'About six miles, I think.' He turned onto the Rowley Road and headed up hill. 'It'll take us an hour. Maybe less. We'll have plenty of time for a walk. I asked my father the best way of getting there and he advised me to go via the Lye Waste.'

She shuffled herself comfortable in the seat. 'Does your father know you're seeing me then?'

'Oh yes.' He turned to feast his eyes again on her face. 'He sends his regards.'

'That's kind of him.'

At the top of the hill he avoided looking in the direction of the toll house on the right, but flicked the reins again. The horse broke into a trot and soon they were passing Tansley House.

'I always think your house looks so grand,' Poppy commented.

'Mausoleum, Poppy. It's an absolute mausoleum. Costs my father a fortune to run and maintain. We need our own railway just to ferry in coal for the fires.'

'I bet you could build one.'

'A railway? Maybe we should build a spur from one of the Earl of Dudley's pits.' He chuckled at the thought. 'I must suggest it to Father.'

'Well, Aunt Phoebe tells me that's what you Crawfords do. You're civil engineering contractors, she says. So, has the family firm ever built any railways?'

'A section here and there. But the mania for building new railways is over now. The best days are gone. There's no money for it any more and even less enthusiasm. We've been mostly concerned with other public works, like reservoirs, inclined planes, sewers and docks. We tendered for work on the Oxford, Worcester and Wolverhampton, but my father's a shrewd old devil, you know. He put in a price that he knew they wouldn't accept. Said they were bound to get into financial straits, in which case he might not get paid. It looks as if he might have been right. They shut up shop for lack of money and the damned line ain't finished. Of course, they're looking to the Great Western to bail them out, but we hear rumblings as well that Rufford's, the bank that supports them, is a bit suspect. Despite all that, it seems they can't agree on far too many points of policy.'

'It's a shame,' Poppy said from the heart.

'A shame it is, and no question . . . But enough of this talk of business. I'd hoped for lighter conversation . . . I want to know about you, Poppy. Tell me about your family. Tell me how you came to be Aunt Phoebe's companion. You suddenly appear in our lives like a wondrous vision.'

Poppy pondered what she should tell him. She didn't want to tell him any lies because it was against her nature. Yet she could hardly tell him the truth, for the truth was too demeaning and would almost certainly mean being shunned in future. So she decided to stall until she could think of how to answer.

'How is your younger sister?'

'Well, I believe. She writes regularly from school.'

'What's she like?'

'Oh, she's an absolute pest when she's home. Let's not discuss her.'

Poppy laughed at that. But it was not Elizabeth she was

interested in anyway. 'Have you heard from your brother Robert since?'

'Nothing since. But they say no news is good news. I mean bad news travels fast, don't it?'

'How's his fiancée taken his going away?'

'Ain't seen her, Poppy. She's been to Tansley House since Robert went to Brazil, I believe, but not when I've been there. Anyway, you were about to tell me all about you and your family.'

'My family, yes . . . My family are in railway building . . .' She looked up at him and beamed, defying the apprehension she felt inside if Bellamy's questioning became too intense.

He hooted. 'Well . . . now there's a coincidence if ever I heard one! Fancy that. Nobody said, you know. What are they working on now?'

'To tell the truth I'm not sure. My father had to go away to work . . . last summer . . . He met with an accident and died. Now—'

'Good Lord!' he interjected. 'That's damned bad luck. You lost your father, eh? My condolences, Poppy. I wouldn't have mentioned it . . . I often worry about my father meeting with an accident on one of the sites, you know. He wants to be involved in everything. He's always on site with the men. Can't keep him away. I think he's got a secret yearning for the muck and the mud, and the men's swearing. It reminds him of his youth, I suppose. Sounds as if your father was the same.'

Poppy smiled angelically. She had told Bellamy no lie. But to her surprise he had likened what she'd told him to his own family's situation. Well, there seemed little sense in allowing him to think otherwise.

'And what about your mother?'

'My mother thought it would be a good idea if I went away

. . . to see a bit more of the world . . .' To see why the rest of the world fared better might have been nearer the truth. 'I was told about this lady . . . So I presented myself at her door one day . . . She turned out to be Aunt Phoebe.'

'Well, I'm blessed. Just think. If you hadn't, you and I might never have met. Aunt Phoebe deserves to be beatified. Anyway, it's so obvious she thinks the world of you, Poppy.'

'I think the world of her. She's been so good to me . . .'

They fell silent awhile as Bellamy negotiated the cobbled streets beyond St Thomas's church. They drove down the Pedmore Turnpike Road where they crossed the unfinished and unloved Oxford, Worcester and Wolverhampton Railway. Seeing it again brought a lump to her throat. It was deserted, save for some young lads playing on part of the levelled strip of land. No navvies, drunk or sober, populated it now.

On to Pear Tree Lane. The landscape was desolate here, devoid of vegetation. Not one blade of grass dared show itself against the clammy black earth that glistened with mud and melanite puddles in the bright sunshine after days of enduring April rain. Both sides of the road were afflicted with the dismal spoils of coal mining. Slag heaps loomed, some higher than several houses, and the primitive headgear of pits looked like the skeletons of automata picked clean by some monstrous vulture. Scores of chimney stacks, idle on God's appointed rest day, pierced the sky, which was, for once, blue and free of smuts. Tomorrow, the same chimney stacks would come alive, volleying upward great columns of acrid smoke. A little further on they passed the Earl of Dudley's burgeoning ironworks. Its dark furnaces, even on a Sunday, were as hot as Hades, and endless plumes of smoke – vast, brown, woolly serpents – reared up into the atmosphere. Locomotives, like well-trained animals, hauled slag for tipping, iron bars as thick as tree trunks for puddling.

Neither Poppy nor Bellamy commented on the bleakness. It was part of everyday life, something that was visually tolerated but financially encouraged, for wealth grew out of it; a landscape wilfully ravaged by man in his relentless quest for prosperity. A necessary evil. Poppy had never minded it; she had never known anything different until she had spent some time in Aunt Phoebe's lavish garden, shut away from it all. In that quiet idyllic corner, she might have been a hundred miles away from the industrial canker that blighted the rest of the Black Country. So it must be for Bellamy. So it must have been for Robert.

They pressed on, Bellamy making little jokes about this and that in an effort to make Poppy laugh. They passed through an area of stubbly fields and small impoverished farms until the road led them among rows of shabby cottages, close packed, with angled roofs crowded this way and that, miserably poor. A place known as the Lye Waste, built on the side of a hill and in fear of sliding down it. The air was heavy with smoke. Poppy held her nose and felt like retching at the sickening stench.

'What's that stink?' she exclaimed, forgetting herself. 'It's 'orrible.'

'Burning clay from the brick kilns apparently,' Bellamy told her. 'My father said it might reek a bit.'

Stunted children in rags ran barefoot through the dirty, muddy streets. Men, drunk on cheap beer, tottered from one alehouse to another till their money was gone, urinating in any convenient alley, behind any corner. Young women, with the haunted look of the old and weary, stood on their front doorsteps and gossiped with neighbours, with nothing to look forward to but tomorrow. Tomorrow, and the chink of hammer on anvil as they wrought one iron nail after another with mind-numbing, soul-destroying monotony in the hot forges in their back yards. Poppy saw them and her heart bled. Never had she seen such grim poverty, such woeful conditions. The navvies' encampment at Blowers Green was gruesome enough, but it was a paradise compared to this. It served as a grisly reminder of just how fortunate she had been lately.

'Do we have to come back this way, Bellamy?' she asked. 'I don't fancy going through that place again.'

'I'm not sure. Perhaps we can avoid it.'

But just as quickly as they had come upon the Lye Waste, they passed through it and were surrounded by countryside as pretty and smiling as anywhere in England.

Soon they were near Hagley, at the very foot of the Clent Hills. They reached the village of Clent through lanes that were fairy grottoes of overhanging trees, their budding limbs casting an intricate tracery of shadows in the slanting sun. They drove on up, past a pretty church, the hill becoming steeper.

'D'you think we ought to get out of the gig and walk?' Poppy queried. 'Make it easier for the poor horse?'

'Poor horse be damned,' Bellamy replied. 'He's well cared for. He's fed and watered regularly, groomed. Let him earn his keep.'

Poppy shrugged. It was not the response she had anticipated. She felt she should get out anyway. She had some sympathy for the animal, but was reticent about asking Bellamy to stop, lest he refused and made her feel silly. Perhaps ladies were not supposed to consider the welfare of animals. She would ask Aunt Phoebe.

On and on they went, climbing higher and higher, until the road levelled out and they were on a high ridge. A vast panorama stretched out before them. Bellamy stopped the gig and stepped down.

'That's quite a view, Poppy.'

He walked round the gig and took her hand to help her down. She went to the other side and looked out. They were facing north, the slanting sun peering over their shoulders. He came up to her and stood beside her.

'What can you see?' he asked.

'I'm not sure.'

'Right there on the horizon . . .' He put his arm around her proprietorially, leaned his face towards hers and pointed. 'Dudley Castle keep. Can you see it?'

'Just about.'

'And there's the spire of St Thomas's . . .'

'Oh yes . . . But all those chimney stacks, look . . .'

'And that conglomeration over to the right, look . . . That must be Birmingham.'

'Have you ever been to Birmingham, Bellamy?' she enquired, the thought of it appealing to her sense of adventure.

'A few times. Have you?'

'Never . . . Someday, maybe . . .'

'Someday I'll take you.'

Well, someday he might, but she would not press for it.

'At the moment we – Crawford and Sons Limited, that is – are involved with the Borough Council and the Commissioners there over the planning of a huge project, to build a new sewerage and drainage system. We are awaiting the order to proceed. It will keep us occupied for years and make us a fortune.'

'So you will be rich, Bellamy.'

'We don't do so badly now.'

She smiled. 'Shall we walk on? Up there?'

'Let's . . . I'll tether the horse to the fence.'

'I bet he could do with a drink of water, Bellamy.'

'There'll be a trough in the village on the way back,' he answered indifferently.

He took her hand and they began walking, climbing a grassy knoll. It was hard going and he had to hold on to her hand and pull her. At the top they found a bench and sat on it, glad of the rest.

'I can't get over the view,' she said pensively. 'You know, if I can see these hills from my bedroom window, I wonder if I can see Aunt Phoebe's house from here.'

Bellamy looked at Poppy and was enchanted by the look of earnest curiosity on her face. He was moved to put his arm around her shoulders again and hug her. 'I suspect not,' he said quietly. 'I imagine it's too far distant to see without a telescope. See how small even the castle looks . . .'

'Pity. We could've waved to her.'

He laughed. 'Oh, Poppy, you're such a delight . . .'

'No, I bet you anything she's looking towards this place now wondering why she can't see us . . . Don't laugh. I bet it's true.'

He looked at her adoringly. 'Will you accompany me often, Poppy? Will you agree to see me as often as you can?'

She stared at some cows that were lying down chewing cud in a field below. 'I wonder what the time is. Is it time we should be starting back?'

'Please answer my question, Poppy.'

She looked into his eyes apprehensively, a look he mistook for one of expectancy. He was thus encouraged, and cleared his throat nervously. 'Listen . . . I confess I'm fairly taken with you, Poppy . . . No, more than that . . . I'm mesmerised.'

A shadow crossed Poppy's face. She avoided his eyes now and looked down at her gloved hands, primly held together in her lap. 'You shouldn't say such things, Bellamy,' she replied, feeling suddenly hot in the cool air, her voice little more than a croak of uncertainty.

'Why not, pray? I can't help being taken with you. It's not something I choose.'

'No? But you could turn away from me. If that's how you really feel, you could resist.'

'Why should I resist? Besides, I don't have that sort of willpower.'

'I think it would pay you to resist, Bellamy.'

She was reminded of having to ward off Jericho and his lustful advances – more than once. She remembered how she was then; a waif in tatty clothes, but evidently appealing none-theless, ignorant of the finer things in life, but aware there must be something infinitely better than allowing herself to sink to the life of a navvy's doxy. Of course, at that time she was suffused with desire for Robert Crawford, but uncertain as to his feelings for her . . . Funny how nothing had changed in that respect, for all her finery now, for all Aunt Phoebe's tutoring. She might speak a little differently in company these days but she had to think about it still; it was not yet second nature to sound all her aitches and form her vowel sounds more roundly. She had to remember to hold herself with greater elegance and bearing. She had to consciously assume an air of confidence that she did not entirely feel, even though she believed she had fooled many people, including Bellamy. Her feelings for Robert Crawford had not changed though. She was still holding out for him, however slim the prospect of attaining him.

'I'm sorry,' Bellamy exclaimed. 'I'm going too fast, I suspect. I apologise, Poppy. I should give you time to get used to the idea of how I feel about you. I should give you time to think. Gracious, you must have scores of admirers . . . I admit to being impatient, you know . . . Well, now at least you know how I feel . . . that I want you for my own.'

'I'm flattered, Bellamy. But I can't—I don't—'

'Why not, Poppy? I don't see why not.'

'Because I don't want to become romantically involved. I like you, Bellamy, but don't expect anything more than that.'

She met his eyes steadily now and tried to read them. They were so like Robert's in shape and colouring; even the faint creases around the lids . . . Yet something was missing. They did not have the look of gentle, warm compassion that Robert's eyes exuded. Oh, Bellamy's were not unkind, not thoughtless nor giving any hint of deceitfulness, but there was this look of self-assurance – a sort of arrogance that comes from having everything you set your heart on – that was never present in Robert's look.

'Don't say anything else now, Poppy. Don't put too much stress on it. I mean, it's not as if I've asked you to marry me. I've merely let you know that I am very much taken with you.'

She hesitated before she said, 'Oh, Bellamy, what can I say? I don't know how else to answer you.'

'Answer me in the positive.'

'But I wasn't expecting this. I had no intention of inviting it.'

'But you'll think on what I've said? You'll consider it?'

'I shall think of it,' she answered. 'In the sense that it will be on my mind . . . But I don't think I can be what you want me to be.'

'What do you think I want you to be, Poppy?'

She shrugged, uncomfortable with this insistent line of questioning. 'It's obvious. You want me to be your woman.' It was a phrase, a concept from her past life. Perhaps she should not have uttered it. It implied too many things, most of them considered improper in the society she now graced.

'My woman?' He hooted with laughter. 'I'm not sure how to interpret that. I would like you and me to be a courting couple. I would like you to be my regular companion in private and in public, at social events, to be accepted by all and recognised as such. If, after a decent time, we proved to be compatible, we could even contemplate taking it a step further. That, I don't think, is unreasonable. But let's not take anything for granted yet. Such happenings would be a long way off.'

'Have you ever been in love before, Bellamy?'

'God, yes. I'm not totally without experience where women are concerned. I've been blooded, too, if that's not too impolite an expression. I've had affairs. I know what it is to feel desire, to feel tenderness. Even to feel protective towards a girl.'

'But these affairs, as you call them, never amounted to anything?'

'They were not the right girls, Poppy.'

'How do you know that I am?'

'I feel it, I sense it. I knew it the moment I set eyes on you. I saw how you looked at me, as well . . .'

'Oh, if I did, it was only because you reminded me of somebody else . . .' She hoped he would not be astute enough to pick up any clues as to whom.

'So is there somebody else, Poppy? I had the distinct impression there was not.'

She did not answer.

'Who?'

'That, I would never tell you . . .'

He uttered a little laugh that had a ring of mockery in it. 'Even if there is somebody else, that won't put me off. And if there is, he certainly ain't with you here, is he? Therefore, as long as he ain't here, I've got a chance. And I won't give up, Poppy . . . I'll win in the end. I always get what I want . . .' He smiled broadly. 'So be warned.'

* * *

The following day, Poppy received a letter from the Reverend James Caulfield Browne confirming her appointment as assistant to Mr Timothy Tromans, the schoolmaster of Baylies's Charity School, working mornings only at seven guineas a year. She was to report for duty on the following Monday, the twenty-ninth of April.

Poppy duly sat down and wrote back, joyously accepting the offer, and looking forward to her new situation. After all, she would be following in the footsteps of Aunt Phoebe to some extent, and that realisation elicited pride. It was evidence of her personal achievements, achievements she would have regarded as impossible much less than a year ago, gigantic achievements for a girl who was navvy-born and navvy-bred. But they were achievements that were only made possible in the first place because of Robert Crawford and his interest in her. Because of his love and his compassion. How could she ever turn her back on him? She was eternally in his debt, but it was a debt she welcomed and relished. With or without Bellamy's confession and his promised further attentions.

She put the pen down and folded the letter to Reverend Browne. As she tucked it into the envelope a powerful wave of sentiment gushed over her. The justified pride in her achievement, the gratitude she bore to Robert and Aunt Phoebe for the transmuting of her thoroughly base life into something infinitely more precious, and the confusing revelation by Bellamy, all combined to produce a white-hot alloy of heightened emotion. She gazed out of the library window as she sat at the oak desk and thought her heart would burst. Clay was out in the garden tending the lawn. Tears welled in her eyes till he was indistinct in her vision, and the grass, the trees and the sky melded into one hazy blur of blue and green. She clenched her fists in an involuntary fervour of passion that was manifesting itself not in her success, but in her failure.

That singular failure was losing Robert, however temporarily. If only she could have clung on to him when she had him. If only she had refused to leave his side when his emotions were running high, when he confessed his love for her. She closed her eyes tight, squeezing out the tears, which ran unchecked down her gently rounded cheeks, and she cried bitter tears for him.

Oh, Robert, where are you now? Do you think of me as often as I think of you? Do you ache inside like I do, longing just to be with you, to feel your arms around me, dying to taste your kisses, even after all this time? Do you lie alone in your bed and wish I was with you, like I wish you were with me? Does your heart thump hard when you think of me, like mine does when I think of you? Do you weep for me at night like I weep for you? Do you wonder what I am doing like I wonder about you? I am afraid for you in Brazil, Robert. I worry about you always, hoping, praying that you are safe, that you are well. I miss you more than I could ever have imagined. I miss you more even than I miss my own family. You would be so proud of me now if you could see me. I am not quite the same Poppy I was, but much more to your liking, I believe. I don't think you would be shy of being seen out with me anymore, either. When are you going to come back? How soon before I can feel the warmth of your body again, pressed against me? I know you will choose me rather than the girl you are engaged to. I feel it, as a certainty. If you have already made up your mind, please come back now and claim me and let us be happy together for the rest of our lives, never to be apart again. I love you so much, Robert. Please, never forget it. Let the memory of our love stay with you and strengthen you and give you wings to fly back to me at once.

Chapter 22

Poppy worried privately about whether she would fail Aunt Phoebe, Mrs Green and herself at Baylies's Charity School. She worried too whether she would be accepted, about the work, and about what would be expected of her. Aunt Phoebe had said she would be regarded as a sort of pupil teacher, but since she had never been a pupil at a school, more especially a pupil at a boys' school, she was concerned that she would be entirely out of her depth and out of place. What if some boy wanted help on a problem of arithmetic or grammar that she was unable to answer? What if she was asked a question about geography? Goodness . . . Geography . . . The only places she knew anything about, apart from Dudley, were Brazil, which she had seen on the globe, Edinburgh because of Robert's university days, and Mickleton where her father had met his death.

All these things and more were going through her mind as she walked to the school for the first time on the cool morning of the last Monday in April. She arrived five minutes early and was greeted cordially and put at ease by Mr Tromans, the schoolmaster. After a brief conversation she followed him outside into the yard that was chilly, lying as it was in the grey shadow of the glassworks and its huge cone. He blew his whistle and the boys, of varying ages, rushed about keenly to form lines straight enough to put a smile on the face of an army general. They stood erect, their heads held high, as they waited for Mr Tromans to call the register.

'Quickly and quietly, file into the classroom,' Mr Tromans ordered when the job was done.

By the time they had all filed quickly and quietly inside, Reverend Browne had appeared. He led them in prayers and they sang a hymn to Mr Tromans's faltering harmonium accompaniment. Reverend Browne then addressed the school, introducing Mr Tromans's new assistant, Miss Silk, whose services they were fortunate to have secured. Every boy would treat her with the respect and courtesy afforded any young lady of standing, under pain of death. Reverend Browne then went on, indoctrinating the pupils sufficiently early in their lives he hoped, to talk about the evils of drink and the virtues of abstinence, before they sang another hymn.

It was a bit of a novelty for the lads at Baylies's Charity School to find they were blessed with the pretty young woman they'd seen a week or so before, now helping Mr Tromans in their classroom. The older boys were inclined to flash optimistic grins at her, designed to outshine their rivals. Others remained expressionless but could not take their eyes off her, while some of the younger ones were too shy to hold any eye contact at all. Mr Tromans realised early the effects Poppy was having and was all the stricter for it, inhibiting any notions of inappropriate behaviour any of them might have been nurturing.

At first she found herself handing out chalk sticks, cleaning the blackboard when requested. The older boys were allowed to use pen and ink and she was asked to top up inkwells, even when it was obvious they did not need topping up. When Mr Tromans was engaged with one pupil, others would attract her attention and ask for help with their work. Some did not actually need her help but they requested it just to gain proximity.

'Are you married, miss?' one whispered.

'No, I'm not married.'

'Will you marry me then?'

'Perhaps when you grow up,' she deftly answered, which immediately earned her the respect of those within earshot.

'You smell nice, miss,' another boy whispered cheekily as she collected written sheets of paper from him to hand to Mr Tromans. 'Better than my sisters.'

'Thank you,' she replied courteously. 'But I wouldn't tell your sisters that.'

That first morning passed quickly and with no undue trouble or embarrassment, and Poppy decided to pay a visit to Minnie Catchpole afterwards to tell her all about it, and to keep her up to date with the other events in her life. It was no more than a three-minute walk from the school, and Poppy was glad to see her friend.

'I got meself respectable work, Minnie,' Poppy declared proudly, but lapsing into her old mode of speech with which she felt comfortable when talking to her oldest friend; after all, there was no point in putting on airs and graces for Minnie. She sat down on the sofa, took off her gloves and laid them on her lap primly. She told Minnie all about her work.

'Lord, how you've gone up in the world,' Minnie remarked when her friend had finished. 'You always wanted to be a lady, and now you am one.'

'Oh, it's nice being a lady. It's nice having a clean bed in a warm room, and eating good food off bone china and silver cutlery. I love everything about it . . .'

'But?'

'But there's something else . . . And I don't know what to

do about it . . .' Maybe Minnie could offer some sound advice. 'You remember Robert Crawford, the engineer?'

'The one you had a bit of a fling with?'

Poppy nodded. 'Now his younger brother's all over me. He keeps coming to Aunt Phoebe's. Not to see her, to see me.'

Minnie shrugged. 'So what's up with that?'

'He's serious, Min. He says he loves me. He wants us to start courting.'

'Is he as 'andsome as his brother?'

Poppy tutted impatiently. 'That's beside the point. I like him, yes. He's good company. But I don't *love* him. I could never love him. Well . . . I suppose I could put up with him, but why should I put up with second best? I'd never love him like I love Robert. Anyway, what if I say yes to him and Robert comes back home for me? What happens then?'

'You still clingin' to dreams of this Robert?'

'Course. Why shouldn't I?'

Minnie gave a mocking laugh. 'You? Look at you. You'm like a princess. You could have your pick of any number o' chaps now. Real gentlemen.'

'Robert's a real gentleman.' She watched a woodlouse crawl along one of the square quarry tiles and conceal itself under the skirting board. 'But I don't want any number of chaps, Min. I want Robert, and I know he'll come back for me. That's why I have to keep putting this Bellamy off.' She sighed heavily. 'Any other girl would be glad of his attentions, I know that. I mean, he's handsome. His prospects are good, coming from a wealthy family. But I can't tell him *why* I don't want to start courting him. If I do start, then I change my mind again when Robert comes back – which I would . . . D'you see what I mean?'

'Yes . . .' Minnie replied pensively. 'But you could still have fun with this Bellamy. Maybe you should tell him your secret . . .'

'No, I could never do that. He wouldn't understand. He's really serious about me. I'm sure he'd be jealous.'

'Then it's best you give him no encouragement, Poppy . . . not yet at any rate . . . But what about if this Robert comes back and he don't want you after all? What if he comes back to marry the one he's engaged to?'

'Oh, don't say that, Minnie. I know he'll come for me.'

'Well, I hope you ain't mistaken, and give up the chance with his brother. You would be a fool . . . Have you mentioned it to Aunt Phoebe?'

'Yes.'

'And what does she say?'

'Same as you. Don't encourage him.'

'There y'am then . . . Any road, I've got a sort o' problem an' all.'

'Oh, Minnie, what?' Poppy asked with alarm.

'There's this young woman what keeps coming to see me, trying to get me on the straight and narrer . . .'

'So who is she?'

'Says her name's Virginia. Can you believe such a name? I reckon she *is* a virgin an' all . . . And she's older than me.'

'I'm a virgin as well, Minnie. So don't mock. It's something to be proud of in this day and age.'

'Proud of? It's nothing to be proud of, keeping your virginity. Virginity's no use to anybody. It's only any use after you've lost it.'

'Well, maybe you wish you'd still got yours.'

Minnie chuckled. 'It makes no odds to me.'

'Are you going to make a cup of tea, Minnie? I'm parched.'

'Course, if you want one.'

'Then you can tell me how you got on with that Captain Tyler.'

'Oh, Captain Tyler . . .'

Minnie got up to put the kettle over the coals, then picked up the teapot with the intention of introducing a couple of teaspoons of fresh tea leaves. Some cold tea remained inside, so she took the lid off, opened the door and hurled the contents outside into Gatehouse Fold. At once there was a mild scream of protest and Minnie put her head out to see whom she had drenched.

It was Virginia. She stood at the door with wet tea leaves clinging to the front of her fine mantle, the brown liquid trickling off and staining the unadorned flounces of her skirt beneath.

'Oh, it's you again, miss. I'm so sorry. I dint mean to drown yer. Come in and I'll wipe you clean. I was just talking about yer.'

'Please don't worry, Minnie,' Virginia replied, obviously disgruntled at this violation of her dignity. 'But might I suggest that before you throw your slops out next time, you look to make sure there's nobody there.'

'Like I say, I'm that sorry, miss—'

'Virginia,' Virginia corrected, regaining some poise.

'I'm that sorry, Virginia.'

A stone sink bled waste to the outside, and near it was a damp cloth. Minnie reached for it and began wiping Virginia's mantle and her skirt.

'By the way, miss—Virginia . . . this is Poppy Silk . . .'

Virginia looked embarrassed when she turned and saw a well-dressed young woman already in the house with Minnie. Poppy, however, smiled openly and stood up to greet the stranger, as Aunt Phoebe had taught her. She offered her hand and said in her best voice, 'How do you do?'

'Virginia Lord, Miss Silk. How nice to meet you. I only wish I had not been showered with cold tea first.' She smiled self-consciously. 'It would have been a far more conventional

353

introduction, I think.' Virginia then laughed at her predicament, and the warmth of her demeanour, despite the suddenly inflicted disadvantage, appealed to Poppy. 'I do hope I have not called at an inopportune moment.' She looked enquiringly at Poppy with soft, brown eyes.

'Not at all,' Poppy replied. 'I was about to go. I happened to be close by.'

'Oh, please don't leave on my account, Miss Silk.'

'No, you'm all right, Virginia,' Minnie confirmed. 'I was about to brew a pot o' tea. You'm welcome to a cup . . . Down your throat this time, not down your cloak.'

Poppy found it difficult to hide her amusement, but she did so, adequately. 'Minnie says you're also trying to talk some sense into her,' Poppy said, diverting them all from the unfortunate accident. 'I hope you succeed where I've failed.'

Virginia smiled, relieved that she had encountered what she believed to be a kindred spirit. 'Oh, it's so reassuring to meet another person who is doing good and much needed work among these girls. Tell me, Miss Silk, whom else do you see?'

Poppy flashed Minnie a quizzical glance, uncertain how to respond. She saw a flicker of devilment in Minnie's eyes as she looked up from tending to Virginia's flounces, suggesting they let Virginia's misreading of the situation prevail.

'Not the same girls as you,' Poppy replied, going along with the deception. 'Except for Minnie here.'

'So it would seem. I've asked Minnie a few times now if she is prepared to join me in worship. God alone is our saviour, you know, Miss Silk. I am convinced she will find joy in God's sanctification, in the forgiveness that comes from Him who only *can* forgive.'

'Oh, I'm convinced of it too,' Poppy said mischievously,

perceiving the joke could be turned to backfire on Minnie. 'Why don't you go along, Minnie? Miss Lord is right. You would benefit greatly from embracing God for a change.'

Minnie stood up. She had done as much as she could to Virginia's dress and mantle. She put down the damp cloth on the table.

'Then I will, Miss Silk,' she replied, mimicking Poppy's reassumed superior voice and accent with a twinkle in her eye. 'If you'll come with me . . .'

Poppy flashed daggers at Minnie, but Minnie merely smiled angelically, defying her friend to refuse. 'The kettle's boiling. I'll make that tea.'

'Which is your usual place of worship, Miss Silk?' Virginia asked with genuine interest.

'I normally go to St Thomas's.'

'Well, I have an idea. Why don't all three of us go into a place of worship – one that none of us would normally attend – and pray together for Minnie's salvation. Let us together ask God to guide her away from the path of wickedness on which she has so sinfully embarked. That is not to say that Minnie is the only sinner among us, of course. We are all sinners in the eyes of the Lord. We could all benefit from His forgiveness.'

'Oh, and how would *I* benefit?' Minnie asked, tiring of repeated interference and personal disparagement of her life from this Virginia. 'I feel no sin. And why should I? Sin is doing bad to other folk, not enjoying what you do. I don't do nobody no harm. In what way do I sin? I just enjoy what I do. How is that a sin?'

'Your sin is in the selling of your body for money,' Virginia replied earnestly. 'It is putting temptation in the way of men who might be married with families to look after. It is against God's law. I want to bring you into the light, Minnie, so that you can freely acknowledge this sin. Then you will feel the forgiveness, the joy of salvation. Salvation is the gateway to eternal life, Minnie.'

'And Gatehouse Fold is the pen what holds me back, is that it?'

'Since you put it like that . . . Look, meet Miss Silk and myself one morning—'

'It would have to be an afternoon,' Poppy interjected.

'One afternoon then,' Virginia assented. 'We'll find a quiet place to pray together.'

'Oh, all right,' Minnie said reluctantly. 'Anything for a quiet life . . .'

'Wonderful,' Virginia said, and they arranged it together.

Poppy and Virginia met a week later, at three in the afternoon of the first Monday in May. The venue was, as Virginia had suggested, neutral territory. She chose the Friends' Meeting House in High Street, opposite the Old Bush where Poppy and Minnie had spent their first nights of freedom from the navvies' encampment. As they waited in the clear May sunshine for Minnie to arrive, Poppy was reminded of it, and privately reflected again on how much had happened since then, how radically her life had changed.

'Tell me something about yourself, Miss Silk,' Virginia said, interrupting Poppy's thoughts.

'Why don't you call me Poppy?' she replied amicably. 'And allow me to call you Virginia. Sometimes this formality is too much to bear.'

Virginia smiled and touched Poppy's arm in a gesture of companionship. 'I do agree. It does tend to keep people at arm's length who might otherwise be wonderful friends. Thank you, Poppy, for taking the trouble to suggest it.'

'It just seems common sense to me.'

'So are you from these parts?' Virginia said, resuming her original line of enquiry. 'I don't think I know any Silks.'

A cart rattled past, heading towards the Town Hall and its market.

'Oh, you wouldn't. Their business is elsewhere,' she answered economically. 'I am staying with an aunt.' It was sufficient information, and not entirely an untruth.

'How long have you known Minnie?'

'Oh, a long time.'

'What? Three months? Six months?'

'Oh, more than six months.'

'Sometimes, you have to work with these girls longer than that. You only hope that by the time you do reach them it's not too late . . . I wonder how long Minnie's likely to be? Is she normally late, do you know?'

'I've always found her to be very reliable, Virginia, but she has got a funny fob watch that's unreliable. Maybe she doesn't know the right time . . . Minnie's not all bad, you know. She's as honest as the day is long, especially where money is concerned. She owed me a tidy sum once, but she quickly paid it all back. Her problem is that she's too fond of men. She actually loves what she does. Nobody's forced her into prostitution. And she does it on her own account, without a pimp.'

Virginia could just see the clock of St Thomas's church. 'The sins of the flesh, Poppy. She's a lost cause then, do you think?'

Poppy shrugged. 'In that sense, maybe. Unless somebody comes along who'll sweep her off her feet.'

'Do you mind if I make an observation, Poppy?' Virginia asked gently.

Their eyes met and Poppy smiled affably. 'Depends what it is.'

'You seem very young to be volunteering for this type of work. Too young, I would have thought, to be confronted with such sin . . . And yet on the other hand, I suppose it enables you to approach and communicate more easily with those very young girls who have fallen into a life of prostitution.'

'I *am* seventeen, Virginia,' Poppy protested. 'And I do other work. Anyway, how old are you?'

'Twenty-one.'

'There. You're not exactly old yourself then, are you?'

Virginia smiled. 'I suppose not . . . So what other work do you do?'

'I work in a school.'

'Oh, you teach?'

'Well—'

'Oh, I long to teach, Poppy. I'm sure I would be a very good teacher. I feel I could do so much good.'

'Then why don't you become a teacher?' Poppy craned her neck, scanning the streets for sight of Minnie.

'That would mean going against the express wishes of my father. I couldn't possibly do that.'

Poppy looked at Virginia with a puzzled expression. 'Why should your father not want you to teach?'

'Because in his opinion it would be too demeaning.'

'Oh . . .' Poppy was not sure of that last word's meaning, but guessed it all the same and gave no indication that she could have felt slighted. 'The way I see it, Virginia, if it helps somebody to get on in life, then there's nothing wrong with it at all. If I were you, I would deliberately go against my father. I would stand up for what I believe in.'

Virginia laughed aloud. 'Oh, I do just adore your spirit, Poppy. Would that I had the courage.'

'It doesn't take courage. To me it's common sense.'

'Oh, Poppy. You have such an outrageous defiance about you that I so envy. Where have you been brought up? In the colonies?'

'It doesn't matter where I was brought up. I've seen so many children deprived of learning. They live in such poverty, and poverty makes them ignorant of the world. How can they better themselves without being given the opportunity to learn? The world would be a better place if all children were allowed to learn reading and writing, if somebody would open the door for them to the world of culture.'

'Oh, such noble beliefs,' Virginia enthused. 'I do admire your attitude enormously.'

'What's so important about your father that you wouldn't dare defy him?' Poppy asked.

'Well, his position.'

'He's *so* important?'

'In his world he is *very* important. In his world it would not be seemly to have a daughter with an independent streak in her. No, I dare not fall out of line.'

'And yet you mix with prostitutes,' Poppy goaded.

'He doesn't know that.'

'Oh . . .'

'None of my family are aware of it,' Virginia went on to admit. 'It's something I do when time permits. I have this inner need – a compulsion – to try and do some good in this world.'

'And you go to church regular . . . ly?' Poppy almost forgot her grammar.

'Oh, yes. But the Established Church is not evangelical enough for my tastes. Tell me, Poppy, when was the last time somebody from St Thomas's, say, went out in an effort to save souls? Never, I suggest, with the exception of yourself.'

'Well, I don't really—'

'No, they are too steeped in worthless tradition. The Anglican clergy are too complacent in their safe livings. They are sons of the wealthy and the well-to-do, almost to a man. How many of them go to the trouble of seeking to save the errant souls in the coal pits, the ironworks, or among the railway navvies, for instance?'

'I've never seen one outside of church,' Poppy agreed.

'My mother, you know, was a Quaker,' Virginia declared, and Poppy thought she sounded proud of it, whatever it was.

'A Quaker?'

Virginia smiled her kind, gentle smile. 'I think I get my compulsive evangelical urge from her. Of course, when she married my father – who belonged to the Established Church – she was disowned.'

'Disowned?' Poppy queried with a frown. 'I don't understand.'

'Of course . . . If you've never had anything to do with the Society of Friends – which they like to be known as – then you wouldn't understand. So I'll explain . . . Anybody who marries out – that is, marries somebody who is not a Quaker – is disowned, excluded. A ridiculous policy, in my opinion, when you consider that membership is declining because of it. But then, I'm in no position to change the rules. Nevertheless, I admire the Quakers and what they stand for. I always have.'

'So that's the reason we're standing waiting outside the Friends' Meeting House?'

'Yes, I confess it,' Virginia said with a broad smile that showed her crossed front teeth. 'Anyway . . . It seems that our friend Miss Catchpole is not going to keep her appointment with us, Poppy. A pity. I had the feeling she was a candidate for repentance.'

Poppy glanced at St Thomas's church clock. It said twenty

past three. 'No, I don't think she'll come now. Even if her fob watch is ten minutes slow. She'd have been here by now.'

'Could I invite you, Poppy, to join me sometime at one of the Society of Friends' Meetings?'

'What for?'

'Well . . . As a regular churchgoer in the Anglican tradition, you might find the difference uplifting. The Friends' Meeting House is not like a church. There are no ministers as such. Nobody preaches. They worship in silence . . . and yet they feel the benign ambience of God's love in their collective silence. When somebody feels moved by God to speak, they speak.'

Poppy sighed frustratedly. 'I have to tell you, Virginia, that I am not the religious person you think I am.'

'All the more reason to join me then,' Virginia replied without hesitation. 'I am driven by God's love, by his desire to save souls.'

'I am driven more by common sense, Virginia.' Poppy hoped she did not sound disparaging or impatient.

'How do you mean?'

'Well, for instance . . . Is your father's refusal to let you become a teacher based on religious grounds?'

'More the principle of respectability, I suspect.'

'Ah . . . Respectability . . .' That word again. 'So this respectability, which we are all supposed to strive for, does not reach out to benefit the poor and underprivileged? Those illiterate souls such as the miners, ironworkers and railway navvies you mentioned earlier?'

Virginia looked thoughtful for a few moments and, finding it hard to read her expression, Poppy wondered whether she had gone too far, expressed too much disapproval.

But Virginia sighed. 'The way you put it makes him sound so hypocritical. I confess that such thoughts as you have expressed have been taking shape in my own mind. Your direct way of interpreting it has indeed given form to such thoughts. Your notions would certainly be embraced by the Quakers, and that's why I think I am so drawn to them. Will you not reconsider, Poppy, and join me here one First Day at the Friends' Meeting House?'

'First day?'

'Sorry. The Friends' parlance for Sunday.'

'I don't know, Virginia. I always go to church with my aunt . . .'

'I beg of you. You have a fresh way of thinking. You are clearly unfettered by the shackles of conventionality, and certainly not inhibited by it. For myself, I feel I could benefit greatly from your way of thinking. Not that I wish to become a rebel. Merely to be shown and to appreciate another point of view. I have the strongest feeling we could be close friends, Poppy. We are opposites, aren't we? And opposites do attract . . .'

When Poppy left Virginia that afternoon, she decided to call on Minnie. It was unlike her to miss meeting somebody when she had agreed the arrangement, and Poppy wondered whether she was ill. So she walked through the town towards St Edmund's church and made her way to Gatehouse Fold. Even on this warm, sunny day, she felt a chill as she entered the courtyard, as always feeling that unseen eyes were watching her. She looked around apprehensively as she reached Minnie's door. She tapped it with her knuckle and waited. There was no answer. She stepped back and looked up at the upstairs window, anticipating Minnie opening the sash and peering out. But there was no curtain up at the window. There was no curtain at the downstairs window either. How peculiar. Minnie must have gone. She must have left the house for good.

Chapter 23

Poppy was uncertain about Virginia Lord. The girl meant well, she was obviously concerned for the well-being of anybody in moral jeopardy, but her religious fervour was too intense. Poppy, too, cared about anybody who was less fortunate than herself, but it did not mean she had to have the imagined support of the mythical God everybody expected her to believe in. Most people, she believed, were innately good. Even the majority of the railway navvies she had lived among and knew so well were not evil. So what if they relished a good brawl and drank themselves to oblivion, seduced each other's women and stole the occasional pair of boots? That did not mean they were evil. They were merely ignorant; ignorant of the finer things of life, of culture, of refinement, of the other more satisfying existences the great wide world had to offer; even the limited amount she had seen. They had no idea of the wonderful things they could aspire to because, as she had said to Virginia, they were the poor unfortunates who had never been allowed exposure to them. Her own mother, Sheba, was certainly not an evil woman and she had never been near a church. Virginia, however, might perceive her as such, since she'd had several bed partners in only a few weeks. Virginia, in her narrow, moralistic conviction, would doubtless never be able to grasp why it had been necessary. Well, maybe Virginia should be aware of the unpalatable truths that constituted raw life which existed outside the drawing room. It would do her good to live in a navvy encampment for a while.

Poppy had agreed to meet Virginia again. She had consented to go with her to a Quaker Meeting, their equivalent of a church service. Virginia had said how close her views – Poppy's views – were to her own and the Quakers'. Well, however close, such closeness was unwitting, but she was flattered and curious to hear it, so the arrangement was made.

She was surprised to see Virginia driven to the Friends' Meeting House in a shining black brougham driven by a man in livery. Her family must be really something if they rode around in a contraption like this. The liveried driver stepped down, opened the door and obsequiously helped Virginia to alight.

'Thank you, Homer,' she said graciously and flashed a broad smile at Poppy as she approached her. 'Poppy . . . I'm so happy you were able to make it. Did you have any difficulty?'

'Oh, my aunt was none too impressed when I told her I was going to a Quaker service with a new friend.'

'Oh, what did she say?'

'Her very words? You don't want to hear them, Virginia.'

'It's so strange how so many people are still prejudiced against Quakers. I don't understand it. So many big and successful businesses are founded on Quakerism. They do so much good. They're so generous to the people they employ.'

'Well, my aunt said something about the way they talk and the way they dress. "Don't come back here with their quaint talk and big white collars," she said. I told her you didn't talk funny nor wear a funny collar.'

Virginia laughed. 'Peculiarities. Quakers have always been proud of their Peculiarities. In the past, Peculiarities set them apart, made them instantly recognisable to each other. So they flaunted them. But all that's changing, Poppy. There aren't so many *thee*s and *thou*s nowadays, except among the older ones who still embrace the old ways. And most Quakers are starting to wear the clothes they feel comfortable in, not necessarily the Friends' uniform.'

'So do you know many of the folk who come here?' Poppy asked.

'None,' Virginia replied. 'I have never been to the Dudley Meeting before. Shall we be brave and go in?'

Poppy was chilled by the silence. A few people, soberly dressed, were already seated, silent, their upright wooden chairs facing one way in that plain, unadorned room. On tiptoe, so as to be as quiet as possible, Virginia took one of the chairs that lined the room and placed it behind the group that was already seated, careful not to scuff the floor and make a noise. She signalled Poppy to do likewise. Then they sat down, and the rustle of their skirts was deafening. The seconds and the minutes passed to the slow, rhythmic ticking of a large wall clock. Another couple entered and, equally silently, took chairs and sat on them while Poppy glanced up at them briefly. One of the chairs creaked, like the groan of an injured cat, as somebody shifted position. Quiet again . . . but for the insistent tick-tocking . . . The sound of breathing, a faint snore and somebody being nudged. A cough that was smothered quickly. It seemed to go on for ages.

'When does worshipping begin?' Poppy whispered, peering round her bonnet at Virginia and nudging her gently.

Virginia opened her eyes. 'When you begin to worship.'

Poppy shuffled about on her chair to relieve the numbness in her bottom. She could see no point in this. She would have been better entertained going to St Thomas's with Aunt Phoebe. At least there you stood up regularly so your bum didn't go to sleep, except maybe in the sermon. At least in a church they sang hymns and she was getting to know a few of them, pleasant stirring tunes with words that made sense. She could never get the hang of psalm-singing, though. There had to be some arcane rules that were denied the congregation when it came to singing psalms. Nobody seemed to know which words to stress, on which words or syllables the notes of the tune changed. Except the choir. Only the choir had access to such secrets . . . And Reverend Browne would read the lessons. She couldn't always understand what the lessons were supposed to teach, but some interesting sounding names like Nebuchadnezzar and Shadrach, rich words like *frankincense* and *omnipotence* sometimes spilled from his mouth, which she repeated to herself, mouthing them silently. But where were the words here? Nobody spoke. Not even prayers. Where were the hymns, the psalms? Nobody uttered a word. Nobody sang a note.

Poppy's thoughts ran on, inevitably, to Robert Crawford. Maybe this was a good time to say a silent prayer for him, to ask for God's protection for him as he lived and worked at the mercy of Brazil's undoubted and unfamiliar terrors. So she said her prayer and asked that he might be returned to her soon in good health, in good spirits and in love with her still. It was appropriate to say a prayer too for Bellamy, whose attentions were still insistent, despite a continued lack of positive response. She said a prayer for Aunt Phoebe, for Esther, and for Dolly who was to be wed in a month. Then Minnie. Yes, she had to say a prayer for Minnie, wherever she was. Minnie was becoming quite a worry now. Poppy had heard nothing from her for more than a week.

But how long could you make the most articulate, all-encompassing silent prayers last? Certainly not long enough to fill the time she was sitting here in this uncomfortable, hushed stillness . . .

Indeed, nobody at the meeting that day was moved to speak, which was quite usual although Poppy did not know as much, and it abruptly ended. She rose to her feet with all the others and stretched her legs as she watched men putting their hats back on and everybody shaking hands. Several folk shook her hand – and Virginia's – and she smiled politely at those who were endeavouring to welcome two fresh faces, although she felt out of place and much too colourful in those austere surroundings in a bright blue dress. Poppy was glad when, in murmured conversation, everybody made their way to the door.

Outside the sun was shining.

'Did you feel the power and reaching energy of the Lord, Poppy?'

'I can't say that I did.' She'd said a few personal prayers and hoped they would be answered, like the time she prayed for new boots and Robert bought her a pair.

'Oh, but I did. I felt the pureness and innocence and right-eousness of God being renewed in me through Jesus Christ. I think I can truly say that I saw the Inner Light, which inspires all Friends. One day I hope to join them.'

Poppy most certainly had not seen any such Inner Light. 'Why not join them now if you're so suited to them?' she suggested. 'Why wait?'

'Well . . . because it's not yet the appropriate time . . .' For a fleeting second Poppy thought she detected some sadness in Virginia's eyes, but if so it was short-lived. Suddenly her face lit up again as another thought struck her. 'I told my mother and father all about you, Poppy. They are very curious to meet you.'

'Then I hope they won't be too disappointed if they do,' she answered uneasily.

Virginia looked expectantly at her new friend with all the

wide-eyed admiration that new friendship engenders. 'Oh, I don't think so at all. They'll adore you.'

St Thomas's church clock struck the hour.

'If I go now, Virginia, I'll be able to meet my aunt coming out of church.'

'Yes, you must, Poppy. She would welcome that.'

Poppy hesitated to go. She said, 'Virginia, I don't think I'll ever get any particular – I think you would call it "spiritual joy" – from going to church. Especially to a Quaker Meeting Hall.'

'House, Poppy. Strictly, it's *Friends'* Meeting House.'

'Friends' Meeting *House* then, if it's so important to call it that. I'm not like you. I've never been brought up to be religious. I can live quite happily without religion.'

Virginia smiled her kind, patient smile. 'Oh, I understand. But it doesn't matter greatly about that. Don't you see? It's our differences that make us so complementary to each other. I said to my mother, "I'm not sure that she will enjoy the Friends' Meeting, or even understand what's going on, but she's agreed to come".'

'And what did your mother say to that?'

'That we cannot all be the same. I think she's rather happy for me that I've found a new friend with such stimulating ideas, although she forbids me to go against my father's wishes where teaching is concerned. I told her what you said about that too.'

'Oh dear,' Poppy remarked, sorry now that she'd said any such thing. 'Oh, listen . . . I know what I was meaning to ask you . . . Have you seen anything of Minnie since last time we saw her together?'

'Unfortunately not. I intend to visit her tomorrow, in fact.'

'Save yourself the trouble, Virginia. She's gone. I don't know where she's gone, but she's gone.'

'Gone?' Virginia repeated incredulous.

'She's left the house she was living in. It's why she didn't turn up when we'd arranged to meet last Monday. I'm worried about her, Virginia. I don't know what's happened to her.'

'My goodness! Do you think she's been abducted? Goodness, in the world she inhabits, she might have been murdered. Maybe she's lying in some ditch with a knife in her back.'

'Oh, please don't say such things, Virginia . . . No, she wouldn't have bothered taking her curtains down if she'd thought she was going to get murdered. I reckon she's found somewhere else to live, or has taken to sharing with somebody.'

'But this is very worrying, Poppy.'

'Yes, it's the not knowing.'

'I shall pray hard for her.'

'I already did, Virginia.'

'You see . . . You do find some comfort in prayer.'

'Who said I found comfort in it? It's all I can do till I know where to find her.'

'God will guide us to her. Of that I'm convinced.'

'I wish I had your conviction, Virginia.'

'Promise to let me know just as soon as you know where she is.'

'Course I will.'

The rattle of a carriage's wheels over the cobbles of High Street made them turn their heads. 'Look, here's Homer come to collect me . . . You would be very welcome to join me and my family for Sunday dinner, you know, Poppy.'

'That's very kind, but my aunt will be expecting me, Virginia,' Poppy said, with a mixture of disappointment and relief.

'Of course, I understand. Perhaps another Sunday?'

'Perhaps,' Poppy said unsurely. She did not relish the

thought of sitting through another Quaker Meeting. So she said, 'Why don't we meet one weekday?'

Virginia's face lit up at the prospect. 'Yes. I could meet you almost any afternoon. But not for a few weeks, unfortunately. Tomorrow my mother, my sister and I are going to Leicestershire to stay with her sister.'

'When you come back then,' Poppy said.

'Yes, when I come back . . . In the meantime, we could write to each other . . .' She looked at Poppy expectantly.

'If you like. Do you want to write down my address?'

'Oh, yes, please.' She searched in her reticule and pulled out a small notepad with a blacklead attached, then wrote it down as Poppy dictated.

'Of course, I'll write. When I return we could arrange to meet and eat somewhere, Poppy . . .'

'If you like,' she answered pleasantly.

Virginia grinned broadly. 'Well, then . . . That's settled.'

Poppy smiled back affably. Despite the girl's assertive attitude, she liked Virginia. She was all enthusiasm, all energy, all commitment, not satisfied with half measures.

The brougham pulled up at the kerb, Homer got down from the driving seat and helped her up, while Virginia turned and waved.

'Have a lovely time in Leicestershire, Virginia.'

The following day, Aunt Phoebe received a note in the post from Captain Cecil Tyler to say that his ailing mother had passed away the previous week and the funeral was being held that very day.

'Well, I wouldn't be able to go even if I wanted to,' she complained when Poppy returned home from the school. 'Not at such short notice. Why Captain Tyler couldn't have let me know before this I'll never know.'

'Perhaps he's been too busy, Aunt,' Poppy suggested, untying the ribbons of her bonnet.

'Busy? I would have thought he'd have let me know. I would have thought he might have graced me with a visit and told me himself, rather than sent a note. I would have loved to have seen the old lady before she died. We got on very well. I do hope Cecil has provided an appropriate burial. Lord knows he'll be able to afford it now.'

It was while Virginia was in Leicestershire that somebody else met Poppy as she came out of school. Minnie Catchpole was waiting for her. At first Poppy did not recognise her. She looked so different, fresh and ladylike in a beautiful summer dress in blue checked taffeta and a matching bonnet.

'Minnie! Oh, Minnie . . . What a surprise. I've been worried sick about you. Where've you been, where've you been? You look so well.'

'I thought I'd best come and explain,' Minnie replied. 'D'you wanna walk with me to Johnson's coffee house?'

'Johnson's coffee house?' Well, for Minnie it was a change from a tavern. 'If you like. So what've you been doing?'

'I've been spending time with Captain Tyler,' Minnie replied and, for the first time in her life, looked bashful.

'Captain Tyler?'

'Yes. We hit it off pretty grand, me and Captain Tyler.'

'Go on . . .'

'Well, we'm a-courting,' Minnie said, laughing at the absurdity of it. 'He don't know as I've bin on the game, though. I never took him back to Gatehouse Fold. I always met him somewhere.'

'But he's a lot older than you, Minnie. He's an old man.'

'He ain't old, Poppy, although he is gettin' on a bit, I grant yer. But he's kind . . . And he's got plenty life in him an' all between the sheets, I can tell yer.' She giggled at her impropriety. 'His old mother was as rich as a nabob, you know. He's due to inherit a fortune.'

'So have you given up being on the game now?'

'For now.'

'Virginia will be pleased.'

'Virginia!' Minnie said scornfully. 'It's nothing to do with Virginia. I've given it up for as long as this courtin' lark lasts. I have to play the part o' the good girl now. He thinks I'm innocent . . . Or leastwise, he thought I was . . .'

'Virginia will be able to count you as one of her saved souls. Wait till she knows . . .'

'Oh, sod Virginia. She's a pestilence. Have you seen her lately?'

Poppy said she had and explained, by which time they had reached Johnson's coffee house. They found a table, sat down and ordered coffee for two, with a slice of apple pie each.

'So tell me, Minnie,' Poppy said, pulling her chair up and resting her face in her hands attentively, 'what happened between you and Captain Tyler . . .'

Minnie Catchpole was exactly how Captain Cecil Tyler liked his women – young and irresistibly, buxomly, handsome. In his army days he had met many women of all nationalities and creeds, even titled ladies, so he was under no illusions as to Minnie's social standing, or rather, her lack of it. But there was something forthright and decent about the girl, something that appealed, other than just her physical attributes. Besides, he'd had particularly bad luck throughout his career where women were concerned. He was not excessively handsome, nor did he crow about the fortune he would one day inherit, which could have secured him any woman. His confidence had taken a battering in consequence. Some women tired of him, some fell for the charms of others more instantly appealing, and those who actually loved him he invariably had to abandon because his regiment was on the move once again. Thus was the life of an unwed soldier who did not possess striking looks. Here, now, back in England, was this gloriously appealing wench who was showing more than a little interest in him, and he found her impossible to resist. So what if she was from the lower orders and uneducated? The world was changing anyway.

For Minnie, it had been obvious from the moment they met that Captain Cecil Tyler was captivated by her. On the night they had left Phoebe Newton's house together, they had talked for ages in his gig at the end of the street where she lived – or, rather, where she told him she lived. He evidently had no inkling of her chosen profession, and Minnie was inclined to believe it would be an interesting experiment to pretend she was the naive daughter of some insignificant glass blower. Having stepped down from his gig, she then made her way to Gatehouse Fold alone, on foot, across the town that was as usual noisy with drunks. To her surprise she was not accosted on the way, and she felt strangely, sublimely virginal as she entered the seedy little house alone for once. She wanted no other male company that night. Captain Tyler was still very much on her mind.

Neither could she get him off her mind as she lay in bed. She played over and over their conversation, relived the banter they'd shared. He was so much older, so much more mature than most of the men she'd been associated with, and sensible despite having consumed several whiskies at Phoebe Newton's house. A man of the world. He treated her with an inbred courtesy she had never experienced before, and she rather liked his attention.

It all came to a head one evening when Minnie had been

collected from the end of the street where her fictitious home was located, and whisked away in Captain Tyler's gig to a remote place that was unfamiliar. As they sat, cosseted by the gig's comfortable leather seat and taking it in turns to swig whisky from a hip flask, they could see the dark hump of the Wrekin in the distance, edged with a rim of amber. The sun, swollen with the myriad colours it had sucked from the land, transmuted them to gold, and gilded the sky. Minnie enjoyed talking with Captain Tyler as this vivid spectacle developed over Shropshire, and wondered how she ought to respond if he made a pass at her.

'Tell me about your family, Minnie.'

'I don't want to talk about 'em,' she replied flatly. 'I can't stand 'em. I want to shift out o' that house just as soon as I can.' It was her way of priming him. Soon she could tell him that in desperation she had found a little house in Gatehouse Fold. She could hardly keep up the pretence for long, and already she felt that there could be more to this relationship than merely drinking whisky together or watching a sunset. 'So why don't you tell me about your family and your life in the army?'

'Well . . . as for my family, it consists of just my ailing mother,' he said, lighting his clay pipe. He exhaled smoke in a controlled breath. 'Unfortunately, she's dying. The doctors give her no more than a few weeks.'

'Oh, I'm sorry, Cecil,' Minnie said sincerely. 'Is there somebody looking after her?'

'Twenty-four hours a day.'

'So what's up with her?'

'A stroke. Her third. She's a poor, poor soul. It will be a blessed release when she passes on.'

'Wouldn't you rather be with her now then, rather than sitting here with me?'

He turned and smiled at her, then drew again on his pipe. 'There's no need,' he said resignedly. 'As I said, she's being looked after. She doesn't know me anyhow. Not anymore. Besides, you're a breath of fresh air, Minnie. I've done enough sitting in that stinking room holding her hand, pondering our lives, recalling my youth. I came to realise I was a bit of a handful for her when I was a lad, you know. I've made my apologies for being an errant son and hiving off into William the Fourth's army. I neglected her for years as a result.'

'Well, you've had your own life to lead, eh, Cecil?'

The horse shuffled forward as he spied a tasty tuft of grass a little out of reach, rocking the gig a little.

'As you say, Minnie . . . But she was not easy to live with. Even my father, I'm sure, found that out too late.'

'What happened to your father?'

'My father? A pompous man, as I recall. He died when I was a youth, a wealthy man. He inherited a thriving bank from his father, merged it with another and promptly sold his banking interests, with the intention of living off the proceeds and the interest he gained from them. Unfortunately for him, he expired having had no opportunity to enjoy it.'

'But the money kept you and your mother?' Minnie fished.

'I kept myself. I was no burden on my mother. No financial burden, at any rate.'

'Do you have any brothers or sisters, Cecil?'

'There's only me.'

'So you'll come in for a tidy inheritance then, when your mother dies?'

'Oh, a tidy inheritance . . .' He looked at her again and smiled. 'You can be sure.'

'Lucky you.'

'Does that make me any more attractive?' he asked.

'It don't make no difference to me one way or th'other,'

she said. 'It's no nearer me. I'm well able to make me own way in life. I wouldn't ask for, nor expect, any favours from you, nor nobody else.'

He laughed, in admiration of her professed independence. It suggested she was not interested in him for his money.

'I ain't never had no money in me life to talk of, but I manage well enough,' she said. 'Me father never brought much home after he'd spent his wages in the bousing-ken getting fuddled. You learn to live without money.'

'You talk of your father in the past tense, Minnie.'

''Cause that's how I see him,' she replied astutely. 'In the past.'

He drew on his pipe again, and she thought how pensive he looked gazing at the distant hills silhouetted against fleeces of cloud now dyed crimson and purple and green.

'Do you see me in your future, Minnie?' He turned and looked into her eyes earnestly, eyes that reflected back the sunset's rhetoric.

With a coyness that was strange to her but entirely unassumed, she lowered her eyes. 'How do I know who or what's in me future, Cecil? You'm here with me now and you ain't heard me complain, have yer?'

He smiled. He would have expected no other answer from this girl. 'I had hoped we might remain friends for a long time. I had hoped we might become more than just friends . . .'

'More than just friends?' she queried. 'What does that mean? Does that mean you got designs on me? I ain't a girl like that, you know.'

'And I'm very glad to hear it. In any case, my designs on you are more or less honourable . . . I am an officer and a gentleman, you know . . .'

'I reckon the only way you'll prove that is by keeping your hands off me.'

He guffawed at that. 'Is that what you want?'

Minnie made no reply.

'I have a proposition to put to you, Minnie . . .' She looked at him with curiosity. 'You say you dislike living with your folks . . . I – or rather, my mother – owns a house that is vacant. It is fully furnished, very comfortable and in a pleasant area. You could move in there . . . rent-free, of course. It merely needs airing.'

'Show me,' Minnie exclaimed. 'Can you take me there now?'

Chapter 24

'Do you love him, Minnie?' Poppy asked, looking wistfully into the dregs of her coffee cup after she'd heard her friend's story.

'Love? Dunno, Poppy. Maybe I do. Maybe I don't. I ain't really sure.'

'Do you feel you want to be with him all the time?' Poppy could only draw on her own acute feelings and experiences regarding Robert. 'I mean, when he's not with you, do you miss him?'

Minnie shrugged. 'Not partic'ly. I like him, though. I do look forward to seeing him. He talks to me . . . about all sorts o' things. He's always interesting to listen to.'

'So do you think you'll become Mrs Cecil Tyler?'

Minnie guffawed in a most unladylike manner and received resentful glances from a group of respectable women at another table. 'Hey, that'd be a turn-up for the books, wun't it, eh, Poppy? Me wed to a rich chap, a gentleman at that. I'd have to have lessons on how to talk proper, like you.' She chuckled at the thought.

'Well, I must say, you look the part, Min, in your expensive dress.'

'What *he* bought me . . . He's generous with his money, I'll say that for him.'

'I'm that relieved, Minnie,' Poppy said. 'I'm just happy you're not on the game anymore. Anything could have happened to you. Now you've got the chance to be somebody. I hope it all works out well for you, Minnie. I hope you do marry him and have a house full of children.'

'Lor! Just think if I'd stopped with Dog Meat, Poppy . . .'

'I know. None of this would have happened.'

'I'm glad I left the encampment when you did. I knew Dog Meat would never be any use. And when I found out he'd sold me to Jericho for a gallon o' beer . . . I wonder how Jericho is now? I wonder where he is?'

'You were in love with Jericho, weren't you, Min?'

Minnie smiled dreamily. 'I thought I was. But when it come right down to it, he was no better than Dog Meat. Any road, Jericho had his eye on you.'

'I know.' Poppy laughed. 'For all the good it did him.'

'Have you heard anything more about him who's the love of your life?'

'You mean Robert? He's well, they say. Bellamy said they'd had another letter from him. Yes, he's well, thank God.'

'And how's this Bellamy? Is he still chasing yer?'

Poppy nodded and smiled bashfully. 'I still see him. I do like him. He calls for me and takes me out sometimes. Generally on a Sunday afternoon if the weather's fine.'

'He ain't given up then?'

'It doesn't seem like it. But I've been honest with him. It's not as if I've led him on.'

'Does he know you're hankering for his brother?'

'No, course not.'

'I wonder when he'll be coming home? Have you heard?'

'Nobody's mentioned it. He said he'd be away about a year. It was the start of last August when he went. It's now the end of May.'

'June, July,' Minnie said, counting the months on her fingers. 'Two more months. How long does it take to sail from Brazil to England?'

'I've no idea, Min. I'll ask Aunt Phoebe . . . And talking of Aunt Phoebe, I'd better go. She'll be wondering what's happened to me. I'll go and pay . . .' She shifted her chair back to get up from the table. 'By the way . . . Am I allowed to tell her about Captain Tyler and you?'

'Best not, for the time being. Let's wait for him to tell her.'

Poppy stood up. 'If he's as sharp about it as he was telling her his mother had died, he might never let her know.'

Minnie laughed. 'That's true. But I'm sure he will. In fact, I'll ask him to.'

Over the weeks, Poppy received several short letters from Virginia extolling the virtues of the Leicestershire countryside, and giving a serialised account of an intense love affair she was having with Ulysses, her aunt's brindle Great Dane. Poppy replied, of course, giving Virginia the news that Minnie had now reformed, although she was careful not to mention her meeting Captain Tyler, or that it was due to him alone, and nothing to do with Virginia's evangelism. Virginia's letters were warm and friendly and Poppy enjoyed receiving them. They were building a strong friendship and Poppy looked forward to the girl's return so they could meet again and get to know each other even better. Virginia wrote to say she was returning to Harborne on the fifth of July.

At the end of June, an envelope arrived in the post, addressed to Mrs P Newton and Miss P Silk collectively. It was a wedding invitation. Captain Cecil Tyler and Miss Minnie Catchpole requested the pleasure of their company at St Edmund's church on Sunday the seventh of July at half past two, and afterwards at The Dudley Arms Hotel.

'I am flabbergasted,' said Aunt Phoebe.

'I'm not,' Poppy admitted.

'You mean you knew?'

'I saw Minnie a while ago. She met me as I came out of the school. She'd left her little house in Gatehouse Fold and I wondered where she'd gone. She told me Captain Tyler had set her up in a furnished house his mother owned.'

'Good gracious! Poor Ariadne, his mother, would turn in her grave if she knew he'd been keeping a woman.'

'Well, at least he's making an honest woman of her now, Aunt Phoebe. It's the best thing that could have happened to Minnie.'

'Let us hope it's the best thing that could have happened to Cecil. He always was wayward, unconventional, an absolute rebel. The worry of his mother's life, you know. I doubt whether she would have approved of him marrying such a girl.'

'What do you mean, Aunt Phoebe? Minnie's a likeable, honest person. She's down-to-earth, I admit, but hardly more so than me.'

'I don't dislike her, but you are refined, Poppy. It is tempered in you. I am not unmindful of your similar backgrounds, but you have raised yourself way above the level of a navvy's woman. I fear she has not. Nor ever will.'

'Perhaps you could give her some of your excellent coaching, Aunt. It worked for me.'

Aunt Phoebe shook her head. 'The old saying is true, I'm afraid. You cannot make a silk purse out of a sow's ear . . . But such short notice gives us so little time, Poppy. We shall both need new dresses, bonnets, shoes and no end of new accessories. I think a visit to Mrs Gadd is urgently necessary.'

So to Mrs Gadd, the seamstress, they went and chose new dresses for the wedding. For Poppy, being measured again and choosing new clothes was hardly a chore. Excitedly, she chose a pale green taffeta material, to be made up into a dress with high neck, tight bodice and flounced skirt over a wide crinoline. She enjoyed the final fitting a week or so later and knew she looked good when Mrs Gadd stood back to admire her own work, displaying a look of self-satisfaction.

At last the big day came. Clay drove Aunt Phoebe and Poppy to St Edmund's and Poppy recalled the time she'd met Robert Crawford outside this very church when he'd taken her to the Old Priory and given her her first lessons in reading. Clay waited outside the church perched on the driver's seat while Captain Tyler took Minnie Catchpole to be his lawful wedded wife.

Unfortunately, Poppy did not think much of Minnie's wedding dress. It was cream – to the bride's credit, not claiming absolute innocence by wearing white – but the fit was not exquisite. Minnie was inclined to be buxom and it was too tight where it might have been less so. But the bride seemed happy and she smiled contentedly, looking up frequently into the groom's eyes with obvious admiration.

During the service Poppy was so intent on keeping her eyes on Minnie, that she failed to see her most recently acquired friend, Virginia Lord. Virginia was sitting in the congregation on the groom's side, wearing a dress of blue-grey tarlatan, very plain, except for the pristine white edging to the skirt's flounces. She was also accompanied. Poppy gasped with surprise when she saw her. So Minnie had invited her too. That was not only very thoughtful, but also very brave, considering the reason they'd got to know each other in the first place. Maybe Minnie had confessed her past to Captain Tyler. It never occurred to Poppy that those sitting on the same side of the church as the groom were traditionally connected with him. They caught each other's eyes, waved discreetly and smiled. Poppy thought how well Virginia looked, how happy, with a definite sparkle in her eye. Maybe she and Ulysses the Great Dane had become engaged. The thought elicited a wry smile.

Bride and groom emerged from the vestry having signed the register, and made their way down the aisle, man and wife, smiling happily. It struck Poppy that there was no bridesmaid. She herself might have been asked to perform the function, but maybe Minnie considered that it was all too short notice and decided to do without. The small congregation filed out slowly behind them into the warm July sunshine, and spilled out onto the pavement of Castle Street. At once, Virginia made her way towards Poppy and they greeted each other eagerly.

'Fancy seeing you here, Virginia.'

'I know. Isn't it a surprise?'

'It was good of Minnie to invite you, wasn't it? You see, she doesn't forget her friends.'

'In fairness—'

'Have you had a lovely holiday, Virginia? You look ever so well.'

'Thank you. So do you.'

'So how's Ulysses?'

'Ulysses . . .' Virginia smiled radiantly. 'Oh, we fell in love good and proper, Ulysses and me. Such a beautiful animal. I enquired of my aunt if I could adopt him, but to no avail . . . I'm here with my mother and father and my sister.'

'That's your mother and father?' Poppy queried, wondering why they should be in attendance as well. 'I imagined it must be.'

'Yes, and I've told them all about you and they're dying to meet you. I'll introduce you when we get to The Dudley Arms Hotel. Look, everybody's moving on now . . .'

'And I must introduce you to my aunt,' said Poppy, glancing in her direction.

'I've also had the most wonderful news, Poppy. I'm so excited. I'll tell you all about it later.'

Poppy watched Virginia rejoin her parents and make their way to their shining black carriage that had pulled up behind the bride and groom's, but a little way in front of Clay.

'My friend Virginia's here,' Poppy said to Aunt Phoebe when she returned to her side. 'It's good of Minnie to invite her. Her family as well, which is a bit of a surprise. Maybe they're here to make the numbers up. After all, there aren't that many guests, are there?'

'My dear, they are the Lords. I recognise *her*.' Aunt Phoebe moved towards Clay and the waiting clarence. 'It never occurred to me that the Virginia you had befriended was their daughter.'

'So you know them, Aunt Phoebe?'

'I have only once ever been in their company. Come, my dear. It's only a short drive to The Dudley Arms but we must arrive in style.'

Captain and the new Mrs Cecil Tyler stood just inside the upstairs assembly room they'd hired and greeted their guests, thanking them for coming.

Poppy flung her arms around Minnie and gave her a hug. 'I'm so happy for you, Min,' she said sincerely. 'The change in fortune for me was dramatic, but it's even more so for you. I do hope you'll be happy.'

'And you'll be next, I daresay, when your chap comes back, eh?'

'Oh, let's just get him back. I'll worry about getting wed later.'

Poppy moved on to Captain Tyler and he greeted her with a broad grin. 'Thank you for coming, Miss Silk, and for bringing Mrs Newton.'

'Congratulations, Captain Tyler,' Poppy said affably. 'You've chosen quite a girl to be your wife. But I believe you've chosen very wisely.'

'There was nobody else in the world for me once I'd spent an hour in her company,' he replied proudly. 'I couldn't snap her up quickly enough.'

'She's a prize, and no mistake,' Poppy affirmed. 'I've known her longer than anybody . . . and I know.'

She moved on so that Aunt Phoebe could give him her congratulations, and looked for Virginia, who had already spoken to the bride and groom. A waitress carrying a tray of drinks intercepted Poppy and she took a glass. It was champagne and the tiny bubbles seemed to burst in profusion just under her nose. As the waitress moved away, Virginia was at Poppy's side again.

'Do come and meet my parents, Poppy.' She leaned closer to Poppy and spoke in a low voice. 'They have no idea of Minnie's past, of course. Doubtless if they did they would disapprove wholeheartedly of the match.'

'I'm glad for Minnie,' Poppy replied in a conspiratorial whisper.

'So am I. I am delighted.'

'He's made an honest woman of her. It's what we both wanted for her, Virginia.'

'I couldn't agree more. I had to pretend we'd never met when we offered our congratulations.' Virginia chuckled at the collusion.

She took Poppy's hand and led her away. Poppy was in awe of Ishmael Lord, an imposing man, tall, with greying hair, and fresh-faced for a man in late middle age. She remembered that Virginia's mother, Rebecca, had once been a Quaker before she was expelled for marrying out. She still bore the hallmarks of a Quaker; her dress was sombre grey and very plain, she wore no jewellery except a wedding ring, and her hair was unadorned and unstyled beneath her plain bonnet. However, she was slender and elegant for all that, and she smiled kindly at Poppy.

'We have heard so much about you, Miss Silk,' Mrs Lord said in her quiet, unassuming voice. 'I have been very keen to meet you. My daughter tells me that you have attended a Friends' Meeting House together.'

'Yes, it's true, Mrs Lord.'

'And what was your impression?'

'It made no impression,' Poppy answered honestly. *Except on my backside*, she wanted to add.

'I told you she was outspoken,' Virginia said.

Rebecca Lord laughed. 'Don't tell me. You found the silence a little unnerving.'

'I'm more used to an ordinary church where they sing hymns and say their prayers aloud.'

'So am I now. But I hold the Friends in very high regard still, and always will.'

'Enough of this talk of Quakerism,' Ishmael Lord said affably, keen to get in on the conversation. 'I thought I'd saved you from all that when I married you.' He winked at Poppy.

Rebecca turned to Poppy and glanced at her husband with a look of mischief. 'What my husband won't tell you, Miss Silk, is that his own father was a Quaker, but he too was disowned when he married my mother-in-law, who was a Methodist. So you see, he has no reason to denigrate Quakers at all, has he, Miss Silk?'

'Please call me Poppy.' She liked these people. They were evidently wealthy, but very amenable for all that. Neither superior nor stand-offish.

'You must visit us, Miss Silk,' Mr Lord said with an expansive smile. 'Arrange it with Virginia. Come for dinner. Stay the night. Stay a fortnight if you want to. I know she's very taken with you. It's my belief that you could be a very moderating influence on this unsavoury religious fervour she's got.'

Poppy looked at Virginia and smiled matily. 'Oh, I don't know about that, sir. It's just that I've got no religious fervour, as you call it, at all.'

'A girl after my own heart,' Ishmael Lord declared, and took a defiant swig from the champagne he was holding.

'Excuse me, Father, but I'm keen to tell Poppy my good news. I'm sure it will all come as a complete shock to her.'

'Very well. We'll see you later, Miss Silk. In the meantime, see if you can get my daughter to drink a glass of champagne. It would be a singular achievement.'

'You know I don't drink alcohol, Father,' Virginia admonished. 'It's the cause of so many problems in this world . . .' She turned away and led Poppy to the far end of the room away from other ears.

Poppy sipped her drink and looked at Virginia attentively. 'What I don't understand, Virginia, is why Minnie would invite your mother and father and your sister to her wedding, when she doesn't know them from Adam.'

'Oh, we are not guests of Minnie. We are guests of Captain Tyler.'

'Captain Tyler? I don't understand.'

'It's a long-standing family connection. Captain Tyler's father was a banker, you know, like my own father. In fact, old Mr Tyler and my grandfather merged their banking businesses more than thirty years ago. They formed what is now known as Tyler's and Lord's Bank.'

'I had no idea,' Poppy said.

'Mr Tyler then sold his interest to my grandfather, but they retained the name of Tyler's and Lord's. Nowadays my father runs the bank.'

'And yet Captain Tyler has nothing to do with it now.'

'Of course not. Because his father sold his share of the bank to my grandfather.'

'Yet you are still friends with the Tylers?'

'Oh, yes. My father attended Mrs Tyler's funeral just a few weeks ago. Our two families have always kept in close contact. In fact, I think old Mr Tyler and my grandfather were related by a marriage somewhere along the line.'

'So the fact that you know Minnie just happens to be a coincidence?'

'Oh, certainly,' Virginia affirmed. 'And what a coincidence! I was on a mission to save somebody and I happened to see Minnie . . . with another girl – very slender with yellow hair, rather the colour of yours, Poppy – being picked up in Dudley one evening as we were driving through. I was on my way to dinner at the home of my fiancé at the time . . .'

Poppy felt herself redden. The girl with Minnie must have been herself. It must have been that night they were picked up by the chap in the carriage, the driver of which, James, had tried to rape her over the Oakham fields.

'Anyway,' Virginia went on, 'I returned another evening just to see if I could spot those two girls again. I was determined to save them from a life of sinful prostitution. Such young girls . . . Well, lo and behold, I did see Minnie – though not the slimmer girl with the fair hair – and I followed her home. When the opportunity presented itself later, I called on her and I found her quite amenable. I've no idea what happened to the other poor lost soul. I haven't seen her since.'

'Fancy,' Poppy said, for want of something else to say. 'Didn't you ask?'

'Oh, Minnie said she hadn't seen her since.'

Thank goodness Virginia did not recognise her as the other girl. It was time Poppy turned the conversation, time she averted her friend from any inkling that it could have been her. 'So, you have a fiancé . . . Your good news then . . . You are engaged to be married?'

'Oh . . . That's not my news. I've been engaged almost two years now.'

'And yet you never wear a ring . . .'

'Adornment, Poppy. You must know by now how I find adornment distasteful. I don't need a ring to say I'm engaged to be married, that I'm in love. It's something that lives in my heart.'

'So tell me your news . . . Oh, I know . . . You've named the day . . .'

'Not quite. He went away, you see, my fiancé. He felt the need. Some complication . . . But the wonderful news is, I heard yesterday that he'll be back home soon.'

Some dark shadow seemed to lurk over Poppy with an instant oppressiveness at this revelation. 'Why?' she asked, her throat suddenly dry. 'Where's he been?'

'Brazil.'

'Brazil?' Of all the places. Poppy nearly choked and she spilled her champagne. 'What's his name?'

'Robert. Robert Crawford. Do you know him? Oh, he's such a dear. Oh, you wouldn't believe, Poppy . . . I'm so happy . . . And yet so apprehensive . . . Oh, goodness! When I think about it I really could do with a drink of champagne to steady my nerves.'

'Have a sip of mine if you want.'

Virginia shook her head. 'No. I would never resort to it, but thank you . . .'

Poppy was utterly deflated. She felt her legs go weak and found it difficult to stop herself trembling. If she'd known Virginia was her rival in love, of course she would never have allowed them to become friends. Now the whole situation was impossible. It was farcical. She smiled sadly and drank what remained of the champagne to steady her own nerves a little.

'Well, Virginia, that's the best news anybody could have. That and Minnie's marriage . . .' She felt tears stinging the back of her eyes and managed to push them back with a great effort of will. 'So tell me – if you don't think I'm prying, that is – why this . . . this . . . Robert Crawford went away in the first place. What sort of complication arose?'

'Oh, Poppy, it was such an enormous shock to me,' Virginia answered, with the candour Poppy had hoped for. 'I'll tell you, because I know I can confide in you. And you can give me your best advice too . . . It caused me considerable heartache . . .'

'Go on . . .'

'Well, we were all ready to get married. Our union had been eagerly anticipated and endorsed by both families. They have been connected for years, you know. Robert and I have known each other for many, many years. When I was only ten years old I knew I would marry him someday. But he revealed to me last summer that he'd been emotionally diverted by another girl and needed time away from both of us, so as to flush her from his thoughts and purge his mind. I was heartbroken. Oh, you can't imagine. Whether this girl was suitable, whether she was worthy of Robert or not, I did not know, nor do I still, Poppy. I did not *want* to know. I wanted to know nothing about her. It was enough that I had a rival. In fact, it was too much. Nevertheless, I realised she was a mortal soul and loved by God. So I prayed for her, whoever she was, that God might help her recover quickly from the emotional turmoil of having loved Robert.'

'You prayed for *her*?'

'Of course.'

'So how did you learn of his coming home?' Poppy enquired, her heart languishing in the pit of her stomach. Yet she might find out so much more by quizzing Virginia. 'Did he write to you from Brazil?'

'Oh, no. When he went, he told me he would write to neither me nor this other girl, for fear of being swayed by a reply. Nor has he. Well, not to me at any rate, and I trust him not to have written to *her* either. No, a note arrived from his mother yesterday. He was due to sail from Rio de Janeiro towards the end of June. He should be back home at the end of this month.' She put her hands together as if saying a prayer, and closed her eyes momentarily. 'Oh, Poppy, I can't wait to see him again . . .'

'I can imagine . . .'

'But I'm on absolute tenterhooks. I mean . . . He went with the intention of trying to forget this girl. But what if he's decided he loves her after all and not me?'

Poppy was suddenly filled with renewed hope. All was not yet lost. 'If he did, would you be able to forgive him? Would you be able to forgive her?'

'I have already forgiven him. Harbouring a grievance like that can only add to the hurt and humiliation. No, I'm not strong enough to withstand such feelings, Poppy. It's so much easier to forgive. But her? Whether I would release him from his promise to marry me so that he could marry *her* . . . Well, that's a different matter . . .'

'Maybe you should say some more prayers, Virginia.'

'I pray that Robert will regain his common sense and return to the straight and narrow a wiser, more mature man . . . What would you do in my situation, Poppy?'

Poppy took another glass of champagne from the waitress who was hovering close by with the tray and pondered her reply.

'Are you sure you won't have a glass, Virginia? I can strongly recommend it in your position. It can do you no harm.' She turned to the waitress. 'Thank you. I think my friend will have one after all . . . Take it, Virginia. Sip it. Don't be afraid of it. Even Quakers must sup sometimes . . . Go on . . . Take it . . .'

Virginia took the glass from Poppy. Tentatively, she put it to her lips, moistening them with the liquid. Even more tentatively she touched the tiny drop of champagne that lingered there with her tongue, all the time looking intently at Poppy.

'It doesn't taste of much . . . Slightly bitter, if anything . . .'

'Well, have a good old mouthful. Give it a chance . . . Go on, drink it.'

Virginia sipped it tentatively, then immediately rubbed the tip of her nose with the back of her hand. 'It tickles my nose,' she said with a grin. 'No, it's not so bad, is it?'

'It's not so bad. You don't have to drink gallons of it. Just a couple of glasses will do you no harm at all. It's when folk drink to excess . . .'

Virginia nodded her agreement. 'So tell me, Poppy. To hark back to my situation . . . What would you do?'

'I'm possibly not the best person to ask,' she answered honestly. 'I don't know, and that's the truth. You know how strong your own feelings are for him, though.'

'Yes. They're intense. Oh, they're so intense, Poppy.'

'Then you have to suppose that the feelings this other girl has are no less intense. You have to suppose that her love is at least as strong as yours, Virginia.'

'Goodness, yes. I suppose so. I'd imagined it to be trivial, but you could be right.'

'Somehow, Virginia, I can't see any sense in competing for him. He must be coming back home because he has made his mind up which girl he wants . . .'

'Yes, I suppose so . . .' Virginia conceded. 'You see, I knew you would see things clearly.'

'So we—*you* must respect his decision. There would be no sense in trying to change his mind if he told you he wanted the other girl. There would be no sense in trying to blacken her name, for instance.'

'Just so long as this other girl realised it too.'

'Oh, I'm sure she will—would, Virginia . . .'

They remained unspeaking for a minute or so. Poppy was still reeling from the shock, mulling over the import of what she had learnt. It was Virginia who broke the silence.

'Poppy, may I ask a favour of you?'

'If it's something I can do . . .'

'Would you come with me to meet Robert that first time? I should feel so much more confident with you there to lean on. I mean, what if he turns away from me?'

'Oh, I don't think that is a very brilliant idea, Virginia. I really don't.'

Chapter 25

Poppy did not stay till the end of the wedding reception. What she had discovered had shaken her inexorably and she no longer felt comfortable in Virginia's company. She was overwhelmed with feelings of guilt over concealing information and facts that directly affected Virginia, which could materially alter the whole course of her life. Despite her concern for her own aching heart, Poppy was sensitive enough to acknowledge it. What if Virginia had somehow uncovered her secret or guessed it? What then? How foolish, how fiendish would she have felt, making a friend of the woman whose intended she was bent on acquiring? Best make herself scarce while the going was good.

That was the main reason she felt she could not stay. Besides, it would have meant moving from The Dudley Arms to St Thomas's church for Evensong. The prospect of more religion on top of what she had just learnt was too much to contend with. She'd had enough of anything and anybody remotely to do with religion for the time being. She politely made her excuses to Virginia and even before the wedding meal had begun she told Aunt Phoebe that she felt unwell and must return home.

'Indeed, child, you do look rather peaky,' Aunt Phoebe agreed. 'I'll ask for my cloak and bonnet.'

'No, Aunt. There's no need for you to come as well. Besides, you'll want to go to church after. I can walk. The fresh air will do me good.'

'Walk alone? In this town? I wouldn't hear of it.'

'But it's Sunday afternoon. Everybody will be out walking.'

'If you don't feel well, then you will not feel like walking. Go to Clay and ask him to take you home. He can return for me when it's time for church.'

'Thank you, Aunt.'

Poppy found Clay and he returned her to Cawneybank House. Esther met her at the front door and when she knew she wasn't feeling well, made a great palaver.

'Oh, please don't fuss, Esther,' Poppy pleaded. 'I just need to go to bed and rest. I'm weary.'

'Shall I bring you a cup of tea, miss?'

'You're very kind, Esther. Would you bring it to my bedroom, if it's no trouble?'

'Course, miss.'

Poppy dragged herself up the stairs. Never in her life had she felt so disappointed, so humble and so foolish. The effects of the champagne exaggerated it all, of course, rendering it even more of a calamity. It made her feel lethargic, yet her emotions were running high and her desolation was intense. She undressed, throwing her fine new outfit across a chair without bothering to hang it up properly. Feeling very sorry for herself she donned her nightgown and drew the curtains to shut out the daylight. Esther brought in her tea. Poppy drank it gratefully and slumped sullenly onto her bed.

There, at last, in the privacy of her own room, in the sanctuary of her own bed, she cried.

If only she'd known. If *only* she'd known, she would never have befriended Virginia in the first place. Yet, having befriended her, she liked the girl and even admired her. How could she now realise her dream of being Robert Crawford's wife, when achieving it would mean stealing him from Virginia, who loved him as much as she herself did? It was some shock to the system to meet face to face a rival in love, to know and understand how they felt, to realise that it was within your power to render that person an emotional wreck. Best not see Virginia again. Best avoid her in future. If she saw her, she was likely to confess that she herself was the other girl, the interloper who had diverted Robert in the first place.

She tossed and turned. The day had been sultry and warm and her bedroom was overpoweringly hot in consequence. She kicked off the bedclothes and lay sprawled, uncovered except for her nightgown.

And Robert would be home in four weeks.

Robert would be home in four weeks.

The shock of learning that alone . . . How would he let her know what he had decided? With a visit? By letter? A verbal message? Well, it was academic now. Even if he'd decided he wanted her after all, she could no longer accept him – on account of Virginia. Poppy would be heartbroken, but she could not respond to Robert in the way that, until today, she dearly wanted. She'd been living in a world of hope, of expectation, certain that Robert would take her and make her his. Only now, after getting to know Virginia with her inborn goodness and moral strength, did she realise how shaky this belief was. After all, she had never seen Robert and Virginia together. She did not know how they got on. She tried to imagine them in an embrace, but the image was too disturbing to sustain, so she shut it from her mind.

And anyway, she pondered – shearing off at a mental tangent, her indignation rising in proportion to the effects of the alcohol – why should she play the obedient little woman and hang on Robert's every whim and fancy? For nearly a year she'd pined like a witless lapdog waiting patiently for its master to decide whether he wanted to throw a morsel of food from his plate. She was no lapdog. She was a young woman, a respectable one at that these days. Why should she sit, anxiously waiting like some poor exploited hound, immobilised in thought and deed by a blind and senseless faithfulness that might never be rewarded?

Look at the admirers she'd got. She could take her pick of any number of men, gentlemen who were actually available, gentlemen who were not stuck in some snake-infested jungle because of some harebrained, namby-pamby notion that they were emotionally confused. What kind of man was this Robert? Would he always be so indecisive, so immature? At least Bellamy was not like that. He knew what *he* wanted, and had to be admired for his perseverance in trying to get it. Well, maybe it was time Bellamy was rewarded . . .

The alcohol got the better of Poppy and she drifted off into sleep, still mentally at odds with herself. She was awakened by an ominous crack of thunder. It was dark now and she wondered what time it was. Her window was open and through it she heard the unmistakable roar of a heavy downpour outside. Flashes of lightning, diffused by the curtains, pulsed in quick succession, to be followed almost at once by raucous, ear-splitting explosions from all directions. Poppy slipped out of bed and parted the drapes. She loved to watch a storm. The landscape flickered with a pinky, silvery sheen as nature set off its random display of monstrous fireworks, and she thought how beautiful, how spectacular it all was. A torrent of swirling water flowed down Rowley Road like a river in full spate. For some time she watched. She was fascinated by the huge spots of rain that splashed on the ground like transparent butterflies frozen motionless by brief lightning flashes.

Reflected in the glass of her window, she became aware of the glow of an oil lamp as her bedroom door was opened. She turned around, half in alarm, half in curiosity.

'I see you are watching the storm,' Aunt Phoebe said softly, standing in her nightgown like a plump cherub. 'I came to see if you were sleeping.'

'The thunder woke me.'

'Doesn't it frighten you?'

'No, I love it . . .'

'Are you feeling better now?' She rested the oil lamp on the tallboy and stood by Poppy at the window.

'I think so, thank you, Aunt.'

'Was it something you ate, do you think?'

'I don't think so.' She glanced guiltily at Aunt Phoebe and gave a little laugh of embarrassment. 'More likely what I drank. I polished off three glasses of champagne and finished half of Virginia's.'

'Oh, really, Poppy,' Aunt Phoebe admonished.

'I know . . . Anyway, how was church?'

'Church? Well, the choir was at full strength and in fine fettle. Mr Furnival and Mr Plumbridge were both recovered from their colds, and all the boys were present as far as I could tell. They sang a wonderful anthem. The Hallelujah Chorus from *Messiah*. It was very stirring.'

Poppy turned and smiled at Aunt Phoebe as lightning illuminated her face. 'I'm sorry I couldn't go . . . To tell you the truth, Aunt, I was too upset . . .'

'Ah . . .' Aunt Phoebe put her hand on Poppy's arm and gave it a reassuring squeeze. 'I suspected as much. Do you want to tell me about it . . . or can I guess?'

Poppy withdrew from the window and sat on her bed. She ran her fingers through her hair and sighed heavily. Aunt Phoebe turned around and watched her.

'I feel so stupid, Aunt . . . and so guilty . . .'

'Go on . . .'

'How can I possibly harbour ideas of marrying Robert now I've made a friend of Virginia? I had no idea when I met her that she was Robert's fiancée. If I'd known, I would've avoided her. But indeed I quite like her. She's a good, decent soul. How could I do such a thing to her as to take her man? Well, I couldn't . . . So I have to let go of the dreams I had . . . They were foolish dreams anyway.'

'Has she told you that Robert has come to a decision as to whom he wants to marry?'

'Oh, no, Aunt. She doesn't know any more than I do. But she loves Robert so much. It would break her heart to lose him. I couldn't let myself be the reason for that. I never had him anyway. He was never really mine. Nor was he ever likely to be, if I'm realistic.'

Aunt Phoebe sat on the bed beside Poppy. She wanted to hold her, to comfort her. She understood Poppy's dilemma, why her poor heart was aching, yet she did not want Poppy to think she was patronising her. So she sat with her hands clasped together in her lap.

'Then if Virginia is no wiser than you, she is in exactly the same situation as you. Therefore, you each have the same two alternatives. You both either respect Robert's ultimate choice, which might be you, or you withdraw now.'

'I withdraw now,' Poppy said unhesitating.

'And if Robert chooses you?'

She shrugged. 'He's too late. He'd have to make do with Virginia.'

'It's my guess he'd make do with nobody in that event. Why should he content himself with the girl he's come to consider second best?'

'He should have held on to me when he'd got me. I've been

399

a fool, hanging on for him, waiting, pining like some lovesick Cinderella. Who does he think he is? There are plenty more fish in the sea, you know, Aunt. I should have made him realise that when he decided to leave me.'

Thunder, like the splitting, cleaving trunk of a giant tree, crackled directly overhead and rumbled through the distant hills.

Aunt Phoebe said, 'If the boot were on the other foot, Poppy, do you think Virginia would withdraw in favour of you?'

'I wouldn't expect her to.'

'But neither would she expect her rival to, I imagine.'

'Virginia asked for my advice, you know . . .' Poppy laughed with derision. '*Me* . . . Ironic, isn't it, Aunt? I told her it's up to Robert who he chooses and that she should accept his decision, even if it goes against her.'

'Do unto others as you would be done unto, Poppy. If Virginia is as devout a Christian as you say she is, she will live by that creed. If she is prepared to accept *you* as Robert's choice, all well and good. To my mind, you should confess that you are her rival and make a clean breast of it.'

Poppy shook her head. 'I couldn't do that. Anyway, I think he's treated her terrible, Aunt.'

'You mean *terribly*, Poppy . . .'

'I mean, getting mixed up with me in the first place. If I'd known he was engaged when we started to get friendly, I would've had no truck with him. But by the time I knew, I was hooked like some stupid fish.'

'But you were not to know that a love affair would result from your friendship. It must have seemed unlikely, even to you, considering the differences in your social backgrounds . . . At the time, I mean, of course . . . Besides, if you'd had no truck with him, you and I would never have known each other.'

'Yes . . . That would have been sad, Aunt.' Poppy leaned her head on Aunt Phoebe's shoulder, inviting a consoling embrace.

Feeling Aunt Phoebe's caring arms around her elicited more tears. They did not come in a great flood, just a gentle trickle. She did not wail this time, merely wept silently as she pondered the past year. She was here, a cherished friend, resident and welcome in Aunt Phoebe's house because of Robert Crawford. He had been responsible, directly or indirectly, for a monumental change in her life. She must respect him if only because of that. He had been good to her, giving her his time and risking his own reputation. He wished her only well. That they had fallen in love along the way was as unintentional as any accident. Of course she loved him. Even after a year her hunger for him had not waned. It would never wane.

The rumble of thunder was becoming more distant. Like Poppy's crisis of emotion, it was passing over. She raised her head and looked at Aunt Phoebe through tear-filled eyes that glistened by the light of the oil lamp.

'You know, Aunt Phoebe,' Poppy said, the light of realisation beginning to dawn on her. 'I reckon that advice I gave to Virginia was good. We must both abide by Robert's decision, whatever it turns out to be. We've both waited this long. She'll wait another three or four weeks, and so will I. There'd be no point either in trying to sway him, if it's not the decision we want to hear. In any case, he might return from Brazil married to some Brazilian girl, for all we know.'

'Lord, that would really set the cat among the pigeons,' Aunt Phoebe said.

During his crisis of indecision more than a year ago, Robert Crawford had responded to an advertisement in *The Times* for a qualified and reliable engineer to survey routes for a proposed railway in Brazil. The timing could not have been better as far as he was concerned, for it would enable him to make the break he needed from the emotional confusion that had both delighted and tormented him. In Brazil, he would be far enough away to shun any inclination to rush home and dive headlong into a commitment he might later regret.

His interview in London meant taking a trip there by train, and he relished it. He recalled that Robert Stephenson, one of his heroes, had walked the ground between London and Birmingham twenty times before deciding on the best route for the railway. He, Robert Crawford, could be just as judicious in Brazil if he were granted the opportunity. On his train journey, he looked with professional admiration at the fine bridges of the London and Birmingham Railway, which had begun a full service nearly eleven years earlier. The Kilsby Tunnel, itself a monumental feat of civil engineering, had consumed some thirty-six million bricks in the lining, all laid by hand. The magnificent portals, through which you entered and exited, served to enhance the immediate landscape, not scar it, and gave no hint of the massive problems the engineers had encountered within.

In London, Robert had taken a four-wheeled growler to the offices of a consortium of investors in Oxford Street. There he was told that the Brazilian government was anxious to expand its exports of coffee and sugar cane. Railroads, of which there were none, were therefore necessary to transport the commodities to the main ports. Britain enjoyed a world monopoly in railway construction, and the consortium had been formed following a fact-finding visit to London by representatives of the Brazilian government. Depending on the results of the initial surveys, and following the official ratification by the Brazilian government, a company would be set up in London to manage and finance the project, and shares would be issued. Robert Crawford was offered the position of assistant engineer at three guineas a day plus all expenses, an enormous enticement. He estimated that he could return a year later about a thousand guineas better off, a handsome sum.

Robert sailed first to Lisbon, a city that impressed him. In Lisbon he embarked on a Portuguese ship for the Atlantic crossing to Rio de Janeiro. The spectacular landscape of Rio astonished him, and he was surprised also to find a cosmopolitan city of a quarter of a million disparate souls who wanted for nothing.

The actual surveying was neither as glamorous nor as sophisticated, however. On one occasion after heavy rains, the bullock cart drawn by eight oxen that conveyed him, the driver and two others with their food, water and equipment, foundered in mud. It took two days to recover it all. Travelling thus was mucky and slow, and a distance of twenty miles could take as long as seven days, hampered by swamps and swollen rivers. It was also obvious that the contractors, when the first line was sanctioned, would have to contend with blasting many tunnels, and building many viaducts and bridges. It would be a massive undertaking.

After three months in Brazil, one of Robert's colleagues, Charles Rabbitt, died of yellow fever. Robert was devastated, as was his remaining co-surveyor, Phillip Rose, a single man the same age as himself. Robert assumed leadership of the project and they pressed on steadily towards São Paulo, over rough terrain. He realised that the potential here for railway building was enormous. He could envisage lines running from Belém in the north, via Fortaleza, to Recife on the northwest coast. Another line would eventually run from Recife, crossing the São Francisco River to Salvador, then on to Rio de Janeiro and São Paulo. Hundreds of miles. Years of work.

Many of the tribulations of the terrain he encountered, Robert took in his stride. They were trivial compared to his personal predicament, which for months seemed unsolvable, and was still greatly concerning him. He had to make a choice between the two delightful but entirely different women in his life. Both were seldom far from his thoughts. Many a subtropical night in the stifling heat of a humid Brazilian summer, he'd lain in his tent pitched beneath a Paraná pine, tormented as he tried uselessly to get to sleep. He'd recalled Poppy's sweet face and her unruly mop of champagne curls. He relived her delicious kisses and remembered their faint but pleasant peppermint taste. He imagined over and over the warmth of her body as she sat in his lap, her easy weight a delight in that huge chair in his office. He vividly recollected how they mesmerised each other with desire, which was to remain unfulfilled. How he'd longed for her. How he'd wished she was with him, lying beside him in that tent. He remembered with affection her awful dresses, those unspeakable clogs, the stale odour of cooking that sometimes lingered in her hair, and smiled. These things did not matter. They were not really so awful. They were part of her. They made her what she was: a decent girl, quirky by dint of being deprived of privilege and the niceties of life but through no fault of her own. Yet, neither the deprivation nor her unsavoury roots had spoiled her. She was honest and forthright, with a childlike innocence one minute and a startling worldly wisdom the next.

Robert would turn over restlessly onto his other side and shake the thin blanket that covered him to dislodge any intruding termites. The blanket, too, protected him from the possibility of a *jararaca* snake joining him as a bed partner, an intruding lizard that might be huge, or even an armadillo, as he slept alone on the hard ground.

Poppy Silk was an enigma. She would always occupy

Robert's heart. He was determined not to let his heart rule his head, however, which Virginia Lord occupied. Common sense told him he should marry Virginia Lord. Her family was enormously influential and rich from generations of banking. They owned and ran Tyler's and Lord's Bank. And because his father's long-established firm, Crawford & Sons Limited, civil engineering contractors, enjoyed a close and lucrative relationship with them, jeopardising that connection could have far-reaching consequences.

Virginia was not only serenely beautiful, she was also kind and compassionate. She was intelligent and immensely loyal, but stricken with a religious fervour that he did not take particular pleasure in. She was also a committed humanitarian. 'How can you possibly allow yourself to work in a country that still operates a system of slavery?' she had asked him when he told her he was going to Brazil for a year. Typically, the tyranny under which many slaves suffered was her first thought. The absolute disappointment of having to postpone or cancel her wedding and the heartache that would entail was only her second consideration. Whatever happened, Robert knew she would wait for him to make his decision with an unwavering commitment.

However, Virginia did not kiss with the same commitment and consummate fervour as Poppy Silk. She did not feel soft and warm and inviting like Poppy Silk. Nor did Robert desire her like he desired Poppy Silk. Oh, he would have been content enough settling down to a comfortable married life with Virginia, to have a house full of children, servants and nurses to look after them all – had he not encountered Poppy. Poppy had dealt a considerable blow to his straightforward expectations of matrimony. However unwittingly, she had made him realise there was another side to man's coalition with woman: desire. Good, hard, sexual desire. It was the engine that drove all mankind, he now realised. It was the hinge on which a relationship pivoted.

Sometimes one person's choice of sexual partner baffled another, but its impact on that person could never be denied. And surely that was God's way. Instinct somehow dictated the person of the opposite sex who appealed most. You didn't even have to think about it. Indeed, you had no control over it. Why fight it? You saw the girl and you simply knew. Thus it had been with Poppy Silk. Such a liaison must therefore be right, decreed by nature and condoned by God.

But God, like the prospect of marriage to Poppy, was an illusion. A successful marriage with Poppy, like the promised existence of God, defied logic. Virginia remained the choice of common sense.

Chapter 26

Robert Crawford arrived back home on the first Friday in August after a brief sojourn in Lisbon. He had been gone little more than a year. It struck him that if *SS Great Britain* had been working the route, the crossing would have been quicker and he would have had the chance to see at close quarters Brunel's vision made manifest of the steam-driven future of ships and shipping.

When he arrived at Tansley House, delivered on the last leg of his journey by cab, he took time to talk with his mother and father before deciding he must go to bed and rest.

'I think I shall sleep for a week,' he declared.

'Tomorrow evening,' his mother said, halting him at the door of the drawing room, 'we are holding a party to celebrate your return.'

'Oh?' He smiled, pleasantly surprised. 'Where is it to be held, this party?'

'Here, at Tansley House. We have hired extra servants and engaged a band.'

'So there will be dancing, eh? That's wonderful. Thank you.'

'Unfortunately, your sister Elizabeth hasn't returned from school yet. She's been staying with a school friend for the first part of the August holiday and is not expected back for another week.'

'I trust she's well.'

'Oh, yes . . .' Clarissa hesitated, poised to say something else more pressing. 'Robert, I have taken it upon myself to send Virginia a note, to say that if they wish, the Lords can visit us tomorrow afternoon prior to the party and their overnight stay.' Clarissa was entirely ignorant of the emotional upheaval that had prompted Robert to go away in the first place. 'I hope you approve. You will have the opportunity to get to know each other again. After all, a year is a long time to be away from your sweetheart.' She regarded him admonishingly.

'That's very considerate, Mother,' he said without conviction, for he did not appreciate what he considered to be her meddling. 'However, it may be a little premature. I have reports to write, a lengthy account of my expenses to tally. No end of things to do.'

Clarissa smiled patiently. 'My dear Robert, don't you want to see Virginia after all this time? You will have all the time in the world to accomplish those things afterwards. Please don't shun your fiancée for the sake of such trivialities when you have been away so long.'

'No, of course, Mother. You are quite right. I wouldn't dream of shunning her. It will be good to see her again after so long. Of course I've been looking forward to it. We have so much to talk about . . .'

'You have a wedding to talk about.' She turned to her husband. 'Does he not, Ridley?'

'Indeed, son,' Ridley agreed. 'It's high time you named the day . . . It's high time we talked of your joining Crawford and Sons. We are desperate for an engineer of your calibre and experience. Especially since the new Birmingham sewerage project we have on hand is so close to being finalised.'

'Sewerage? Is it big?'

'It's huge.'

'We'll talk about it, Father – naturally – once the party is behind us.'

At three o'clock on Saturday afternoon with the weather hot, sunny and humid, the shining black brougham belonging to the Lords rattled into the drive of Tansley House. It deposited the Lords and a very nervous Virginia. She stepped down from the carriage and was at once greeted by Robert. He smiled his broad, open smile and she ran to his arms.

Four hundred yards away at Cawneybank House, Aunt Phoebe and Poppy were going through the latter's wardrobe to decide what she should wear for the party.

'I could wear the dress I wore for Minnie's wedding, Aunt . . . But on second thoughts, no. It brought me bad luck. I think I'll wear this blue satin one . . . The one I wore for my own birthday party. Everybody liked that.'

'Certainly all the men liked it,' Aunt Phoebe said with a knowing look. 'I'm sure they were all tantalised by your small waist and sight of your pert heaving bosom.'

'You sound jealous of my pert heaving bosom,' Poppy said saucily.

'Indeed I am. Gone are the days . . .'

'Well, a pert heaving bosom is quite the fashion, Aunt,' she said like a seasoned socialite. 'Besides, I need every advantage if I'm going to tempt Robert.'

'Hussy!'

Poppy laughed at Aunt Phoebe's good-natured jibe. 'I know. It's the navvy's daughter coming out in me.' She took the dress from the wardrobe, held it up in front of her and looked at herself in the long mirror.

'So, the blue satin dress it is, Poppy. I must confess, you do look very striking in it.'

'Thank you, Aunt . . .' She tilted her head and arranged the folds of the dress to assess the look. 'I wonder what Virginia will be wearing. Something very plain but very elegant, I expect. Something to enhance her slenderness and her classic good looks. I'm not really looking forward to seeing Virginia again . . . But I can hardly wait to see Robert. Does he know I live here with you now, I wonder?'

'Perhaps. If Bellamy's mentioned your name.'

'Oh, blimey! Let's hope Bellamy hasn't.'

'Such cursing, Poppy . . . We must get Esther to do your hair up. She's very good with hair.'

'I must take a bath as well, Aunt. And dab some *eau de cologne* behind my ears. It's important to smell sweet.'

'Why don't we take a walk in the garden?' Virginia suggested to Robert when the niceties and formalities of the Lord family's arrival had been taken care of. 'It's such a beautiful day. We should take advantage of it.'

'If you like,' he replied.

They got up to go outside, leaving their mothers and fathers smiling at each other with anticipation. The Crawfords were content that their middle son was reunited not only with them but also with the girl who, two years ago, he had asked to become his wife. It seemed a tortuous path, strewn with hazards, getting them to this point, but they were together again now.

'How was the weather in Brazil, Robert?' Virginia asked, turning to look at him with a girlish twirl as they went through the door to the extensive grounds at the rear of the house. 'You look so tanned. Like a farm worker.' She chuckled at the teasing slur.

'Well, it was hot.'

'Hotter than this?'

'Much hotter.'

'I don't know how you could tolerate it, much hotter than this.'

'You get used to it,' he said. 'January and February are the hottest. It's the height of summer then. A tropical summer.'

'Have you missed me?'

'Of course I've missed you, Virginia.'

She looked at him with eyes that told again of her uncertainty. 'How formal you sound. How remote. Have we been apart so long?'

'A year. More or less.'

'Yes,' she sighed. 'A year in which you had to live away somewhere, to get away from me. A year that I thought would never end . . . I'm terrified, you know, Robert, to ask what decision you came to – presuming you came to one at all. Yet I don't have the patience to wait for you to tell me . . .' She looked at him earnestly. 'I presume you came to a decision?'

'Let's sit on that bench over there . . . It's in the shade. Nor shall we be seen from the house.'

She wanted to take his hand or his arm but could not be so presumptuous. Not while she did not yet know whether he still wanted her. They walked to the bench unspeaking and she sat down primly, a very intent look upon her face. She looked into his eyes and smiled with all her commitment and unending patience.

'Well?'

'It has not been easy, Virginia, I should hate you to think otherwise. It was not something I did lightly, either, my going away. I have to thank you for your enduring patience. A lesser woman would have told me to clear off for good. But not you.' He took her hand and held it tenderly. 'Your loyalty was something I never doubted . . .'

She smiled graciously, flattered that he thought so, and

411

encouraged by his words. But she needed something more positive, some other, more potent reassurance. 'Your mother was . . .' She looked into his eyes beseechingly. 'She was talking to me while I was settling in my room. She gave me the distinct impression that you wanted to discuss with me naming our wedding day . . .'

'Did she now? She always did like to interfere.'

'It's a matter I've already given a great deal of thought to, Robert, while you were away. I think either Christmas Day or New Year's Day, don't you? Which would you prefer?' It was the oldest trick in the book, giving two choices and asking him to pick one.

'Which would I prefer? Oh, out of the two I would prefer Christmas Day, undoubtedly. But let's not—'

'Oh, Robert!' She let go his hand and flung her arms around his neck. 'Oh, thank you, Robert. I love you so, I've missed you so . . .'

He took her wrists and peeled her arms away from him gently, held them at her side and looked into her eyes reprovingly. She was going too fast, trying to coerce him into the decision she wanted, when he had not yet had the chance to seek out Poppy Silk, wherever she was. He must see Poppy; he must know how she felt now. It was only fair . . . not least on himself.

'Oh, Robert,' Virginia said again, but with a great sob, her tears of unbounded joy turning instantly to sorrowful weeping as she realised his lack of intent. 'Don't tell me it's not to be. I can't stand it. Honestly, I can't . . .' Her shoulders shook with her blubbering, her face was a contorted mask of anguish. 'I've waited all this time . . . All this time, hoping, praying that you still wanted me . . . that you would finally see sense and turn your back on *her* . . . that our wedding would . . . Perhaps I should go home—'

'No . . . Don't be foolish, Ginnie.' He sighed and put his comforting arms around her as he imagined the response of her parents if she returned to them distraught. He would be to blame and it would have repercussions.

She shunned him, and stood up. 'Yes,' she snivelled. 'It will be for the best.'

'No, Ginnie . . .' He could not suffer to see her cry in any case. He was such an inconsiderate cad bringing her to such depths of misery after such a short time in his company, and after such a long time absent. 'It would not be for the best. Sit down . . . You are jumping to conclusions. No doubt you are oversensitive to my comments, my actions.'

'You have been away from me for so long. How do you expect me to feel?'

'I know, I know,' he said soothingly. Maybe Poppy Silk was miles away anyway, living in some squalid railway encampment, the lie-by of some buck navvy who had already filled her belly with his brat. 'I understand that you want us to be wed. Of course I do. I am not opposed to it, Ginnie. You mustn't think that. It would be the common-sense thing to do . . .'

'But?'

What had he been thinking? What stupidity had possessed him? Poppy Silk knew no better than to become the whore of some buck navvy. It was to be expected of her. She had been only sixteen when they parted. At such a tender age her attentions would have been quickly diverted. There was not the remotest possibility that she would still be in the Dudley area, much less hankering for him. How could he entertain such stupid fantasies when all the time this wonderful girl beside him, this lovely, chaste, devout, loyal girl, was breaking her heart because for too long he had been too blind to see the obvious.

'Let us plump for Christmas Day, Ginnie,' he said.

* * *

413

Poppy towelled her fair hair dry while Esther emptied the bath and nimbly skipped down the stairs with pails of soapy water.

'Aren't you hot, Esther?' Poppy enquired.

'A bit, miss,' Esther replied.

'I'm hot and I haven't been running up and down stairs like you.'

'But you just got out of a hot bath, miss. You'm bound to be hot.'

'D'you think my hair's dry enough yet?'

Esther inspected Poppy's clean hair as Poppy sat down in her dressing gown. 'Hold your head over your knees and run your fingers through it to get the warm air to it. It'll soon be dry enough. I bet you'm looking forward to the party tonight, ain't yer, miss?'

'Yes,' said Poppy, her voice muffled under her mass of curls. 'In a way. In another way I'm dreading it.' Poppy lifted her head up, revealing her flushed face. She had no desire to expand on things of such an emotional nature with Esther. 'Oh, come on, Esther, I'm sure it must be dry now. It feels it . . .'

'All right, miss. Let's make a start . . .'

As Poppy was having her hair done, she heard the doorbell. Esther put down the brush and comb with the intention of going downstairs to answer it, till she heard voices and realised Aunt Phoebe had answered it.

'Listen,' Poppy said excitedly. 'I can hear a man's voice.' She made to get up, but Esther pressed her back down in the chair by the shoulders.

'Your hair ain't finished, miss, and you ain't dressed decent neither.'

'Go and see who it is, Esther. It might be Robert Crawford. If it is I want to see him. Quick, so's you can come back and finish my hair.'

Her heart was beating fast. He mustn't see her like this. She would have preferred him to see her regaled in her blue satin dress, looking beautiful and desirable, but if it *was* him she would make the best of herself and see him now. She was dying to see the expression on his face when he saw her, for he would hardly be expecting to see her here at Aunt Phoebe's . . . unless Bellamy *had* mentioned her.

She heard Esther's footfalls as she ran back up the stairs.

'It's Bellamy, miss.'

'Bellamy?'

'Yes, miss. He's talking to Mrs Newton. He's called to see you.'

'What's he want, I wonder?'

'You'll know in a bit.'

Poppy sat fidgeting while Esther tended to her hair, wondering about Bellamy. Had he brought her a message from Robert? Robert said he would let her know his decision through Aunt Phoebe. This must be it. His long-awaited message. Curiosity and anxiety were tumbling through her simultaneously. Oh, that agony of waiting . . .

'Have you done yet, Esther?' Poppy looked up at herself in the dressing-table mirror. Her hair looked finished.

'Patience, miss . . . There . . .'

'Which dress do you think, Esther?'

'Your day dress. The one you just took off. It's clean. You always look nice in it.'

'No, I want a fresh one.' She rummaged through her wardrobe, found one she fancied and put it on. Then, she briefly checked herself in the long mirror and ran downstairs.

'Poppy!' Bellamy greeted enthusiastically. 'My, you look radiant.'

'Flushed, more like. I've not long stepped out of the bath. How come you're here? Do you have a message?' She looked from Bellamy to Aunt Phoebe. Aunt Phoebe shook her head discreetly. 'So how's your brother Robert? Returned safely I presume?'

'Yes, he seems well enough. Not that I've seen very much of him yet. Virginia seems to have monopolised him since she arrived.'

'Virginia? She's there? Already?' A cold shudder ran down her spine. 'How long has she been there?'

'She arrived just after lunch with her family and a corps of maids. And enough bags to sustain her in clothes for a week, I shouldn't wonder,' Bellamy replied. 'Of course she's staying the night, but why she needs all that stuff I know not.'

Poppy's heart sank to the very depths of her being.

So that was it.

It was all over.

Virginia had won.

Virginia was there with him already. Poppy could just imagine them meeting after a whole year apart, the fond embrace, Virginia overflowing with tenderness, her soft brown eyes creasing into shy smiles, the familiar touching of hands. Of course, he'd let Virginia know as soon as he'd arrived back, invited her to spend an intimate afternoon before the party when he would announce the date of their wedding. Right now they would be professing their love for each other, their undying devotion. Virginia would be plying him with the sweetest of kisses, moving before him tantalisingly with her delicate, lovely body. Poppy gave a great, shivering sigh of desolation. So this was how it felt to be forgotten, to be overlooked. She had not foreseen this nightmare. She really had not expected this, not in her heart of hearts, so confident had she been of securing Robert's love for herself. But how could it have been otherwise? She had been living in cloud-cuckooland if she had expected it all to turn out any differently.

For long seconds she stood without moving as a shaft of slanting sunlight penetrating the front window mirrored the sun's stealthy creep across the afternoon sky. She was warm still from her bath, but she trembled as if chilled to her bones. In the brief silence she heard the slow ticking of the grandfather clock echoing hollowly across the tiles in the hall, like a metronome setting the turgid measure of some death march.

'Do they seem happy together?' Poppy's voice was a tight thread, stretched to the limit with emotion.

'I would say so, from what I've seen of them. Virginia seems very happy. Mind you, I would expect her to, having not seen old Robert for a whole year. She must be glad to have him back.'

'And does he look well, Bellamy?' Aunt Phoebe enquired.

'In robust good health, I would say, Aunt.' He turned to Poppy. 'My reason for calling on you . . . It occurred to me that . . . well . . . perhaps you would like to attend the party as my guest tonight. I would be entirely honoured, Poppy. I dearly want to show you off – especially to Robert. I haven't mentioned you at all. I wanted to surprise him with the most stunning girl. He was always the one to introduce some pretty girl or other before he and Virginia became engaged. Well, now it's my turn. You'll be far and away the loveliest girl there tonight. What do you say, Poppy? I could collect you and Aunt Phoebe in the brougham. Make a grand entrance and all that.'

This appealed not only to Poppy's sense of defiance, but to her basic hunger for Robert's acceptance. She cast her mind back to the times when he had all but pleaded with her not to submit to the demands of Jericho. His jealousy had shown even then. Well, no doubt she could work the same trick again, but this time with his own brother, and before his very eyes. Robert would have the shock of his life, and serve him right. And there was another aspect to this, which was beginning to dawn on her: she had diverted Robert before. She must possess some quality that Virginia lacked, even as a lowly navvy's daughter. She was evidently blessed with some magic string or other that she could pull, that would have Robert dancing to her own tune. Tonight, she would look her absolute loveliest. Tonight, she would be tantalisingly charming, attentive and utterly vivacious . . . with Bellamy . . . Robert had only ever known her as an impoverished waif from a railway cutting. He had no notion of the confident, elegant young lady she had become. Well, he was in for quite a surprise. The humble caterpillar had turned into a dazzling butterfly.

Poppy smiled sweetly at Bellamy and glanced at Aunt Phoebe for her consent, receiving a faintly amused look and a barely noticeable nod of the head in reply.

'I think that would be a splendid idea,' she said eagerly, eyes sparkling with impishness. If all else failed, if she couldn't have Robert after all, she could have the next best thing, his younger brother . . . and it would truly be one in the eye for Robert . . .

'Excellent,' Bellamy said with a broad grin of satisfaction. 'Shall we say quarter to nine? I want to make as grand an entrance as possible with you on my arm, Poppy.'

'It sounds perfect,' she said.

Most of the guests had arrived and had been greeted by Robert, with Virginia proprietorially at his side, parents hovering in the background. Slowly, everybody made their way to the large, oblong room at the rear of the house that had been adapted to resemble a ballroom. Sofas, chairs and tables had either been shifted or removed so that couples would have room to dance in the centre. The four-piece band were performing at one end and there was a table with drinks at the other, close to the door through which everybody was drifting in a haze of tobacco smoke and a rumble of conversation intermingled with laughter. Built into the long wall that faced the garden was a marble fireplace, devoid of any fire on this warm, sultry night. Set in the opposite wall was a French window, open to allow the free circulation of air. Already, the candles were lit as daylight began to fade.

Men patted Robert on the back matily, and fawned with a simpering attentiveness over Virginia, who looked flushed and shy and demure.

'Good evening, everybody,' a man's voice boomed, obviously trying to gain the attention of every person in the room. It was Bellamy.

Beside him was a flaxen-haired young woman who was radiantly beautiful, her pale skin smooth and flawless with the translucence of the finest Dresden bone china. Her slanting blue eyes sparkled and danced as they reflected the tiny flames of the several candelabra. Her lips, as she smiled so appealingly, revealed her perfectly even teeth. Everybody turned to look and a hush descended over the room at the sight of her. The envious glances of not only the men but the women as well, as they raked the length of the girl's body, statuesque in a gown of blue satin, told her how desirable she looked.

Robert Crawford saw and he gasped with incredulity. The girl looked astonishingly like Poppy Silk. But it could not possibly be, for Virginia shrieked with delight and rushed over to greet her, and she did not know Poppy Silk from Adam. Astounded at the likeness, he scrutinised her more as he was left standing alone.

'Poppy! Oh, how delightful to see you,' Virginia gushed, 'and looking so utterly ravishing . . . Bellamy, I never knew you and Poppy were friends. Such a coincidence. Such an astonishing coincidence. I must introduce her to Robert at once . . .' She turned back to Poppy excitedly. 'Poppy, do come and meet my fiancé, Mr Robert Crawford. But fancy you knowing Robert's brother. You never said . . . You *are* a dark horse . . .' She took Poppy's hand and led her eagerly over to Robert, with Bellamy in tow.

'I would have said,' Poppy declared, 'but I had no idea that Bellamy was the brother of your fiancé. I didn't even know you had a fiancé till last time we met, Virginia.'

'Of course, that's true. How silly of me not to realise . . . But isn't it a wonderful coincidence?'

They reached Robert, and Poppy's heart was pounding like a drum. He looked leaner, fitter and his skin was tanned, which she thought made him look even more handsome. She wanted to run to him; to slip her arms around him and hug him to her. This was the man she had yearned for, for so many long and empty months, for so many empty nights alone in her bed. She wanted to feel his arms embracing her, squeezing her tight, whispering words of love in her ear. She wanted to sniff his skin, be as intimate with him as she had been before.

'Robert, I want you to meet my friend, Miss Poppy Silk,' Virginia said. 'Poppy, Robert Crawford . . .'

'Miss Silk,' he said, and there was an audible tremor in his voice as he offered his hand. 'It is indeed a pleasure to meet you . . . and such a *pleasant* surprise . . .' His eyebrows twitched, which elicited a smile from Poppy. Could she assume from his look that he was all at once agonised with some inner struggle which he had not anticipated, and which he must unexpectedly endure?

Poppy was stumped for words but it did not matter. Virginia was gushing, bubbling with vivaciousness.

'Poppy and I have been close friends for a while, Robert,'

she explained. 'She has such common-sense notions about the world. You must discuss them with her sometime.'

The rest of the guests turned their attentions back to each other and resumed their conversations.

Robert said, 'So you are a friend of my brother Bellamy, Miss Silk?'

'Oh, please call me Poppy,' she said, finding her voice at last, and feeling a little mischievous. She gave him a devastating smile that had him reeling. 'Already I feel as if I have known you ages.'

'Really?' he answered. He turned to Bellamy, unsmiling. 'You have kept it quiet about Miss Silk, Bellamy.'

Bellamy smiled proudly. 'I wanted to surprise you, Robert. I wanted you to see that your younger brother is just as capable of attracting a pretty girl. And you have to admit – Poppy is stupendously pretty.'

Robert scanned Poppy again and their eyes met briefly. 'She's not just pretty, she's beautiful. Far too beautiful for you. Have you known each other long?' He looked from one to the other.

'Ever since her seventeenth birthday in April. Aunt Phoebe put on a marvellous party for her.'

'Aunt Phoebe?'

'Yes . . . Of course, you are not to know, Robert . . . Poppy is Aunt Phoebe's companion—'

'Companion? Ah! Yes, I see.' A hint of a smile flashed through his eyes.

'I understand you have been in Brazil these past twelve months,' Poppy said, meeting his gaze full on. 'Did you achieve what you set out to achieve?'

Their eyes held and electricity surged between them.

'Oh, Poppy,' Virginia exclaimed. 'You remember what I told you about Robert and his going off to Brazil . . . Well, now he's back we've named the day. We're to be married on Christmas Day.'

Poppy believed that her insides had suddenly dropped as she felt a vast emptiness within her. 'Is it true?' she said to Robert, controlling herself admirably.

'Well . . . I . . . We . . .' He avoided her eyes to spare his embarrassment, his disappointment and his guilt.

'Congratulations,' Poppy managed to utter, 'to you both.' Tears stung the backs of her eyes. But they must not witness them. She turned to Bellamy, reached for his hand and looked up at him beseechingly. 'I'd love a drink, Bellamy.' She turned her back on Robert and Virginia as her bottom lip began to quiver.

'See you later,' Virginia called.

'My word, Poppy, you downed that rather swiftly,' Bellamy said with obvious admiration. 'Let me get you another.'

'Thank you. I never realised sherry was so nice.'

Within a second or two he'd handed her another. She swallowed some and felt its warmth spreading through her.

'Take it easy with this one, else you'll be soused. Then Aunt Phoebe will castigate me for trying to lead you astray.'

I won't take much leading, she felt like saying. Well, she had nothing to lose now. Robert had made his decision and was going to be wed. Whatever she did now was of no consequence to him. She might as well give herself to Bellamy; he deserved her. Poppy felt discarded, disenchanted and heartbreakingly disappointed. No wonder Virginia was so buoyant. She'd got what she wanted. But at Poppy's expense.

The musicians had just started playing a waltz. Poppy said, 'Shall we dance, Bellamy?'

He smiled, delighted she'd asked. They stepped into the centre of the room where the carpet had been taken up and the woodblock floor conscientiously polished by the maids to a slippery shine. Poppy turned to face Bellamy, forcing a smile through her pain of emptiness, longing, and grief over her lost love. He received her into his arms with a self-satisfied smile.

'Hold me tight, Bellamy.'

'Of course, little Poppy,' he answered warmly.

Her dance steps, which should have been light as she swirled around, making her skirt whirl attractively, seemed heavy and contrived. She had to force herself around the floor as if the weight of all the world's woes were pressing down on her. Robert was going to marry Virginia. That's all she could think of. Robert was going to marry Virginia. He hadn't even sent her a message to say *sorry, dear Poppy, but I've chosen Virginia after all.* As she turned, feeling Bellamy's hand hot in the small of her back, she was barely conscious of anything other than this indescribable ache in her heart. Faces flitted past in a blur, some familiar, some not, and then she spotted the friendly face of Minnie who was waving to her. She waved back and pressed her head against Bellamy's shoulder.

'Would you prefer to take a walk outside?' he asked, misinterpreting her actions.

She looked up at him and he saw tears glistening in her eyes.

'You're crying.'

'No, it's the smoke in here.' She smiled reassuringly and nonchalantly wiped her eyes with the backs of her hands and sniffed. 'It always makes my eyes run. Maybe it's a good idea to go outside and get away from it for a while.'

He took her hand and led her away, through the French window and out onto the lawn.

'I was worried,' he said. 'I thought maybe I'd trodden on your toes and you were too polite to complain.'

That made her smile. 'Believe me, you'd have known. I would have very likely socked you one.'

He laughed. 'Oh, wonderful.'

Moonless night had settled on the land, but already the stars were as thick as meadow flowers. A touch of indigo lingered in the western sky, the last remnant of daylight, and Poppy could just make out the fleeting shadows of bats as they flew between the trees. She looked back towards the house and saw the warm yellow glow from the party room. Through the French windows she could see people standing, drinking, talking. She heard the clink of glasses, the strains of the quartet as they struggled to be heard over the buzz of animated conversation and the peals of laughter.

They walked on and came to an ornamental fishpond. Bellamy stopped, turned towards her and put his hands to her small waist, 'I've dreamed about this moment, Poppy,' he breathed. 'For ages I've wanted to bring you here on a night such as this and hold you by starlight and feel the warmth of your body against mine.'

'And here I am,' she said, content to submit to Bellamy's fantasy, for none of hers were forthcoming. 'Kiss me, Bellamy.'

He bent his head towards her, searching hungrily for her lips. She met him halfway and half-heartedly, felt his mouth on hers, and allowed herself to be kissed . . . Oh, it was not as pleasant as being kissed by Robert, but it was infinitely better than Jericho's slobbering. And yet . . . if she responded more ardently, with more enthusiasm. If she put her heart into it . . . Yes, that was better . . .

'Bellamy!'

It was a man's voice.

It was Robert's voice.

Poppy and Bellamy broke off their embrace.

'What?' Bellamy answered, irritated at the interruption.

'Sorry to disturb you. Virginia has just informed me that she has never danced with you, Bellamy. She's free right now. Perhaps you would care to oblige her . . . Don't worry, I'll take care of Miss Silk . . .'

Chapter 27

'So, Poppy . . . I find you fastened by the mouth to my brother.'

Poppy could hardly see Robert's face in the darkness so she was unable to read his expression. However, his voice was intense, his words sarcastic. 'Fastened by the mouth?' she queried, her heart beating faster over this startling encounter than over her embrace with Bellamy. 'That's a funny way of putting it. Is that what they say in Brazil?'

'Who cares what they say in Brazil?'

'So are you criticising me, or mocking me with your sarcasm?'

'Neither. It was merely an observation,' he answered stiffly.

'Good,' she said. 'Because the only reason I was "fastened by the mouth" to Bellamy was because you have no interest in fastening me by the mouth to yourself. So, if you'll excuse me . . .' She threw her head back in defiance and walked away.

He grabbed her arm. 'Wait, Poppy. I need to talk to you.'

His hand was warm on her skin, his touch electrifying. 'Let go of me,' she said coolly, finding it the most difficult thing in the world to say.

'We must talk, Poppy.'

She hesitated, impeded by her own desire for him, but even more so by the need to say her piece. 'Then let go of me . . . Thank you . . .' She tried to recover her poise. 'I don't think there's anything left to say. You've evidently got what you came home for. Thanks for not letting me know sooner.'

He sighed profoundly and raised his hands, palms up, in a gesture of sincerity. 'I didn't know where to find you, Poppy. Besides, I had no time to look. My mother had invited Virginia to stay with us almost as soon as I returned.'

'Your mother?'

'Yes, my mother. She always was inclined to interfere. Please don't entertain the notion that it was me.'

A light breeze rustled the leaves in the tops of the elms. Poppy turned her face to the cloudless ink-blue sky, clenching her fists to release the tension that had built up inside her, thankful to learn it had not been him who'd arranged to see Virginia before seeking her.

'The last time I saw you, Robert,' she said, 'you handed me Aunt Phoebe's address on a note. You said that through her you would let me know when you had arrived back. It was the main reason I went to see her in the first place. And yet the first I heard of your returning was from Virginia.'

'Only because my mother let her know without my knowledge or consent.'

'Your mother must have been very anxious for her.'

'Very anxious that we marry, I admit. Anyway, I can't believe that you and Virginia know each other.'

'Oh, it was by accident, not by design. I certainly didn't know she was engaged to you when we met. Nor did she have any inkling that I was her rival. She still doesn't, I'm sure. We befriended each other, Virginia and I. I actually like her, Robert . . . The fact that she's your fiancée has taken the shine off it, though. Still . . . I know she's very much in love with you. I'm sure she deserves you. I'm sure you deserve her.'

'You've changed, Poppy.'

'Oh, tell me something I don't know.'

'You've changed for the better, I mean. I had the shock of my life when I saw you. Aunt Phoebe is to be applauded.'

'I'll pass on your plaudits, unless you prefer to tell her so yourself. But it wasn't all Aunt Phoebe's doing. Doesn't it occur to you that I also had to put in some effort?'

'Forgive me. Of course you did . . . You were always enchanting, Poppy, but now you are the most beautiful creature I have ever had the privilege of setting eyes on.' His voice was as soft and warm as a caress.

'And to think I was yours for the taking,' she answered with a spurt of provocation.

'But not any more?'

'I waited for you, Robert. For a whole year I pined. I ached for you, I cried for you. And for what? You come home and you are still promised to Virginia. You've even named your wedding day. You've obviously considered your choice carefully.'

'You are far more grown up, you know.'

'It's of no matter to you whether I am or not,' she answered, the spirit of defiance still aflame within her, fanned by the hurt she felt.

'The change has made you infinitely *more* appealing. There is a new assertiveness about you.'

'I am also more socially acceptable now, don't you think?' she said cuttingly. 'Now that I wear well-made, fashionable clothes and shoes, and speak a little differently. I am more socially acceptable now that my navvy roots and navvy boots have been concealed, aren't I?'

'I loved you with your navvy roots, Poppy. I loved you with or without them. I could hardly love you less for being more complete now.'

It was the first real inkling that he still felt something for her. Her heart seemed to bang like a drum at his words, thudding in her head as her blood surged hot and swift through her veins. Was he implying that he loved her *still*?

'As I said, Robert, it's of no matter to you any more.'

'But could it be, Poppy?' There was a plea in his voice. 'I have been too hasty since I returned home. I have allowed myself to be swept along on a tide of events that flowed much too quickly. Virginia made me feel extremely guilty over my going away. She wept piteously. It was so obvious she had suffered a broken heart and I felt so moved, so *sorry* for her, so *obliged* to make amends . . .'

'So to ease your guilt and to make amends, you agreed to name the date of your wedding. Is that it?'

'Virginia was so nervous when I saw her again, like a child almost. And so visibly upset. I felt for her. I felt deeply. I'm not so indifferent that I could not be moved by it. Would you rather I was so heartless?'

'No . . .' she answered pensively. 'Of course not,'

'I cannot bear to see a woman upset, Poppy.'

'So should I weep buckets to get the same response?'

'I can assure you, Poppy, it isn't necessary. Virginia is just a sweet and sensitive girl.'

'Oh? Aren't I a sweet and sensitive girl?' she challenged.

'Of course you are. But a little more worldly than she. She's also been very loyal.'

'And you think I haven't?' she blurted.

'With my brother Bellamy around?'

'Yes, even with your brother Bellamy around. I've been loyal despite Bellamy. Ask Aunt Phoebe. But there's many a girl who wouldn't have been – he's quite something, you know.'

'I'm sorry. I shouldn't have implied anything. It was entirely the wrong thing for me to say . . . Oh, would that Virginia had not been invited here before I'd had the opportunity to speak to you, Poppy. Things might have been different.'

'Might?' she queried.

'Would, Poppy. Things *would* have been different. Always assuming you still feel the same as you did. Do you still feel the same?'

She sighed, her true emotions surfacing through her anger. 'I thought I did. Before it was plain Virginia had got in before me. Now I feel forgotten and overlooked. It's not a nice feeling, Robert,' she pouted, looking beyond Robert. She was suddenly distracted by figures silhouetted against the light spilling out of the French windows. 'Damn! Bellamy and Virginia are coming back.'

He glanced over his shoulder.

'Will you meet me, Poppy?' he whispered urgently. 'There's so much more to talk about. I beg you.'

'Tomorrow night. After church.'

'Where?'

Her mind raced to think of a suitable venue. Where did they meet the very last time? 'Outside St Edmund's. Where we met before. Remember?'

He nodded. 'How very appropriate.' With a smile, he turned to greet Virginia who was clinging to Bellamy's arm in sisterly fashion. 'I was just saying to Poppy what a beautiful evening we have for the party,' Robert said easily. 'Perhaps we should have hired a big marquee and held it here in the grounds.'

Bellamy edged his way towards Poppy and felt for her hand.

'Bellamy is a much better dancer than you are, Robert,' Virginia said, still full of the dancing and not heeding Robert's words.

'Well, he's had a damned sight more practice.' Robert looked at Poppy from under his eyebrows. 'You don't find many assembly rooms in the Brazilian jungle.'

'I'm surprised you enjoy dancing, Virginia,' Poppy said lightly, trying to conceal the mischief she intended. 'Aren't

Quakers opposed to it? Don't they regard it as flippant, or flamboyant?'

Virginia cast an apprehensive glance at Robert. 'I hope I haven't altogether lost my sense of fun, Poppy.'

'Tell me, Bellamy,' said Robert. 'Is Poppy a good dancer?'

'Tolerable. Or rather I should say she's a better dancer than she is a pianist.'

'How unkind,' Poppy said, pretending to be hurt. 'You've cut me to the quick, Bellamy. That's the last time I dance with you.'

'Don't be so touchy, Poppy.' He squeezed her hand and looked at her with an apologetic smile. 'What I was suggesting is that your talents lie in other areas.'

Poppy continued to pout and Robert looked at her lips with an acute ache of longing. He was reminded of how they felt on his when they kissed. He yearned to take her in his arms again, to tell her how much he still loved her.

'Well, if Poppy won't dance with Bellamy anymore,' Virginia said, turning to Robert, 'perhaps you should take her to the floor, Robert. Then you can judge for yourself how well she dances.' Such a suggestion would dismiss Poppy's notion that she considered dancing a frippery.

'A splendid idea,' Robert answered, seizing the moment. He looked at Poppy for her consent.

'I have no objection,' she said, trying to hide her excitement at the prospect of feeling Robert's arms around her again.

'Excellent.' He offered his arm theatrically. 'Miss Silk . . .'

'While you assess Poppy's dancing,' Virginia said, 'I shall take the opportunity to speak to the new Mrs Cecil Tyler. I've had no chance yet. Come, Bellamy. I will introduce you.'

Robert's and Poppy's footsteps were soft on the cool grass as it yielded beneath their feet. She clung to his arm, exhilarated, keeping close to him as, entering the house, they received nods, smiles and admiring glances as they nudged through the throng of people that edged the area of polished floor reserved for dancing. As they reached the floor, the quartet was playing a polka.

'Not my favourite step,' Robert commented disappointedly.

'Nor mine either,' Poppy agreed.

'Maybe if we stick it out we could be rewarded with something a little less strenuous.'

She smiled up at him, her true feelings manifest in her eyes. She hoped he was right. All this energetic whirling about to the polka was preventing her from being in his arms.

At last their patience was rewarded. The leader of the quartet announced that the next dance would be a Strauss waltz, and they waited while some couples left the floor and others arrived. They stood awkwardly close together, each yearning to be in the other's arms, illogically feeling conspicuous, that all eyes were on them.

'Who is this new Mrs Cecil Tyler, I wonder?' Robert said, referring to Virginia's comment. 'She seemed vaguely familiar when I met her, but I couldn't place her.'

Poppy giggled, beginning to feel more at ease with Robert. 'Of course, you don't know, do you? Do you remember my friend Minnie Catchpole from the encampment?'

'The flighty one with the loose morals? Tipton Ted's daughter?'

'Shhh! Folk will hear. Yes. It's her. She's now Mrs Cecil Tyler.'

'Good Lord! How on earth did she pull that one off?'

'She met him at Aunt Phoebe's one night after my party. They fell in love.'

'Good Lord!' he said again. 'She has no finesse. And he married her? He obviously didn't know what she was like.'

'I don't think it would have mattered. Let's face it, he wasn't in the front of the queue when they were giving out hand-some faces. And stranger things have happened.'

The band struck up and those dancing began swaying sedately to the steady rhythm of the Lorelei Waltz. Robert took Poppy in his arms and they glided off.

'So you met Bellamy at this birthday party of yours?'

'Yes.'

'Would that I had been there myself . . . with you.'

'So you say now.'

'Oh, I believe you know it to be true,' he said, his voice low. 'I can scarcely believe I'm here now, dancing with you.'

'But still promised to Virginia,' she goaded.

He made no response.

'We are no further forward, Robert. *You* are no further forward. If you still love me – and I have a suspicion now that you still might – things are just the same as when you went away. You left to sort out your feelings. If you still love me, why haven't you done it? You've had plenty of time.'

'I did. I sorted out my feelings. But on my way back to you I got shunted into a siding by Virginia, her family and my mother.'

'Then all I can say is you lack determination. You lack the resolve to get out of it.'

'Well . . . I can't deny it, under the circumstances . . . However, there was another aspect to the way I reacted. I imagined you must have moved on with your mother and family, and the rest of the navvies. In which case you could have been anywhere in the country and unreachable. I imagined that you might have eventually been seduced by that brute Jericho . . . even had his child—'

'Ugh! You thought that of me?'

'All these things went through my head, Poppy. And not unreasonably. How was I to know otherwise? All these thoughts influenced me. Of course they did. Then . . . almost as soon as I'd arrived back here, Virginia was here. Yet I wanted *you*. Oh, I dearly wanted you, Poppy . . . but I was certain you had gone from me. With Virginia I still had someone . . . and that was so important to me, coming back home starved of the love of the woman I wanted. She at least had been waiting for me—'

'As I was.'

'But I'd imagined you gone, Poppy, just a memory to plague me for the rest of my life.'

'Well, as you can see . . .' She looked up at him defiantly. 'I am not just an affliction of your memory.'

'And I am delighted to note it.' He smiled when she looked into his eyes. A warm smile that elicited a lovely warm glow inside her. He bent his head towards her. 'I am still head over heels in love with you, Poppy. Nothing has changed in that respect.'

She sighed, a deep, satisfied sigh of relief, and gave him a squeeze. She closed her eyes, oblivious to everything and everybody, and smiled to herself as they swirled around in time to the music. This was the reward for suffering a horribly uncertain day.

He looked into her eyes again and smiled warmly. 'Now that *I* have confessed, it's *your* turn.'

'Don't you already know?' she asked earnestly. 'Isn't it obvious? Do you think I would have waited a whole year if I didn't love you with all my being?'

'Say it then. Tell me you love me.'

'I love you, Robert,' she breathed, meeting his eyes directly. 'With all my heart and soul I love you. Only you ever doubted it.'

'So there really is no romance with Bellamy?'

'Of course there's no romance with Bellamy . . . But there

could have been . . . There was no prior "fastening by the mouth" as you cynically put it . . .' A smile lurked behind her sombre façade. 'Although I know him to be fond of me,' she went on. 'Perhaps too fond. He's asked me to be his, but I've never agreed to be. I've always kept him at arm's length. It would've caused too many problems.'

'As if we didn't have enough.'

'It might still, if he's of a jealous nature.'

'Another bridge to cross when the time comes.'

'So what do you intend to do now as regards Virginia?' Poppy asked.

'Nothing, till you and I have had the chance to talk in private and at greater length. Virginia is staying the night, and so are her parents. I presume they'll return home tomorrow after tea.'

'Her parents are here? I haven't seen them.'

'They're in cahoots with my own mother and father, shut away in one of the other rooms. Do you know the Lords?'

'We've been introduced. They seem very nice.'

'As indeed they are. My, how you have inveigled yourself into society, Poppy.'

While Poppy and Robert were dancing, Virginia sought out Captain and Mrs Cecil Tyler, with Bellamy in tow. They engaged pleasantries, although it soon became obvious that Mrs Tyler was the worse for drink. Virginia was thus content for Bellamy and Captain Tyler to lead the conversation.

'Rumour hath it that there is likely to be a tie up between Peto's and Treadwell's to complete the Old Worse and Worse at last,' Captain Tyler remarked. 'I wonder that Crawford and Sons are not in the fray.'

'Not our cup of tea, Cecil,' Bellamy replied and sipped his beer. 'Whatever arrangement anybody makes they'll no doubt get their fingers burnt. That's my father's view, at any rate. We have other fish to fry.'

'But don't forget that in the last session of Parliament, an Act was passed to raise the unissued capital of the OWWR by preference shares. Talk is that Peto's and Treadwell's will join forces to complete the line on the strength of it.'

'Are you likely to acquire any such preference shares?' Bellamy enquired.

'Depends what they're offered at, of course.'

'Sounds risky to me, if you don't mind me saying so. It's been beset with problems from start to finish, that railway.'

'Gosh! All this talk of contracting and high finance,' Virginia said in an aside to Minnie. 'I get utterly confused by it all. I swear my father rues the day he realised he would have to make do with daughters. I'm sure it's one of the reasons he is so fond of Robert. I'm sure he would love to groom him to take over the bank eventually.'

Minnie took a slug of the gin and orange juice she was drinking, emptying her glass. 'I thought he was an engineer, not a banker.'

'Did I tell you he was an engineer, Minnie? I don't recall.'

'You must've,' Minnie said, trying to cover her slip up. 'There he is, look. Busy dancin' . . .' She nodded her head in his direction, to divert Virginia's attention away from herself.

Virginia looked. She thought it odd that, for relative strangers, Robert and Poppy were dancing awfully close; that Poppy ought to have more propriety than to allow such familiarity, but she made no comment.

'I want another drink,' Minnie said petulantly. 'Cecil, will you get me another drink?'

'How many have you had already?' he queried, excusing himself from Bellamy.

'Who's countin'? You said you like me when I'm tiddly. Fetch me another drink, eh?'

Bellamy drained his own glass. 'I'll go. Would you like another, Virginia?'

'I'll have a little orange juice, please.'

Captain Tyler and Bellamy headed to the drinks table together.

'Have you not had enough alcohol, Minnie?' Virginia asked apprehensively. 'Maybe you should stop drinking now.'

'Stop drinkin'? Oh, Virginia, you ain't gunna start preachin' at me again, am yer?'

'Gracious no. You're a married woman, the responsibility of your husband . . . But one question has been intriguing me . . .' She glanced around to ensure nobody was listening. 'Does Captain Tyler know you were once . . . you know?'

'Course not. And don't you tell him, neither. I'm reformed, me. I'm a one-man woman these days. Strictly a one-man woman.'

'Oh, Minnie. I'm so glad. I've prayed for it to happen. You obviously idolise Captain Tyler.'

'I do that.'

Virginia glanced around anxiously for further sight of Robert and Poppy. She witnessed him whispering into Poppy's ear and the girl was responding with a gratified smile. Virginia felt a searing pang of jealousy, a sensation she did not particularly like, but one she could not dismiss on account of his infidelity before.

'Poppy is such a pretty girl, Minnie, and so clever. I question whether I have done the right thing by suggesting she and my fiancé dance together. It seems to me that she is being a little forward with him, the way she's dancing so close.'

'There's nothing wrong with that. She always was a friendly sort of a wench . . . 'Specially if she likes the chap, I mean.'

'Is that true?' Her tone revealed her disapproval. 'How long have you known Poppy, did you say, Minnie?'

'A good many years,' Minnie slurred. 'She's me best mate.'

'Fancy . . . I thought you'd only fairly recently met.' Virginia looked extraordinarily interested. 'How did you meet?'

'When we was kids.'

'No, *how* did you meet, Minnie . . . ?'

'Oh . . . Our fathers was navvies.'

'Poppy's father was a navvy? I find that hard to believe. Are you quite sure?'

'Listen . . .' Minnie beckoned with her finger for Virginia to get closer and leaned towards her ear. 'It's a secret, so don't get blabbin' it about. If it ever gets back that you said anythin', I'll know who said it.' Minnie realised she had phrased her sentence ridiculously in her inebriation, but her meaning, she believed, was clear.

'But I don't understand, Minnie. Poppy's no navvy's daughter.'

'You wunt think so to look at her now, with all her airs and graces. But we left the navvies' encampment together a twelvemonth ago. We shared that house I had in Gatehouse Fold for a bit.'

'Last summer, you mean?'

'End o' September time.'

'You mean that dainty, fair-haired girl you used to walk the streets with was Poppy?'

'I 'spect so.'

Virginia was not convinced. She had to be sure. 'The first time I saw you, Minnie – the time I was alerted to you – you were with another girl, very pretty with fair hair . . . I lost track of her, but I suppose, yes . . . it could have been Poppy. That night, you were under the arches of the town hall and a carriage stopped. I watched you talk to the man inside the carriage – negotiating your price, I suppose – then you both got into the carriage and it drove off.'

'Yes, that was Poppy. Oh, that was a night . . .'

'Gosh!' Virginia exclaimed. 'Goodness gracious!'

Virginia was utterly astounded. Poppy had been a prostitute, although evidently now reformed. Or was she even reformed? The way she was dancing so close to Robert, perhaps she was not. Perhaps she had turned herself into one of those discreet, high-class prostitutes who graced society, but only ever with their eye on taking a fortune from men. You would never have guessed. To look at her, butter wouldn't melt in her mouth. She had fooled everybody, it seemed. Now she was trying to make a fool of Robert. Yet, maybe she already knew Robert from his working on the Oxford, Worcester and . . .

'Listen, Virginia,' Minnie said looking as serious as she could in her drunken state. 'That's a secret 'tween you an' me. I shouldn't never have told yer. Her'd kill me if her knew I'd told yer. Swear to me as you won't repeat it.'

'Look, here are Captain Tyler and Bellamy with our drinks. I'm going to catch Robert's eye. It's time he danced with me.' Bellamy handed her a glass of orange juice. 'Thank you, Bellamy. Shall we intercept Robert and Poppy now? They've been dancing together quite long enough.'

Chapter 28

The end of Evensong could not come soon enough for Poppy. She suffered several hymns, two readings from the Bible, the abstruse chanting of two psalms as well as the *Magnificat* and the *Nunc Dimittis*. The choir sang an anthem, followed by an unfathomable sermon from Reverend Browne and yet another hymn. Only then was she allowed to escape down the stone steps to the street and the warm air of that summer evening. Aunt Phoebe insisted that they drive her to St Edmund's church at the other end of the town to meet Robert, not content that her charge should walk there alone.

Poppy had had a long conversation with Aunt Phoebe that morning, and told her all that had transpired. Aunt Phoebe intimated she was glad she was not in her shoes, and warned that she should be prepared for difficult times if Robert refused to marry Virginia after all, and Poppy was recognised as the cause of it.

'I know,' Poppy replied. 'But he has his own life to lead. Nobody can live his life just to suit somebody else, and neither should anybody expect it. I'll fight any person tooth and nail who says different.'

'But sometimes it's unavoidable,' Aunt Phoebe tried to reason. 'Princes have married princesses for the greater enrichment of their family or their country, without a thought for themselves, with love never entering into it.'

'But we're neither prince nor princess,' Poppy argued, 'so we don't matter. Anyway, Aunt, if he asks me to marry him, I shan't refuse.'

'I suspect it won't be quite so cut and dried, Poppy my dear. There is a great deal at stake.'

The clarence rattled to a stop and Poppy saw that Robert was indeed already waiting.

'It looks like rain, Poppy,' Aunt Phoebe said, peering up to the sky. 'Don't get caught in it. These summer storms can be quite severe.'

'I won't, Aunt.'

Eagerly, she made her exit and, with a broad smile, ran across the street to greet Robert. Aunt Phoebe watched from her seat in the clarence with a great fund of sympathy. She offered a little prayer that Poppy, who was her whole life, should not end up devastated as a result of this love affair.

'You didn't forget me,' Poppy said as she hurried to be with him.

'How could I?' His eyes were warm on her and he planted a welcoming kiss on her cheek. 'I'm only glad that Aunt Phoebe didn't want to chaperone you.'

'Oh, she might have wanted to, but I would have resisted with all my being. I take it Virginia didn't stay too long?'

'She and her family left after tea, as I thought they would.'

He took her hand and looked her up and down admiringly. She looked bewitching in her Sunday-best dress and bonnet, and her dainty boots that he glimpsed briefly beneath her skirt as she walked. This girl was so outwardly different from the navvy's daughter he used to meet before, the one he was not so keen to be seen with in public because of her impoverished clothes and unspeakable clogs. For all his self-consciousness then, he had found it impossible to keep away from her. She tantalised him with her angelic face, her slanting blue eyes, her loveable, impish ways, her intelligence and her natural grace, all of which made her the enigma that she was. Now, she surpassed his every dream. She still had all the qualities that had captivated him in the first place, but a year later she possessed a grown-up charm, style and confidence as well, yet none of the arrogance that might have accompanied it.

'You look astonishingly beautiful, Poppy. I can't get over you.'

'Thank you,' she said, mightily pleased.

'Shall we walk through the castle grounds?'

She smiled up at him. 'That was where we said our good-byes a year ago,' she answered softly.

'It's where we can cancel them out and say our hellos.'

'Tell me about Brazil,' she said as they entered the gates. 'Tell me what it's like, and what you did.'

He told her what he had seen, what he had done. He told her about the friends he had made, the good times and the hard times they'd shared and the sadness they'd felt over losing a colleague. He held her spellbound. 'The potential for railway building there is colossal,' he said. By this time, they were looking down on the area that used to be the old race-course. It was due to become Dudley Station, but was a building site now. 'I'm in half a mind to apply for the position of Chief Engineer on the line from Rio to São Paulo when work is scheduled to begin.'

Suddenly, her heart was so full of pain that she believed it would burst. 'You mean you want to go away and leave me again?'

'But you would go with me next time,' he said tenderly. 'I wouldn't leave you here again. I presume you would agree?'

She smiled, as quickly relieved. 'Of course I'd go. I'd go with you to the ends of the earth.'

They ascended into the Triple Gateway that gave access to the courtyard, which in turn was surrounded by the ruined Tudor great hall – the buttery, the kitchens, the stables and the living apartments of the castle. Like most Sunday evenings in summer, there were plenty of other people around, courting couples, couples with young families, some strolling, some sitting on the grass in the centre watching the world go by.

'Bellamy asked where I was going when I went out,' Robert said.

'Oh dear. What did you say?'

'That I was going to meet a friend I hadn't seen since I left for Brazil.'

'Well, that's partly true,' she said. 'When have you arranged to see Virginia again?'

'I haven't. But I shall have to . . .'

He sat down on the grass and tugged her hand, indicating that she should sit beside him. She sat facing him, but side on to him so that her legs and his kissed.

'I take it you intend to tell her about me . . . about us?' she said, arranging her skirt around her shins.

'Yes, little Poppy, and I'm not looking forward to it.'

'So do you love me enough to see it through?' She was hugging her knees and watching him with adoration glistening in her eyes.

'Of course I do. Please don't doubt my love for you. It's been tested for more than a year in Brazil, a year when you weren't there and I longed to be with you.'

'Absence makes the heart grow fonder, Robert. Now I'm no longer absent, maybe you'll take me for granted.'

'Never. Horsewhip me if ever you think I'm guilty of it.'

'So what shall you tell Virginia?'

'That I've seen again the girl who was her rival and I have come to a final decision . . . That I intend to marry this girl.'

Her heart leapt at this revelation and she smiled. 'And will you tell her it's her good friend Poppy Silk?'

'I hadn't considered that. Perhaps not.'

'I think she should know. Let's get it into the open. What's the point of hiding it? There's also the question of her willingness to release you from your betrothal.'

'Yes . . . I know . . . I wish to be as honourable as I can, Poppy. I would relish her willing release. But if she refuses to give it, then I shall have no alternative but to be dishonourable about it and take the consequences.'

'Your mother and father will not be pleased.'

'Either way, they will not be pleased . . . Nor hers, either. There'll be ructions.'

'Just as long as you know what you're letting yourself in for. If you think you cannot face it . . . If you want to change your mind, Robert . . .' She picked a daisy that was growing beside her and fingered it gently, twirling the fragile stem between her thumb and forefinger. 'Maybe now would be as good a time as any to tell me. I will walk away . . . heartbroken, of course, knowing that you love me and would prefer me. I won't bother you ever again. I'll leave you and Virginia in peace . . . If that's what you want . . .'

'That's not what I want, and it's not what I ask of you, Poppy. I love you. I intend to make you mine, come what may.'

'Oh, Robert,' she whispered. 'I've waited so long to hear you say it. Now I have to wait for the outcome with Virginia.'

'Whatever the outcome, it won't alter what I feel for you, my love.'

'That's what I'm afraid of, Robert.'

'What?'

'First you say there will only be one outcome, then you say "whatever the outcome".'

'There can only be one outcome. And you know what that will be. I'll go and see Virginia tomorrow after dinner. I'll set the record straight.'

It was dusk when they descended, arm in arm, back down the steep winding path that led back to the road known as Castle Hill, and St Edmund's church. They had spent more than an hour getting to know each other again, reviving the rapport they enjoyed before. As they walked through the town they were oblivious to everybody, their attentions focused only on one another. They heard not the babble of men darting from one alehouse to another as they sought oblivion from the banal reality of life. They were wrapped up in each other, content to be in each other's company after so long apart.

'I used to lie awake in my bed at night as we camped under the stars, miles from civilisation,' Robert told her. 'And I would think of you.'

'Tell me what your thoughts were,' she pleaded.

'Oh, Poppy, I dare not. They were a mite too racy.'

Her laughter was like a bell tinkling. 'I'm not a prude, Robert – I grew up with navvies. I know what people get up to in their beds, whether they're alone or not. In fact, I bet your thoughts were not half as racy as mine.'

'Then tell me yours,' he chuckled.

'I will not,' she said, feigning indignation. 'At least, not until you've told me yours.'

'Well . . . If you really want to hear it . . . I would try and imagine you lying beside me on the hard ground, beneath my blanket—'

'And would I be naked?'

'Oh, eventually.'

She laughed approvingly.

'I would remember your kisses, Poppy . . . I would lie with my eyes closed and imagine your lips on mine and remember the taste of you. Then I would smother your body with soft kisses, every soft mound, every lovely crevice, and I would hear you sigh with pleasure . . .' He turned to look at her. 'Were your thoughts ever anything like that?'

'Oh, yes,' she responded dreamily. 'I would put my arms around myself and imagine they were your arms. I would gently feel my breasts and imagine it was you . . .'

'And?' he prompted, a lump in his throat. 'Was there more?'

'Oh, yes . . . But you'll think me a real hussy.'

'I can only love you the more,' he said with tenderness. 'Knowing you have thought of me in that way.'

'Well . . . Then, I would . . .' She hesitated, not sure how to say it. 'I would touch myself . . . You know . . . I would feel myself . . . Between my legs, I mean . . .' She realised she was blushing and was glad the dusk concealed it. 'I would imagine it was you doing it . . .' Her voice was low, barely audible. 'I wanted so much for it to be you, Robert. It was so heavenly.' She looked into his eyes then with a candour that was unnerving.

'And did we . . . go all the way?'

'Oh, yes,' she said emphatically. '*All* the way.'

'We did in my thoughts too,' he said. 'I could never sleep for thinking about it.'

'Nor me either.' They both laughed and their eyes met lovingly at these most intimate secrets shared. After a pause, Poppy said, 'Did you ever think such things about Virginia?'

'Never.'

'I bet . . .'

'I have never felt any such desire for Virginia. And that's the gospel truth.'

'She told Minnie she would remain a virgin till she married.'

'Oh, she'll probably remain a virgin long after she's married,' Robert suggested wryly. 'But Minnie Catchpole, you said . . . Your friend?'

'Yes. It was about the time Virginia and me first met. Minnie had turned to prostitution, you know—'

'I didn't know.'

'Of course you didn't.'

'But it doesn't surprise me. She was always wayward, you said.'

'Always. I tried to turn her away from it. I was scared stiff what could happen to her.'

'And poor old Cecil Tyler married her. He couldn't have known.'

'Oh, he had no idea. But that's his concern. Anyway, Virginia was trying to save her, trying to put her on the straight and narrow. She'd spotted her somewhere and made it her business to get to know her. It was at Minnie's little house when I called once that I first met Virginia. For some reason, known only to herself, she assumed I was also trying to save Minnie.'

'She would. That's the way her mind works. She always was an extreme busybody where spreading the word of God was concerned.'

'She took me once to a Quaker meeting, you know.'

'A Quaker meeting?' he scoffed. 'Lord, I bet that was fun.'

'She has ideas of becoming a Quaker when she's married. Her mother used to be one.'

'Oh, I know. So had my grandfather. It's just another reason not to marry her. I can't imagine being married to Virginia, she with a straight, pious face, tight-lipped, unsmiling and wearing those dowdy clothes they wear, preaching the gospel to me with a pair of knitting needles in her hand and a ball

447

of wool in her pocket. They knit perpetually, you know, Quakers.'

'I didn't know.'

'It's so that they're never idle. When they have nothing to do they knit. I'm sure they must knit in their sleep. They knit useful things, I grant you. Gloves, stockings . . . anything . . .'

'But they are very . . . devout – I think that's the word – good people . . . and kind. She would want your children raised as Quakers as well.'

'What children?' he laughed. 'I wouldn't have the desire . . .'

'Why not? She's quite beautiful, in a quiet, austere sort of way.'

'Yes. That's a good way of describing her. Austere. And eminently respectable.'

'I'm surprised you don't fancy her. A good many would.'

'Well, I don't. I like her and respect her, of course . . . But I couldn't go through a marriage that was destined to be like that – devoid of any passion, any desire. It would be a complete waste. I gave it a great deal of thought while I was in Brazil.'

They walked on for a minute or two in a companionable silence. It was Robert who broke it.

'Tell me how you came to leave the Blowers Green encampment.'

'Oh, yes . . .' She began to giggle. 'That's quite a tale . . . You remember Tweedle Beak?'

'The one who—'

'The one who was bedding my mother after my father left.'

'Yes, I do recall him. I didn't like him. He was a surly so-and-so.'

'He was a swine. He tried to raffle me off, but he fixed it so that he won the raffle and I would be his to do his bidding.' Robert looked at her aghast. 'He planned to leave my mother

448

and tramp off with me. When the others found out, he got hounded out, but I left afterwards anyway – with my mother's blessing – with most of the takings from his raffle.'

'Serves him right,' Robert commented.

'Minnie left with me. She wanted to get away from Dog Meat. The encampment was due to close anyway in the October. Treadwell's stopped all work because the OWWR had run out of money. Anyway, I bought Minnie and me some new clothes with Tweedle's raffle takings. We thought we were proper ladies.' She chuckled as she recalled it. 'Anyway, we stayed a few nights in The Old Bush Inn before Minnie rented this house in Gatehouse Fold. I stayed with her for a week or two. I had the intention of finding work as a maid. Then I found Aunt Phoebe's address you gave me and went to see her. I thought she might know somebody who wanted a maid. We hit it off right away.'

'You seem happy with Aunt Phoebe, Poppy.'

'She's my mother now. She regards me as the daughter she never had. I love her dearly.'

They were walking past Tansley House by this time and quickened their pace unwittingly. Poppy hoped that Bellamy would not see them, and said as much to Robert.

'He won't see us in the darkness. At some time I'll have to tell him about us. It's not something I look forward to. But if he had no prior claim on you . . .'

'None, Robert. I saved myself for you . . . And your two-wheeled riding machine . . .' She laughed again. 'What happened to your machine, Robert?'

'Oh, it's in one of the unused stables. I'll dust it down soon and take it for an outing.'

'Don't forget to call for me on the way. Do you remember when you took me for a ride on it?'

'Could I ever forget?'

'I was hoping all the time that we would fall off and roll together in the grass . . . that we would end up making passionate love . . .'

He chuckled again with approval. 'You *are* a strumpet.'

'Oh, given the chance . . . I dreamed about it. I used to imagine it.'

'You never!'

'I did.' She laughed at this other secret admission, glad that she'd told him, glad to witness how it excited him. 'And what about when you gave me reading lessons in your office and we sat in your chair and kissed and kissed and kissed?'

'I carried those kisses with me all the way to Brazil and back.'

'So you can return them to me?'

'Yes, so I can return them.'

'I can't wait, Robert.'

'Neither can I.'

'Then let's not wait any longer,' she breathed.

They had reached Cawneybank House and slowed their step. A chestnut tree stood at the end of the drive and a late bird flapped noisily from it and flew off to his own roost as Robert opened the gate.

'Let's walk on the grass,' Poppy suggested in a whisper. 'Our footsteps will crunch on the gravel else, and Aunt Phoebe might hear.' She took his hand and she led him past the front of the house where a light was glowing through the fanlight over the front door. 'There's a light in Aunt Phoebe's bedroom, look.'

'Where are you taking me?' he asked.

She put her finger to her mouth.

The air was sweet and cooler now. She glanced up at the sky and saw that clouds were blanking out the stars. Maybe the rain Aunt Phoebe had predicted would materialise after all. But she was home now and it was not raining yet.

How different today had been. She'd hardly slept last night for thinking of Robert and Virginia. She'd been on tenterhooks all day, waiting for evening to come when she would meet Robert. She'd hardly eaten a thing, so nervous had she been. During the afternoon she had sat in the summer house trying to make herself comfortable, propped up on a pile of cushions while she'd tried to get interested in *Ivanhoe*. But she could not concentrate on the novel. Her thoughts were only of Robert; her head was full of him.

But now she was leading Robert past a rose bed that Clay had been working on earlier that day. The scent of the blooms delighted her as they brushed past, to walk around the stable. Poppy put her forefinger to her lips again and pointed to the room above the stable where Clay lived and slept. A light burned within. She prayed they would not encounter him exiting the privy. They crept past more rose beds. Even in the twilight you could make out the roses and new buds with little splits of colour which were difficult to determine in the darkness, and half-hidden among the dark foliage of the bushes. They crossed another lawn, turned at a large rhododendron bush. There they beheld the summer house.

On the steps up to it, she turned to him, her head at the same height as his, and she slipped her arms around his neck and smiled with such joy on her face.

'I've longed for this moment,' she whispered as the cloud cleared momentarily to reveal a sliver of new moon that lent a silver lambency to her complexion.

He opened his arms to her, enchanted by the warmth of her affection, which she gave so unstintingly. He held her close, and their lips met. The agony of waiting was over. Their kiss was hungry as her hands went between them and held his face to her. He was pressing against her and she could feel his warm body. Oh, she had ached for this.

'Let's go inside,' she breathed. 'There are some cushions I was sitting on earlier . . .'

The door creaked as she opened it and she halted, cringing that the sound might have disturbed Clay. She tried again . . . carefully . . . Inside she could just discern the cushions, strewn as she had left them on a wicker sofa; at her suggestion they laid them on the wooden floor of the summer house. She untied her bonnet and threw it on the sofa.

He scooped her up into his arms and laid her gently on the bed of cushions as if it were fit for a bride, and lay beside her. She turned her face to him and smiled conspiratorially, all her love exuding from her clear blue eyes, which reflected the sickle moon still visible between the clouds. She closed her eyes and felt his lips caress her smooth eyelids, with the lightness of a butterfly's wings. He found her mouth and she tasted him with tantalising pleasure. She ran her fingers through his hair in an ecstasy of bliss at her absolute love for him, and at her brazenness in bringing him here.

He was unfastening her Sunday-best dress at the back with inexpert fingers, so she raised her shoulders to make it easier for him.

'Wait,' she whispered, realising the awful potential for farce. 'Let me take it off. It'll be such a palaver otherwise. The things we girls have to wear, it's no joke, I swear.'

He watched in awe as she stood up and undressed. Soon, she was standing before him entirely naked, her slender body pale but exquisitely beautiful in the insipid, intermittent moonlight. She lay beside him on the cushions again. He rolled onto her and kissed her on the mouth once more, one hand cupping her firm young breast.

'In my thoughts, when I was trying to get to sleep,' he sighed, 'I used to kiss your breasts—'

'And every soft mound and every lovely crevice, you said.' Her prompt was a soft whisper.

His mouth skimmed her breasts delectably, his tongue teasing her nipples till she thought they would burst. He kissed her warm belly, then between her legs. She lay sprawled, clenching the soft curls of his head between her fingers. 'Oh, Robert,' she sighed, paralysed and astounded with pleasure.

Too soon he raised himself up to remove his jacket and his shirt. He sat down, pulled off his boots, then his trousers. He was as naked then as she was. She watched him. Her lust, simple and shameless, was increasing inexorably as he knelt beside her.

'My angel . . .' He looked at her longingly, appreciatively, and ran his fingers lightly up between her thighs till they settled at her crop of soft fair hair. She was warm, soft and deliciously wet, and she parted her legs a little to make herself more accessible. 'Oh, my angel,' he breathed again, as though she had no other name. He bent down to her, kissed her lips and gently lay on her. As she felt the pressure of his warm naked body, his smooth chest against her breasts, she sniffed his skin, breathing in her ardent desire that seemed unquenchable.

'Robert,' she sighed with longing. He entered her and she winced. 'Oh, Robert,' she murmured again.

He drew back at once. 'I'm so sorry, my love. I don't want to hurt you.'

'It's just a little twinge. It's to be expected first time.'

He kissed her closed eyelids, her soft, round cheeks and her neck. He was inordinately gentle, afraid of hurting her, but each sharp pain that accompanied each tender, tentative push was a dizzying delight, and she raised her legs to accommodate him the more as he probed deeper, deeper into her. The pain seemed to be numbed as the pleasure increased with each tempered, careful movement, and they soon found themselves locked into a steady rhythm that grew more compelling the longer they were joined. Her breathing came in short gasps as she rubbed herself more firmly against him, intensifying the pleasure, until all knowledge, all sense of who or where she was, was gone.

There was only Robert and this glorious sensation in the pit of her stomach and her groin. Her world was him entirely, his quickening breath, his heart hammering against her own. She held onto him ardently, clinging to his shoulders, then around his waist in a fervent hug of passion as he thrust into her harder. He groaned . . . and sighed . . . and eventually ceased to move . . . Tears ran down her cheek as she cleaved to him, tears of relief that the heartache of waiting, that a whole year of uncertainty, was over and done with. This was the way it would be from now on. This was the future. It was also the present and, for now, she wanted time to stand still, to exist only in this moment. She wanted this wonderful feeling of peace, which emanated from the very centre of her body and seemed to spread up into her head, to last till eternity.

He felt her tears wet against his cheek. 'My angel! You're crying.'

'I know,' she whispered and hugged him. 'Tears of happiness . . . Tears because too soon we shall have to part, that I shall have to go to my bed without you, that you will have to go to yours.'

'More's the pity,' he said, with intense feeling.

Then they lay silent, each aware of the enormous significance of what they had done, aware of the forbidden heights of ecstasy they had scaled, and not regretting it. Certainly not regretting it. It was done and there was no turning back. He rolled off her and she felt moist with perspiration where he had lain on her, a little sore where he had been, but content. Oh, utterly content. All she wanted then was to sleep in his arms, to awaken with him at dawn and smile into his soft eyes . . . and make love like that again.

'Can you hear the rain?' she whispered. 'Aunt Phoebe said it would rain.'

He opened his eyes and slowly, reluctantly sat up. They could hear the spots of rain pattering on the roof of the summer house. It came heavier, squalling as the breeze got up, beating on the windows, rasping through the leaves of the trees outside. She cuddled up to Robert.

'We'd better get dressed,' he said, giving her another hug. 'Otherwise we'll catch our deaths.'

Reluctantly, she stood up while he watched her with ultimate contentment.

'You're watching me,' she said, amused, as she stepped into her skirts.

'I'm trying to. But in this light I'm rather straining my eyes.'

She laughed. 'I wonder what my hair looks like. I do hope Aunt Phoebe's gone to sleep. I should hate to meet her on the stairs with my hair everywhere. She'd guess what we'd been up to.' She put on her bonnet and tucked her hair inside it, then tied the ribbons. 'Maybe I'd better go in by the back door and up the back stairs.'

'I wonder what time it is,' he said.

'It can't be very late. Aren't you going to get dressed? Or do you intend to walk home naked?'

'Well, at least my skin is waterproof,' he replied.

When he was dressed, they stood holding each other, the rain hammering on the roof of the summer house.

'When shall I see you?' she asked.

'I don't know. I have to see Virginia very soon.'

'I know.'

'Of course, if you gave me your permission to call . . .'

'You're mocking me . . .'

'Not at all . . . For the sake of propriety, I mean.'

'How can you talk about propriety after what we've been doing?'

'Aunt Phoebe doesn't know what we've been doing.'

'Then I will tell Aunt Phoebe that I have given you permission to call on me. She won't be a bit surprised.'

'Then I shall call on you . . . But better not expect me tomorrow.'

'I know,' she answered. 'Virginia . . . Come on, let's make a run for it . . .'

Chapter 29

Robert Crawford awoke next morning to the pearl-grey light of a high summer dawn. In the split second of waking, while the mind is sluggish and all thoughts are gathered and sorted, last night registered as vivid as an enamelled picture. He lay awhile and hungrily relived every sensuous moment in Aunt Phoebe's summer house, how he and Poppy had committed themselves so deliciously, so whole-heartedly to each other. If he were a cad he would run a mile now, avoid her as if she had typhoid. He would ignore her if ever he saw her out or in company, or act as if nothing had ever happened . . . if he were a cad. But he was no cad. His commitment was equal to hers. It was serious, deadly earnest and sincere, and it promised a lifetime of contentment.

Now, it remained for him to make the other players in this drama aware of his true feelings and his plans. First, he should have a man-to-man talk with his father about his reluctance to marry Virginia. It was only fair to let him know his intentions before visiting the home of the Lords to inform Virginia, as gently as he knew how. He could not live his life for Virginia. He could not live his life to please her parents or his own. There was also Bellamy to consider . . . He got up from his bed and rang for some hot water. When it was brought to his room, he shaved, cleaned his teeth, washed and dressed.

He was first in for breakfast. It was a working day and his father and Bellamy would be travelling to the office and yard together at Burnt Tree, a mile or so distant. Soon they would be joining him at the table. Robert sat alone meanwhile, steeped in thoughts of Poppy, reliving still their erotic encounter, and yearning for more.

It was the custom in the Crawford household not to have servants lingering in the breakfast room, because the nature of the family's conversation, often orientated towards business, warranted confidentiality. So Robert went over and helped himself from the silver dishes deposited on the sideboard. He chose bacon, eggs, black pudding, mushrooms and fried bread, and took it back to the table, ravenously hungry.

Bellamy entered, wished him a brotherly good morning and poured himself a glass of freshly squeezed orange juice.

'Have you seen anything of that girl Poppy Silk since the party?' Robert asked experimentally.

''Fraid not.'

'Oh?' This was encouraging news. 'Doesn't she appeal any more then, Bellamy?'

'Oh, she appeals all right, Robert. She's a looker if ever I saw one. But she blows hot and cold and you never quite know where you are with her.'

'She doesn't suit then?' he suggested hopefully, and shook pepper over his plate.

'Oh, on the contrary, she'd suit admirably. I'm very taken with the girl. She's so eminently beddable.'

That remark irritated Robert. 'But you're not going to bed her, by the sound of it.'

'Oh, I don't know . . . She puts palings around herself, as if she's some exotic species of tree in a park, and won't allow me near her. But, at your party, she'd taken them down. She seemed a little more inclined. She seemed to be warming up encouragingly.'

'Oh? Did she?'

'Till you came along and interrupted us with Virginia's request that I dance with *her*. She seemed positively keen then . . .' Bellamy sipped his orange juice as he pondered those moments. 'She hinted once, you know, that there was some other chap she was waiting for . . . Well, you *know* women. It's not the thought of their man's fine looks or prowess that gets 'em, though, is it? Especially when he's absent. It's not the heroic soldier far from home that carries the day, but the chap who happens to be on the spot.'

Robert picked up his knife and fork and cut a piece of bacon which he pressed onto his fork. 'I take it, then, that your intentions are not entirely honourable.'

'Honourable enough, I would've thought. I could quite happily spend the rest of my days and nights bedding Poppy Silk. If it takes a proposal of marriage, then so be it.'

'I suggest to you, Bellamy, that there's more to marriage than merely bedding the bride regularly.'

'Yes, I imagine there is. But I am serious about the girl. Maybe it's time I made the move. Strike while the iron's hot and all that . . . Tell me, Robert, have you made your mind up yet to join Crawford and Sons?'

'It's something I intend to discuss with father,' Robert answered sharply, annoyed and relieved at the same time that Bellamy had diverted himself from the sacrosanct subject of Poppy Silk.

'Excellent. We urgently need somebody of your expertise and qualification.' He twirled his glass between his fingers as he sat opposite. 'By the way, did you hear the rain last night?'

'Hear it? I was caught in it. Got soaked. Didn't make it home early enough to avoid it. I should have taken a cape.'

'Cleared the air a treat, though, eh? So, where did you get to? Who did you see?'

'Oh . . .' He loaded more egg and bacon onto his fork. 'Somebody from the OWWR works I wanted to see.'

'There's a chance they'll be restarting soon. Did you know?'

Robert put the loaded fork to his mouth and ate. 'It'll be a pity if they don't,' he said eventually. 'All the work that's been put in so painstakingly already. Actually, I wouldn't mind seeing it through . . .' His face brightened as he looked up to gauge Bellamy's reaction. 'If Treadwell's will have me back, of course.'

'I thought you said you were going to join us.'

Robert shook his head. 'I didn't say that, Bellamy. I said I intend to discuss it with Father.'

'I'm sure money would not be an obstacle.'

'Money is not the obstacle.'

'So what is?'

'The same as ever, Bellamy. My independence.'

'I'm afraid I don't understand your obsession with independence.' Bellamy stood up and went to the sideboard.

'Well, it's easily explained. I have no wish to be beholden to anybody. I want to do what *I* want to do. I see various ways forward . . .'

Ridley Crawford entered the breakfast room like a stiff breeze.

'Good God, Robert, you're up early. Dare I hope it is your intention to visit the works with Bellamy and me?'

'Not today, Father. I have too many other things to do. Reports and things for the Brazilian venture. They have to be completed.'

'Of course. So when *do* you intend to pay us a visit?'

'He's not sure he wants to, Father,' Bellamy answered for him.

Robert glanced coldly at Bellamy, then looked at his father. 'I do need to discuss things with you, Father. If you are not too tired or too busy this evening . . . After dinner, perhaps . . .'

'Very well,' Ridley said agreeably. 'After dinner.'

After dinner, Robert was able to steer his father into the study for the promised *tête-à-tête*. Ridley sat at his big oak desk, assuming the business persona he'd shed earlier when he left his office.

'So, Robert . . . You wanted to talk.' He sat back in his leather chair with his elbows resting on the armrests, his fingers steepled. 'I trust it is about your future.'

'Yes, Father,' Robert said deferentially, taking the chair at the other side of the desk. It reminded him of when he was being interviewed for the situation of engineer at Treadwell's. 'As Bellamy rather blurted out this morning, I don't quite see my future in Crawford and Sons.'

'It's a pity,' Ridley replied with obvious disappointment. 'I would have thought your sojourn in Brazil might have made you see sense.'

'It's rather less to do with Brazil and more to do with Ginnie, Father.'

'Oh?' Ridley looked surprised.

'The fact is . . . even though I am technically engaged to Ginnie . . . and even though *she* has already decided when we are to marry, I intend to ask her to release me from the betrothal.'

Ridley's expression manifested both his disapproval and horror. 'I believe that would be a very grave mistake, Robert. I really do. There is a vast amount at stake here. Whatever your reason, I urge you to reconsider.'

'While I was in Brazil, I thought about it till I was blue in the face. I thought of little else.'

'So what are your reasons for wishing to jilt Virginia? Let us see if we can find some way around this . . . Your mother will be devastated. Come on, lad. Out with it. You can talk to your father.'

Robert coughed nervously. 'Before I went to Brazil . . . some months before, actually . . . I met a girl. I found her totally enchanting. She was everything that Virginia was not, and nothing like what Virginia was. Well, to cut a long story short, we fell in love. Head over heels in love.'

'And she knew that you were engaged?'

Robert nodded. 'She knew I was engaged. I knew it too, so you cannot blame her,' he added defensively. 'Anyway, I believed that my year in Brazil would erase this girl from my mind and from my heart . . .'

'But it has not,' his father prompted.

'Indeed it has not. I have seen her a couple of times since my return and I am even more certain of my feelings for her now than when I went away. I truly see no point in agreeing to marry one girl when I am so utterly in love with another.'

'I do see your dilemma,' Ridley said, not without some sympathy.

'You do?' Robert exclaimed, not without some astonishment.

'Of course. I am not totally unworldly in matters of the heart.' He smiled expansively. 'You youngsters tend to think us older generation were never young. You seem inclined to believe we have never been capable of love, of emotion. You see us all as old fogeys, never touched by love or desire. I swear the younger generation is content to believe it was created by immaculate conception.'

Robert laughed at his father's little joke, cheered by his benign attitude. 'I fear Ginnie and I have tended to veer in different directions in any case,' he went on. 'She has some notion, I understand, about dragging me into Quakerism. I believe she would convert now, but for the fact that she would be disowned when she married me. Well, now she can . . . Convert, I mean.'

'So who is this girl who has stolen your heart so consummately, Robert?'

Robert smiled. 'Poppy Silk.'

'Poppy Silk,' Ridley mused. 'The name is familiar . . .'

'You have met her. More than once, I believe. She is Aunt Phoebe's companion.'

'Oh, Poppy Silk. Indeed . . . Yes, I have met her. A delightful little bundle, I do concede. I can quite see the attraction . . .' He looked at Robert squarely. 'Does she have money?'

'I think not, Father. She is not of a moneyed family.'

'Her father doesn't own a bank, therefore?'

'No, sir.'

'Mmm . . . Then we have a problem . . .'

'A problem?'

'Yes. A not insignificant one at that.'

'It's not a problem to me. I want to marry Poppy for herself, not for money.'

'That's very romantic, Robert, but not entirely practical. You see, Crawford and Sons, as I believe you already know, have tendered for the construction of a new sewer and drainage system in the Borough of Birmingham and we have heard – unofficially – that our tender has been accepted. You are obviously not aware, however, how massive an undertaking it is. We, Crawford and Sons, are scheduled to make a considerable amount of money from it by the time it's finished. It'll be highly profitable work, barring any huge unforeseen hazards . . . and we have reckoned on some, to be sure. It will benefit us all greatly. Work is to begin within the next two to three months. In order to commence the project, we have to employ literally hundreds of men – excavators, navvies, brick-layers and masons, carpenters, labourers, blacksmiths, miners. You know the business, Robert, so you know exactly what is involved. You can therefore imagine the wages bill, before we have even turned a sod. There will be the hire of perhaps two hundred horses, a similar number of carts, the purchase of thousands of pounds worth of materials and equipment. Although Birmingham council will be contracted to pay us in stages, we shall not see any of it till the first agreed section has been completed and finished to the satisfaction of their inspectors. We cannot fund what has to be funded for that length of time by ourselves. It is a financial impossibility. For us to be able to finance such a vast amount we need the support of a sympathetic and flexible banker. As it happens, Robert, we already have one, don't we? Tyler's and Lord's Bank, owned, as you are well aware, by Ishmael Lord, the father of the girl to whom you are engaged.'

'Yes, I am aware of that, Father,' Robert said softly, dreading where this was leading.

'Then understand this . . . I am not in the business of alienating those who are my lifeblood, which is my money supply – people who would inevitably be alienated if *you* fail to fulfil your promise to Virginia. I cannot be party to such an arrangement, nor can I allow my son to be, on whose head now rests the success or failure of our well-established firm.'

'Then you would have to use another bank.'

'These days, I am afraid there are too many shaky banks,' Ridley replied patiently. 'What if we were to court the wrong one and it went down? We would go down with it. It is not a risk I am prepared to take, Robert.'

'I see,' Robert said tartly. 'So you wish me to sacrifice my future, the rest of my life and my future happiness, for the sake of Crawford and Sons' bank account?'

'It cannot be such an arduous imposition. You obviously don't dislike Virginia, else you wouldn't have asked her to marry you in the first place. There must have been some attraction, some spark of devotion . . .'

'And so there *was*, Father. But already our aims and desires are different. We are going in different directions, Ginnie and me. In any case, mating the woman of my parents' choice with the plans of two families on me, and my clear duty before me, is not my idea of an ideal marriage.'

'Nevertheless, I expect it of you.'

'Then I am sorry, Father. You are about to be disappointed. I am a grown man—'

'You have obligations, Robert. Obligations to your fam—'

'I have obligations to myself and to Poppy only,' Robert said, raising his voice. 'I shall of course defy you.'

'You also have an obligation to Virginia . . . Unless she will discharge it . . .'

Robert sighed and stood up. 'I see no point in discussing this further. My mind is made up. I shall seek Virginia's release from our engagement and I shall marry Poppy Silk.'

It suddenly became clear to Ridley that he no longer had the command over his wilful middle son that he once had. It was one thing to allow him to go and work for another contractor – he would gain valuable experience, which would be useful when he eventually entered the family firm – but it was another to allow him to put the family into a position where financial ruin was a distinct possibility.

A shaft of sunlight suddenly fell on Ridley's desk as the sun slid from behind a cloud. It rendered visible tiny motes of dust that hung suspended in its slanting path.

'If . . .' Ridley said, and immediately his tone was conciliatory. 'If I agree . . . If I place no obstacle in the way of you marrying your Poppy Silk eventually . . .'

'Eventually?' Robert queried.

'Yes, eventually . . . Would you agree to postpone that marriage to a later date? Would you agree to postpone telling Virginia and her family that you wish to be released from your promise?'

'Until Tyler's and Lord's have agreed in writing the facility to overdraw on Crawford's account, you mean?'

'Broadly, yes, that's what I mean.'

'Isn't that bordering on the dishonest, Father?'

'Not entirely. If I swear that I knew nothing of your intention to marry another woman . . .'

'I was thinking also in terms of my dishonesty towards Virginia. I presume I would have to maintain the charade that we were to get married until the last. She's expecting it to be Christmas Day, remember.'

'Yes,' Ridley said. 'I remember. When did you hope to marry Poppy Silk?'

'We have not discussed a date.'

'Then that at least simplifies the matter.'

'It might simplify it for you, but not for me.'

'You need only call on Virginia once a week to maintain the illusion, Robert. On a Sunday, say. Go for dinner. When she's keen to go to church be seen there with her . . .'

'In the meantime, I have to deceive poor Poppy as well. I wouldn't wish to lose Poppy because of it.'

'Then explain it to her. She's not unintelligent as I recall. She'll understand.'

'I hope she does . . . All right, Father . . . I will accommodate you. But I will expect some consideration in return . . . the freedom to do as I wish with my career. I shall expect no opposition either from you, from Mother, or anybody else when Poppy and I eventually announce our engagement.'

'Fine. It is agreed. Shall we shake hands on it, my son?'
They shook hands.

That evening, Robert worked on his surveying reports till late. It was hard going; his head was full of the discussion with his father and the disappointment of not having resolved the issue of his engagement to Virginia. So, he must continue to pay her court, and to allow her to think he was still in love with her. It would be cruel, and it was totally against his nature to deceive, but he had agreed to do it rather than thrust Crawford and Sons into financial jeopardy. He hoped with all his heart that Poppy would understand.

Poppy . . . Sweet, sweet Poppy . . .

His mind meandered once again to their lovemaking the previous night and he felt a potent stirring inside his trousers. He looked at the clock. It was ten minutes past midnight. The house was quiet. Bellamy had returned two hours ago. Everybody, including the servants, had retired to bed. He closed the notebook in which he was writing, put down his pen and stood up. His legs ached from too much sitting in one position. He would take a walk. Yes, he felt the need to stretch his legs, to get some fresh air in his lungs. Last night's rain had cleared up; it had been a pleasant day. It would be a pleasant night. It was August, after all. So, without even picking up his hat, he let himself out quietly by the front door and walked on the grass – to save the crunching gravel of the drive announcing his unanticipated outing.

At Dixons Green Road he turned left. He seemed drawn that way, like a moth is drawn to a burning lamp. It was only because Cawneybank House lay in that direction. At the toll house, he took the right fork, then the left one which, of course, took him right to the front gate of Aunt Phoebe's house.

There, he loitered. The house was in darkness. Nothing stirred but the leaves sighing in sympathy in the treetops. What was he doing here? What purpose did he hope to achieve? He wondered whether Poppy was asleep. He longed to be lying with her in her bed, to feel her firm young body next to his, to stroke her silky smooth skin, to taste her lips . . .

He stepped onto the grass, again avoiding the gravel . . . except to stoop down and gather up a few sharp pieces in his hand. He was certain the other room on the front, the one that didn't have a light in it last night, was Poppy's. He approached the house beneath his target window and carefully aimed a piece of gravel at it. It clattered on the windowpane and fell back silently to the grass. He tossed another . . . and another . . . In the darkness he could just make out the slit that appeared in the curtains . . . the shape of an indistinct face . . .

He stepped away from the house, to the middle of the lawn, and waved his arms about like a lunatic, then waited.

A slight figure draped in white, like an ethereal eidolon, appeared from the side of the house.

'Robert?'

'Poppy!' He hurried towards her and she took his hand, pulling him into the more complete darkness at the side of the house where they would not be seen.

'What are you doing here at this time of night?' She could hear his breathing, as fast as if he'd been running.

'You gave me your permission to call on you,' he answered glibly.

'At this time?'

'I've missed you, Poppy. God, I've been longing for you.' He took her in his arms and felt her skin, warm and soft and inviting beneath her nightgown. 'I couldn't get you off my mind. I had to come, in the hope that I might see you.'

'I'm glad,' she breathed, her heart jumping as if she'd tripped coming down the stairs. 'I was thinking about you as well . . . about last night. I haven't stopped thinking about us all day.'

He felt her shiver in his arms as the cool night air penetrated through that single layer of cotton. 'You're cold, my love.'

She nodded against his chest. 'But I'm warm inside now I'm with you.'

'Kiss me.'

She tilted her head, offering her lips, and they kissed . . . a long, lingering kiss that inflamed their mutual desire.

'Let's go to the summer house,' he suggested. 'You'll be warmer there.'

'Quiet, then . . .' she answered biddably.

With the stealth and purpose of a rutting stag with his doe, they crossed the lawn at the rear of the house. An owl hooted; only he had eyes wide enough and round enough to witness this secret meeting in the darkness. The door to the summer house creaked again as Poppy opened it and she swore to herself that she must find an oilcan and oil the hinges tomorrow. She wouldn't have the nerve to request it of Clay lest he asked her why. In the safety of concealment, they fell into another embrace, more passionate, and he lifted handfuls of nightgown and ran his hands hungrily over the bare flesh of her small round buttocks, drawing her to him. She felt him hard against her and with nervous, shaking hands, undid the buttons of his trousers, thrust her hand inside, and held him, tenderly stroking.

'Let's put the cushions on the floor again,' she said eventually. 'It's so much nicer if we lie down.'

Without shame or inhibition, she pulled her nightgown over her head and lay naked on the cushions, while it took him a few moments to undress. He lay beside her and she nudged herself under him and shivered with pleasure as he rolled onto her. Both were panting like hounds after a run. Her hands gripped his buttocks, pulling him into her, and she sighed with little whimpers of pleasure as they settled into an easy rhythm that belied their inexperience. Before long, the indescribable sensations became mesmerising, growing and growing inexorably into a crisis of ecstasy that had them both gasping.

They lay in silence for a while, still gaining familiarity with each other's bodies as their hands affectionately roamed cooling skin.

'I had a word with my father today,' he whispered as they rested afterwards. 'I told him about you, that I wished to call off my engagement to Virginia.'

'And?'

'There is a slight problem, Poppy . . .' He explained about the financing of the sewers project and how it radically affected the timing of his breaking the news to Virginia. 'It means that from time to time I shall have to see her, just to maintain the illusion that everything is all right between her and me. Of course, it will mean nothing. But for the sake of my family . . .'

'But that's not fair on her,' Poppy said typically. 'Will she have to wait till what she believes is the eve of her wedding before you can tell her?'

'I hope I can tell her sooner than that.'

'I hope so too, Robert.'

'Even so, I'm glad you understand. It's such a load off my mind.'

'Yes, I do understand . . . Maybe you should count your blessings that I do.'

'Oh, I do.'

They lay unspeaking again for a while, still in each other's arms.

'Bellamy called earlier.'

'Oh? What did he want?'

'He asked me to marry him.'

Robert sat upright in indignant astonishment. 'He what? What did you tell him?'

'That I'd think about it . . .'

'Seriously? Are you serious?'

'Serious that he asked, or serious that I said I'd think about it?' There was a tormenting catch in her voice.

'Well, both . . .' He tried to read her face in the darkness, tried to catch something in her tone that would define whether she was teasing or not.

'Oh, he asked all right,' she said evenly. 'He was in earnest.'

'And your reply?'

'Yes, I was in earnest too.'

'You honestly told him you'd think about it? As if you might consent?'

'Why not? *You* are still engaged, Robert. Why shouldn't I be? It'll put our *affaire* on a more equal footing.'

'You are a complete strumpet, Poppy Silk. You realise the trouble this will cause . . .'

Chapter 30

Poppy would never deny to Robert that she was considering Bellamy's offer of marriage as long as he remained engaged to Virginia. His jealousy, his knowledge and belief in the existence of a rival were her only insurance that when the time was right, he would extricate himself in the greatest hurry from his promise to marry Virginia. So, for the sake of appearances, their affair remained clandestine, and grew more intense because of it. Robert's first nocturnal visit and their repairing to the summer house had, of course, already shaped the form of their secret meetings. Aunt Phoebe had no idea as to the physical extent of their involvement, but both Dolly and Esther thought it strange that small muddy footprints should some mornings have appeared on the tiles by the back door, obviously left after they had gone to bed the night before.

'So do you still intend to see Bellamy?' Robert asked, gathering her close into his warm embrace as they lay on the cushions again one such night, soon after he had sprung the shock of having to deceive Virginia a while longer.

'Why shouldn't I?' she answered with some defiance. 'You continue to see Virginia.'

'I feel you are holding a gun to my head, Poppy, my love, when there truly is no need.' He stroked her soft cheek with

472

the back of his forefinger. 'And encouraging Bellamy won't make things any easier when my break with Virginia becomes official and generally recognised. I shall also have an estranged brother to contend with. Don't you see?'

'I didn't say I was encouraging him. We talk, usually with Aunt Phoebe close at hand, except for the odd times he's taken me for a drive. It's all very proper, Robert. We don't get up to the shenanigans you and I do.'

'I should hope not indeed.' A frown furrowed his brow. 'All the same, he has designs on you.'

'And I'm flattered.' She turned over to lie on her belly and propped herself up on her elbows to look into his eyes. 'If you *do* eventually decide it's impossible to give up Virginia, I shall most likely consent to marry Bellamy. I'm quite sure that on our wedding night I could make him believe I was still a virgin.' She chuckled saucily.

'I'm sure that would be an excellent ploy if you could contrive it,' Robert said with some surprise. 'But Bellamy would be second best. You don't love him. You know you don't love him.'

'Oh, and how do you know I wouldn't grow to love him?'

He sighed with frustration. 'This isn't fair, you know, Poppy.' He was feeling threatened and very vulnerable. He turned onto his side, his head propped up on his elbow. He looked at her arched back, lissom and pale in the half-light, at the smooth curve of her small round buttocks that reminded him of a delicious peach. 'My hands are tied and you know it,' he went on. 'I have to maintain the pretence that I'm still earnest about Virginia, so I can hardly question Bellamy about his intentions towards you. To do so . . . to demand that he withdraw in favour of me, would be to declare my own interest in you prematurely. He would be vindictive enough to report the fact to Virginia and so mess up everybody's schemes.'

Robert was thus thwarted by his inability to resolve anything. However, Poppy's unstinting willingness to love and be loved, her intense passion, excited Robert and their affair blossomed beyond his wildest imaginings. As autumn set in, the chill of evening did not at first inhibit their sorties to the summer house on prearranged nights, where they made love with growing expertise and refinement. But it was not solely for these intimate sessions that he adored her. She was a soulmate. They laughed at the same things, they understood each other. Each got to know what the other was thinking without a word having to be said. In all, they were entirely comfortable with each other.

Then, one bright day in November, Robert was waiting for Poppy as she left Baylies's Charity School. She was not expecting him in the daytime, for he had just been reappointed engineer with Treadwell's who, along with the contracting firm Peto's, were about to recommence work on the Oxford, Worcester and Wolverhampton Railway, the problem of finance having been resolved at last. She did not see him at first, only the gig he used for travelling to work.

'Poppy,' he called. 'Climb aboard, I have a surprise for you.'

'Robert!' She smiled with pleasure at seeing him. 'You gave me quite a start.'

'Come on, I've got a surprise for you.'

'What?' she asked, approaching the gig.

'I can't tell you, it's a surprise.' He handed her up.

'Oh, Robert, you can be so annoying sometimes,' she said as she sat down beside him. 'If you can't tell me what it is, why did you say you have a surprise for me? It's not logical.'

'The place I'm taking you to is the surprise. That's why I won't tell you – it would spoil it.'

'I think it's just an excuse to abduct me and have your

wicked way, now that it's too cold at night to visit the summer house.'

He smiled with amusement as he flicked the reins.

'Where are you taking me? Tell me.'

'You'll see.'

'Tell me how far then.'

'You'll *see*.'

She thumped his arm playfully. 'You're so annoying. Can't you at least tell me how far? I'm only worried that Aunt Phoebe will be expecting me back soon.'

'Well, you'll be late home today and that's all there is to it.' There was a look of smugness in his eyes, as if he would be admired for this outing. 'We're heading towards Brierley Hill and Stourbridge. That's all I'm telling you.'

As they left the confines of Dudley town, the road became more bumpy and the gig lurched and jolted.

'I shall have bruises all over the cheeks of my bum at this rate,' she said. 'This bouncing about doesn't befit a lady.'

'Then I myself shall take great pleasure in massaging the cheeks of your said bum till they're better, which will benefit you hardly at all but benefit me no end.' They both laughed. 'And yet, when I think of it, you enjoyed riding before you became a lady. Even on my two-wheeler. And you must've ridden a horse. Why should you cease to enjoy bouncing about just because you purport to be a lady now?'

'I don't purport, Robert, whatever that means,' she replied, feigning a haughtiness that thoroughly amused him. 'I *am* a lady.'

They drove on, past the vast smoke-belching iron works belonging to the Earl of Dudley, and through a small town that Robert announced as Brierley Hill. The road was level for a while, then descended. Eventually they turned right, off the high road.

'Nearly there.'

Poppy looked about on both sides and could see the chimney stacks of brickworks to her left, the red-brick cones of a bottle and glassworks to her right and, of course, the horse gins of the coal pits. There were a few houses, taverns, a chapel . . . She had no idea where she was. They drove on, chatting about all sorts of things but nothing in particular. Then, on a patch of waste ground she saw it.

'A navvies' encampment!' she exclaimed, delighted. Her eyes beamed even brighter when she realised what this meant, and why Robert had kept it secret. 'My mother . . . my sisters . . . my brothers . . . Are they here, Robert? Oh, please tell me they're here.'

He nodded, a broad grin on his face, elicited by witnessing her joy. 'Yes, they're here. I saw Buttercup yesterday and caught sight of your mother this morning.'

'Quick, then. Let's hurry . . .'

Poppy jumped out of the gig and ran as fast as she could. Robert had difficulty keeping up with her, and she reached the encampment before him. There were few people living there as yet. At the periphery of the haphazard conglomeration, she stopped, turned and waited for him, breathless, eager anticipation lighting up her face.

'Over here,' he said.

He led her towards one of the slapdash constructions of wood, tarpaulin and recently cemented-in bricks. The hut had a full complement of glass reinstalled in the windows, but how long that might last was questionable.

'Should we knock?' he suggested.

Poppy tapped on the door excitedly . . . and waited . . .

Eventually, a familiar young woman answered it, with a baby in her arms.

'Mother!'

Sheba shrieked with surprise and delight. 'It's our Poppy! I can scarcely believe it.'

Poppy flung herself forward, wrapping her arms around Sheba and her baby. She was too overcome to say anything, but clung to her mother, her eyes filling with tears. The baby began complaining at being squashed between them, so Poppy let go and cooed her apologies to the little mite.

'The baby,' she said, looking up tearfully. 'What have you called it?'

'It's a him. I'd already made me mind up to call it Jack if it was a lad. After your father. What else? But look at you, our Poppy . . . I'd never have recognised you. Why, you'm all growed up and quite the young madam.'

'I have Robert to thank for that,' she answered, turning to him. 'It's a long story.'

'Come inside,' Sheba said warmly, standing aside to let them in. 'Have you got time for a mug o' tea or a tankard o' beer?' She looked enquiringly from one to the other. 'Have you ate? Am yer hungry?'

'That's very kind,' Robert replied. 'But I have to get back to work. I daresay Poppy's ready for a cup of tea, though. Poppy, I'll call back for you as soon as I can to take you back.'

So Robert went about his business, leaving mother and daughter to bring each other up to date with their lives.

'Do you have any honey, Mother? I just fancy some bread and honey.'

'There's some cheese.'

Poppy took the baby, her youngest brother, from her mother and held him in her arms as she told her story, interspersed with sips of tea and mouthfuls of bread and cheese. Sheba listened, fascinated.

'So how about you, Mother?'

'I'm content,' Sheba said simply. 'Buttercup's me man, and

we'm happy. He's bin lucky enough to have got the ganger's job, so we've been able to rent this hut. We shall let the other room to lodgers, like we used to at Blowers Green.'

'Where's Buttercup now?'

'Gone with Jericho to try and round up some o' the lads what worked on the Blowers Green section.'

'Jericho? He's here as well?'

'Lives in this hut. He's one o' the family now.'

Poppy chuckled as she recalled her unsavoury experiences with him. 'Good gracious . . . So how long have you been here?'

'Less than a week. Buttercup heard as how they was starting up again so we tramped all the way from Hereford to get here. We'd been fruit pickin', see, and doin' farm work. Work starts again next month on this section to Stourbridge. They'm a-getting' everythin' ready.'

'So I'll be able to come and see you.'

'If he'll bring yer . . . Is that the same chap you was friendly with, who used to be an engineer up at Blowers Green?' Sheba asked, nodding at the spot where Robert had last stood.

'Yes.'

'Am yer married to him now or summat, our Poppy?'

She shook her head. 'Not yet. But I hope to be . . . soon.'

'You've done well for yourself. I always knew you would. I can scarcely believe how you've changed. I'm that *proud* o' yer. If only yer father could see yer.'

'I know . . .' she answered wistfully. 'Anyway, what about Lottie and Rose and Jenkin? And little Nathaniel?'

'They'm all about somewhere, getting to know the place, I reckon. They'll be back soon, I daresay.'

'I'm dying to see them. I imagine they've grown up.'

'Oh, Lottie's quite the young madam now. Just like you was, our Poppy.'

'I can't wait to see them all again. And Buttercup. How is he?'

'A good father to your brothers and sisters. A good man to me. I couldn't wish for better.'

'I'm glad, Mother. Every day I've thought about you all, wondering where you were, if you were all right. I've missed you. Oh, wait till Aunt Phoebe knows I've found you again. She'll be dying to meet you. We'll have to arrange a get-together.'

'And this Aunt Phoebe's been good to you, our Poppy?'

'You wouldn't believe how good. I think the world of her.'

'You sound different an' all.'

'I know. Minnie often reminds me.'

'Minnie Catchpole? You still see her?'

'Minnie's married now, Mother.'

'Married? Good God!'

'To a very rich man . . . She's Mrs Tyler now, and quite the fashionable young thing.'

'Best keep that from Tipton Ted . . . if he ever shows up. He'll be trying to tap up this Mr Tyler otherwise. Wait till Dog Meat knows.'

And so they gossiped, till Robert returned for her. On the way home, they stopped so that Poppy could buy a jar of honey, then proceeded to Cawneybank House and Aunt Phoebe. She was delighted to hear Poppy's news, even though she couldn't help feeling a little jealous of Poppy's mother.

Virginia Lord's plans for her wedding were well advanced. Her wedding dress was made and hanging in her wardrobe, awaiting the fateful day when she and Robert would be joined in holy matrimony. The arrangements had been made with Reverend Bartholomew at St Peter's parish church in Harborne, for the ceremony to take place after morning service on Christmas Day, which fell on a Wednesday. The guests would then repair to Metchley House, the home of the Lord family, on the outskirts of the village. All that remained was for the banns to be read.

Virginia understood that Robert was unable to pay her court more frequently than once a week due to his commitments at work and the geographical distance between them, and she accepted it without qualm. That Robert had chosen her at last, after so many heart-rending doubts, was reason to be thankful that she saw him at all. Of course, when they were finally married on Christmas Day, they would be together every evening and most of the weekends. Meanwhile, she had enough to keep her busy. Supervising the fittings of the bridesmaids' dresses and the suit for her pageboy were alone enough to contend with. Her mother, too, could not decide what to wear. Then there was the question of what flowers would be available, as well as worrying over the rest of the trivialities that generally beset a nervous and excited bride-to-be.

The couple were expected to live at Metchley House at first, and a private apartment had been created for them, at great expense, on the first floor of one wing of the house. Robert was suffering extreme pangs of guilt that all this money was being expended to benefit a marriage that would never take place, when, with just a word or two, he could have prevented it. This deceit, which went so much against the grain of his nature, was a travesty that he must lay at his father's door.

It was in such a mood of frustration that he called at his father's office to discover why there was such a delay in setting a starting date for the sewers project, and thus the inception of the necessary overdraft arrangements with Tyler's and Lord's Bank. Robert tapped politely on his office door and waited for the call to enter.

'Good God, Robert, what brings you here?' Ridley exclaimed testily. 'Come to spy on us for Treadwell's, have you?'

Robert perceived that his father was not in the best of spirits. 'May I sit down?' he asked neutrally.

Ridley gestured that he should. 'To what do I owe this unexpected pleasure?'

'Virginia Lord,' Robert responded evenly. 'A fortune is being spent on my supposed marriage to the poor girl, a fortune that they could have avoided squandering, if only I could have told her that I have no intention of marrying her. I have kept my part of the bargain to protect Crawford and Sons, Father, but I am losing patience. I am feeling inordinately guilty as well. I can assure you, the Crawford name will be mud when this fiasco is over, and I shall be castigated as the biggest cad in Christendom.'

'Hmm,' Ridley said gravely. 'You have been very patient, Robert, and I am grateful for your indulgence. I do have some news, however. We received a letter only this morning.' He picked it up off his desk and waved it at him.

Robert regarded him expectantly. 'So this charade can soon be ended?'

Ridley nodded. 'Indeed, it can be ended without further ado. The letter does not confirm the council's acceptance of the tender, as we had anticipated, though. No, Birmingham council has decided to reorganise itself first. Something to do with its constitution, I understand, abolishing the old town commissioners and increasing the power of the town council. In consequence, all civil engineering projects have been shelved indefinitely, and no contracts will be signed, pending the formation of a Committee of Public Works, when the sewers and drainage project will be put to tender again. But not until sometime next year. Neither is there any guarantee that we shall win it next time, since those who would have

481

been the losers this time will doubtless submit reduced tenders.'

'Then I shall pay my respects to Virginia today.' He got up to go. 'I'm not looking forward to it.'

Metchley House was an impressive affair, designed and built by the architect James Wyatt. As befitted the Quaker family who commissioned it at the turn of the century, it was plain and unadorned. Its semicircular portico, set in the centre of its symmetrical façade, was the only concession to grandeur. It stood in immaculately manicured grounds, tangential to a gravelled drive that swept before it in a great arc through an arbour of tall elms and horse chestnuts. Robert drove his gig to a halt at the portico and rang the bell. A maid answered it.

Naturally, Virginia was surprised to see him, but greeted him with an affectionate smile and asked what brought him there as she invited him into the drawing room. 'I was writing a note to Mr Beese the florist, about my bridal bouquet.'

'I'm sorry to have disturbed you.'

'Not at all, Robert, it's lovely to see you,' she said brightly. 'I thought you were working today.'

'The hard work hasn't begun yet, Ginnie,' he said solemnly, sitting down on a huge sofa. 'I was able to get leave for a day. Slingsby Shafto is covering for me.'

'How is Slingsby?'

'Oh, as argumentative as ever. He'll never change.'

'It's nice of you to think of me,' Virginia said. Coupled with the fact that he was visiting on an unusual day at an unusual hour, she read his serious demeanour with apprehension as she sat primly at his side, twiddling her fingers in her lap. 'Is something amiss, Robert?'

482

'I'm sorry to say that there is, Ginnie. Something radically amiss.'

'So . . . Out with it. It can't be as bad as your face makes it out to be.'

'Ginnie, I'm afraid it is,' he began. 'I have misled you . . . rather seriously.'

'Misled me?' The colour drained from her face and the sparkle seemed to leave her eyes. 'How have you misled me?'

'When I returned from Brazil I rather foolishly allowed myself to go along with your notion that we should be married on Christmas Day—'

'Christmas Day was your idea,' she corrected. 'Are you saying that you wish to postpone it to a later date? Does it interfere with your work?'

'No, not postpone it, Ginnie . . . cancel it. I want you to release me from my promise to marry you.'

'That is such a pity, Robert.' Her heart was pounding inexorably, her face an icon of anxiety. 'I always think of Christmas Day as a combination of Sunday morning and Saturday afternoon. I never mind the Sunday morning part, the going to church, but the Saturday afternoon I find a bore. I was so looking forward to this Christmas being somewhat different . . .' Tears were rolling down her cheeks. 'I trust you have good reason for disappointing me.'

'When I returned from Brazil,' he said again, nervously concentrating on his fingernails so as to avoid her eyes, 'I had actually made up my mind to tell you that I was no longer in love with you. I was about to tell you that I wished to marry the girl that had diverted me in the first place. Unfortunately, my mother seemed to have other plans. Because of her interfering I was diverted. I also felt extreme guilt at the misery I had caused you by going away. I could not find it within me to cause you more . . . Not then. I felt compelled to appease you . . .'

'But all the time, your real wish was to ask for my release so that you could marry this other girl?'

'Yes.'

'Such self-sacrifice, Robert . . . For me . . .' She took a small handkerchief from her pocket and dabbed her eyes. 'I presume this other girl still feels the same about you after your time away?'

'Yes . . . Without question.'

'Ah! May I presume therefore that you have been seeing her meanwhile?'

'Yes.'

'You should have let me know sooner, Robert. We are to be married in a month.'

'I know.'

'All the arrangements have been made.' She changed tack and got up from the sofa in a state of high agitation. 'My father has gone to the enormous expense of converting the top floor of one wing of Metchley House into an apartment for us, and that only because the house he is having built for us as a wedding gift won't be ready in time.'

'What house?' he queried, incredulous.

'A house situated on Oakham Road, on the bend near to the hangman's tree.'

'Why has nobody mentioned this house to me before?'

'Because it was to be a surprise,' she said earnestly. Letting him know about the house at this moment was designed to make Robert feel even more guilty. But Virginia did not know Robert as well as she thought she did.

'Well, it's certainly a surprise, Virginia. But I'm amazed. Did it not occur to either you or your father that I might want to decide on my own house? And pay for it myself? I am not entirely without money.'

'You are angry?'

'Yes . . . but amazed and disappointed too . . . that you believed I would accept your father's charity.'

'It was to be a gift, Robert. It can hardly be construed as charity. It is being built as much for my benefit as for yours. Don't you see?'

'As if I couldn't have provided something equally grand, is that it?'

'No, Robert, that's not it. My father regards you as his own son. He thinks the world of you. I don't know what he'll think when he knows you don't approve of his wedding gift . . . that you wish to let me down . . .'

'It is with very deep regret that I have to let you down, Virginia,' he answered quietly.

'You keep calling me Virginia . . . not Ginnie.'

He shrugged. 'So what? It's of no consequence either way. It alters nothing. Will you please say that you release me from my betrothal?'

'I don't believe I can do that, Robert.'

'But what is the point in not?' His impatience was rising on the back of his indignation over the gift of a house. 'What chance of success would a marriage between us have now in any case?'

'It is more a question of my honour, don't you think?'

'Your honour will remain unsullied. You may tell the world that I am a cad, and everybody will declare you well rid of me.'

'First you have to tell me who my rival is. Do I know her?'

'If I tell you, will you agree to release me without further ado?'

'It depends.'

'On what? Whether you know her, or whether you approve?'

'Oh, you can be sure I shall not approve, whoever she is. Even if she were the Queen of Sheba.' Robert smiled to himself at the irony in that. 'She is responsible for breaking my heart, for luring you away . . . I presume she is beautiful and wealthy?'

'Oh, she's beautiful, but as poor as a church mouse.'

'Then I might even approve of her . . . eventually. So tell me who she is.'

'Poppy Silk,' he said.

'Poppy?' Virginia shrieked. 'Oh, Robert, you don't know what you're doing. You cannot marry Poppy Silk. She is utterly beautiful, I grant you, but you cannot *marry* her.'

'Why not indeed?'

'Well, for a start, she is not what she seems. Neither will I be responsible for Bellamy's unhappiness if I have it in my power to prevent it. You must surely know *he* has asked her to marry *him*?'

'Yes, I'm well aware of it. I'm also aware that she hasn't consented, even if he lives in hope. It has only occurred because Poppy and I have had to keep our liaison secret . . . But I'm also confused, Virginia . . .'

'How so?'

'You say you are anxious to prevent Bellamy from being unhappy, yet you obviously don't give a fig whether I am or not.'

'On the contrary, Robert. I happen to know that you would end up the unhappiest of men if you married Poppy Silk. Thus, I cannot let you do it. I will not let you do it. You will thank me in the long run.'

'So you will not release me?'

'Under no circumstances. It is for your own good, Robert.'

'I see. Then I shall have to be dishonourable about this . . .
I shall, of course, speak to your father.'

'I wouldn't bother yet, Robert. You'd get short shrift there.'

'No doubt I shall.'

'It might also be premature.'

'I think not. Goodbye, Virginia.'

'No, it's not goodbye. I shall see you at the altar on
Christmas Day.' She then remembered the solemn vow she
must make on her wedding day. It would be appropriate to
say it now. '*I will*, Robert . . . Believe me . . .'

Chapter 31

At dinner that evening Robert was last to take his seat at the table. His older brother Oliver and his wife Clare had been invited, but not their children, who remained at home being cared for by their nanny.

'Oliver . . . Clare,' he greeted with a smile. 'Good to see you both.' Robert was not in great admiration of Oliver. He loved him as a brother but believed he was too much dependent upon his father's whims, lacking the backbone to stand up for himself. Clare, however, was an intelligent girl, the same age as himself, with dark eyes and a pleasant smile. Robert liked her and wondered what it was she had seen in Oliver, although she was evidently happy and made the best of her marriage.

Robert cast a glance at his father at the head of the table, polishing his steel-rimmed spectacles on his table napkin. Bellamy, slim and neat, handsome and fair-complexioned, was at Robert's left. Bellamy was always easy-going and care-free. He had never known what it was to be short of money, to be away from home, or to be in danger. Robert glanced at his mother, a stately and chilly woman. She was fumbling absently with a gold cross and chain and watching the serv-ants with a supervisory eye as they brought in soup and served it.

Already dominating the conversation was the disappointment of not being awarded the Birmingham contract for constructing the new sewers and drains.

'I think it's appalling that they couldn't have let us know sooner,' Oliver commented predictably. 'We could have directed our resources elsewhere, rather than holding back and waiting for it to materialise.'

'I agree,' said Ridley. 'And my response to the council will be very much along those lines. I am very disappointed. We invested a great deal of time and money in tendering for that work. It would have been a highly profitable contract. But there are other fish to fry.'

'Let's hope that when next it's up for tender they will mean it,' Clare said sympathetically, misconstruing the reasons. She tilted her soup bowl to collect the last dregs. 'It all smacks of insincerity, I think.'

The soup was finished, the empty bowls were cleared away and the next course was brought in and served. When the servants had left the room, Robert cleared his throat and took a gulp of wine.

'I, er . . . I have an announcement to make,' he said hesitantly. 'It's perhaps an appropriate time to make it – with the exception of dear Elizabeth, we're all present this evening . . .'

Suddenly, all eyes were on him.

'I, um . . . I visited Virginia Lord this morning . . . and sought release from our engagement . . .' Silence fell on the table as he peered across at his mother to gauge her reaction.

Clarissa, predictably, gasped with horror. 'You have done *what*, Robert?'

'I have asked to be released from my promise to marry Virginia.'

'Oh, my goodness,' she said, as if he had announced the end of the world. 'Did you know anything about this at all, Ridley?'

'I have been privy to a few basic facts,' Ridley replied economically, hoping he would not be too deeply incriminated.

'And yet you said nothing to me?' She turned again to Robert. 'Are you out of your mind? What has brought on this madness?'

'Oh, you may be sure, Mother, that Virginia has typically refused my request. She is absolutely certain I shall marry her come what may, but on what she bases such a tragic notion I'm at a loss to understand.'

'You cannot back out at this late stage, Robert. You will marry her if I have anything to do with it. Virginia is blessed with some sense in not giving way. But why on earth would you *not* wish to marry her? She is such a sweet, unspoilt girl who idolises and adores you. She must be heartbroken. And she the daughter of Ishmael Lord.'

'The truth is, Mother,' Robert said, 'I wish to marry somebody else.'

'Some—somebody else?' She looked at Ridley, seeking support. This was a severe blow to her contentment and social esteem, with the added potential for a scandal of monumental proportions. 'And are we allowed to know who this girl is?'

'Indeed,' Robert answered. 'Especially since she will shortly be your daughter-in-law. It's Poppy Silk.'

There was another momentary silence while everybody digested the information before them. Robert sensed Bellamy's sudden but expected agitation.

'Poppy Silk?' Clarissa at last queried, as if speaking the name left a nasty taste in her mouth. 'Aunt Phoebe's young companion?'

'The same.'

'But she hasn't got two ha'pennies to rub together.'

Bellamy dropped his knife and fork onto his plate with an

indignant clatter. 'But I have asked Poppy Silk to marry *me*.' He looked at his mother beseechingly so that she might run with his cause.

'I know you have,' Robert answered. 'But she hasn't consented, has she? In any case, Miss Silk and I have been close friends for nearly two years now. Long before she met you, Bellamy.'

'You mean you have been conducting a secret affair with her all that time?'

'Why? Did you expect me to conduct it openly and have no regard for Virginia?'

'Openly or covertly,' Clarissa hissed, 'you have obviously had precious little regard for poor Virginia.'

'Then this Poppy Silk is a hussy,' Bellamy complained, petulantly pushing his dinner away unwanted. 'And on two counts . . . One, for having an affair with you, Robert, discreet or not, and two, for allowing me to think she was available.'

'I understand,' Robert said calmly, 'that she did intimate to you that she was interested in somebody else. She merely did not name me. That there was somebody else obviously didn't deter you. Is that because you believed you had something better to offer?'

Bellamy did not answer directly. 'Evidently, she's making fools of both of us,' he said instead.

Clarissa put down her table napkin in a state of obvious distress. 'I am much too upset to discuss this now,' she said to Robert. 'But I shall be visiting your Aunt Phoebe Newton tomorrow to see what is to be done. I shall also confront Miss Silk.'

'You most certainly will not, Mother.'

'Indeed I shall.'

'Listen, I am a grown man. I know my own mind. I am able to make my own decisions.'

'I fear you cannot be trusted to make decisions that are sensible, Robert.'

The doorbell rang and everybody fell silent.

'Damn! What a time for somebody to call,' Ridley said, and threw his napkin down on the table.

As the front door was opened by one of the servants a cold draught blew under the dining-room door, chilling Clarissa's ankles.

'Who can it be?' she complained impatiently. 'How inconsiderate for anybody to call at this time.'

The door opened and a maid said, 'Miss Virginia Lord to see you, ma'am.'

Clarissa put her hands to her face. 'Oh, the poor child. She's here. Ask her to come in, Barnes.'

Virginia entered, looking pale, in a state of obvious consternation, and shivering with cold.

'Oh, my child,' Clarissa fawned. 'I have just heard . . . You must be distraught . . .' She turned to the maid. 'Thank you, Barnes. That will be all.'

Virginia greeted everybody at the table, including Robert. 'I do apologise for interrupting your dinner. I had not intended that . . . The drive did not take as long as I thought it would, for some reason. But it is bitterly cold out.'

'Come and sit down, Ginnie,' Robert suggested softly, his guilt rising again at seeing her upset and knowing himself to be the cause of it. 'Oliver, please give the fire a poke.'

'Thank you, Robert,' Virginia said and looked around for a spare chair.

Seeing her difficulty, Robert got up and pulled another chair to the table between himself and Bellamy. 'There,' he said. 'Would you like a glass of brandy to warm you?'

'Don't be silly, Robert.' She forced a smile to soften what was a mild rebuke. 'You know I don't drink.'

'I was merely trying to be hospitable.'

'I'm sorry to burst in on you like this, but I had to come,' Virginia said to Clarissa, from whom she knew she would gain maximum sympathy. 'I suppose, Robert, that you have told everybody of your decision?'

'Indeed, I have. Just. Mother is still reeling from the news, you may be sure.'

'Well, it is convenient that you are all gathered here this evening . . . Because I don't think I could bear to repeat what I have to say.'

'Which is what, Virginia dear?' Clarissa asked supportively.

'I have come primarily to tell Robert that I forgive him for his faithless adventure, but also . . .' she sniffed, full of self-pity, 'to tell you all that he has made a prodigious blunder. Not simply in wishing to be rid of me, but in his choice of bride. I think too much of him to allow him to make such a grave mistake, to make such an absolute fool of himself.'

'I think you are very brave in coming here, Virginia,' Clarissa said indulgently, 'and I am also very happy to hear you question his revised choice of bride. It proves beyond doubt your mettle and your integrity, of which Robert should also take note.' She shot a withering look at her second son. 'Would you like some hot tea, Virginia, or a glass of water, perhaps?'

'A glass of water would be most welcome.'

Robert reached for a clean glass and filled it from the crystal jug on the table.

'Thank you.'

'So do tell us in what way you feel Robert has made a colossal mistake,' Clarissa urged. 'I for one will be very interested to hear of it.'

'It concerns Miss Silk, of course.' Virginia sipped the water and put down her glass carefully, all eyes upon her. 'As you may be aware, Miss Silk and I are already acquainted, and I would like to tell you of the circumstances under which we met.' She wiped her eyes with her small handkerchief, an action that Robert realised was calculated to elicit more sympathy. 'You see, unbeknownst to my own family, I took it upon myself to try and help some of the young women of this town who had fallen by the wayside. I had this urge to help them give up their sinful ways and live good and godly lives. One such fallen woman – and I am dreadfully sorry to have to reveal this – was Minnie Catchpole, whom you know now as Mrs Cecil Tyler, the wife of dear Captain Tyler . . .'

There was a murmur of surprise from those seated around the table. This response encouraged Virginia and she grew more assured in her measured delivery.

'I had not intended to compromise Mrs Tyler,' she went on. 'Indeed, it was my earnest wish that I should avoid it, but as she is an integral part of the story you will see that I have no alternative. I therefore beg you to respect and keep this information strictly between ourselves. Mrs Tyler is of course now, mercifully, reformed and I like to think it was a direct consequence of my intervention. However, the very first time I saw Miss Catchpole – as she was then – was while she was negotiating a price for her services with a gentleman in some sort of carriage – a carriage with a driver. Another girl accompanied her, slender and quite pretty, with fair hair. Both girls climbed aboard the carriage when the deal was struck. On another occasion I followed Miss Catchpole, which is how I discovered where she lived, but I lost track of the other girl and did not know then what had become of her, and neither did Miss Catchpole at the time. Or so she said.'

All attention was focused on Virginia. She dabbed her eyes again and sniffed.

'The first time I met Miss Silk she was visiting Miss

Catchpole. Not unnaturally, when I saw such a well-dressed and glossy young woman, I assumed she was also trying to save Minnie in the same way that I was. Thus I befriended her. I liked her vastly. She seemed a very cheerful character and irreverently forthright, which amused me. But with hindsight, I also perceive now that she was very worldly for a girl of such tender years. Anyway, sometime later – at Robert's welcome home party actually – I was informed by Minnie, who was by this time Mrs Tyler, that she had known Poppy Silk since they had been quite young. When I enquired as to the circumstances, she told me that their fathers were both railway navvies . . .'

Virginia paused for this gem to register.

'So this . . . this Poppy Silk, whom my son wishes to marry, is a navvy's daughter?' Clarissa challenged, her face expressionless like a carving in alabaster.

'I'm afraid so.'

'Then it is entirely possible – even likely – that she is illegitimate in any event, if what I have read about the navvies is anything to go by. I hear some dreadful things. Who's to say she hasn't had a child herself already?'

'I'm to say,' Robert exclaimed huffily. 'I know it for a fact. Look, I *know* she is a navvy's daughter. I'm aware of it. But so what? That's how I met her in the first place. Her father was working on the OWWR. There's nothing wrong with her. She is sweeter than any girl I know, more talented, more intelligent . . . Bellamy will testify to that. So what if she is a navvy's daughter? Who cares? So what if she's illegitimate? It's not her fault if she is. And anyway, you wouldn't know it to look at her.'

'It's not merely that she is a navvy's daughter or illegitimate, Robert,' Virginia said patiently. 'One could forgive that, since plainly she cannot help it. But when I questioned Minnie further, she confirmed that Poppy was the girl who accompanied her on the night I saw her get into the carriage with that man. Don't you see? It means that Poppy Silk herself was a prostitute . . . and might still be, for all we know. I believe that by raising her social status she has merely raised the standard of her clientele.'

'That's preposterous,' Robert protested vehemently. 'Poppy Silk is no more a prostitute than you are, Virginia. You should be ashamed of yourself for even thinking it, for tainting the minds of my family with such malicious speculation.'

'But, Robert, I saw her with my own eyes getting into the carriage with that man,' she said earnestly. 'There can have been no other motive. Don't you see? It is already established beyond doubt that Minnie was working as a prostitute. It must be obvious even to you, who sees Poppy Silk through rose-tinted spectacles, that she is also.'

Robert remained as silent as death after this, his thoughts at once searching desperately for some clue that might either confirm or deny Virginia's persuasive allegations.

'It is convincing enough for me,' Clarissa proclaimed. 'Robert, I expressly forbid you, in the good name of Crawford, to have anything else to do with this . . . this navvy's daughter. You too, Bellamy, if you were so fooled as to have designs on her as well. Thank you, Virginia, for having the courage to speak to us about her. I intend to visit my sister-in-law Phoebe Newton tomorrow in any case. I shall tell her what we have just learnt. There is no doubt in my mind that she will not want a woman of the streets, reformed or not, living under the same roof.'

'Indeed, Clarissa,' said Ridley, who till this moment had remained silent, content to swig his wine and listen, 'methinks it would behove me to do it. It's rather a delicate matter to be tackled by a woman.'

'Nonsense, Ridley. There are none of us women here so squeamish that we couldn't talk one woman to another about such things. Best left to me.'

'Virginia, have you discussed any of this with your father?' Ridley asked.

'Indeed not, Mr Crawford. I didn't wish to upset him prematurely. Nor my mother either, when it seemed that it might be unnecessary. I was certain you would take the stance you have.'

'You were very wise, Virginia.' Ridley turned to Robert. 'I am so sorry, my son,' he said, telling no lie. 'I appreciate that this girl Poppy Silk meant something to you. But we all of us make mistakes.'

Virginia leaned towards Robert and touched his hand. 'I'm so sorry too, Robert, to shatter your illusions about Poppy Silk,' she said softly, privately, and kissed him gently on the cheek. 'But I know you'll thank me for it someday. Of course, I understand that you will need a little time to recover from the emotional distress of having to give her up, but I will make allowances for that. I am very patient. It will all be for the best, believe me.'

'Oh, God, I *do* wish you weren't such a bloody martyr, Virginia,' he said acidly, as he got up from his chair. He left the room.

In the privacy of his bedroom he blew out the lamp and stood at his window looking out into the darkness. The sky was clear and already there was a hard frost. He was thinking about Poppy, could see her smiling face. If only she were with him now so that he could bask in the warmth of her presence. He slumped onto his bed, tortured by doubt, and wept bitterly. How could they be so cruel as to annihilate his most cherished dreams with such icy detachment? Despite having consumed several glasses of wine, his mind was wildly active, preoccupied. They had talked about the sweet girl he loved, denigrated her, turned her into nothing more than a common whore, a piece of dirt worthy of no more than being trodden underfoot. But Poppy was no piece of dirt. She was a living, breathing soul, kind, generous, witty, chock-full of vitality and oh, so much love. They did not know her like he did. They had never been privy to her warmth, her laughter. They had never experienced the infectious joy she imparted to all that took the trouble to get to know her.

But Virginia's words, those potent words that had sown the seeds of doubt, kept returning. Powerful words. *'I saw her with my own eyes getting into the carriage with that man. There can have been no other motive. Don't you see?'* He could still hear her controlled voice, the spite she felt for Poppy deliberately suppressed so that she would come across as reasonable, rational, impartial. *'It is already established beyond doubt that Minnie was working as a prostitute. It must be obvious even to you, who sees Poppy Silk through rose-tinted spectacles, that she is also.'* It was all there – resentment, scorn, revenge. He knew it was there. Virginia could not hide these negative emotions from him. For all her religious beliefs, her kindness, her fine education, her professed compassion for lesser mortals, she was vindictive, bent on vengeance. He knew every catch, every falter that would be imperceptible to anybody else, in her calm, quiet delivery. She was so sure of herself, and so confident she would win him back with this attack, deliberately enlisting the willing help of his mother.

However, one thing irked Robert more than anything else: the possibility that Virginia might be right. What if she was right? What if he'd been wrong about Poppy all along? What if he had been entirely bedazzled by her angelic face, her firm, delightful body? What if her winsome charm, her amorousness, her tenderness were all an act calculated to deceive?

While he was away in Brazil languishing, agonising over her, had she been with anybody else? Well, if it was true that she had been picked up by some man in a carriage with Minnie Catchpole – and he knew Virginia well enough to realise that she was essentially not a liar, despite her other flaws – then it seemed to prove that Poppy must have worked the streets while he was away.

No. It could not be. Poppy was too plausible. She was too sincere in her love. She was so much in love that she gave herself gladly and whole-heartedly . . . Perhaps she had given herself too easily . . . as if she were used to it . . . And if she *could* give herself so easily to him, she could just as easily have given herself to others. Perhaps her love for him was a sham after all. Perhaps she saw him merely as a meal ticket, an entrance to a fine house with servants and silver cutlery, as a means to a pampered life. Lying on her back, wriggling beneath him, would indeed have paid such dividends . . . had she not been found out.

He dried his tears and cast his mind back inevitably to that first delicious encounter, that first time they made love, naked on the floor of Aunt Phoebe's summer house. Poppy had been totally uninhibited about undressing, about showing herself. Virginia, by contrast, would never be that brazen. He tried to recall the actual moment he entered her the first time, whether she winced, gasped, let out a little shriek of pain as you would expect from a young virgin of seventeen. His emotions were etched in his memory, as was the absolute elation of experiencing the ultimate commitment of their love for each other. As for the actual mechanics . . . It had not been that easy to penetrate her, but with her coaxing and a little bit of gentle pushing he accomplished it. It all seemed convincing enough . . .

Then something clicked in his mind . . . something she'd

said . . . something frighteningly ominous now he recalled it
. . . that if she ever married Bellamy she would be able to fake
her virginity . . . His heart lurched at what it implied. How
had she phrased it? They were lying on the cushions in the
summer house at the time . . . Concentrate . . . Yes . . . it was
coming back . . . something like *'I'm sure that on our wedding
night I could make him believe I was still a virgin.'* That was
it. He remembered his response to it as well: *'I'm sure that
would be an excellent ploy if you could contrive it.'* Well, she
must be a dab hand at contriving it. She must have contrived
it on the occasion of their own first dabble together. He
wondered how many other times she had contrived it. Perhaps
even with that blackguard Jericho, the handsome buck navvy.

More detestable things entered his mind to hurt him. He
imagined Poppy had endowed Bellamy with her sexual
favours, despite her denials. He visualised them making love,
she with as much apparent commitment and pleasure as she
demonstrated with himself.

Thus was Robert tortured. The more he thought about
these things, the more plausible they seemed in this new
narrow, distorted view, and he convinced himself that it was
so, making himself utterly miserable.

The case against Poppy was beginning to look bad, not
only among his family but in his own mind too. Wouldn't he
look a fool if he persisted with the affair in the face of the
evidence that Virginia had presented? He'd wasted a whole
year on some puerile notion that he couldn't make his mind
up between two women. One of them, a whore, had already
taken him for a fool; the other, utterly devoted, was whole-
some and good in the old-fashioned sense, even if she did
not excite him. The two women could not be more different.
And to think he was prepared to bring the family name into
disrepute and the firm into financial ruin, or at the very least

embarrassment . . . because of a whore. Well, it was all over now. It had to be over. What if he married her and the man with whom she had had that assignation which Virginia had witnessed was ever in their company? If he owned a carriage he must be a man of some substance, so it was likely he might even know him. How would he cope with such a situation? Could he really afford to risk Poppy's former clients whispering behind cupped hands, boasting that they had had his beautiful young wife when she used to work the streets? God forbid. No, he could not risk embarrassing himself or his family by persisting with a love affair with a whore. Thank God it had all gone on very discreetly.

Next morning, as she had said she would, Clarissa Crawford made her way on foot to Cawneybank House like a frigate in full sail. She was not aware that Poppy would be out, helping at Baylies's Charity School. Indeed, she had never given it a thought, so little did this girl and her feelings matter, who had fooled them all. She pulled on the front door bell and waited, huffing herself up under her mantle in self-righteous readiness for the unpleasant assignment with which she had invested herself. Esther opened the door and let her in.

Clarissa was annoyed at being left to wait, standing on the cold tiles of the hall while the maid announced her and admitted her to the small sitting room that Aunt Phoebe preferred to use in the wintertime.

'My dear Clarissa,' Aunt Phoebe greeted cordially. 'What a pleasant surprise.'

'A surprise it might be, dear Phoebe, but pleasant it is not.'

'Do sit down,' Aunt Phoebe said fussily. 'I'll send for a pot of tea. Or would you prefer coffee?'

'I'll take tea, if I may.'

Aunt Phoebe rang for Esther to return. 'So to what do I owe the pleasure?'

'An unpleasant task, I fear.'

'Then out with it.'

'It concerns your young companion, Poppy Silk, and my son.'

'Do you mean Bellamy or Robert? They are both visitors here from time to time.'

Esther entered the room and Phoebe Newton ordered tea.

'I am mostly concerned with the welfare of Robert and his engagement to Virginia Lord.'

'So how can I be of help, Clarissa?'

'It appears that Robert has been foolishly conducting a clandestine affair with your Miss Silk over the past months, to the detriment of his betrothal to Miss Lord. As a result, he has asked Miss Lord to release him from his promise to marry.'

'Which he is perfectly entitled to do, as I see it,' Aunt Phoebe said defensively. 'I am aware that he and Miss Silk are inordinately fond of each other and he is, after all, a grown man, capable of making his own decisions.'

'You would think so, dear Phoebe. However, Robert has made a rather serious blunder in getting mixed up with a girl like Poppy Silk. A mistake that could have had very serious financial and social consequences for all of us Crawfords . . . However, I will not go into that right now—'

'You say "a girl like Poppy Silk" as if she is dirt,' Aunt Phoebe interrupted, and her irritation at Clarissa's disdain was obvious. 'I am well aware that she was raised on navvy encampments up and down the country, but she has risen above all that by her own efforts. To my mind that is eminently commendable.'

'But are you altogether aware of the rest of her past?'

'I fail to see what you're implying, Clarissa.'

'Then allow me to enlighten you. It has come to our attention that before Poppy Silk came to you she was a prostitute, working the streets of Dudley. That being so, you will therefore appreciate—'

'Poppy? A prostitute?' Aunt Phoebe laughed with contempt at the accusation. 'I have no notion who you have been talking to, Clarissa, but Poppy Silk is no more a prostitute than you or me. Nor ever was.'

'My information is rock solid, Phoebe, I can assure you.'

'Your information, Clarissa, wherever it has come from, could not be further from the truth. Wherever or whoever its source, it reeks of spite and vengeance . . . which rather points the finger at Virginia herself.'

'She was seen—'

'Oh, appearances can be so deceptive . . . Let me just enlighten you a little about Poppy Silk, just to set the record straight. She sits in my house night after night, improving herself. She studies literature after your son Robert recognised her intelligence and gave her her first lessons in reading when she was indeed the daughter of a mere navvy, living on a navvy encampment. The girl is sensitive, affectionate, eloquent, and extremely considerate. She studies music, is learning to play the piano, is now adept at needlework and drawing. She studies geography, elocution and religion, and attends church regularly on a Sunday. She is particular about what she wears, that she is clean, that she makes no social gaffe that might embarrass me. Most edifying of all, she tries to make sure that I am content. She worries about *me*. Just a little while ago she came home all excited that her poor dear mother and her brothers and sisters were in the area again, none of whom she had seen for fifteen or sixteen months. She *cares*, you see, Clarissa. Such qualities are not consistent with the hardness and insensitivity of a common whore, and I demand that you retract your allegations and apologise to me for their gross offensiveness.'

'That I cannot do, Phoebe.' Clarissa puffed herself up like a ruffled pigeon. 'I know what I know, and I cannot allow my son to be associated with such a strumpet. If she nurtures ideas above her station, ideas about marrying Robert, as seems the case, then she can forget them.'

'I suspect that Robert is old enough and wise enough to take his own counsel on matters that affect him directly. I feel certain that he would not have approved of your coming here this morning bearing such vile poison.'

Esther tapped on the door and entered with a tray.

'Thank you, Esther, but Mrs Crawford will not be staying for tea.' Aunt Phoebe got up from her seat and turned to Clarissa. 'Thank you for calling, my dear. I shall pass on your kind regards to Miss Silk. I am sure she will be extremely interested in what you have said.'

Chapter 32

That fateful day when Poppy returned to Cawneybank House, she remained in the library for at least an hour, gazing vacantly out of the window where Clay had been pruning the rose trees. Aunt Phoebe had told her about Clarissa's visit, and Poppy was numbed by what she'd heard, by the ridiculous accusations levelled against her.

'You don't believe it, do you, Aunt Phoebe?' she had asked.

'Not for a minute, my dear. Not even for a second.'

'It's why I escaped Minnie Catchpole,' she asserted tearfully, 'to get away from such goings-on.'

'I know, my dear,' Aunt Phoebe murmured consolingly.

'But it means I have no future with Robert now. Bellamy will never speak to me again either. Their minds are poisoned against me forever.'

'We don't need the Crawfords, my dear.' Aunt Phoebe took Poppy's hand as she sat beside her. 'And the truth will out, one way or another.'

'But only when it's too late,' Poppy groaned. 'Only when it's too late.'

'Would you rather I left you alone for a little while, Poppy? I understand if you would prefer to be by yourself awhile.'

Poppy nodded tearfully. As she sat alone, her head was filled with little incidents that had occurred while she and

Robert were together, some of which had amused her at the time, though she was unable to laugh now. She got up from the sofa and just stared blankly out of the window, her heart as cold as ice, wishing with all her might that she could turn back the clock to that summer they met. She recalled how they had contrived to meet as if by accident around the encampment, how she had enjoyed her lessons in reading and writing and kissing in his office when everybody else had finished work and gone home.

She came out of her daydream and began weeping again as the hard reality engulfed her in another shuddering wave of sorrow. Having never felt so wretched in her life before, she dragged herself upstairs to her room and lay on her bed. She took the book he had given her before he left for Brazil, *Pride and Prejudice,* and gazed at it through misty eyes for a long time, realising that she was the victim of both misplaced pride and vengeful prejudice. She clutched the book to her, whispering his name to herself, wishing that she could fall asleep and never wake up to suffer more this agonising pain of emptiness and longing, this grieving for lost love.

Aunt Phoebe tapped on the door, came in and roused her to ask if she wanted any dinner. When she saw her sorry state she put her motherly arms around her to console her, and succeeded in making her worse. A torrent of tears ensued from both. Poppy said that she would still prefer to be left alone, and Aunt Phoebe went out again, wiping her own tears, and undertook to allow neither Esther nor Dolly to disturb her.

Next day, Poppy went conscientiously to Baylies's Charity School, though she was unable to concentrate on anything she was doing. She was in a perpetual daze, a hazy world where things were happening all around her, but where she felt not a part of it. As she went about her work, trying to help the younger boys with theirs, her eyes would fill up with tears as she reflected on moments she and Robert had shared.

It was obvious that Robert would not visit her to explain things. He would be carefully watched. In any case, what would be the point of him coming? Even for a man of his years and his independent nature, he would be obliged to comply with his parents' demands on a matter as serious as her alleged whoring. She understood that. Such was the essence of respectability. Respectability was at stake, and she was perceived now as being not respectable. Respectability had spawned a method of control, a code that dictated who was considered acceptable and who was not. Respectability created its own pride, its own prejudices. However much she protested her innocence now, she could not overcome the Crawfords' injustice. As far as they were concerned, she was a pariah.

As the days progressed, Poppy missed Robert overwhelmingly, and the heartache became infinitely more acute with their passing. She felt no anger that he should also consider her to be what his parents and Virginia had conditioned him to believe, only sorrow that she had been given no chance to protest her innocence directly to him. And yet, on the other hand, why should she have to protest it? Robert knew her well enough. He must surely realise sooner or later that the accusations were entirely false, trumped up by Virginia with no other purpose than to secure the wearing of his wedding ring on Christmas Day. It begged the question: how much did Virginia really love Robert if she was prepared to see him trapped in a marriage where she knew she would be unloved and undesired? Surely, in the long run, it would break her heart as well as Robert's. Or was she simply prepared to sacrifice herself for what she believed was saving him?

She wanted to know how Robert was, what he was doing. She hadn't seen him, or caught even the merest glimpse of him. Being without him was intolerable, and she was certain it was going to take years to get over Robert Crawford, if indeed she ever could.

'I am worried about you,' Aunt Phoebe said one day, about a week after Poppy's break with Robert. 'As each day passes you look paler than the day before. You pick tentatively at your meals as if they are tasteless, yet you cram down spoonfuls of honey spread thickly on bread and butter as if your life depended on it. Honey is a wonderful food, Poppy, but honey alone is no diet for a young woman. I think I am going to write to Dr Grice asking him to call and see if he can prescribe you a tonic.'

Dr Grice received the letter and duly called a couple of days later. He examined Poppy thoroughly, asked her when she had last seen her monthly visitor and pronounced her pregnant . . . whereupon Aunt Phoebe fainted and had to receive the doctor's ministrations as well.

'But my dear,' Aunt Phoebe said, after Dr Grice had brought her round and departed with his shilling fee, 'how can you possibly be pregnant? Dr Grice must surely be wrong.'

Poppy shook her head sorrowfully. 'No, he's not wrong, Aunt. Robert and I were lying together quite regularly.'

'You mean you—'

'We were lovers, Aunt,' she said without shame. 'We were passionate lovers.'

'Passionate? Oh, spare me the particulars, Poppy . . . When did you find the time, and where on earth did it happen?'

'I'll spare you the particulars, Aunt.'

'Don't be so flippant, child. This is hardly something to be flippant about. Do you understand the seriousness of your situation? Do you understand the position in which you place me as well as yourself?'

Poppy sighed resignedly. 'Yes, I do, Aunt, and I'm truly sorry for that. I never wanted to embarrass you. I never wanted to ruin your respectability.'

'You understand well the meaning of the word now.'

'Oh, yes, I believe I understand it better than anybody.'

'You realise that your condition, once it becomes apparent, will only lend credence to the Crawfords' belief that you were once a prostitute.'

'It doesn't follow, and I don't see why it should. Anyway, I don't give tuppence for what they think. I know what I'm like better than anybody. I know I'm no prostitute, and that I lay with Robert out of love for him. I'm not sorry for that. Where I come from it's the most natural thing in the world. I'm not ashamed that I'm carrying his child. Why should I be? We are in love.'

'But he should know, Poppy. He should be told.'

'Why, Aunt?' Poppy protested. 'It's nothing to do with him now. He's gone. He has his own life to lead among his own kind. I am no longer any part of him. Leave him be. Let him get on with the life he's obliged to live. I don't want to burden him anymore. He has problems enough, I imagine . . . There's only one thing I can do now. I shall go back to my mother. She and Buttercup will look after me.'

'To the new navvy encampment, you mean?'

'Please don't look so shocked, Aunt. That's where I belong, isn't it? There'll be no wagging tongues or pointing fingers. I'll not be reviled there just because I'm carrying a child out of wedlock. Nobody will turn a hair. I'll be welcomed and cared for. They might be barbaric in the eyes of society, they might be godless, but at least they look after their own. And, by going there, I shall not be an encumbrance or an embarrassment to you.'

'But you are worthy of so much better, Poppy.'

'Maybe I am, maybe I'm not. I tried to better myself, with your help, Aunt, but I fell prey to the one beast that is most girls' undoing at some time – love. The only sin, though, was falling in love with somebody who was really way out of my class. I was a fool not to have realised it at the outset. I could've saved myself a lot of heartache.'

'Perhaps you'll have your baby and fall in love again . . . when you are older and wiser. You're still very young.'

'No, Aunt. I shall carry this love for Robert Crawford forever. It'll be the cross I bear through my whole life. I could never love another man like I love him. I loved him the first moment I saw him and I shall love him to the end. No other man could ever take his place. I hope you won't think too badly of me, Aunt Phoebe, for falling in love with your lovely nephew and for willingly consenting to do the things with him that can only produce a child.'

'Oh, Poppy,' Aunt Phoebe sighed. 'You are not the first, nor will you be the last. But I feared from the start that you would end up with a broken heart. It never occurred to me you might end up with a broken heart *and* a baby, however. I knew you would have an uphill struggle to oust the likes of Virginia Lord. Her family have too much of a hold on the Crawfords.'

'But promise me you won't be fooled by them, Aunt.'

'Fooled?'

'Yes, fooled. Don't let them ever fool you that I was nothing to Robert. I was, and I still am the whole world to him. I know him well enough to know it's true. He loves me just as much as I love him, no matter how many Virginias he might marry. When two people have been as close as we have, you just know. When he goes to bed at night with *her*, he'll be wishing it's me lying beside him . . . No, please don't be shocked, Aunt. I know it, and I draw some comfort from it. But all this has made me realise at last that we can never be together . . .'

'Oh, Poppy,' Aunt Phoebe whimpered.

'We each want what we want, don't we, Aunt? All of us. And we pay no mind to whether it's suitable, or convenient, or wise.' Poppy sighed, a sigh as profound as her words. 'But we have to live with what meagre scraps life allows us, even though nothing else in the world will satisfy us except our hearts' true desire.'

Tears filled Aunt Phoebe's eyes. 'I have loved you as if you were my own daughter, Poppy.'

Poppy took Aunt Phoebe's hand. 'I know you have. And I love you. I always will. I know that this is hurting you as much as it's hurting me.'

'Indeed it is. I feel somehow that I have let you down.'

'You, Aunt Phoebe? Let me down? Never. I've been the instrument of my own undoing, not you. Never you. I've let *you* down. I'm the one who should feel ashamed . . . And yet I don't. I can't. Not for carrying Robert's child.'

'Did you have any notion before Dr Grice diagnosed it that you were pregnant?'

Poppy smiled. 'Oh, yes, Aunt. And before Virginia thwarted me with accusations about my past, I was certain that telling Robert would be the greatest wedding gift I could give him. I'd planned to tell him on our wedding night. He would have been overjoyed. Now, sadly for him, he must never know.'

'What is your mother likely to say to you if you go back to her?'

Poppy smiled again as she imagined the sort of lewd

comment Sheba might make, and Aunt Phoebe was relieved to see a sparkle in her eyes after so much misery.

'Well? What might she say?'

'That I should have kept my legs crossed . . . or some such.'

Aunt Phoebe laughed. 'No other reprimand?'

'My mother is in no position to tell me off. She was fourteen when she conceived me, she's had a house full of children since, and has never been married . . . Such wantonness must be in my blood, Aunt Phoebe.'

'I shall be very sad when you leave me, Poppy. I don't want you to go. I can give you my support here. But I cannot keep you from your mother, if that's where you think you should be.'

'It will be for the best, Aunt.'

'Just so long as you make me one promise . . .'

'Whatever you ask of me, I promise it.'

'That you shall not forget me . . .' Another flood of tears rolled down Aunt Phoebe's cheeks. 'That you shall visit me as often as you can, and bring your baby as well when your time comes . . .' She lifted her spectacles and wiped her eyes.

'Oh, Aunt Phoebe,' Poppy sighed, her own eyes glazed and red. 'Of course I promise it. You are my other mother. I love you no less than my real mother. Of course I shall visit you. You'll not be able to keep me away.'

'Then God bless you always, Poppy.'

It was the first Saturday in December, the seventh, that Poppy was driven by Clay to the new navvy encampment in Brierley Hill. Sheba was surprised to see her daughter, but even more surprised to see that she was accompanied by a trunk.

'Does this mean you've come back to live wi' we?' Sheba

asked, her hands in a bowl of water, peeling vegetables, as she stood at the stone sink in the communal kitchen that occupied one side of the hut.

'It's where I belong, Mother.'

'Belong?' Sheba scoffed. 'Here? No, you can't fool me. You'm too grand to come back to a navvy hut out o' choice. What's up? Did you fall foul o' your Aunt Phoebe?'

'Not exactly.' Poppy sighed as she took off her gloves. 'Do you understand the meaning of the word respectability, Mother?'

'Yes. I reckon I do.'

'Well, I find myself carrying Robert's child, so my situation is not deemed to be respectable. To make matters worse, he'd already vowed to marry somebody else. So, to save Aunt Phoebe any trouble, I deemed it best I left.'

'You've been doing a lot o' deeming, our Poppy. All them funny words . . .'

As Poppy had expected, Sheba made no comment whatsoever about her carrying a child.

'So where you gunna sleep?' she asked.

'Are there any lodgers yet?'

'Why, do you fancy sleeping with one of them?'

Poppy laughed. 'No, thank you.'

'Nor with Jericho?'

'Definitely *not* with Jericho.'

'He'll be disappointed.'

'That's his affair. I'll sleep with my sisters.'

'And what about when the babby's born?'

'I'll still sleep with my sisters . . .' She opened the travelling case and began sorting her clothes, ready to put them away. 'Where's Buttercup and the others?'

'Out. At work.'

'Does he get drunk?'

'Not drunk. Not Buttercup. Thank God. Here, let me help you with this lot while the babby's asleep.'

Together they emptied Poppy's case and Sheba admired her beautiful clothes as they put them away.

'D'ya think e'er a one o' these'll fit me, our Poppy?'

'Try one on if you want.'

'Another time, eh? When I ain't up to me elbers in water. But they'm too good to be wearing around this dump. Ain't you got nothing old? Summat you can't spoil?'

'Aunt Phoebe made me throw all my old things away. Well, they were horrible . . . But I've still got the blue frock that I bought with the money Buttercup made me take with me when I left Blowers Green. I expect it's at the bottom of the case.'

'Well, I should wear that for now, our Poppy. What with all the mud what's collecting round here, anythin' decent will be ruined.'

'Well, I have to keep something decent for my work.'

'Work? What work?'

'I work at a charity school in Dudley. I shall still do it.'

'But it'll be a tidy walk there and back.'

Poppy shrugged. 'I'll do it till I begin to show. After that, it wouldn't be seemly in a boys' school. Meanwhile, the exercise will be good for my constitution.' Her eyes lit up in the realisation that after that, she might still be useful. 'After that,' she said, suddenly fired with enthusiasm, 'I can teach my brothers and sister to read and write . . . and do arithmetic.'

'That's just what they need,' Sheba agreed. 'Don't yer think it'd be better to start teaching your brothers and sisters straight away, rather than tramping to Dudley and back every day?'

'Yes, I suppose it would. But I'll have to let them know at Baylies' first, that I can't go there any more. It's only right.'

* * *

514

A wet and foggy darkness had fallen over the Brierley Hill encampment that day. The breeze had been non-existent and you could see the mist descending, veiling the surrounding hills, then sinking into the valleys. When the late afternoon came, nothing changed, except that the grey gloom darkened to black.

Work on the Oxford, Worcester and Wolverhampton Railway had recommenced with a vengeance, and the fog did not muffle the sound of colourful language, of picks thudding into the stone-cold earth, nor the scrape of shovels as men probed and dug by the light of lanterns. You could see their indistinct shadows, ghostly figures fringed with soft halos, as they strove with barrows to load the wagons that would tip the shifted dirt further along the temporary line, to be used as infill for an embankment. An engineer appeared in the dimness with a tape measure, a field book and blacklead. He did some calculations by the feeble light of a lamp and went away, shivering with cold, as if all the woes of the world had come to rest on his shoulders.

'We got *him* back again, have we?' Jericho remarked quietly to Buttercup, pointing with his thumb over his shoulder at the young engineer behind him. 'Crawford, his name is. I remember him from Blowers Green. He was sweet on Sheba's daughter, Poppy.'

'Still is, according to Sheba,' Buttercup replied. 'There's talk of 'em getting wed.'

Jericho leaned on his shovel as he watched Robert Crawford disappear into the fog. 'There's no accounting for taste.'

'Whose taste?' Buttercup queried. 'Hers or his?'

'Hers. What's *he* got?'

'Money . . . class . . . learnin' . . . Not to mention good looks and fine manners.'

'That's twattle. Women like their men rough.'

'Is that what thou think'st?' Buttercup scoffed. 'Well, no wonder thou hast no luck with decent wenches, once they get to know thee. Women like to be treated like ladies, Jericho. They like to be treated as if they'm the only thing in the world that matters to a man. They respond better to love and respect than to roughness and rudeness . . . and drunkenness.' He picked his watch out of his waistcoat pocket and peered at it by the light of one of the lamps. 'Nearly six. Time to pack up, eh, son? I'm starved. I could eat a scabby hoss.'

'There's enough hacks in the stables,' Jericho said. 'Pick yourself one.'

'No, not I. I'll mek do wi' the rabbits and the few taters what Sheba's cooking.'

They picked up their tools and carried them on their shoulders as they headed back towards the encampment from the new cutting that was already taking shape, followed by several other navvies, all sore and aching from the day's grind. There was a rude orderliness about the huddle of newly constructed huts that came with their freshness. There was no huge midden heap yet, hardly any rubbish and litter scattered about. But it was just a matter of time . . . Buttercup wondered why it had to become degraded over time, and wished it wouldn't. Already the grass that had clad the land hereabouts was muddy from the rain and the constant tramping of scores of boots every day.

'One day I'm gunna get out o' this rut,' Buttercup said to Jericho. 'One day I shall find meself some genteel employment and live in a quiet country cottage with Sheba, away from all the squalor that goes with navvydom. There's more to life than the back-breaking work that me and thee have to contend with.'

'You're getting soft in your old age,' came the predictable reply.

'Aye . . . soft and sentimental, me . . .' He shot a knowing look at Jericho, who picked it up and grinned.

They were at the door of the hut, which had not yet been given a nickname, stamped their feet to shake off the mud, and went inside. It was warm, and the heady aroma of rabbit stew filled their nostrils.

'How's my wench?' Buttercup affectionately asked Sheba, as he took off his boots. 'Bin busy, Old Shoe?'

'Yes . . . We've got a new lodger . . .' She glanced from Buttercup to Jericho to gauge their level of interest.

'Oh, ar. What is he? A navvy, a brickie, a blacksmith?'

'He's a she,' Sheba replied smugly.

'A she?' Buttercup's eyes met Jericho's and registered their mutual curiosity. 'You mean a wench?'

'Aye, a wench, o' course. What else did you think I meant – a she-man?'

'Who is it?'

Poppy had heard the exchange from the communal bedroom and appeared at the door wearing the blue dress she'd bought when she left Blowers Green. Jericho looked at her and was speechless, not so much at the refined loveliness he beheld, but at the sight of a woman he had desired and had not expected to see ever again.

'By cock and pie!' he exclaimed. 'It's Poppy Silk.'

The year and a quarter had not marred his handsome face nor his physique. His skin was clear and healthy despite his dirty face, and his eyes shone with enthusiasm at seeing her. He had a big droopy moustache that reminded Poppy of her father's and which made him look even more masculine. Oh, Jericho was the same rough-hewn earth god she had known before. She smiled with pleasure at seeing him again.

'How lovely to see you, Jericho,' she said with ladylike aplomb. She turned to the other man. 'You too, Buttercup.'

'By Christ, thou'st changed, wench,' Buttercup said warmly. 'Thou'st growed up. It's good to see thee.'

'You'm here for good?' Jericho queried, his eyes widening at the prospect.

'For good, yes.'

Quickly overcoming his shock, he sat down on the nearest available chair and pulled off his boots. 'Did your mother tell yer I'm one o' the family now?'

'More or less.'

'More or less,' he repeated, almost with contempt. He looked at Sheba in an earnest appeal. 'Why didn't you tell her?'

''Cause I thought you might like to tell her yourself.'

'Tell me what?'

'I'll tell her,' Buttercup chimed in. He turned to Poppy. 'I dunno what all the fuss is about. It's simple. It turns out that Jericho's me own son.'

Poppy's eyes were wide with surprise at this news. 'Fancy,' she said. 'How did you find out?'

'We was working together one day and we got to talking,' Jericho announced, eager now to relate the story to Poppy. 'We got to talking about where we come from and where we'd been. Buttercup said he'd worked in Wiltshire, and I told him that's where I come from. Then he said, "What town do you come from?" and I said "Chippenham". "What was your mother's name?" he axed me, and I answered "Sadie Visick". "Sadie Visick?" said he, and I said, "Yes". "Have you got any brothers or sisters?" he axed, and I said "No". I said, "Me mother never married". So he says, "Then you must be the little bastard she had o' mine," he said. He said, "How d'you do, son? Nice to meet you."'

'And that was it?'

'That was it. Since then, we've bin inseparable. I'm pleased

518

as Buttercup's me father, 'cause I reckon he's a decent sort, and I like him.'

Decent enough to disappear when he learnt poor Sadie Visick was carrying his child, Poppy thought, but made no comment. 'What happened to your mother, Jericho?' she asked instead.

'I ain't seen her for a couple o' years now. I ought to go back and see how she is.'

'You really ought. She might need you. What if she's poorly? What if she's starving?'

'She might be in the workhouse,' Jericho said flippantly.

'Would you want her to be?'

'No, she works. She used to work as a cook at an inn in Chippenham. I expect she still does.'

'You should write to her,' Poppy reproached.

'Write? I can't write. You know I can't write.'

'Then I'll teach you. It's easy if you put your mind to it. I learnt to write in no time.'

'And you'll teach me, Poppy?'

'Yes.'

'But Mother can't read, so it's no use.'

'But if you learn to write, she can get somebody else to read your letters to her.'

'Oh, aye, that's a good idea . . .' He pondered the prospect for a moment. 'Can we start tonight?'

'Yes, if you like. When we've eaten . . . We can all start. The young ones as well.'

Chapter 33

Lessons in reading and writing thus began at the new encampment. Within a day or two, Jericho had acquired a blackboard, an easel, writing books and blacklead pencils from somewhere. Nobody asked from where he'd stolen them, for stolen they must have been. Poppy enjoyed her role as teacher, drawing on her experience with Mr Tromans at Baylies's Charity School and Aunt Phoebe. She felt she was doing some good, fulfilling in a small way a need that she knew had always existed . . . and it helped take her mind off the heartache she was suffering. If only she had been taught to read as a child, as she was now teaching her brothers and sisters and the other children that lived on the encampment.

Despite the fact that she was in the early stages of pregnancy, she felt well. She'd experienced none of the sickness that women often suffer. Rather, her skin glowed and her hair shone as if in defiance of her condition. She had become resigned to her fate. Her adventure into wealth and society was something she would not have missed for the world – it gave her a more balanced outlook on life – but it was in the past now.

When the navvies complained about the rich and what evil, conniving bastards they were, she could always turn around and say that not all were evil and conniving. She would obstinately declare that the vast majority were decent, law-abiding folk who strove merely for a decent standard of living and to be thought well of by their friends and neighbours – for respectability. As far as Poppy was concerned there was nothing wrong with that. Wealth was infinitely better than poverty. If you were wealthy, you had the potential to help somebody in poverty. If you were poor, you had nothing to offer anybody, except for a sorry tale or two and expressions of envy. She could also tell those who felt most hard-done-by that many wealthy people were conscious of the plight of the poor, of their sad lack of education, of the exploitation of the very young, and they genuinely wished to address those issues. But it could never happen overnight. Even if there were a revolution, things could never happen as quickly as everybody might want. Such reforms must evolve. There was a growing, common will to improve the lot of the poor; things would inevitably change for the better, but all in good time. Having listened to conversations over dinner that had taken place at Aunt Phoebe's and elsewhere, Poppy had gleaned that already the railways were having a benign effect on trade and intercourse, and that prosperity for all must surely follow. Robert Crawford had taught her that enterprise was the key, and that nothing was impossible.

Sheba had so far told nobody that Poppy was pregnant. After she'd been living on the Silver End encampment a couple of weeks, Jericho plucked up the courage to ask her to go with him one evening to a public house he'd discovered and liked to use. It was the week before Christmas and bitter cold. She wrapped up warm and he took her to The Old Crown, a place not normally patronised by navvies, although Jericho was recognised as one by his mode of dress. He was tolerated, but at arm's length, as long as he was alone, and as long as he behaved. That night, when he entered with a pretty, fair-haired girl who looked as though she should have had more about her than to dally with the likes of him, he was suddenly regarded with envy and a little more respect.

A warm fire blazed cheerily in the grate at one end of the saloon, sprigs of holly and mistletoe hung in clusters from the ceiling. A group of men sat round one table smoking clay pipes, supping ale, muttering and nodding as they put the world to rights. Others were accompanied by their women in fancy bonnets, happy to be out of the house for a change. The spirit of Christmas had begun to manifest itself in their laughter and gaiety. Poppy and Jericho sat down at a vacant table and when Jericho had fetched them drinks, they talked desultorily.

'So where've yer bin since you left Blowers Green?' he asked at last.

She related all that had happened, describing her life at Aunt Phoebe's, how she had been tutored and thrust into local society. She told him about the religious friend she had made who had ideas of becoming a Quaker, how she had been introduced to bankers and the cream of industrial society. Yet she made no mention of Robert Crawford and his part in her life.

'You done well for yourself, Poppy,' Jericho remarked, and took another swig of ale from his tankard.

'So did your old sweetheart Minnie Catchpole,' Poppy said.

'She was never my sweetheart.'

'But you bought her,' she said disapprovingly. 'You used her. And she was in love with you.'

Jericho shrugged. 'What's a man to do when his mate says, "Here, you can have a go on my wench for a gallon o' beer"? And she was comely enough. I'm just a man, Poppy, with a man's needs. Don't hold that against me.'

'I don't,' Poppy asserted. 'Anyway, she's done well for herself since. She's married now to a wealthy man a lot older than she is. She's respectable at last.'

'I'm happy for her. It's good to hear o' folk doing well for theirselves . . . What I don't understand, Poppy, is where that engineer Crawford fits into your adventures, and why you've come back to navvydom when you was living the life of a princess.'

'Oh, it's a long story and I'm quite sure you wouldn't want to hear it,' she said.

'Me, I'd love to hear it. If it means you ain't having nothin' to do with him any more, I'd like to commend meself. You know well enough how I always wanted you to be my woman.'

She smiled at him with sympathy in her eyes. 'Oh, I know, Jericho . . .' she said softly. Self-consciously, she averted her eyes.

'But you was always out o' my reach then . . . If things have changed . . .'

'Things *have* changed, Jericho . . .'

His expression brightened at the implication. 'Then you could do worse for yourself than let me look after you. I've changed an' all, you know, Poppy. I ain't so wild as I was. I reckon I could just as soon take to religion now.'

'You?'

'Aye, me.' He gave a self-mocking little laugh. 'I don't drink nowhere near as much. Dog Meat made me realise how stupid drinking was when he needed drink that bad as he had to sell his woman. He was a useless wastrel, Poppy.'

'What happened to him?'

'Lord knows. I daresay he'll turn up sometime, looking for work . . . And when I found out as Buttercup was me father . . . That changed me as well. I decided I wanted to be like him. I always liked him and admired him – not for runnin' off and leaving' me mother with a bellyful of me – but for his calmness, the way he listens to folk, his compassion. I tell yer, your mother's found a decent bloke in Buttercup, and he thinks the world of her an' all.'

'I know,' Poppy answered wistfully.

'I'm more like him now, Poppy.'

'I think you are,' she said with a growing regard.

'Well, then . . . Do you think we might give it a try, you and me, if things am different for you now?'

She made no reply, peering into her glass.

'Would it help if I told you how much I think of you, Poppy? How much I've always thought of you? I never said that to any wench afore, you know. 'Cause it was never true afore. But 'tis true now.'

She understood the courage it had taken for Jericho to admit as much. 'Buttercup took on five children,' she said, deciding to test him. 'And my mother was carrying Lightning Jack's baby as well. I couldn't see you doing that.'

'Well, there's no need. You ain't got no kids.'

'No, that's right.'

'So why mention it?'

'But what if I was carrying a child, Jericho? What if I was pregnant with somebody else's child? I'll wager you wouldn't feel so drawn to me then.'

'Well, you ain't carrying nobody's brat,' he said. 'Your belly's as flat as a board . . . I noticed . . . You'm too slender to be carrying.'

She smiled, her blue eyes meeting his for a second, candid, giving too much away.

'You ain't carryin' somebody's brat, are you, Poppy? Oh, tell me you ain't . . .'

A group of carol singers entered the inn, men and women,

bringing in a gust of cold winter air. For Jericho it was the cue to rush to the bar before they did.

'Same again?' he asked Poppy and she nodded.

The carol singers did not require refreshment, however – not then, at any rate. They stood in a group, one of them carrying a lantern, and began their festive singing with smiles on their faces that were rosy red as they recovered from the outside cold. First they sang a bouncy 'God Rest Ye Merry Gentlemen', by the end of which Jericho had returned from the bar with two more drinks.

'If you am carryin' somebody's brat, Poppy, it don't matter to me that much,' he said earnestly as he sat down. 'Buttercup did it, and I want to prove as I can be as good a bloke as Buttercup.'

She smiled again and felt tears sting the backs of her eyes, so touched was she by his offer. 'You are a good man, Jericho, and I appreciate your offer—'

'So you am pregnant then?'

She nodded, without looking at him.

'And do you accept me? I'd be able to look after you. I'd be glad to look after you. And your babby.'

The carol singers struck up with 'Ding Dong Merrily on High', which at once caught the attention of everybody in the room, even diverting Jericho. Poppy listened to the bright, clever harmonies and pondered at the same time what it had taken for Jericho to make such a self-sacrificial offer.

She was tempted . . .

Oh, she was tempted . . .

He looked at her, catching her glance, and he gave a smile that for him was tender. 'Well, Poppy? Am yer gunna be me wench? Am yer gunna let me be your chap? Am yer gunna agree to jump the broomstick wi' me?'

But the difference between them was too great. What little

learning she'd enjoyed, crammed into but a year and a quarter, had created too much of a gap between them. Jericho was unlearned, ignorant, albeit through no fault of his own. Yet he would be deemed by his peers to be the superior of the two if they paired up. She was so much wiser by dint of her learning and her innate common sense, however. He would come to resent her cleverness, for a woman must never be cleverer than her man. Jericho, it was true, was a changed man. He was infinitely more mature and more considerate. But he was not Robert Crawford. Nor would he ever be like him.

Her first instinct to get away from the navvies, the instinct that had manifested itself a year and a half ago, was still alive within her. Oh, she loved her mother and her brothers and sisters, but she did not enjoy the navvy life and all that went with it. If she agreed to be Jericho's woman she would be trapped in it forever and her own resentment of her situation would be poison to Jericho. Eventually, she must make a life for herself and her child away from the navvies. She would set off again into the big wide world when she'd had her baby. She would become an experienced teacher and respectable. She would pay somebody to look after her child while she worked. To explain the presence of a young child, she would fabricate some story about her past, a story that would satisfy the old ladies who were so set on their high moral conventions and their immovable respectability. She could buy a cheap wedding ring and say she was a young widow . . .

There was a ripple of applause for the carol singers as they ended their carol and began singing a slow, lilting 'The First Nowell'. It sounded so pleasant, so joyous.

'I can't be your woman, Jericho,' she whispered. 'Oh, I appreciate your offer, but it would be too big a sacrifice for you to make.'

'I'll be the judge o' that,' he responded.

She shook her head and held his hand across the table. 'No,' she said firmly. 'I am the better judge of it, believe me. You could never love my child as much as you would if it were your own, and I couldn't stand to see it spurned. But the father of the child as well . . . You see, Jericho, I loved him dearly and I still do. I shall love him to my dying day, to the exclusion of any other man. You would never be content with that, waiting for me to drop some crumb of love, like a dog waits at the feet of his master for a piece of gristle to be tossed from his plate. I wouldn't expect it of you. It would be too demeaning, too degrading, for such a worthy man. You deserve so much better.'

'He's a lucky man,' Jericho replied quietly. 'I'm proper jealous of him. But I tell yer straight – if it was me that was the father, I'd be with yer now. I wouldn't have sloped off like he's done and left yer in the lurch . . . like Buttercup did with my mother. Not I, Poppy. Not now as I know what it's like to grow up without a father . . .'

'The man I love doesn't even know I'm carrying his child, Jericho,' she added defensively.

'Crawford? He took his pleasure. It's time he did know.'

She shook her head, smiled sadly and squeezed his hand as the singing filled the room. 'No . . . Believe me, it's best that he doesn't.'

'I don't understand you, Poppy. If he left yer in the lurch, how can you not tell him? Why don't you want him to know, if you love him as much as you say you do? It don't make no sense.'

'Well, he'd already vowed to marry somebody else . . .' She shrugged, indicating her acquiescence. '*And* she told him I used to be a prostitute when I left Blowers Green.'

'You, a prostitute?' he scoffed aloud, which prompted her

to put her forefinger to her lips. 'You ain't no prostitute, Poppy. You got too much about yer.'

She shrugged. 'He thinks I was . . . Well, he does now at least.'

'What a stupid bastard! So when's he getting wed?'

'Christmas Day.'

'Christmas Day? Jesus Christ, that soon?'

The haunting melody and tender delivery of 'Silent Night' hung in the air with the tobacco smoke, sung with such feeling that both Poppy and Jericho felt compelled to listen again. Jericho was seething, however. Only his new-found self-control was preventing him from exploding with anger and frustration at what he had heard. Soon the carol finished, and the revellers in the inn began applauding.

'So would you have him back?' Jericho queried.

'What do you think?' she replied. 'Of course I would. But what chance have I got? He thinks *that* of me, and he won't be persuaded otherwise now. And anyway, it's cutting it a bit fine now.'

'He don't deserve you, Poppy. It's best you leave him be.' Jericho finished his drink. One of the women who had been singing the carols approached him, clutching a gentleman's top hat, taking a collection. 'What's the collection in aid of, missus?' he enquired.

'It's in aid of those poor girls who are abused and left with child,' the woman said with a kind smile.

'I'll gladly put a shillin' to that,' Jericho said, and delved in his pocket.

Through gossip that he had overheard among the navvies working on the Oxford, Worcester and Wolverhampton Railway, Robert Crawford discovered that there was a girl, described as extraordinarily pretty, teaching reading, writing and elementary

528

arithmetic to the children, and indeed some of the adults, on the Silver End encampment. He was curious to ascertain her identity, since the circumstances and timing suggested it must be none other than Poppy Silk. Especially so, since he had discovered her mother was a resident and had himself taken Poppy there. Yet he could not reconcile the possibility that Poppy Silk could have given up her comfortable existence with his Aunt Phoebe to return to the squalor and immorality of a navvies' encampment. So he sought out Bilston Buttercup, whom he reckoned should be able to confirm or deny it, and found him alone one afternoon on his way to the site hut.

'Aye, 'tis true, Mister Crawford,' Buttercup verified. 'I ain't privy to the whys and wherefores, but it seems the wench is doing some good.'

'Thank you,' Robert said. 'I'm very pleased that she is.' In a strange way, he felt that some good, some betterment of those poor children who were compelled to live on the encampment, had resulted from his affair with Poppy. 'But please don't mention that I asked,' he added with a wink. 'Eh, Buttercup?'

'Me? I'm the very soul o' description, me. I won't breathe a word, Mister Crawford. Have no fear.'

'Thank you.' He touched the brim of his top hat and smiled to himself at Buttercup's unwitting misuse of a word. 'I'll be on my way.'

That evening, Robert decided to pay a visit to Aunt Phoebe, to try and find out the circumstances under which Poppy had left. He was beginning to feel guilty that his rejection of her had caused her to give up unnecessarily the pleasant life she loved so much. After all, that was not what he had intended. Unless, of course, Poppy had admitted that she had been a prostitute and Aunt Phoebe, unable to contemplate such a notion, had asked her to leave.

The air was cold and clammy, and threatened snow. It would be a delightful thing if it were to snow on Christmas Day, to add a romantic touch to a day that would actually be lacking any, despite his marriage. He arrived at Cawneybank House and tapped the door with the cast-iron knocker. While he waited for somebody to open it, it occurred to him how many heady nights he had slipped from his bed and crept round the back of this house to wait for Poppy to steal down from her bedroom and join him in the summer house. It was a wonder they had never been caught, a miracle nobody had ever found them out. He had a strange, compulsive feeling that if he crept there now, Poppy would be waiting for him, warm, loving and eager to give herself to him, as she always had been. Of course, it was nonsense, but he sighed as it struck him again exactly how much he missed her.

Esther answered the door.

'Well, it's Mr Crawford,' she beamed. 'Hello, Mr Crawford. Come to see your aunt?'

'If she's at home, Esther.'

'I'll just ask.'

Robert smiled to himself at Esther's demeanour as he waited in the cold hallway, holding his hat in his gloved hands. The maid returned and ushered him into the small sitting room. A coal fire blazed in the grate.

'Please don't get up, Aunt.' He bent down and gave her a kiss on the cheek. 'I thought it was time I came to see you . . .'

'Came to see *me*?'

'Well, I understand Poppy has left you,' he said, catching her meaning. 'I'm told she's gone back to her mother on the new navvy encampment at Silver End near Brierley Hill.'

'Unfortunately so.' Aunt Phoebe's demeanour was cold; her face was set in stone.

'I hope it was not as a result of my . . . my inability to pursue our *affaire du cœur*.'

'Why else would she leave, Robert? She was happy here.'

'So why did she leave?'

'Because she did not wish to be an embarrassment to me after the despicable accusations your very silly fiancée made.'

'I'm so sorry, Aunt,' Robert said, still holding his hat and his gloves. 'It was not my wish that Poppy should leave you. I know how much you thought of her. I'm in no doubt that you miss her very much.'

'Don't *you*?' Aunt Phoebe asked pointedly.

'Yes . . . As a matter of fact, I do . . . Vastly.'

'It's such a pity you don't deserve her, Robert. For obviously believing her to be what Virginia accuses her of being.'

He made no reply.

'Do you honestly believe that dear, sweet Poppy was a prostitute, Robert? Do you?'

'I don't want to believe it, Aunt. I certainly don't. But Ginnie's evidence is overwhelming. She witnessed her getting into a carriage with a man . . .'

'And didn't it cross your mind that such evidence is no more than merely circumstantial?'

'Unfortunately, that evidence is supported by what her erstwhile friend Minnie, Mrs Cecil Tyler, also revealed to her.'

'Oh? Which is what?'

'That Poppy lived with Minnie for a time, sharing a house for the purpose of prostitution.'

Aunt Phoebe sighed with exasperation. 'I suggest that this is all a beastly misunderstanding, you know. If I were you, I would pay Captain and Mrs Tyler a visit and discreetly ask Mrs Tyler to confirm Poppy's innocence. Virginia has either misinterpreted what Mrs Tyler said or jumped to the wrong conclusions – obviously. You will soon find out for yourself that Poppy's sojourn with Minnie was under duress and meant to be temporary, while she sought employment as a maid. Unable to stand Minnie's goings-on any longer, she came to me seeking work, because you had given her my name and address. She was desperate to get away. We were immediately taken with each other, and she took little persuading to come and live here with me. Poppy is not a prostitute, Robert, nor ever was. In your heart of hearts you know it. She is too warm, too sensitive . . . and far too sensible.'

'I do hope you are right, Aunt. I must confess, I've had my doubts about the veracity of Ginnie's interpretation of—'

'And have you considered Virginia's motives?'

'Her motives?' Robert looked puzzled.

'Oh, Robert . . . Men! You are so naive when it comes to the wiles of women. Virginia was afraid of losing you to Poppy, was she not?'

Robert nodded. 'She believed she had already lost me.'

'So . . . to get you to change your mind she had to vilify Poppy. She had to make sure the girl was seen as socially unacceptable to you, but even more so to your family, who would do everything possible to restrain you. What better way than to claim she was a woman of the streets? She has succeeded.'

'I never regarded it in that light, Aunt Phoebe.'

'Then maybe you should. But the greater damage has been done. Virginia knows that even if she is wrong, Poppy's reputation is already ruined. She could always argue that there is no smoke without fire. Besides, the girl is the daughter of a common navvy with no breeding whatsoever. Virginia was very quick to reveal that as well, a revelation that in itself is enough to render the poor girl totally unacceptable socially, despite her acquired finesse.'

Aunt Phoebe was tempted to tell Robert that Poppy was

carrying his child, but remembered and respected her wish that he should not know. It would complicate things too drastically when they were already complicated enough. No, let him live in ignorance of his unborn child. As Poppy had said, it was simpler, and cleaner. He would have enough to contend with, without that knowledge.

'So you honestly feel I should have a quiet chat with Minnie, do you, Aunt?'

'Yes, if you still feel the need to be convinced. Go on. Ask her outright. Was Poppy Silk ever a prostitute? I predict she will laugh in your face.'

'You are already convinced, Aunt.'

'Robert, I have lived with Poppy a long time now. I know her every feeling, every emotion. I am familiar with her inner-most secrets . . . Oh, yes . . . And don't look so doubtful about that.' Aunt Phoebe looked at him reproachfully. 'She even told me how close you two had become . . .' Robert blushed to his roots. 'A girl who openly divulges something as intimate as that would certainly have no qualms about divulging whether she had been a prostitute or not. Don't you agree?'

'Perhaps.'

'Well, the only thing she ever declared to me about such things is that she might eventually have been forced into it through circumstances, had she not escaped the malign influence of Minnie Catchpole. But she had the sense to get out. Of course, we acknowledge that Minnie has since reformed and is socially acceptable as the wife of Captain Tyler. Or, rather, she was, before silly Virginia let the cat out of the bag.'

'I think Virginia has a lot to answer for,' Robert said.

'That is for you to sort out, Robert. It must be on your conscience as well as on hers now.'

'I shall be happy just to clear Poppy's name and reputation. I am resigned to the fact that as the daughter of a navvy, my parents would never accept her as their daughter-in-law anyway.'

'Well, now it's of no consequence either way. You are to be married on Wednesday to the girl they adore.'

'Yes,' said Robert, very quietly. 'I know it only too well.'

Chapter 34

Work on Christmas Eve came to a close at the usual time, with no concession for the fact that tomorrow was Christmas Day, and a holiday. Nobody minded the end of the working day. The earth was hard and unyielding to pick and shovel, and the icy cold air foretold of snow. Jericho and Buttercup joined their workmates in a celebration drink or two at The Red Lion, which had become the navvies' favourite public house. Since word had got around that it was the main drinking annex to the new encampment, it was becoming a target for hawkers. That night, being Christmas Eve, there were even more hawkers than usual, selling everything from poultry to jewellery.

'A bit o' goose wouldn't be amiss for our Christmas dinners, eh, Jericho?' Buttercup commented as he saw one hawker touting a late example. He took a swig from his pewter tankard then placed it on the table before him, seriously pondering the prospect. 'I fancy a bit o' goose wi' some taters roasted in the juices.'

'The thought's makin' my mouth water an' all, Buttercup,' Jericho replied, wiping froth off his big moustache with the back of his hand. 'Will Sheba be able to roast summat as big as a goose?'

'Roast it? Aye. She'd draw it an' feather it an' all.' Buttercup tapped his nose with the side of his forefinger. 'Sheba's a bostin' little cook.'

'Then let's have one, if you can afford it.'

'Aye, no trouble.' He hailed the hawker who was offering the goose to other men.

The man approached. 'What can I do for you, sir?' he asked deferentially.

'How much is the goose?'

'Six shillings I'll take.'

'Six shillings?' Buttercup scoffed. 'Nay, that's more than the price of a half a gallon o' whisky. Nay, lad, thee'll have to do better'n that.'

'It's a big bird. See?' He held it up. 'Just feel the weight . . . There's many a square meal to be had off that.'

Buttercup felt the weight and was impressed. It would feed the whole hut, lodgers and all. Why not treat them all to a decent Christmas dinner?

'I'll give four shillings for it.'

'Four bob? Nay, my mon.' The packman made to walk away with his goose.

'Won't thee at least barter with me?'

'Five and six,' the seller said, staying.

Buttercup shook his head. 'Four and six.'

The other hesitated a second or two. 'Five bob and it's your'n.'

Buttercup winked at Jericho, but presented a serious face to the packman. 'Th' bist a robbing bleeder . . . but go on then, I'll gi' thee five bob . . .' He felt in his pocket for the money and handed it over.

'A merry Christmas to yer, sir, and thank you.' He took the money and handed over the goose, which Buttercup laid on the floor at his feet. Then he finished his beer.

Jericho went to the bar to buy two more tankards of beer.

When he returned, he nodded in the direction of another hawker. 'There's a bloke over there selling trinkets. I've a good mind to get Poppy a Christmas box.'

'Aye, it's sure to stand thee in good stead,' Buttercup said wryly, but the sarcasm was too subtle for Jericho.

Over the hubbub and the tobacco smoke he hailed the man, who acknowledged his call. When he had finished the transaction that was keeping him, he made his way over.

'Let's see what you've got,' Jericho said. 'I want summat for a nice pretty wench. Summat with a bit o' quality.'

'Summat plain then,' the hawker suggested, wishing to be helpful. 'Pretty madams want summat less pretty than they am . . . A locket, eh? Worn on a chain?'

'Got anything heart-shaped in silver?'

'Aye.' The packman picked out a silver locket and chain. 'Hallmarked, it is. See?'

Jericho looked, but in the dim light could make out nothing. 'How much?'

'Half a guinea.'

'I'll give you eight shillings,' Jericho said, trying to emulate his father and mentor.

'Ten bob,' the man replied. 'It's the best I can do.'

'Will yer settle on nine bob?' Jericho asked.

They agreed on nine shillings and sixpence. The exchange took place and both men were happy.

Jericho grinned proudly at Buttercup as he put it in his pocket. 'See, I can barter an' all. And Poppy'll be pleased with the trinket.'

'Th'art as saft as a ballyache shit,' Buttercup said with a grin.

'Nay, I'll be thought plenty of for this. It might even do the trick.'

'Oh, I doubt that. Not the way Poppy's mind is set. But

mebbe we ought to get a few other things. A few oranges wouldn't come amiss for them poor kids. A few nuts an' all, mebbe. Canst th' see anybody selling oranges or nuts?'

'There was somebody outside,' Jericho proclaimed.

'Come on, let's finish our drinks an' have a piddle.' He picked up the goose by the neck and stuck it under his arm. 'We can buy some oranges and stuff on the way.'

Outside in the darkness they navigated their way to the privy. Buttercup tried to relieve himself while still clutching the goose under his arm but found the combination of activities too complicated and too restricting. So he let it fall to the floor where it landed with a squish on the wet, evil smelling flags. When he had finished and returned his nether parts into the warm, nestling comfort of his long johns, he reached down for the goose and wiped the wet away with the sleeve of his jacket.

'Hast finished?' he enquired of Jericho.

'Aye. Just about,' Jericho replied to the diminishing music of his concluding trickles.

'Then let's find that chap selling oranges.'

At about the same time that Jericho and Buttercup were leaving The Red Lion, full of festive spirit, laden with sodden goose, fruit and other oddments, Robert Crawford was harnessing his horse to his gig. He was being joined by surveyors and the resident engineer in The Old Crown for a drink to celebrate both Christmas and his last night of bachelorhood, before making his way home for a late dinner with his family. It had begun to snow and Robert eyed the dark sky warily; his breath was steam in the cold, damp air.

'Who wants a lift?' he asked.

'We'll walk, Robert,' answered Slingsby Shafto. 'We'll not be far behind if you're the one paying.'

Robert threw himself into the gig, flicked the reins, and drove off.

Close by were glassworks, bottle works, brickworks, iron works, coal mines and fireclay pits. Other workers had had the same idea and stopped by on their way home for seasonal drinks with their mates, so already the public house was busy. The room was noisy, thick with smoke and the sweet, dark smell of beer. The well-stacked coal fire at the far end of the room was burning with bright blue flames.

Robert ordered four tankards of beer and guarded them assiduously while he waited for his three colleagues. This cold, grizzly night was to be his last night of freedom before taking on a whole new host of marital responsibilities. By this time tomorrow it would be all over. Virginia would be his wife, the Lords would be his in-laws, and he would be well and truly manacled. He had capitulated as regards the house Ishmael Lord was having built for them, although doing so had gone against his inclination. The implication was that he would be unable to provide anything as fine, unable to maintain Ishmael Lord's daughter in the manner to which she had always been accustomed. Well, in good time he would show them. For Virginia's sake he had not taken issue with them. To have done so would have been churlish in the extreme. Instead, reluctantly, but with forced affability, he'd offered his thanks for their unbounded generosity and consideration. Ishmael Lord had made no bones either about his intention to groom somebody to take over Tyler's and Lord's Bank. He had not pointed his finger directly at Robert, but it was obvious he considered Robert a prime candidate. After all, in the absence of a son of his own, who better to make extremely rich than a decent and honest son-in-law, the husband of his elder daughter?

Robert supped his ale as he stood at the bar waiting, steeped in thoughts of this imminent marriage. Men unwittingly jostled him as they crowded against the bar waiting to be served by landlord, wife, or barmaid. He moved aside as best he could to allow them more room, and pondered more. His family had had their way as regards his ideal bride. Of course, there could never have been any doubt. He always knew there would have been a bloody battle to get his family to recognise Poppy Silk as a worthy bride, but never had he supposed their strength of feeling would have run so deep. But their total hypocrisy staggered him. At first they evidently liked the girl . . . until they realised she was the daughter of a common navvy, born and reared in one of those beastly shanty towns. As soon as they knew it, she was not to be touched, as if she were contaminated, escaped from some leper colony. They were still labouring under the misguided belief that she was a prostitute, but Robert himself had dispensed with such vile notions after his visit to Aunt Phoebe. Aunt Phoebe was right; Poppy was too sensitive and far too sensible.

He sighed to himself, a profound sigh, as he pondered Poppy again. Theirs was truly an affair of the heart. He would never love and be loved like that again. Marriage to Virginia could never be as satisfying as marriage to Poppy would have been. At best it would be superficial, at worst farcical. Already, he had contemplated that for sexual satisfaction he would be driven to the arms of other women. Already, it was in his mind that he could never remain faithful to his spotless bride; not after he had tasted love of the quality and intensity of Poppy Silk's.

Poppy remained a total enigma. When he returned from Brazil and saw her transformed into the essence of femininity, elegance and breeding, his love for her blazed anew, but with an even more intense heat. Her navvy breeding still showed through – to him if to nobody else – in her consummate lack of inhibition. What ordinary girl would admit to the erotic dreams and fancies she'd harboured? What well-bred girl of seventeen would throw off all her clothes without a second thought and stand before him naked, unabashed, willing and anxious for him to take her, never constrained by the likely consequences? But these things only ever excited him. Her candour, her openness, her sauciness, her honesty, her directness, her simplicity, all were part of her delicious character, the very qualities that fomented his love and his desire for her. To him it mattered not at all that she was the daughter of a navvy. As well as being more of a challenge than any other woman he had known, she had more to offer, mentally, spiritually, and physically.

He was not proud of himself for having surrendered under pressure from his family and from Virginia. His feelings had not changed; only his obligations had been pointed out more assertively. He still loved Poppy Silk with a fervour that he knew would never leave him. He knew that when he grew old and grey and cantankerous, he would sit in his chair and still his heart would be aching and his mind would be full of Poppy Silk. He knew that even in those far off days he would be wondering where she was and what she was doing. He would be regretting having never done what his heart was begging him, as a young man, to do right now . . . He would regret bitterly having never followed his heart, for the sake of his so-called obligations to his family, to Virginia, and to Ishmael Lord.

He felt a tap on his shoulder, and turned around. It was William Round, one of his colleagues, the friend he had asked to be his best man in preference to Bellamy, with whom relations were now strained.

Robert smiled, leaving behind his thoughts. 'Here . . .' He reached over and lifted one of the tankards from the bar.

'I wager it's gone flat,' William said with a grin and sipped the beer tentatively.

'Not at all. It's a decent drink,' said Robert.

The other two joined them almost immediately and, after some friendly banter, they got to talking about work. William ordered four more drinks and they discussed the relative advantages of Brunel's broad gauge over narrow gauge. It ended up as a heated discussion with Slingsby Shafto, as usual, doing his best to needle Robert over his views. And so it went on . . . until the four had sunk several more tankards of ale, and talk was about women in general, with references to Robert's marriage tomorrow.

'She's a fine girl, is Virginia,' Slingsby Shafto said, slurring his words. 'Far too good for you, Crawford. You're a very lucky man, you know.' He turned to the others unsteadily, spilling some of his beer. 'I've met Virginia, you know. Lovely girl . . . Her family owns Tyler's and Lord's, you know. *Lord* knows what she sees in this reprobate, though.' He laughed at his own weak pun.

'As if owning a bank had anything to do with it,' Robert protested, also inebriated by this time. 'I couldn't give a toss about their money, or their damned bank.'

'It's funny,' said Slingsby, with a wink at the other two, 'but it's always those who have money who are the first to assert its unimportance.'

'I don't shee that,' slurred Robert. 'It's important to have money in this day and age. It's what we all work for.'

'But those that have it in abundance reckon it's unimportant,' Slingsby argued. 'Such folk should feel destitution for a while. It's only when you have no money that money becomes important . . . And *I* should know.'

Robert remembered that he was supposed to be dining with his family that evening and took his watch from his fob to check the time. 'Lord, I'd best be off, else my Christmas Eve dinner will be as black as the grate. Let me get you another drink apiece before I go.'

'Let me,' Slingsby Shafto insisted.

Robert scoffed. 'Can you afford it?'

'Yes, I can afford it,' Slingsby retorted with a sudden seething resentment that was triggered by the alcohol.

'But you were the one pleading poverty a minute ago.'

'Oh, it's all right for you, Crawford. Marrying your rich girl tomorrow, aren't you?' He looked hard at Edward Lister. 'Why did you have him back after he'd buggered off to Brazil?'

'Because he's a good engineer, Slingsby. And the experience won't have done him any harm.'

'Left that poor sweet girl for a whole year, didn't you Crawford?' William Round taunted, more to rile Slingsby than Robert.

'Oh, which one?' Slingsby asked pointedly. 'Poor, dear Virginia, or that little slut who used to live on the encampment at Blowers Green?'

Incensed at the slur on Poppy, Robert grabbed Slingsby by his lapel and thrust him hard against the wall. 'Don't ever call that angel a slut again, Slingsby, or I swear I'll throttle you,' he rasped into his face. 'She's better than you'll ever—'

'Lads! Lads!' Edward said with a plea in his voice. He edged himself between them, glancing anxiously in the direction of the landlord. 'You'll get us chucked out, brawling like drunken navvies. Behave yourselves, or you'll have me to contend with Thursday morning.'

'Maybe it's time we went,' William said diplomatically. 'Any more booze and these two'll be killing each other. Save your coppers, Slingsby. I'm off anyway when I've downed this. Are you coming, Edward?'

'It'd be as well, yes . . . Robert . . .' Edward offered his hand. 'Congratulations and the very best of happiness to you and your bride tomorrow.'

'Thank you, Edward. I have a sneaking suspicion I shall need it.' He turned to Slingsby. 'Are you going too?'

'I'm not staying here with you to be insulted,' Slingsby replied sullenly.

'What about you, William? You are to be my best man tomorrow.'

'And I'll be there. But I must be off too, dear chap. I have a wife and child awaiting me . . . and it *is* Christmas.'

'Then I'll stay here and get fuddled on my own.'

'I thought you had to be home for dinner.'

'Sod dinner. Sod home. Sod 'em all.' He turned his back on his colleagues as they left. 'Give me a very large whisky,' he said awkwardly to the landlord's wife.

She almost filled a tumbler and Robert began drinking it as if it were a tankard of ale. The laziness of his eyelids made manifest the effects of the alcohol. He finished off the whisky and asked for another. What the hell. He felt miserable and wretched already. He needed the oblivion alcohol would very kindly bestow. As the woman filled his glass again, he felt an ice-cold blast as the door opened. A flurry of snow was blown in with four more customers.

'Merry Christmas, Mister Crawford,' Buttercup said deferentially as he sidled up to the bar where Robert was still managing to stand upright.

Robert focused his eyes on Buttercup. 'Oh . . . Mishter Buttercup . . . And a merry Chrishmas to you too. Let me buy you a drink, Mishter Buttercup.'

'That's generous, but there's four o' we.'

'That'sh all right, I ain't skint yet.' He turned around to see who was accompanying him and saw Jericho, then Sheba, their clothes whitened with a thin covering of snow . . . And then he saw Poppy, a snowflake slowly melting on her long eyelashes and taking on the appearance of a tear. Their eyes met and held, and Robert wished with all his heart that he was not drunk, that he could instantly sober up and be lucid if she deigned to speak to him, for he detected no animosity.

'Miss Shilk . . .' His attempt at formality was rendered silly by his slurred words.

'Robert,' she said unsurely. 'Fancy seeing you . . .' She risked a half smile.

'Is it shnowing?' he asked stupidly.

'Beltin' it down,' Buttercup replied.

'Good God. What will you have to jink? It'sh Chrishmash and I want to buy you all a jink.'

'He's pickled to the gills,' Jericho muttered to Buttercup.

Buttercup acknowledged the obvious with a cursory nod. 'I'll have a whisky, thank thee, Mister Crawford.'

'And you, Jericho?'

'I'll have nothing that you're a-paying for,' Jericho said, and received a kick on his shins from Poppy.

'That'sh your choish, Jericho,' Robert replied with a lazy shrug. 'Sheba? I mean Mishish Shilk.'

'A glass of beer would be very nice, thank you.'

Robert smiled exaggeratedly. 'Beer it ish . . .' He turned to Poppy again who was loosening her mantle at her throat. 'Mish Shilk . . . What can I get you?'

'Leave her be,' Jericho rasped. 'She wants nought from you.'

Robert frowned at Jericho, angered by his unreasonable attitude. 'Perhapsh that desh . . . deshish . . . deshishion should be left to Mish Shilk . . . eh, Mish Shilk? What would you like to jink?'

'I'll just have some soda water, please, Robert.'

'Very well . . .' He noticed that she was wearing a locket in the shape of a heart and was confused as to what conclusion he should draw from it. 'I'm drunk, you know, Poppy . . .'

The landlord's wife eyed Robert warily as he called for the drinks. She had seen this young man getting more inebriated by the minute. She had already witnessed his cross words and threatening behaviour with one of his companions earlier, and now he was mixing with folk who, according to their mode of dress and the older woman's quaint hairstyle, were navvies from that new encampment. If they weren't careful, all the damned navvies from that godforsaken site would be descending regularly on their orderly house, earning it a bad reputation.

Robert handed the drinks round as he received them. 'Are you sure I can't tempt you?' he said again to Jericho.

'I'll buy my own beer.'

'Leave it,' Buttercup said in an aside to Jericho. 'He wants to buy you a drink. Be sociable. It's Christmas.'

'Nay, I'll have no drink off him. He reckoned Poppy was a street wench.'

Robert shook his head solemnly, uselessly, for he could not readily form the words to reply.

'Well now,' Jericho went on, eyeing Robert maliciously. 'It's true, ain't it, *Mister* Crawford? She was a street wench, wasn't she, according to you? Well, she must've been, she's had the clap three times, and now she reckons she's got the pox.' Poppy nudged him agitatedly. 'It must have showed up in you by now, *Mister* Crawford.'

'You have a foul mouth,' Robert managed to utter.

'And you have a foul mind, *Mister* Crawford. Don't you believe she's got the pox?'

'Of courshe I don't.'

'Pity. Maybe you should consider it when you'm pokin' your new bride tomorrow. You wouldn't want to pass anything on to your new bride on her wedding night, would you?'

While Poppy looked aghast at the depths Jericho could trawl in his venom, Robert tried to rally himself, trying to shake off the slough of inertia and haziness and stupidity that was impeding his mind and his body. It was as if he was not a part of all this, as if he was watching some sinister act in a bizarre play, its outcome preordained.

'I ought to thrash you,' Robert hissed.

Jericho guffawed, a mocking, sneering laugh.

Robert lurched forward in an attempt to grab Jericho. 'How dare you say such vile things about Poppy?' He stumbled to the floor in a heap, and struggled to get up, while Jericho held him down.

'Leave him be, Jericho,' Buttercup implored. 'He's down. He's fuddled. Leave him be.'

'Aye, he's fuddled all right.' Jericho stooped down over Robert, clutched the lapels of his jacket and lifted him so that their faces were only inches apart. 'Think you'm man enough to fight me, do yer?' he goaded, his face ugly with hate. 'Man indeed! What sort of a *man* would cast aside a young woman who was a-carryin' his child, eh? Tell me that, *Mister* Crawford.'

Poppy knelt down beside them both, desperately trying to intervene, trying to shove Jericho away. 'Leave him be, Jericho, and shut your damned mouth,' she shrieked, her tutoring and respectability leaving her in these anxious moments. She felt so sorry for Robert. To see him thus afflicted was an unpalatable blow to his dignity. 'Hurt him, Jericho, and I'll never speak to you again.'

Jericho ignored her, shoving her aside as his temper got the better of him. 'Did yer know as Poppy was carrying your babby?' he hissed. 'Well? Did yer?'

Robert shook his head stupidly, only half-aware of what was going on.

'No, she reckons you don't know, but I wager you do. Course yer do.'

'Jericho!' Poppy screamed. 'Will you shut your vile mouth and leave him be!'

'Any road, what does it matter?' Jericho ranted. 'She's scum, ain't she? The scrapings from the bottom o' the barrel, that's all she is. But you . . .' He spat in Robert's face. 'You'm like all o' your class. You tek what you want then shit on it. Well, I'll wait, *Mister* Crawford . . .' He let go and Robert slumped to the floor. 'I'll wait till you'm sober afore I fight yer, just to mek it fair.'

Poppy knelt alongside Robert and cradled his head in her arms. 'Robert, Robert,' she whimpered, as her tears fell onto his face and into his hair. 'Oh, Robert . . .'

The landlord was upon them. 'I want you all out. You'm all troublemakers. The lot o' ye. The minute you lot come in here, I could smell trouble. Get out of here. And I never want to see any of you in my house again.'

Robert struggled to his feet, helped by Poppy, and comically went through the motions of dusting himself off. Buttercup, Jericho and Sheba looked on, while Poppy was stupefied by the swiftness with which all this had happened.

'Does he have a mantle or summat?' Sheba asked. 'He'll catch his death.'

'Here,' the landlord said, picking up Robert's greatcoat. 'Get him out of here.'

Buttercup took it and wrapped it around Robert's shoulders as he led him outside. 'Come on, lad,' he said kindly.

'That's his horse and gig,' Poppy said, pointing to the combination standing at the kerb. 'But he can't drive back to Dudley in his state.'

'He'll have to,' Buttercup answered. 'Mebbe the hoss knows the road. He'll have bin up and down it enough times be now.'

Poppy rushed to the gig and, with tears in her eyes, made sure he had hold of the reins. 'Goodbye, Robert,' she wailed, for if she ever cast eyes on him again, she would be looking at a married man. 'Remember me . . .'

Chapter 35

Poppy watched with tears in her eyes as Robert and his gig headed towards Dudley and his irrevocable marriage tomorrow. Soon, he became invisible, lost in the haze of pure white feathers that floated silently down and glittered in the lamplight and lanterns of The Old Crown and other inns and houses. She walked homeward, lagging behind the others, and with disinterest shrugged off Jericho's arm, which was offered as support in case she slipped.

Although tomorrow was a holiday, many furnaces and kilns worked still, their orange glow more noticeable than usual against the cold uniformity of untouched snow. The heavy charcoal sky flared with tongues of flame that leapt over the larger furnaces, while palls of smoke still spewed from the myriad red-brick chimney stacks, as if in the midst of a conflagration.

After his rebuff, Jericho walked on ahead with Buttercup, his head down against the driving snow, his collar up, his shoulders hunched to ward off the cold. Sheba waited a few seconds for Poppy to catch up, then took her daughter's gloved hand caringly.

'It's upset yer seeing him again,' she said, her voice soft with tenderness.

'It's upset me seeing him lose all his dignity through drink,' Poppy snivelled. 'He seldom drinks.'

'Well, it's Christmas. He's entitled to a drink.'

'Christmas or not, he wouldn't get drunk like that, Mother. I know him. He's unhappy. I know he's unhappy. And Jericho didn't help, wanting to fight him. How *stupid*! I thought he'd grown up.'

'Jericho's Jericho,' Sheba proclaimed.

'But I thought he'd grown out of it. He seemed to have settled down . . .'

'He'll never grow out of fighting. And just be glad you ain't had nothing to do with him, 'cause he wouldn't be past clouting you either. He's got a vile temper . . . And listen, that Robert's nothing to do with you any more, our Poppy. It'd pay you to stop grieving over him. This time tomorrow he'll be a married man.'

They trudged on, the hems of their skirts soaking up the wet as they brushed across the fresh snow.

Buttercup stopped and turned round to face them. 'Me and Jericho am off to The Red Lion. It's no place for women, so we'll see thee later.'

Soon Poppy and Sheba were within sight of the encampment. The children were still out playing, relishing the novelty of the first snowfall of winter, throwing snowballs at each other in the darkness from between the huts, rushing about and giggling. The two women entered the hut, and the heat from the stove was welcoming.

'I'm going to bed,' Poppy said miserably, taking off her bonnet while Sheba lit a lamp. 'I need to have a good cry . . . on my own.'

'Have a nip o' whisky afore you go. It'll help you sleep.'

Poppy took off her mantle, shook off the adhering snow,

and hung it on a nail in the door. 'All right. I'll take it to bed with me.'

Sheba took a bottle from a shelf above her and poured a good measure into a glass. 'Here . . . Don't spill it.'

'Thanks, Mother. And don't expect me to get up early. I don't want to even *see* the day that *he* gets married on.'

Alone for once in this spartan family bedroom, Poppy shivered. She undressed, put on her nightgown and slipped into the cold bed. She propped herself up on the pillows and shivered again as she watched her breath turning to steam. She sipped her whisky held cupped in both hands, her mind full of the disturbing events in The Old Crown. Poor Robert. If only she could have helped him. It was not in her nature to hold a grudge. She still loved him and she was resigned to the fact that she always would. But now she was powerless to do anything. If he was miserable it was of his own making. He had chosen his future path, not she. But it had hurt her to witness him, a man of culture and high self-esteem, stripped of his pride yet oblivious to his lamentable state because of too much drink. He was like some pig-ignorant navvy bent on self-destruction. It might even have been best if she'd never seen him again, allowed to remember him the way he always was, kind, considerate, dignified . . . and sober. Now, even her memory of him was tainted.

She finished her nightcap, snuggled down under the blankets and drifted into sleep. Before long, she was awakened by her sisters and brothers boisterously getting into bed. Lottie's cold feet and her cold body were a shock to Poppy's warm skin. Their chatter and giggles kept her awake, but she could not be angry with them. If only she felt as happy herself.

Morning came and the bedroom was filled with the ghostly white light that only a covering of snow outside can bring. On the window a film of ice had formed, intricately patterned with ferns, flowers and crystal stars. Poppy turned over and pulled the blankets higher around her neck to keep out the bitter cold. Today was the day she had dreaded more than any other day in her life: the day Robert would be wed. Well, by now she had accepted the fact, but it still hurt. Yet how soon it had rolled round. It seemed like only yesterday that she had learnt it was to take place on this very day, this Christmas Day . . .

She recalled last Christmas with Aunt Phoebe . . . The preparation, making cakes and mince pies, plum pudding and pork pies with Dolly, enough to feed an army, Clay brewing ale. She recalled helping Dolly – or rather Dolly helping her – to feather and draw a goose, laughing and joking while they did it. She should be helping her mother do the same with the specimen Buttercup had acquired yesterday. Last Christmas she had eaten too much, and so had Aunt Phoebe who suffered the indignity of indigestion and had to slacken off her stays. They'd laughed together at that, she and Aunt Phoebe. Carol singers had also arrived and were rewarded with bags full of the cakes and mince pies, as well as a nip of whisky or brandy each, according to their taste. Well, there would not be quite the same joviality here in this navvy encampment. Not for Poppy at any rate . . .

Virginia Lord . . . What would she be doing now? She'd be on tenterhooks, almost certainly, doing some last minute worrying that everything was ready and in order. Poppy imagined her soaking in a hot bath in her bedroom, making herself sweet smelling and pristine for her initiation with Robert tonight. That notion horrified Poppy; Robert and Virginia in bed together. It did not occur to Poppy that in bed with Robert, Virginia would not be like her. It did not occur to her that Virginia was shackled by her religious beliefs and a deep-seated fear and repugnance of sexual intimacy.

Circumstance had not bestowed on Virginia the gift of being uninhibited and willingly giving herself. Poppy had never considered that well-bred girls were expected to behave differently to her in that respect. She suspected that not all were prim and pure in thought and deed, especially in the privacy of their beds where they could think and do as they pleased. She tried to imagine Virginia in her bridal gown, statuesque as she clung to a posy of flowers imported just for the occasion. She thought of the carriage that would convey her to church, bedecked with more flowers and white ribbons . . .

Lottie awoke and sat bolt upright. 'I want to see if the snow's still here.'

'The snow's still here, Lottie. Go back to sleep.'

But Lottie insisted on clambering across several of her siblings, waking them all up. She rubbed the frost off the inside of a window pane, took off her nightgown hurriedly, shivered, dressed, then ran outside, followed by the others, who were just as anxious to play in the snow. Buttercup snored, disturbing Sheba who stirred and poked him in the ribs in an attempt to get him to turn over. Again, Poppy snuggled under the blankets and returned to thoughts of Robert Crawford and his wedding day.

His wedding day.

Virginia's wedding day.

It could have been her own wedding day.

If only Virginia had not acquired the wild notion that she was a whore and revealed that she was a navvy's daughter. Prior to that, Poppy had been so close to becoming Robert Crawford's wife. His father had given him his blessing to marry her once the overdraft facility with Tyler's and Lord's had been secured. His mother's blessing would naturally have followed, albeit with some reluctance. But it would have followed. Damn Virginia! Virginia had not played fair at all.

Now Robert was lost forever because of Virginia's meddling. Well, her scheming would do her no good and serve her right. Robert would never be happy or content married to her. But even that was no source of satisfaction to Poppy as she wiped fresh tears from her eyes with a corner of her bed sheet. *She* wanted him. *She* should be lying with him tonight, and to hell with Virginia. It was *she* who was carrying his child, not Virginia. And Jericho had either stupidly, or with unwitting wisdom, let him know in his uncontrollable frenzy . . .

Sheba roused herself and slid out of bed.

Poppy put her head over the blankets to see. 'Are you getting up already, Mother?' she whispered.

'There's a lot to do. It's Christmas Day and it's white over outside. Aren't you going to have a look? You'm a-crying again, our Poppy.'

'I know and I can't help it. He's getting married today . . . to *her*.'

'Your eyes'll be all puffy and red. I told you, you have to forget him. Believe me, there's plenty more fish in the sea.'

'I'm so grateful for your sympathy, Mother,' she answered sarcastically. 'A merry Christmas to you as well.' She smothered herself with the bedclothes again and turned over, feeling desperately sorry for herself.

Sheba felt a surge of pity for her daughter, but knew she dare not show it for fear of making her worse. So she moved round to Poppy's bed and good-humouredly pulled the bedclothes off her.

'Stop it, it's cold!' Poppy complained, and sullenly snatched back the blankets.

The disturbance woke Buttercup. 'Noisy pair o' buggers,' he grumbled, then broke wind and belched simultaneously.

'Hark who's makin' all the noise,' Sheba remarked.

The couple dressed and left Poppy to her sorrowing. Very

soon, she could smell bacon frying, which almost tempted her to waive her anguish and get dressed as well, but she stubbornly stayed in bed, determined to grieve, and Sheba took in her breakfast on a plate. After it, Poppy lay down again, still declining to get up, still refusing to relinquish thoughts of Robert Crawford, his wedding, and how she'd had the grossest misfortune to lose him. She knew she should be helping her mother work, but let Lottie come in from playing in the snow and do it. She was old enough.

Poppy fell asleep again and dreamed about Robert's wedding. In her dream it was springtime and she was a guest, dressed in a primrose yellow dress and bonnet. Aunt Phoebe, to her surprise, got up from her pew and vindictively shoved Virginia out of the way, beckoning Poppy to take her place, while the vicar, Reverend Browne from St Thomas's, smiled with benign endorsement. The boys from Baylies's Charity School were the choir, and Minnie Catchpole irreverently lifted her skirt above her waist revealing everything she had, applauded by Captain Tyler. Next, Bellamy was trying to slip a ring onto her finger, since Robert and he had switched places.

She woke up in a state of anguish and confusion.

Sheba was standing over her with a mug of steaming tea. 'Your Christmas dinner'll be ready in half an hour. It's time you got up. Never mind mithering over *his* wedding.'

Poppy frowned at the daylight, her fair hair bedraggled and tangled. 'What time is it?'

'About one o'clock.'

'Oh . . . He'll be married by now. It was to be at twelve.'

'Then it's all over and there's nothing to be done, so get up. Any road, if he could see you now with your red eyes and your fuzzy hair he'd very likely run a mile. Come on, get yourself up. I need some help.'

* * *

556

After her Christmas dinner, Poppy decided to go for a walk. If she could not have the company of Robert Crawford, she craved only her own. In any case, it would be good to wander in the snow alone. It had stopped snowing by then, the sky was clear and the sun was shining, and she was amazed at the mighty breadth of glistening snow all around her. For as far as she could see, everything was shrouded in pure white. Around the encampment, the footprints of the children where they had played were the only evidence of human activity. Elsewhere, the earth, its normal colour black, was dazzling white and pristine. Where the wind had chased the snow, drifts filled hollows, smoothing them out as if a sheet had been draped across them. Gentle white curves transformed the shapes of blocks and bricks, of stumps and jagged rocks. Even the slag heaps had become beautiful, shimmering like snow-capped Alpine peaks as they caught the sunlight. The huts, including the one she had just left, were encrusted with icicles that dripped liquid jewels, and trees creaked under the weight of their resplendent white coats. Red-brick houses, their windows square eyes that stared at her across the icy waste, were the faces of old men, the snow-clad roofs their caps.

It was hard going, walking through snow more than two feet deep everywhere. Her hems and shoes were becoming saturated, her feet were like ice. But it was good to see nature's work, how it could alter a depressingly ugly landscape and turn it into something wondrous. Even the horse gins in the distance looked pretty, bejewelled like the crowns of queens. Poppy made her way towards the new cutting and realised there would be no work for the navvies until the thaw came, and it would take days to melt all this, especially if it all froze over tonight.

She sat down on a snow-covered pile of bricks and looked

around her, strangely uplifted by the transformation she beheld. Everywhere was silent, all sounds deadened by the thick blanket of snow. Nobody stirred. Everybody was either resting or too tipsy to venture out after their Christmas dinners. She was all alone in the landscape . . .

Except for one other lonely figure.

Poppy noticed him descending the hill to her left, trudging wearily towards the encampment. His ponderous movements told of his tiredness as he struggled to keep upright in the snow. His progress was slow, for the depth of snow as well unquestionably impeded him. The way he held himself, his bearing, was unnervingly familiar, however, and Poppy's heart lurched to her mouth as she realised who he was. She watched him, her temples suddenly throbbing, her emotions a mixture of excitement and apprehension as he got closer. She could not help but stand up and call his name.

He looked up, waved frantically in recognition, and scrambled towards her ponderously. As he got closer she could see he was out of breath, his forehead beaded in sweat from exertion. She strove to reach him as quickly as she could, the deep snow clawing at her feet, conspiring to impede her when she urgently needed to get to him. His arms were open, waiting to receive her. She reached him at last, fell into his embrace, and they both slumped to the ground in an ecstasy of relief and longing. They ended up rolling in the snow, clutching each other frenetically, as if to let go would be to lose each other again. Once again her eyes were swimming in tears as she clung desperately to him, silent, unspeaking for long, uncertain seconds.

'How come you're here?' she asked at length, almost dreading his answer.

'I didn't get married.' He half released her, and looked directly into her moist blue eyes. 'Poppy, I didn't get married . . .'

'You didn't?' she queried, uncomprehending.

He smiled at her, love unmistakable and unconcealed in his earnest facial expression. 'How could I?'

'Was it what Jericho told you that changed your mind?'

'Jericho?' He looked puzzled. 'No, the snow prevented me . . . We couldn't even get the brougham out, it was so deep. The horses would have been sliding all over the place. We'd never have got to Harborne.'

'Then thank God for the snow,' she breathed, her face a delightful picture of uncertainty.

'But don't you see? It was nature's way of allowing me to escape a marriage I truly did not want, a marriage that would have suited nobody, not even Virginia. So I decided to grasp the opportunity, and I ran. I ran as fast as I could to escape, to the only girl in the world I'm interested in marrying.'

'So does this mean no more Virginia?'

He swallowed hard. 'Poppy, I'm yours, if you'll still have me. I've been a complete and utter fool, listening to others and not listening to my own heart. I have put you through so much heartache . . . myself as well. I love you absolutely, Poppy. Unconditionally. I want nobody else. I'd be happy with nobody else. Only you. I beg the privilege of spending the rest of my life with you . . . Please say you'll have me . . .'

They were still on the ground, sitting in the snow. She flung her arms around him and wept, unable to say yea or nay for sobbing. But they were tears of happiness, of sweet, sweet relief, and of grateful thanks. Perhaps there really was a God after all, a God who had answered the doubtful, sceptical prayers she'd offered, asking Him to deliver Robert back to her arms, back into her life. Perhaps, after all, there was an unprejudiced God, who even listened to unbelievers as well as those devoted worshippers like Virginia. Robert held her

close, his own eyes filling with tears as his emotions intensified, as he realised just how fortunate he was to have the love
of this exceptional, unique young woman. He had almost lost
her . . . but for the snow.

'Did it make a difference, knowing about the baby?' she
asked between sobs and snivels.

'Baby?' he repeated with a curious frown. 'What baby?'

'The baby I'm carrying, Robert . . . Your baby.'

'I didn't know you were carrying my baby, my love. I came
because I wanted to, because I love you. Not because I thought
it was my duty.'

'But Jericho told you last night. When you had stumbled
onto the floor, he taunted you and told you I was carrying
your child.'

'Did he, begad? Was I on the floor? Where?' He looked
aghast.

'In The Old Crown. Don't you remember, Robert?'

'I know I went in The Old Crown . . . I have a vague recollection of seeing you . . . Nothing else. I realise, of course,
that I was as drunk as a lord. I had a hell of a headache this
morning.'

'I'm surprised you managed to get home. I saw you on
your way.'

'I honestly have no recollection of it, Poppy. As a matter
of fact, I don't feel very grand even now, especially after
trudging through all this snow half the morning. I'm absolutely starving hungry, and so thirsty . . .'

'You've had no Christmas dinner?'

'Nothing.'

'Oh, we'll feed you, Robert,' she promised. 'There's some
goose left. But first you must understand . . .' She looked at
him earnestly through wet, soulful eyes. 'I *am* having your
child. If it's not what you want, if it's not what you want for

yourself after all, then now is the time to say so. I'll understand. I won't hold you to anything. They'll look after me here—'

'If you're carrying my child, Poppy,' he said, interrupting her flow, 'I couldn't be happier. And don't imagine for a minute that I would leave a child of mine fatherless . . . Good God!' He started to laugh, picked himself up off the ground and jumped up and down, frantically waving his arms about, fired with a renewed energy. 'This is the best news I could ever have had. You'll have to marry me now. I'll have to make an honest woman of you anyway.' He twirled round and round like an excited child, then fell over, giddy, exhausted. 'Say you'll marry me, pretty Poppy,' he pleaded, his head swimming. 'Say you'll marry me and we'll do it by special licence just as soon as we can. Tomorrow if it's possible. In the next day or two anyway.'

She fell on him, smothering him with kisses, smearing his face with the cold remnants of her tears. 'Oh, Robert . . . Of course I'll marry you. Of course I will. But what about your family? What will they have to say about it?'

'To hell with them. I don't care a fig what they say or what they think. You are the only person in the world that means anything to me.' He beamed. 'You and my child. If they don't accept it, if they don't accept you, then it's their loss. I'm not prepared to let you go again. Ever.'

'Then that's settled . . .' She grinned with pleasure at this new-found salvation. 'Come on, we'll go and tell my mother and Buttercup, and find you something to eat . . .' She started to laugh.

'What's so amusing?'

'Well . . . Marriage by special licence might be for the better, you know. Just you, me and a couple of witnesses. It just occurred to me what a strange do it would be with my family and yours together in the same church, afraid to mix one with the other because of their class differences, scowling suspiciously at each other across the aisle . . .'

'Oh, to hell with a church wedding as well,' Robert said.

'Aunt Phoebe will be glad about us, you know.'

'I know. Aunt Phoebe will be delighted. She can be a witness to our marriage.'

'She'd love that . . . So where shall we live?'

Robert grinned, fascinated by Poppy's lovely face, her exquisitely animated expressions that alternated between doubt and triumph in a twinkle. 'Oh, I shall buy a fine house. I have enough money.'

'In the meantime, I'm sure Aunt Phoebe would let us lodge with her . . . till we have a house of our own.'

'I'm sure she would.'

'At least after we're married, and until the baby's born.'

'I'm sure she would, yes.'

Poppy stood up and offered her hand to Robert to help him up. 'Come on, let's break the news.'

He grinned with new-found contentment as he stood up.

'Poor Virginia,' she said quietly.

Robert looked at her curiously, unable to acknowledge that she would have any sympathy for Virginia after the agony the girl had put her through. 'The words *poor* and *Virginia* do not sit comfortably together, Poppy.'

She smiled into his eyes as they started walking hand in hand towards the encampment. 'In one sense, yes. But I still can't help feeling sorry for her. She's lost you at the last. I know just how she feels . . . and it's not pleasant.'

'It'll come as no surprise. As soon as she saw how deep the snow was this morning, she would've realised that travelling to Harborne was impossible, and that her chance was gone. I'm sure of it. She finally realised how grossly unhappy I've been. I don't really think she'll begrudge me my happiness. Nor you yours. Especially when she knows you're having our child.'

The winter sun was dipping, red and swollen, yet lacking any heat. The snow, taking on a golden hue, was beginning to freeze, sparkling and crunching underfoot already. Icicles that had dripped water an hour ago were quiescent. Chimneys atop the terraced houses nearby emitted curling smoke as the hearths beneath burned bright, warming the inhabitants within. To their right, Poppy and Robert could just see the canal, winding like a black serpent between the factories.

'I want to sleep with you tonight,' she said. 'I've waited long enough.'

He laughed, once again shocked, but at the same time delighted by her frankness. 'In your hut, you mean?'

'No. Not there. We all sleep in one room there. Imagine what it would be like. Us lying together but not being able to have each other. No, we can go to an inn. My mother will find me a brass ring or something to put on my wedding finger. Folk won't know we aren't married yet.'

'Your mother would do that?' he queried, surprised.

'Yes. And why not? It's the navvies' way. But if you're worried about impropriety we could always jump the broomstick first.'

'Too pagan even for my taste, Poppy. Oh, I was never squeamish about impropriety. I'll be quite at ease with a brass ring from your mother. It will do admirably until I can buy you a gold one. So long as your finger doesn't turn green in the meantime.'

'If it does, it will shock nobody but an old lady or two. I don't think it would shock Aunt Phoebe, though. She knows me too well.'

Rescued from destitution and poverty . . . but at what price?

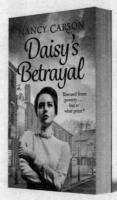

When charming Lawson Maddox asks Daisy Drake to become his wife she jumps at the chance to better herself. But with the honeymoon over he shows his true colours, and Daisy's life descends into chaos.

The appearance of John Mallory Gibson, a sensitive and idealistic painter, offers Daisy the prospect of real happiness, which she finds hard to refuse.

But Lawson will not let go of her, and he embarks on an unscrupulous quest for revenge that threatens to shatter Daisy and her entire family . . .

Only tragedy can save her . . .

When Lucy Piddock meets kind and dependable stonemason Arthur Goodrich, he seems to be the ideal match for her – but he lights no flame in her heart. Lucy dares to dream of love and hankers for Dickie Dempster, the debonair young guard she meets who works on the newly constructed railway.

Prompted by Lucy's rejection, Arthur leaves home to seek a new life in Bristol, leaving Lucy free to pursue her dream of happiness with Dickie.

But when tragedy strikes, Lucy must re-examine where her heart really lies . . .

Sunday's fine weather continued into Monday. Lizzie Bishop walked to work without her coat, her head swimming with dreams and fantasies. The brief, romantic adventure last evening with Stanley Dando was devouring her. It had been so unexpected, but she had relished every minute. In a flash, her emotions had been relentlessly stirred like leaves in a gale, and it was heart-stopping. Now she could hardly wait to see him again, especially after they'd been so abruptly parted when the families went their separate ways. If only she could summon the patience to wait till Wednesday, when they would walk together across the fields by the Oakham farms to the Dingle, where it would be quiet and secluded. She hoped more than anything that he would have the courage to kiss her.

Stanley had set something in train that excited her beyond all expectations. Now she was determined that nothing could stop them or divert them. Strange, she thought, how she'd known Stanley all her life; but not until recently had she thought of him as anything other than family. His dark curls, his even teeth, and his lovely, lovely lips would surely break the hearts of a good many girls. It was up to her to make sure no one else had a chance. Stanley was drawn to her, too, just as surely as a buck is drawn to a doe; that much was obvious. And her eager appetite had been whetted enough.

The clatter and whine of an electric tram travelling through the Market Place roused Lizzie from her daydreams. Stall-holders were loading their trestles beneath the red and white awnings with everything from fruit, vegetables and rolls of velvet, to brass fenders, lamp oil and crockery. Horses clip-clopped over the cobblestones, drawing rumbling carts, and a motor car spluttered as it passed circumspectly in the direction of St. Thomas' tall spire at the top of the town. A man riding to work on a bicycle took pains to avoid getting his narrow wheels caught in the tramlines. Already, awnings were out over many of the shop fronts and Lizzie could see others being drawn down. A hawker was selling fly papers outside the front door of E. C. Theedham's, Ironmongers and Cutlers, where she worked, and bid her good morning.

She saw May Bradley walking towards her from the opposite direction, and waited. They entered the shop together and headed for the passageway at the rear where they generally hung their coats. Today, they had only their baskets to deposit before entering the small back-room to titivate their hair. May looked at herself in the mirror and rearranged a wayward wisp. Despite their age difference the girls got on well. They first met when Lizzie started this job, some couple of years ago, and soon they began to meet socially.

May was down-to-earth, with a ready smile, and a wit that was at first beyond Lizzie. She was an attractive girl with a slender waist and an ample bosom, and she had an abundance of dark, wavy hair that framed a pleasant but hardly striking face. When Lizzie invited May home to tea one Sunday afternoon to meet her mother, it was Joe Bishop, her brother, then twenty-two and looking more like his late father every day, who monopolised the conversation, amusing May with his humorous quips. Later, when it was time for May to leave, Joe offered to escort her home, since it was dark. He insisted there was no need for Lizzie to trouble herself accompanying her friend. May accepted bashfully, thanked Eve for her hospitality, and that was the beginning of their courtship. Eve was hopeful that Joe had found himself a nice, homely girl, at last.

May turned away from the mirror to speak to Lizzie. 'When you was at church last night with your mother, me and Joe went for a drink in The Junction, and while we was in there, we saw Arthur Dowty, your next door neighbour. He says as how him and Bella am flittin'. He says it's 'cause of Jack Hardwick's pigs. Anyroad, when we got back I said to Joe as we ought to think about rentin' that house ourselves. If we could have it, we'd get married. That way, we'd still be close to your mother.'

Lizzie fastened the ties of her pinafore behind her. 'Wouldn't the pigs bother you as well?'

'Oh, I'm used to pigs. Me father always kept pigs. He's a pig himself. Anyroad, if the pigs was there afore we, we couldn't rightly complain.'

Lizzie shrugged. 'I suppose not. But how soon are Bella and Arthur flitting?'

'As soon as they find somethin' else, they said.' May continued to fiddle with her hair in the mirror. 'There's plenty houses to rent. It shouldn't be long.'

Lizzie's smiling eyes lit up her face. 'Another wedding to look forward to. Oh, I'm that happy for you, May. I'm sure that our Joe'll make you a lovely husband, though I say it myself.'

'Yes, and if you get him a big enough piece of wood, I daresay he'll make you one, Lizzie.' May tried to keep a straight face.

'Oh, I think I'm a bit too young yet, May,' Lizzie replied innocently, not having caught the humour in May's comment. Then she said coyly, 'I think me and Stanley Dando might start courting, though.'

'Oh, young Stanley, eh? What's brought that on?'

Lizzie sat down and explained excitedly how Stanley had all but abducted her to the back pew in church, even held her hand, and told her that cousins could marry. But she failed to say that her mother seemed not to approve.

'Well, he seems a pleasant enough lad. He's nice lookin', an' all, there's no two ways. But remember you'm only sixteen, Lizzie. It's no good courtin' serious at sixteen.'

'I know that. But when I'm eighteen, I'll be old enough to get wed. That's less than two years off. A good many girls get wed at eighteen.'

'Not if they've got any sense they don't. It's generally 'cause they've got to if they'm that young. You'd break your mother's heart if that happened, you know. Just remember she's been through all that before with your sister Maude. And look what happened to her.'

'Oh, May, I wouldn't do anything like that. What sort of girl d'you think I am?'

'Like any other, I daresay, so liable to get carried away.'

When Lizzie left school at twelve years old she had found a job at the Dudley Bucket and Fender Co-operative and made a friend of another girl, roughly the same age, called Daisy Foster. They soon bettered themselves at another firm, operating small guillotines, cutting coils of brass into lengths ready to be pressed into parts for paraffin lamps. They stayed for two years, not just learning the job, but learning about life, listening to the other women gossiping over the hollow rattle and thumps of hand presses, and the fatty smell of tallow. Most of the girls they worked with were older, and Lizzie was amazed at the unbelievable things some of them used to tell her about their men, the amazing antics they performed with them and, most surprisingly, how often. Lizzie didn't know such things were possible, but it all sounded intriguing. Those girls told her things she would never have known about had she stayed at home. By autumn, however, the two girls had tired of the oil lamp factory, and found jobs at Chambers Saddlery in Hall Street. Lizzie, however, did not take to working with leather and its dark, sickly odour, whereas Daisy did. Thus they split up when Lizzie left to seek other employment.

'I know a lot of girls *do* do it, May . . . you know? . . . before they get wed I mean . . . But I wouldn't, even if I wanted to. I'd be too afeared of getting caught.'

'Yes, well . . . It's somethin' you need to bear in mind, Lizzie.'

'Do you and our Joe do it, May?'

May registered no outward change in her expression, continuing to preen herself. 'That's between Joe and me.'

'Well, have you ever done it? With anybody, I mean?'

'Lizzie! Honestly!'

'It isn't that I'm being nosy,' Lizzie persisted, trying to justify her questioning, 'but I can talk to you about things. I've got nobody else to talk to, and I want to know about things like that. I want to know what it's like, and everything. I need to talk to somebody about it.'

May turned round and grabbed her pinafore from the hook on the back of the door. 'You'll learn soon enough when you do get wed, Lizzie, and not before if you want my advice. There's no rush . . . Tell me about Stanley, eh?'

Lizzie smiled again, modestly. 'I keep thinking about his lips, May . . . and how much I want him to kiss me. I only have to think about him and my legs go all wobbly. D'you think I'm falling in love?'

May shrugged. 'So you'm not interested in Jesse Clancey any more?'

'Well I would be if he'd asked me out. But he seems more interested in our Sylvia.'